G000141680

THE GIRL FROM

THE

LAND OF SMILES

BY THE SAME AUTHOR

FICTION

CRADLE OF SECRETS
LULLABY OF FEAR
BABY ROULETTE
SPELLBINDER

THE DOHLEN INHERITANCE trilogy:
THE DOHLEN INHERITANCE
HOBGOBLIN GOLD
LADYBIRD FLY

NON-FICTION

A VOICE AT TWILIGHT (*ODD FELLOWS Social Concern Book Award 1989)*
THE GROCKLES' GUIDE (with Jeremy Warburg)
SNACK YOURSELF SLIM (with Richard J Warburg)

KNITTING BOOKS

THE BATSFORD BOOK OF HAND AND MACHINE KNITTING
THE BATSFORD BOOK OF HAND AND MACHINE KNITTED LACES
YARNS FOR TEXTILE CRAFTS
EARNING AND SAVING WITH A KNITTING MACHINE
CHOOSING AND BUYING A KNITTING MACHINE
YARNS FOR THE KNITTER
THE GOOD YARN GUIDE

THE HERITAGE OF KNITTING SERIES
TESSA LORANT'S COLLECTION OF KNITTED LACE EDGINGS
KNITTED QUILTS AND FLOUNCES
KNITTED LACE COLLARS
KNITTED SHAWLS AND WRAPS
THE SECRETS OF SUCCESSFUL IRISH CROCHET LACE
KNITTED LACE DOILIES

THE GIRL FROM
THE LAND OF SMILES

Tessa Lorant Warburg

Thai Proverbs translated by Praphaphorn Phonbuakai

The Thorn Press

Copyright © Tessa Lorant Warburg 2012

http://www.tessalorantwarburg.com

The moral right of Tessa Lorant Warburg has been asserted.

All rights reserved. No part of this publication may
in any way be reproduced, stored in a retrieval system,
transmitted in any form or by any means: mechanical,
photocopying, electronic, recording or otherwise,
without prior permission from the copyright holder.

This is a work of fiction. The characters and incidents
are not based on any actual events, and are entirely the
products of the author's imagination.

Published in 2012 by The Thorn Press, Lansdowne
House, Castle Lane, Southampton SO14 2BU
http://thethornpress.com

ISBN: 9780906374306

DEDICATION

To Colin and Jum, who inspired me to write this novel.

ACKNOWLEDGMENTS

First of all I would like to thank my daughter-in-law, Praphaphorn Phonbuakai, for always being ready to answer my many questions about her home country, Thailand. Her Thai nickname is Jum, and we all know her by that name. Which is fortunate, because pronouncing and spelling Praphaphorn is not easy for a mere Westerner.

Jum has been an invaluable and patient help for quite a long time now, explaining her culture with good grace and great humour. However, I would like to emphasise that this novel is *not* her story, though she did come from an Isaan village, and she is married to one of my sons, a farang.

Jum has also been a great help with the Thai proverbs I use for the chapter headings. I feel these are both humorous and indicative of the Thai spirit – and the fact that some of them sound remarkably similar to some English ones is equally significant. The cultures may be very different, but the human condition is not.

I would also like to thank Robert Savage, originally from the UK but now living in Thailand and married to a Thai. He kindly read an early manuscript and made some very helpful comments.

And I am indebted to the Blue Room members of 2010-2012: Deanna Dewey, Evelyn Harris, Mike Hayward, Jenni Jacombs, Donna McGhie, Mike Plumbley and Ann Roberts. The group has had substantial amounts of this novel read to them and has made a number of very helpful comments.

AUTHOR'S NOTE

The Girl from the Land of Smiles has not been an easy book to put together. I was drawn to write this novel because I noticed that the differences between Thai and European cultures are so very substantial – and so very intriguing. It is not like comparing, say, the French and the British, or even Americans and Europeans; Thai and European cultures are far more fundamentally diverse.

I felt that a book written using the distinct voices of the two protagonists - Taiella Motubaki, the girl originally from an isolated Isaan village, and Luke Narland, a businessman running a small software company based in London – would give a reasonable, and sometimes humorous, approximation to some of these differences. However, the thoughts and words of the Thai characters only give a hint of the way Thais speak. This is because Thai is dissimilar to European languages in a number of ways: for example, there are no tenses, no comparatives, no pronouns.

The novel itself is not based on anything other than my imagination, though my daughter-in-law, Praphaphorn, did tell me a story handed down in her village, that of a fly which led to the body of a murdered villager. The rest of the book is simply fiction.

If any reader feels I have made some fundamental errors in my interpretation of Thai culture I apologise in advance. I would be very grateful to hear from him or her, and to try to put that right.

Any mistakes in the narrative are, of course, my own.

Thai Water Buffaloes in deep Holes

WHITE ELEPHANTS ARE BORN IN THE FOREST

'You very good dancing.' Taiella smiles at me as we take the floor. Buckling my knees. 'Me not very good.'

'I'll teach you.' We're at a party in an upmarket hotel, and the band is playing a quickstep. I encircle Taiella's tiny waist with my left arm and hold her left hand up with my right one. 'Just relax and let me guide you.'

'Guide?'

'You follow me. When I go forward, you go back.'

She giggles, but soon catches on. The music changes to disco, and she's happy twisting and turning to the rhythm.

It's time to go home before I've found out anything about her. Teng Japhardee, my right hand man in Thailand, the one who introduced us, has disappeared. I know I have to get her name, her address. I grab a tuk-tuk, hop in beside her and try to catch what she's telling the driver. Not a hope; my Thai's too rudimentary to catch the words. I pull out a piece of paper and ask her to write down her name and address. In Thai, so a tuk-tuk driver can find it.

She smiles sweetly, but leans away. 'Living with sister.'

Is this the brush-off, or merely a statement of fact? 'Can we meet again tomorrow?'

'English not very good. No understanding.'

'Coming again to see you? Pick you up from your sister?'

'Me working.'

"Pick up" could be misinterpreted. I remember how Teng introduced us: "Kuhn Luke, this is Kuhn Taiella. A real humdinger from Northeast Thailand, from Udon Thani. But she lives in Bangkok now, with her elder sister. And she works in a Japanese department store."

This last sentence to warn me that Taiella is a proper young woman, not a bar girl. 'Of course. I meant in the evening. What about seven o'clock? I could come to fetch you...'

Her body goes stiff, she edges away. 'You having wife?'

There's no point starting a relationship with a lie. 'Yes, I have a wife. Her name is Helga.'

'Not good idea meeting.'

'But we don't get on. We're getting a divorce.' This last bit is wishful thinking. I can feel the idea taking root, can sense this turning point in my life. Oddly enough it was Helga who suggested it last time I was home, when we had yet another of our many rows. I didn't respond, though I do remember wondering what made her say that. Now I think it's a brilliant idea, whatever her reasons for bringing it up.

Taiella's response is yet another variation of the smile. 'Not meeting married man,' she says, slowly, deliberately, still smiling but in a subtly different way.

'Of course. I understand. Not on a date. But I would love to see more of Bangkok, and I find it very difficult to get around on my own. I just thought you might show me something of your beautiful city. The Imperial Palace. I haven't been there...'

'Not understanding. Very sorry.' The tuk-tuk has stopped, she's about to get out. 'Now saying thank you and good night.'

'Hold on one minute, Taiella.' I get hold of Teng on my mobile, ask him to talk to her, suggest she becomes my guide.

'What is your meaning, Kuhn Luke? You having rocks in your head?'

'I just thought she could show me the sights of Bangkok. The cultural ones,' I add hastily.

'You full of bull. Proper Thai girls are in the soup if going out with a man on their own,' he tells me. 'She will be thinking you are in the catbird seat.'

2

'I could invite her sister as well,' I say. As long as I can get to know her I don't really care.

I visit the toy shop in the Japanese department store. Not that I have any need for toys. Helga and I don't have any children. Her choice.

As I walk around the shop, watching Taiella charm what seems like an army of customers into buying handfuls of toys, I realise I'd love to be a father. Apart from her other talents Taiella looks as though she'd make a wonderful mother.

'When is your day off?'

'Free tomorrow.'

'Can we go to see the Imperial Palace?'

She smiles. More customers claim her attention.

'My hotel tomorrow morning?'

More smiles and waves.

It's been a week, and I'd hoped for some sort of communication. Teng assures me Taiella will get in touch – in her own good time.

'You will be off the track if you insist too much, Kuhn Luke. Play the waiting game,' he advises. 'She is testing you.'

No doubt he's right, as usual. He's my bridge to Thai culture. I couldn't do business in Thailand without him.

At nine in the morning, a week later, reception ring me to say I have a visitor.

Teng mentioned he might call in to discuss a couple of problems the Farmer's Bank are having with one of my programmes. 'Just send him up,' I say.

There's an agitated tone to the man's stutters. 'Is young woman. Maybe you meeting downstairs, Kuhn Luke?'

My heart beats wildly as I rush downstairs.

Taiella has turned up, on her own, at my hotel. Dressed in her business clothes; a sort of uniform all Thai girls working in offices or department stores seem to wear. White blouses, navy blue skirts, low heels. Very demure.

In spite of that the receptionist is still agitated. His eyes swivel from me to her and back again, and I can see he's about to call the manager.

'We're having breakfast in the dining room,' I calm him down. And invite her to the excellent buffet the hotel provides.

We laugh a good deal, try to work out what we're going to do. Her response to virtually everything I say is 'hnn'. I take it to be her pronunciation of the English 'yeah'. With a Thai accent, accompanied by variations of the smile. Later I learn it means 'what?' in Thai.

Eventually we set out in a tuk-tuk and drive around Bangkok. Noisy, smelly, fume-filled Bangkok. We stop at various places, but none of them look like the Imperial Palace buildings I've seen on the internet.

The driver is getting impatient. 'Know what wanting? Maybe Imperial Palace?' he suggests.

'Yes, that's it,' I say. And Taiella begins to laugh and laugh.

'Not understanding,' she giggles. And, after two hours on the dusty streets, on a trip which should have taken no more than fifteen minutes, we arrive. And prepare to admire Bangkok's finest wats and palaces.

We enjoy each other's company, eat a meal together, go out to the floating market, learn to communicate. This time, when I drop Taiella off, she agrees to meet again – for another cultural tour.

That first impression, instinct, delight – all confirmed. So now that we've known each other for well over six months, and have put aside all barriers, I've finally persuaded Taiella that it's a good idea for me to go with her to visit her family.

I want to be sure that they understand that I want to marry her, not treat her like some sort of slave wife. I'm pretty clear she knows that, but since most of our communications are based on my English and variations of her smile, I can never be entirely sure.

'When would be a good time to visit, tilac?'

'Good time now, tilac. In dry season now.'

Dry season; a couple of weeks before the Songkran festival, which heralds the beginning of the monsoon. Everything is shrivelled up, mud roads caked solid, the atmosphere dusty. There's an air of expectation, a yearning for a break from blazing sun and cloudless skies. We often long for a warm summer in England. What we don't realise is that too much sun can be much worse than gentle summer rains.

'So now's a good time for your parents, that what you mean?'

'Yes, tilac. Very good timing.' She smiles radiantly, but I notice her eyes blinking rapidly. She twists away when I try to embrace her. I can't really understand her reluctance. Surely I'm proving that I want to do the right thing?

Should be an interesting experience. Teng, his English almost entirely taken from slang expressions he's learned from the fragments Thais picked up when the GIs used Thailand as a playground during the Vietnamese conflict, assures me Udon Thani is "pretty damn as near as you can get to the bee's knees. Might even say it's the elephant's instep, to give it a more local twist." He tries hard, of course. I couldn't do business in Thailand without him, but even my limited knowledge of US slang tells me he often gets it completely wrong, or uses expressions from the wrong decade. Necessitating a pretence at coughing to cover my amusement.

Well, Taiella doesn't come from Udon Thani. She's from Dumden Village, total population, I would guess, around 500. I doubt it's the elephant's instep or even the cat's meow. I just hope the natives are reasonably friendly. Particularly, of course, Taiella's parents.

I can tell she's really nervous. She keeps playing around with her hands, keeps blinking, then smiles radiantly whenever she catches my eye. What's she worried about? How difficult can it be to meet a rural Thai family living in a remote village?

She's even asked Teng to emphasise that the village is very near the Lao border, and that her mother is from Laos. Teng, highly educated, preached at me that Laotians are a Buddhist people inhabiting the area of the Mekong River in Laos and Thailand and speaking the Lao language. It is not the same as Thai, but related to it. Taiella, apparently, speaks both these languages.

She makes it sound like a big thing, though for the life of me

I can't work out what significance it can have for us. I'm more concerned with how her family will react to me, a 'farang', a Western foreigner not always held in the highest regard by ordinary Thais. The cross-cultural differences are hard to explain, hard to adjust to, for both cultures.

There's also a certain anxiety about actually coping with life in the village, even just for an overnight. You get there using a songthaew, a rather primitive form of transport popular all over Southeast Asia. Basically, a truck with two wooden benches facing each other for passengers to sit on. I suspect the local one might even be without a cover to shield against sun or rain. The trip to Dumden will be over mud roads, caked to concrete at this point, and take between three or four hours, depending on the number of passengers requesting stops on the way. Three times the flight time from Bangkok to Udon Thani!

So we'll have to stay the night. Which means braving the mosquitoes which, I know from our excursion to Ayutthaya City, the old capital of Siam and the countryside around it, adore me. As well as having to cope without furniture of any kind.

I shake myself. I'm not an old man yet!

DON'T LAMENT OVER A CHILLI WHEN KILLING A BUFFALO

I worry all the time we are on the plane. Luke's eyes are looking at me like two big question marks.

'What's wrong, tilac?'

'Nothing, tilac.'

It is very sweet the way Luke always using the Thai word for sweetheart. He watches as the ring he giving me is twisting round and round the second finger of my left hand. Even the very small European size is much too large for me, so now I worry the precious ring will be lost on the floor of the aircraft, and slip it off and put it on my thumb. I also worry because accepting a present with the left hand is very bad karma. People in my village believe this is an insult, but in Luke's country the second finger of the left hand is always used for the engagement ring. Maybe it's OK even in Thailand because I'm using only one finger. And Luke did not give me a real engagement ring – not yet, he is telling me, because that would be a lie.

Now he is taking my left hand in both of his, turning to palm facing, and he breathes kisses on the centre. Then he slips the friendship ring from my thumb back on the second finger again – a wide silver band on which are etched two birds touching beaks. He calls them turtle doves, a big symbol of true love in England.

Now Luke puts his arm around my shoulders, pulling my body

to him. I'm feeling safe and snug, a silk moth warm in its cocoon. I allowing this because no one can see what we are doing.

'You're looking rather peaky, tilac.' His big love is enveloping me, caressing me. 'Not feeling sick, are you, Taiella?'

I can see the big dream in Luke's eyes. I know he is longing to have a baby, and his English wife is always refusing him. 'I little bit tired, tilac. I try sleeping.'

It's not pregnancy sickness, and I do not wish to give Luke any false hope. I agreed to having a baby before we marry when we first became lovers. Luke's wife always refusing to have a baby, and their divorce can take a long time perhaps. Luke is nearing middle age, it's not a good idea to go on waiting. My older sister Pi Sayai advising me to have a baby as soon as possible. She warned that divorce outside Thailand can take many years. My lovely sister is truly sympathetic.

People from Northeast Thailand have a very strong belief in spirits, and my parents are always eager to give me their blessings to encourage good spirits each time I visit Dumden Village, the place where I grew up. My mum – Mae – is always going to her special Buddhist temple for fetching white strings before I come to visit. She makes good contributions for the monks, each time giving a few satang if she has no baht. At the end of each of my visits she ties four or five special white strings round my wrists for me – she has a firm belief that this will bring good fortune for me.

This time is very different, this time I need big luck before going home. Older sister Pi Sayai understands this very well. My kind sister invited a special blessings master to her room last night because she knew I would be visiting her to collect gifts for our honourable parents. She provided party food, and invited many friends. All crowding into the small room which is all she can afford for living in.

'We are very happy celebrating the lucky engagement of my younger sister, Nong Taiella,' she told neighbours, holding up my hand and stroking the ring to show it off.

Pi Sayai is quite right. This is a proper time for making sure the good phii spirits are on my side. They are very important for me, and I need them.

The blessings master brushed his fingers from my palms to my wrists, tying white strands round both. He smiled with his whole face, saying my hands are very small, and I could see in his eyes that he approved that I am dainty. Then he brushed his fingers in the opposite direction, from wrists to palms, so encouraging all spiteful spirits to leave. He held my hands in his, and advised me to keep the ties on my wrists for a minimum of three days.

The friendship ring Luke gave me is so very loose on my finger. I thread lucky white strings through it to stop it falling off and try to sleep. Luke and I are flying from Bangkok to Udon Thani, and I only have a very short time to prepare myself for the visit to my parents.

Luke is putting his arm around my shoulders, pulling me to him. 'You'll chafe your wrists if you keep fiddling with those coarse ties, tilac.'

I do not stop Luke from taking my small hands in his big ones, and smile away the many worries I am having. The flight between Bangkok and Udon Thani takes only one hour, but I wish very hard for it to take longer because I am not looking forward to landing. I already know very well we will have big problems, but cannot tell this to Luke. How can I explain my village will not be able to understand Luke's reasons for coming? He is such a sweet man, wanting to behave in the correct way for meeting my parents. My heart has a big ache because my lovely fiancé cannot comprehend Thai village ways, is not prepared for that in any way. Therefore I think it best if I let experience be Luke's teacher while I stand firm by his side. My fingers are creeping to my wrists inside Luke's hands, feathering the white strings with my fingertips. The rounded, firm shapes of the cords comfort me, giving me strength for managing problems I know will be sure to surface in the village.

My dear parents are not racist, but they do not trust foreigners, least of all Westerners. They assume all farang treat Thai girls as ladies of the night. They cannot know, will not believe me, that my lovely Luke always treats me with respect, is always polite. He has such a good heart, which is the main reason I am so much in love with him.

There is one special big problem which is always worrying me.

I cannot allow my dad – Phor – to find out Luke already has a first wife in England. If my dad discovers this he will forbid me ever to see my lovely man again. One thing I know for sure: I cannot go against my father's orders.

COVERING A DEAD ELEPHANT WITH A LOTUS LEAF

The plane lands in Udon Thani at the correct time, meaning we can take the morning songthaew to Dumden. My big worry now is that maybe one of my mum's neighbours will be on this same songthaew that we will take. It is not proper for an unmarried girl to be with a man unless a girlfriend or relative accompanies her. If someone from my village sees me with Luke it will cause a very big loss of face for my parents.

I am very happy when I notice that the benches of the waiting songthaew are empty, so not so nervous now. I worry instead about Luke travelling in a pickup truck with hard wooden benches for sitting on and only a canvas top for shading his delicate, white, western skin from the hot sun. We are at the end of dry season now, the soil almost like concrete, and there is only the dirt road leading from Udon Thani to Dumden Village. This means the songthaew will be jolting like a water buffalo on the hardened ruts. This journey takes a long time, often several hours, and so leaves all passengers very bruised. I twiddle my white strings as I look around and am very glad to see no other passengers coming. I know good luck is more certain if I leave the strings on as long as possible. There will be plenty of time for removing them on this trip. I am more relaxed now because it is almost time for setting out. We are getting ready to climb aboard.

'Not leaving now, younger sister,' the driver calls out to me while strolling over, looking at me with scornful eyes. 'Waiting for mother coming with sick baby she taking hospital yesterday.'

I feel the familiar pang. The driver sees I am an unmarried woman already twenty years or more old, and therefore worthless.

'You knowing name of mother, older brother?' Girls who went to the village school with me are all long married and have several children, and I know all of them.

'Not name, younger sister. Only know mother coming from Dumden Village.'

So I definitely know her. Please, let it not be the younger sister of my mum, Na Att, I now whisper to my lucky strings. Na Att always reminds my mum that a good younger daughter should be staying at home to help her family in the paddies. My aunt is forever complaining that I set a bad example for Nong Wuadon, the beautiful baby girl my mum brought for my aunt from Laos sixteen years ago. Because Na Att is not able to have children, so she was very happy to adopt Nong Wuadon. Na Att is particularly clever at hiding her snake tongue behind her crocodile smile, meaning my mum never has any idea of what is really going on.

The tough hemp scratches my wrists raw as I pull my strings off. The pain this causes me reminds me again that my Aunt Att is a palm tree without leaves or fruit, meaning she cannot have children. So I was worrying for nothing, because it means she cannot be the other passenger the driver is waiting for.

'What are you doing?' Luke, seeing me struggle with the strings, takes both my small hands in his.

The driver scowls at Luke, eyes very hard. He did not realise Luke is with me. So now I am not just unmarried, I am with a farang. The driver will think this very bad.

'Putting white strings in safe place, tilac,' I whisper. It is really important to keep the strings as high as possible. Normally I put them on the little altar in my older sister's Bangkok room. Now I take a tiny silk square out of my pocket, wrap the white strings inside, then put that in the breast pocket of my blouse.

'This farang going with you, younger sister?' The driver's voice cuts across to me, sharp and rough. Such loudness is very impolite.

I pretend not to hear.

Spitting hard to the side of the road, staining the withered vegetation with dark purple betel-nut juice, he turns to us. Bared teeth change to dog-snarl smile when he sees Luke standing tall, very tall compared to Thai men, and frowning at him.

Everyone is ultra conservative, here in Northeastern Thailand. I can tell the driver thinks I must be a lady of the night because I accompany a man who is farang.

'Mother coming,' the driver now calls out in a loud voice, climbing into the driver's cabin.

A village woman, her baby held in a sarong sling in front, with a second sarong holding her belongings saddled on her back, stumbles towards us – very slowly. She is short, and painfully thin, just like my aunt, Na Att. The baby sling is dyed indigo blue, the same colour my mum still uses when she dyes silk or cotton. Is it Na Att, after all? Has a miracle happened, and she gave birth?

The woman is coming closer and I am really shocked to recognise Pi Lai, the only daughter of Na Att's sister-in-law. She's dragging herself along like a lop-sided hen, her face dark brown from too much sun, her skin shrivelled with many wrinkles, lines etched from nose to mouth.

Luke, seeing she is in distress, jumps down from the songthaew, ready to help her. I hurl myself in front of Luke, warning him not to try to help the mother, in English.

'Not good idea, tilac,' I gabble quickly. 'Thai women do not accept physical contact from a male stranger. We are in Isaan Province now, not in Bangkok.'

'I was only going to take one of her bundles...'

'Better for me to help her, tilac.' I walk up to Pi Lai, say 'Sawatdee Kha!' Guilt makes me give an exaggerated greeting by bowing almost to an L-shape, steepling my hands in the traditional wai greeting, lips stretched as wide as I can make them. 'So nice meeting you, Pi Lai.'

'Sawatdee Kha!' Pi Lai returns my greeting, out of breath. She hands me the sarong bundle on her back and returns the wai. 'You travelling to Dumden Village in this songthaew, sister?'

Pi Lai is putting on her widest smile, nodding, glancing at

Luke. Full moon eyes turn to slits as she takes in he is with me.

'Yes, Pi Lai.' Backing away from Luke, putting on a demure smile, I say: 'This is Khun Luke Narland. I am bringing fiancé for meeting my parents. Marrying soon soon.'

Pi Lai is wai-ing at Luke and he returns the greeting.

I give the bundle to Luke, stretching my arm out to its full extent to make sure he cannot brush against me. I offer to take the baby while the exhausted mother wheezes onto the pickup. The baby is so light I hardly feel his weight.

Luke places Pi Lai's bundle on one bench, and sits opposite my former school companion. She is sliding the sarong along to dust the wooden seat, sits down, stares at Luke, devours all the details of his farang body.

I wonder what Pi Lai thinks of the man with me. He has a long nose, like all farang, the reason we call them 'long noses'. But Luke's nose is slender. Many of his colleagues have thick noses, in a dark red colour. And my man is very tall, even for a farang, with extra light skin covered in brown spots he calls freckles, and hair of a ginger colour I have never seen before. We always prize pale complexions in Northeast Thailand. Our girls are famous for this in the whole of Thailand. We call this skin tone khiao, the colour of young rice shoots. So now I am thinking my Luke is looking very handsome, and cannot stop smiling my happiness.

'You staying at hotel in Udon Thani, Pi Taiella?' My cousin's nostrils widen as she scans the clothes I am wearing, also my hair, takes in the ring, eyes looking hard at my waist, down to my belly.

'We arriving with the early plane this morning, Pi Lai.'

Pi Lai sniffs, holds out her arms for the baby. Such a small, thin child. As she takes him from me he starts coughing, bringing up liquid all over his mother. Sighing, she is taking a dented plastic bottle filled with water out of her sarong, together with a filthy cotton square. She wipes herself as clean possible. Liquid spreads all over the bench.

I sit down next to Luke.

'Is this lady from your village, tilac?'

Nervousness has made me impolite, and I forgot to introduce Pi Lai to Luke. 'Yes. She is related with my family, so I know her very well. She is the daughter of Lung Ban's sister. I call him Lung Ban, meaning Uncle Ban, because he is husband to Na Att, that is my Aunt Att, who is my mum's younger sister.'

Luke frowns at this long explanation. It would have been enough to explain that we went to the village school together.

'That means Lai is some sort of cousin, and younger than you, right?'

At first I have no idea why Luke is asking this. Does he really think I look older than this work-worn woman? Maybe he thinks I'm not at all pretty, that I look like Pi Lai, dark skinned and ugly. It is true I have quite dark skin, not like my sister who is very fair. 'Pi Lai is older than me, Luke, by at least two-three months.'

He nods, smiling me on.

'She married at eighteen, and already has three children. Village life is very hard.'

'Indeed.' He's laughing now. 'She certainly looks a lot older than you.'

I breathe a little more freely.

'What I can't understand is why she's calling you Pi. Shouldn't she be calling you Nong?'

Luke does speak a small amount of Thai. He heard the way Pi Lai addressed me, and clearly it puzzled him. It is very true that we address anyone older than ourselves Pi, anyone younger Nong. And we address people as Khun when wishing to be more formal. Luke already knows Thai people consider it very rude to speak to another person without using a title. Many of our customs are hard to explain to a western foreigner – a farang. Thai culture and traditions are so very different from the West.

'It is hard to explain, tilac. She called me Nong when we were children. She calls me Pi now to show respect.'

'Respect?' His eyebrows lift at me. I notice now that they are also that ginger colour, transparent in the strong sun. Making Luke look quite young.

'She shows respect because I have an important position in my world.' I am very proud of my achievements in the big city. 'I am Sales Manager in a big Japanese department store in Krung Thep…'

15

Luke's eyes blink. 'Assistant Sales Manager. And you work in Bangkok!'

'Sorry, tilac. I always forgetting. We calling Bangkok by a different name here, in Northeast Thailand. We call our capital city Krung Thep – meaning Divine City of Angels.'

The main reason Pi Lai addresses me as Pi is because I introduced Luke as my fiancé. Of course she can see he is farang. All farang are rich beyond any village woman's dream, and therefore due the highest respect. And that, of course, transfers to me also.

Luke's blue eyes fade to grey in the bright sun, but he is still laughing. 'So older is a compliment, even if you happen to be younger. Must say that appeals to me.'

Already thirty-eight, a little bit older than me. Here in Isaan we have a saying that an old cow likes to eat fresh grass. Also true, of course, for an old bull. But Luke is only twelve years older than me, not such a big difference. Also, in Dumden Village, no one thinks of me as very fresh grass. They consider me coarse grass, even if not yet shrivelled.

Pi Lai continues to clear up her child's vomit. She has time to study Luke and me, her eyes as brittle as the dry earth. Seeing Luke's arm moving towards my shoulders I jerk away, reminding him in English that this not proper behaviour.

'What are you calling your baby, Pi Lai?'

'We calling Suphat, nickname Deng. Maybe better giving more rude nickname – Ugly Pig good idea, so evil spirits do not want to steal him. Mean spirits always wanting to steal my boys, like two more boys we having.'

'You losing two boys?'.

'Your mum not telling you?'

I smile away confusion. My mum is always saying that Lung Ban's sister is a worm gnawing at her daughter Pi Lai's guts. Many spirits are very unforgiving, and in the village we believe that they are punishing Pi Lai for the sins of her mother.

'My son is nearly six months in this world, but he looks as though he's only two months old. Not like my daughters, they are very strong. I have been taking him to doctors at the hospital. All telling me there is nothing wrong.' Pi Lai's face is shutting down. She brushes the baby's head with her lips. 'The Doctors say I should be eating more protein to make good milk.' Tears are trickling down her cheeks, drying right away in the heat, leaving shadowy streaks. 'Now it's the end of the dry season, water is very low in the river, fish are all gone. My daughters are not clever for fetching crabs.'

She reminds me of my own childhood, when my sister and I looked for small crabs in the cracks in the earth, at the end of the dry season. 'Rain must be coming soon,' I try comforting her. 'We will be celebrating Songkran Festival in a few days, then the rain will come and the fish will be back.' Older sister Pi Sayai and I became very good at finding the little crabs, in the cracks where water is still snailing through in places, even at the end of the dry season. We took our catch back to Mae for our main meal. She cooked the crabs with garlic and herbs, making a tasty topping for our meal of sticky rice. That was the time when my dad was far away, working in Saudi Arabia, and our family was left behind in Thailand, poor like Pi Lai and her family.

'Not lucky like your family, Pi Taiella. You now have money for buying a lake, now owning it. You having fish all year round.' Pi Lai's eyes are smouldering, but she lowers her eyelids so that I won't be able to see her envy. 'My family happy if we having enough sticky rice to fill our bellies.' She takes her left breast out of her blouse and offers it to her child. The boy refuses to wake. 'I know my son is OK,' Pi Lai shouts, her voice strong and high. 'You remember, Pi Taiella, Buddha teaches us that the virtuous are protected by their own own virtue, and therefore it is not necessary to give up hope.'

The baby is sleeping, not even waking when the songthaew bucks like a bronco. Luke puts his arm out to stop me from falling off the bench. I back away, explaining once more that we are not alone, and therefore cannot touch each other, cannot even hold hands. So we enjoy it when the unruly pickup throws us together, allowing physical contact we cannot avoid. This does not escape Pi Lai's cobra eyes.

'Like bird in snare,' she says, pointing at me, her tongue spitting indignation. 'Tangled hands tied with bonds of desire are very hard to cut.' She tries feeding the baby again but cannot wake him.

One thin, elongated breast lies bared. Luke's eyes are wandering, uncertain where to look, gazing above Pi Lai's head. I understand his discomfort because Western women do not show breasts in public.

'Self-restraint is a constant blessing, Pi Taiella.'

The driver stops by Pi Lai's house and I jump off the songthaew, helping the exhausted mother down.

As I do this, and am very close to Pi Lai, I notice many strong marks of virtue deeply etched on her face.

CUTTING THE BAMBOO SHOOT BEFORE SEEING THE WATER

'Want buy?'

Taiella and I jump down from the songthaew, my body tormented and bruised from being tossed up and down on the wooden bench. The voice is loud, demanding – and, quite astonishingly, speaking recognisable English. It sounds assured, used to being in charge. I stand full height, suck in my stomach. Heat tends to distend my abs, a hint of middle age I'm determined to defeat. Taiella's a bit younger than me, but not that much younger.

I turn, look around. Who could that be? No one knew we were coming.

A sudden scuffle in thick dust under a dark canopy of banana leaves – chickens cluck-clucking at being disturbed. But no human to be seen. A strong whiff of manure envelops me, makes me sneeze. I pull out a soggy tissue and wipe my nose, look round. No one that I can see.

I swivel back to the road – a dung-spattered dust-track, hard-surfaced by ox-carts and the hooves of water buffalo – meandering between houses on stilts crowned by Napa-thatched roofs. There's no movement, the scene is like a film set waiting for actors. A disembodied voice? One of the spirits Taiella so often mentions? Ridiculous; how could I even let myself think such rubbish?

Taiella has also disappeared. My eyes adjust, slowly, to the shadows under the banana leaves. She's yanking a pail towards us, dipping a half-coconut shell into it and offering it to me. I gulp down the water, narrow my eyes rather than putting on glasses, search the dark areas under the house we were deposited by, then the parched vegetation. No one, nothing.

I definitely heard a male voice, yet the village looks deserted. Naturally; it's around noon and I assume most of the villagers would be working in the paddies, cultivating the soil one way or another.

I squint against the harsh light, pointing my nose to where the sound seems to have come from. That's when I finally spot him: a short, wiry man blending into a background of scrubby vegetation, standing at the back of the canopy of intertwined banana leaves. His khaki trousers and mottled green shirt provide impressive camouflage. He comes forward, nods vigorously at me, two large but incomplete rows of teeth lighting up his face. Short, muscular arms are hugging his thin frame in spite of the intense heat. His mouth is upturned in the ubiquitous Thai smile, but it looks unsure. Smile-on, smile-off eyes flicker first over Taiella, then scan my face.

Taiella steeples her hands together in an attitude of prayer, pulls them in against her body, inclines her head respectfully, looks demurely down. The obligatory wai. She'd be using the correct greeting for the occasion, of course. I'm no expert in the many variations of the wai but it looked, somehow, filial. Her father, presumably.

'Want buy, OK?' The voice has taken on an edge which flutters away to an uncertain high. Claw-like fingers press into his shirt, then his arms spread apart and he flicks his head and widens his eyes. Ominous-looking sweat stains spider his sleeves, giving off a pungent smell.

I turn to Taiella for a clue on how to react but she's moved away from me and stands to one side, head hanging down. Usual deferential crap. She never openly goes against any of my suggestions, just waits for events to unfold. This is her way of telling me off for insisting on coming here.

'Is this your father, Taiella?' Nervousness gives my voice

20

a mocking tone. I hope she won't misinterpret that. She's extraordinarily quick to pick up nuances, even in English.

She nods, colouring up, eyes fixed firmly on a shallow dip in the caked earth by her feet. She begins to shuffle dirt into it, endangering her prized high-heeled shoes. Already covered in a thick envelope of dust, I wonder why she insists on wearing them. Then grasp she's showing her father – everyone in the village – that she's wearing city shoes, that she has an important city job, that she isn't a village girl any more.

So that's what she's been trying to avoid: her father offering her for sale. Why else would a farang come to the village? She must have known all along. She didn't say so – nothing as crass as spelling things out. She always lets me wallow in my mistakes. Now I understand why she didn't want me to visit. Not simply because her father would offer her for sale – she'd have assumed that – what she's really worried about is that I might accept! My nostrils flare. Haven't I made it clear that I want to marry her? Isn't the very fact that I'm here proof enough?

I take a deep breath. 'We don't do that in England, Lung.' Address her father as uncle, that's the drill. All the same, my attempt to sound nonchalant, normal, as though I make a habit of turning down trades in girls from Thai villages, isn't an outstanding success. He stands there blinking, looking expectant.

I manage to force my face into a toothy grin and spread my palms upward for good measure. Surely an international gesture? Actually, I've no idea – that's the problem. Not just language, body language is different, too. I drop my arms to my side and try to look amiable but determined. Not because of the money, I know I can handle that. No way am I going to offer to buy Taiella, however tempting it might be to get her father off my back. He mightn't have any idea, but I know she'll have me on the next songthaew out of the village – and out of her life – if I show any signs of agreeing to such a deal.

Clearly not understanding he leers at me, winks, then frowns with his lips upturned. A Thai smile variation I haven't come across so far. Then his eyes light up, as if he's just got the right answer on *Millionaire*. 'Two thousand dollars,' he announces, teeth glinting spittle, nodding. 'Very good price.'

Taiella's hair whirls round her face, turns from demure to fetchingly tousled. She glares at her father, forgets the filial stance, the sidelong look. Her tone and gestures, though delivered in a voice so low I can hardly hear it, tell me she isn't translating – she's telling him he's got it completely wrong. I do know some Thai, but I can't pick out more than the odd word or two because of the Isaan dialect, but I know well enough what she's saying.

I don't have to contribute anything. His nostrils widen, his face closes up, he looks away. Obvious; he'd see me as a gangling farang, pink skin unable to cope with tropical sun, not even prepared to pay the modest price he's set on her. Hardly an attractive swain. Worse, too mean to pay for his pleasures.

Does he assume I've taken advantage of his daughter? Well, going by their customs, I wouldn't be here if I had. I don't doubt he's comparing me to local suitors who'd give him proper respect, kowtow to him. Perhaps not altogether for the sake of righteousness. Could be because, as youngest daughter, Taiella's husband's role would be to join the family and help her father run his smallholding, and eventually to inherit it. Thai property is passed down through the female line, and the youngest female at that. Quite different from our first-born male customs.

I shade my eyes, trying to get a better look at the man. Short, gnarled, wizened. Constant exposure to sun isn't beneficial even if your skin doesn't lack melanin. He probably isn't even fifty yet.

As for me, he'd see me as a useless farang, about to deprive him of the daughter he'd expect to rely on in his old age. The best he can do now is to get money out of me for soiled goods. He doesn't even have to worry whether Taiella is still a virgin, which all village suitors naturally expect. What really matters is that we'd been seen together without chaperones, and that this is known about here, in the village – a massive loss of face. Furthermore, he'd be clear that, like all the other farang men who come to his country, particularly to Bangkok, I'd have only one thing in mind: to get a local girl and use her as a sex object. No self-respecting Thai would take her as a wife after that.

I watch the busy eyes in the walnut face take in the bad news, see the mouth tucker into a half-smile. We are, after all, in the Land of Smiles. Doesn't exactly mean his thoughts are amiable, much less that he's given up. He'll offer to sell me something else. He does have another daughter, the older one, in Bangkok! Of course she's already spoken for, but only as a second wife – a minor wife, as they say – to a rich businessman, and could, therefore, be bartered for.

I've brought Wirat Motubaki a splendid present: a Swiss Army knife, a Victorinox with all the gadgets anyone could ever need, housed in a compact package. I'm really pleased with my choice.

He takes it, smiling, opens it. Then his face turns to stone. He gabbles something too low for me to make out, but his sounds are harsh in any language. Blaming Taiella, or cursing her? Is he saying he never wants to see her again?

Concerned, I touch Taiella's arm. She jumps back as if stung by a snake. Damn! No touching in public, least of all in her village, worse still in front of her father. Sure sign, she'd quoted Buddhist lore many times, that "where infatuation reigns outer darkness prevails". 'What's he saying?'

She turns a new, semi-sweet smile towards me, melting me. My heart thumps as her delicate body twists round, eyes big. 'We never giving sharp tool for present, tilac. That destroying friendship, cutting in two.'

Bloody hell! Why hadn't I shown it to her first?

'This meaning Phor must buy from you. Then everything OK.'

Wirat Motubaki draws himself up to full height – a clear head below me, and no taller than Taiella. 'Giving one satang for knife, OK?'

I bow, taking the oily coin he digs out of his pocket. 'That's all right now, is it?' I ask Taiella.

'No problem,' she assures me. She always does.

'Two thousand dollar for daughter,' Wirat persists, slipping the knife into his pocket. A grin, together with an assured flick of his head. 'Good deal. Quality four thousand.'

I nod, my face composed into grave lines, adjusting to a business deal before I'd even been introduced. He's spent time working in Saudi Arabia as a construction worker, leaving his family for several years. The only way to lift them above subsistence level. It shows in his factory-made trousers and shirt instead of home-made gear, as well as the good charcoal cooker I've been told he's bought his wife – and the family's land with a lake on it. A few words of English along the way are a bonus. So is knowing the value of the greenback.

My lips wide, I try to work out how to save face for the father without agreeing a deal. I'm not judging East by West – I'd soon be out of a job if I do anything like that – and I'm not turning him down because I don't want to pay the price. Taiella's worth much more than that to me.

One of Teng's many axioms blunders into my mind from nowhere in particular: "A person with forbearance brings benefits to others as well as to themselves". Could be that my devout Thai associate has a point. I catch on: don't say anything at all, just smile.

So that's what I do. I'm out to marry Taiella, not buy her like some bloody piece of merchandise. She hasn't escaped to a decent job in Bangkok for anything so appallingly crude as being bought by a farang. Nor, downcast eyes or not, do I have any doubts about her strengths: an astonishing ability to pick up English, learn new ways, leave her rural past where it belongs. Not highly educated, no. But intuitive, bright, imitative, quick. I know well enough that that isn't down to me. I also know she'll never go back, in mind or body. She's no longer a village girl.

'If you could just explain to your father, Taiella. We don't buy women in England. We court them and marry them. I'd be keen to have your father's blessing, of course. But I can't pay him for it.'

STUMPS SHOW UP WHEN THE TIDE GOES OUT

At first Taiella just stands there looking at me, that half-smile dancing on and off her face, like the shadows of fast-moving clouds on a lotus leaf. Then the clouds mass as her expression darkens. 'I no can be first wife – Mia Glang Muang - for you, Luke. You already have.'

I breathe in to speak, then out, but only manage grunts. Taiella hands me another half-coconut of water. She's right of course; I *am* still married to Helga. 'Well, yes, I know,' I gurgle through the tepid liquid. 'I was thinking. Couldn't you be my Thai wife, just for the time being?' Ex-pats I've come across in Bangkok have assured me that a man living in Thailand can, legally, have up to four wives. I'm asking her to be second, not fourth.

A gentle hand takes back the coconut-shell and cups it, staring into it. 'Only one first wife, Luke.' She plucks little bits of hair from the outside, flicks them away. 'Law changing in 1935. Now only one legal wife in Thailand.'

I blink at the coconut-shell cup. Quite impressive. I've never seen a bald coconut-shell before. A liquid brown, and shiny, like a mirror.

'Maybe some rich men also still having three Mia Glang Norng – minor wives.'

The shiny coconut catches the sun like a mirror, blinding me. 'Oh.' Could I really have got it that wrong? I thought she said? Surely her sister Sayai, the one she stays with in Bangkok, is a second wife with a son, whose husband visits regularly. Taiella was adamant. Lung Palem is as responsible for Sayai and her offspring as if she were his first wife. 'So what about your sister?'

She looks past her father. His head moves like a swaying palm, from her to me and back again. Can he understand what we're saying? He seems to be listening, carefully.

'Pi Sayai minor wife,' Taiella explains. And shrugs.

I take back the coconut cup and dip it into the almost-empty pail. Second wife was the description I'd been given, but I've forgotten that, in the East, saving face is always more important than western ideas of accuracy. 'And her son? I thought you said he was as legitimate as if she were his first wife?'

Taiella treats me to the facial contortion I've come to recognise as her patient sufferance smile, a special variation to accommodate an ignorant farang's inability to understand Thai ways. 'Already explaining, tilac. Thai man must take responsibility for children fathering on every wife. All children legitimate in Thai law. Even Mia Glang Tasee children.' She dips her fingers into the pail and brushes water over her face and neck.

Her father offers me more water, staring at me. No smile, eyes narrow.

'And what's a mia – well, what you said?' I know there are at least ten ways of saying you in Thai. Now I'm being informed that there are three types of wife.

'Mia Glang Tasee.' Taiella's eyes open wide, drops of water on her eyelashes catching the light. 'Already knowing, tilac. Slave wives. Man pays parents sum money, takes woman. Man owns.'

So that's what her father was getting at, that's why she was quite so upset. I saw him nodding his head, looking glum. No wonder he'd been so nervous he'd even forgotten the traditional Thai welcome. And my instincts haven't let me down. Taiella has in mind being my wife – legal, first, only. Has she really understood that that's what I want, too? Buying her would be to turn her into a kind of prostitute – a butterfly of the dark, as the Thais picturesquely put it. I've heard rumours about sex slaves, how the service industry in Bangkok recruits young girls from the remoter villages. The parents get the cash, the girls get dragged to Bangkok to work. Virtually kept as prisoners, though a number agree to be bar girls. What could I possibly have said that she would even bring it up? Frustration that I couldn't take her in my arms, kiss all the hurt away, makes sweat pour into my eyes.

'You know I'd make you my first and only wife right away if I were free. You know that's what I want, sweetheart. Explain that to your father. But it can't be done overnight.' My voice sounds harsh, much too harsh. I dip my hand into the pail and scoop up a few more drops of water.

There are a couple of Helga problems, none of them insoluble. Strange she'd initiated the idea of splitting. After ten years of marriage her threat of divorce was, I knew, simply another weapon in her campaign to nag, to humiliate, to insult. That had misfired, but the notion had taken root, had seriously affected my feelings for her. I brush damp fingers round my neck. The liquid dries instantly, leaving my skin tight.

My love for Helga was real enough in the past. It lasted through her ill-concealed irritation at what she considers my inferior education, tastes and earning power. She's the dazzling lawyer, she earns almost twice what I do, she always reminds me of that. Until her constant competitiveness reduced my self-esteem to zero.

Helga assumes she's the loved-one, I the supplicant. Not any more. I felt released after that little scene, ready for a new, a gentler lover. And I met Taiella on my very next trip – to Thailand, as it happened.

Unfortunately Helga also brings out my sense of guilt, the nagging feeling that what God has joined together... I square my shoulders. If I want Taiella I have to pull asunder from Helga.

'I'll start divorce proceedings as soon as I get back to England, tilac. Immediately.' Why hadn't I got on with it right away, the moment I'd returned from that fateful meeting at the business party Teng Japhardee dragged me to? Because I wasn't sure? Of course I was, I'd picked up the forms as soon as I got back to London. Just hadn't filled them in. Because I cringed at confronting Helga, knew she wouldn't give up without a fight. And, being a barrister, she'd fight whether she still wanted me or not. Just for the sake of winning.

I turn to Wirat. He has a right to know my intentions, that's why I'm here. 'We no buy England, Lung,' I announce, my voice sepulchral. Stop short, feel myself prickle with more sweat. What an idiotic thing to say. I need help with this, interpretation. 'Taiella explain,' I finish, defeated. I notice my blood surging, start to feel faint in the broiling noontime heat. I prop myself up against a slim nearby tree, desperate for support.

Taiella stares at it nervously. 'That home of family spirits, tilac. Not good for leaning on.'

Is everything against me? Evidently villagers can't afford the fancy little houses of the spirits which one sees, prominently displayed, all over Thailand. They are in front of every private house, every shop, every place of business. In Dumden Village they apparently nominate trees. As teacher Teng also instructed me, "a gift is never insignificant when given with sacrificial intent". 'Sorry.' I close my eyes, move away from the tree, will myself to stay upright.

'Stand under banana tree shade. Very hungry for water because of fierce sun. Fetching more for drinking.' She grabs the pail and disappears behind her father, lifts the lid off an enormous vat, dips the pail into the interior and comes back with another half coconut-shell and the pail heavy. Would I get some kind of ghastly disease drinking stagnant water? I take it gratefully, too thirsty to care, and drink and drink. It tastes wonderful.

Taiella is always helping me, translating for me – literally, culturally, personally. Except for business she's become my right-hand woman whenever I travel to Thailand, more or less from the time I met her, almost six months ago. Interpreter, guide, friend. And finally, about two months ago, lover.

A gentle, quite amiable discussion between father and daughter, with much nodding of heads and soft smiles. That leaves me free to cool down, to look around. I hadn't noticed, but we now seem to be surrounded by at least twenty rural Thais who've arrived, stealthily, silently, and are standing in a semi-circle, a few still dressed in the traditional mor hom – coarse, home-woven blue cotton work clothes – watching us. Most of them, I'm sure, have never been further than the thirty odd miles to Udon Thani.

They've probably never seen a European before. They don't look as though they find the spectacle inspiring.

No longer feeling faint I begin to feel irritable. Isn't this work time, aren't all these people supposed to be in the paddy fields? I've always understood Thai villagers are like Chinese coolies – bent double planting rice seedlings or something, working all daylight hours.

Apparently not. They stand and stare without a single word between them, raising their cheek muscles in a pseudo smile whenever I catch someone's look, their eyes blank. Even the children have gathered round, watchful, arranged in a mute, inner semi-circle. We're standing outside a comparatively large, bamboo-walled building on the inevitable stilts. I take it to be Taiella's parents' house.

Her father, only a fleeting smile on his face as he turns from me, makes an unmistakable and autocratic gesture of dismissal to his fellow villagers. They shuffle off as he beckons me to climb up the short ladder and go inside the house.

I'm careful to take my shoes off on the landing outside the door. You never enter a Thai person's house wearing shoes. Then I stoop under the opening and walk into a large room. There's no furniture, just a couple of rugs – another benefit from Saudi Arabia – on the wooden floor. So where's Taiella's mother? I spot a small door at the far end and guess there's one other room – a kitchen.

WATER FLOODS THE MOUTH

The small door opens slowly, doubtfully. A head wearing a stern-looking face filters round it. Inquisition eyes flick from Taiella to me, then the head retreats and a naked foot with splay toes is followed by a leg covered in brilliantly-dyed cloth. Shiny, like silk. The whole body emerges, the dazzling skirt covered by a dull cotton top. My cheek muscles arrange themselves, ready for a smile of greeting, when a second female darts out. She's young, and lithe, and wearing a skirt of the same peacock-coloured material, this time topped by a blouse in the same shiny fabric.

My eyes, greedy for more, only catch a glimpse of her because, before either Taiella or I could say anything at all, she smiles, radiant but nervous, then wais her way past us and out of the door, down the ladder and away. A vision of pale latte skin, long wavy hair and a Lolita figure.

The woman follows slowly, deliberately. An older, a more solid version of Lai, the young mother who was with us on the songthaew – worn, deep lines between mouth and a broad nose, toes with blackened nails, arms folded.

'Sawatdee khrab, Pa.' I try out the greeting Taiella has drilled into me: Pa is the appropriate Thai word for aunt. Like all Thai relationships it depends on relative ages and whether the person is from the father's or mother's side. I bow but do not wai. 'Always let the Thai initiate the wai greeting,' Teng has been careful to instruct me as soon as I set foot in Bangkok that very first time. I

30

presume the woman is Taiella's mother. Too old for a sister.

I blink my eyes and look again. Probably too young for a grandmother, and clearly unimpressed with me. Well, who else could she be? And where does the young girl fit in? Is there another daughter, a sister Taiella hasn't mentioned? At least that would supply a younger daughter for the parents, someone who might stay and look after them in their old age.

Eyes of an even brown with no highlights look from my head to my feet. No greeting for me, or Taiella. Nothing but a blank stare.

Taiella says something, and I make out the word Mae. Right; definitely her mother. Still no attempt at an introduction, no greeting from the woman. She flicks her head, throws a few words at Taiella, turns, goes back into the kitchen. Nothing at all to indicate pleasure that her daughter has come to visit, has brought someone specifically to meet her.

'Mae cooking rice,' Taiella says, mouth corners working hard to form a smile, but eyelids blinking nervousness. 'She asking help for cooking chicken Phor killing. You sitting down, making comfortable.'

She means on the floor, of course. There is no furniture. It's been a few years since I've sat on floorboards rather than in a chair. Taiella finds one of those hard, Axe cushions – triangular prisms made of three thick rolls of stuffed material on each side – for me to lean on. Still damned inconvenient, my long legs stick out at all angles. But at least I have some support for my back.

'So who was the young girl?' I move my legs experimentally forward, back. Settle for having them straight out in front of me. I had the strangest feeling about her. She reminded me – well, what I could glean about her looks – of Panjim Narcoso, Taiella's best friend in Bangkok. The girl has the same inquisitive features, mischievous body and exciting gestures which make Panjim unforgettable. He's a ladyboy working in the hairdressing franchise of the ZenZam Centre, right opposite the toy department where Taiella works. He – or she, as she insists on being referred to when off duty – is envy-provokingly beautiful. She's invited to all the best parties in Bangkok and insisted on inviting Taiella to a lavish birthday do for Panjim's long-time boyfriend – a Norwegian who spends half his year in Bangkok, the other half in Oslo. Teng knows the boyfriend through a business connection, and dragged me to that same party, the one where Taiella and I met. I am forever grateful to Panjim.

Taiella pulls in her lower lip with an audible suck. 'Nong Wuadon. She my cousin, daughter of Na Att – she my aunt, I already telling she younger sister of Mae.' Her supple body settles near to, but not touching, mine, her mouth a tight white line. 'Nong Wuadon first cousin to Pi Lai.'

'Right.' I go over the relationships in my mind. Not easy when all the names are strange. The beautiful young girl, Wuadon, referred to as Nong Wuadon because she's younger than Taiella, is her cousin because she's Att's daughter. The mother is called Na Att, meaning Aunt Att, by Taiella because Att is Taiella's mother's younger sister. 'You OK, tilac?'

She jerks her spine straight, smoothes the sober colouring of her skirt over her knees. 'Little bit tired after journey.' Manicured hands lift the hem of her blouse as she waves air through it. She still looks hot, unlike either her mother or her cousin.

'Tell me something about your family. Why did your cousin rush off like that?'

'Na Att not wanting Nong Wuadon talking with me. She thinking me not good for daughter, bad influence.'

For some reason Att wants to keep Wuadon away from Taiella. Interesting. 'So why was she here with your mother when they knew we were coming?'

The briefest smile which means it's a question only a farang would ask. 'She not knowing when we arriving. Mae very close to Nong Wuadon. Mae making all clothes for my cousin.' This time her hands twist at the material of her skirt, creasing the hemline. 'Mae very proud my cousin so beautiful.'

The Hollywood devotion to the body beautiful is a constant everywhere in Thailand. Evidently to the extent that Taiella's mother makes wonderful silk clothes for Wuadon, but leaves Taiella to wear sober, bought clothes. 'More beautiful than her own daughters, you mean?'

32

'Already explaining you about Na Att. Many year ago, when stranger from another village coming to old village we living in, he wanting marry Mae, telling Phor already dead because not coming back from Saudi Arabia for long time.'

Of course. I already knew Taiella's father chose to spend several years away to earn enough money to lift his family above subsistence level.

'Mae not liking this man, so she going away to parents' house in Laos, during rainy season. Therefore Na Att, already living in Dumden, looking after older brother Pi Chong, older sister Pi Sayai and also Taiella until Mae feeling well again.'

Right; the mother went back to her own parents to recover from an illness, and Att took the three children, brother Chong, sister Sayai and Taiella in and looked after them. 'So you're very close to Na Att? Is that what you're saying?'

'She our mother for eight months.' Taiella's eyes blink. 'But Na Att not approving Pi Sayai and also me living in Bangkok. She thinking all time Nong Wuadon wanting join us. She worrying much much.'

So Att thinks Taiella will persuade the girl to go back to Bangkok with her. 'Not exactly a surprise, is it?' Taiella looks puzzled. 'I mean, she's young, she's likely to prefer the city. Is she an only child, is that the problem?'

'Already explaining, tilac. Na Att cannot having children. When Mae coming back, only short time before Phor returning from Saudi Arabia, she bringing with her orphan Nong Wuadon, and giving to Na Att. That same time Mae deciding we moving to Dumden Village. Then Phor coming home, sixteen years now.'

OK: Att is barren and looking for a child. Taiella's mother brings a baby girl back from Laos, and also moves the family from her old village to Dumden. Presumably to be near Att.

Taiella is strangely immobile, staring at the door her mother has disappeared through. At last she gives a little shudder, swishes her hair and smiles radiantly. She tucks her legs demurely under her in the practised, modest position I've often admired. 'Please, tilac, you sitting legs crossed? My parents thinking you very rude if pointing feet.'

Idiot. Showing one's soles, the lowest part of the body, is so rude it's unmentionable. The head, on the other hand, is the highest part – which makes it untouchable. No patting kids on the head Teng warned me. I feel aggrieved. Why is the mother entitled to be spectacularly rude, while I have to contort my body into unnatural positions? 'I'm not really used to that, Taiella. OK if I sit like you?'

A frown chisels light lines between her eyebrows, then the smile comes back. 'No problem.'

'Is everything else all right? Your mother didn't seem delighted to see me.' Should I mention I'd noticed the girl's remarkable looks? 'And your charming little cousin disappeared so quickly I only managed to notice her skirt!'

Quick-on-the-uptake eyes search my face. The 'charming' was a stupid mistake. I do my best to look suitably bland.

Taiella's eyes veil. 'Everything fine. Nong Wuadon shy girl, and Mae very quiet, not speaking great deal.'

'Your mother doesn't smile?'

'Not like Thai. She from Laos. People coming from there not smiling, not having much expression.'

Dumden Village is in the top corner of the Northeast, set on the Thai side of the Mekong River dividing Thailand from Laos. Reason tells me the differences between Thai and Laotian could be as substantial as those between English and French, but that's far from clear to my senses. The mother has the same short stature, squat nose and almond eyes as Thai women, though her nose seems broader and her skin considerably lighter. More like Wuadon's, in fact.

When Teng heard I was going to Isaan he lectured me again on the differences between Thailand and Laos. Laotians stem from a different source. The old Sanskrit word for Thailand – *Syam* – means swarthy. Taiella has clearly inherited her skin tone from her father, making her 'ugly' to Bangkokians. Many of them do have lighter complexions, but they're still Thai. I grasp that Taiella's real price would reflect her dark skin – father Wirat Motubaki, having learned commercial ways in Saudi Arabia, asked too much for her.

'You relax, tilac. I go cooking with my mum – Mae.'

No chance. Wirat appears at the outside door, beckons me to join him.

34

'Like eat?'

'Yes, very much.'

Gestures to follow him down the ladder to the space below the house, now rather more restricted because two water buffaloes have settled in. 'Take.' His hands point at a flock of small, skittering birds desperately trying to hide in the shadows and paraphernalia under the stilts and in the surrounding undergrowth.

Am I supposed to catch one and wring its neck? An unexpected twist to fresh organic food.

'Want dwa pho, dwa mia?'

Trying not to retch I call out for Taiella. The walls of the house, built of vertical bamboo slats with irregular slivers of space between them, let the sound through easily.

'Everything OK?'

'I'm not quite sure what your father wants me to do.'

She skips down to join us. 'Pointing to chicken you want eat.'

These are chickens? They look the size of crows.

'Hens having small amount meat, very soft. Cocks bigger, but meat very tough,' Taiella explains.

Apparently I'm to choose between a cock and a hen and, having done that, to choose the particular bird I fancy. I stare helplessly around me. Of course I'm as responsible for eating a dead hen as if I'd killed it myself, but I'm not sure I can actually do the killing.

Taiella points at a cock. 'Picking good one for you.'

Mercifully I'm not expected to kill it, pluck it or take out its innards. Unmercifully I have to watch as Taiella's father – the gentle, polite, sweet father she's so often talked about – plucks the chicken alive, then holds it by its neck.

'Kill slow and meat more tender,' he explains.

BENDING AN OLD TREE IS VERY HARD

I am very grateful to my parents for welcoming Luke with a special feast. My dad – Phor – is preparing to kill our best chicken and my mum – Mae – is making her famous papaya salad, adding lots of chilli. She is famous in our village for making this special papaya dish very hot. Not everyone can manage to eat it, not even all Thais. Mae is smiling at me with big teeth, asking if such spicy food is OK for Luke. I am proud to explain that Luke likes hot Thai food much much, and therefore I am very confident he will love it.

Mae is also frying rice with egg and fish – kauphat. I do not like this dish but my mum always insists it is a big favourite of mine from childhood days long gone and so she always makes it for me, every time I come to visit my parents. Also Mae is very proud to show me that she is cooking Jasmine rice tonight, not sticky rice which the family eats normally. Of course I know this costs my dad big big money, but Mae insists they must honour a guest coming to visit the family home with this special rice.

Now is the time to explain to Luke that our custom is for men to start drinking sato before the meal. My dad's home-made sato is forty percent strong, I warn Luke. I explain that the men drink while the women cook. After this the men eat before the women who wait, staying in the kitchen. But this evening I must be interpreter, therefore I join the men in the big room. But I don't feel comfortable there, as the only woman with my dad, my

36

elder brother Pi Chong and Luke. Therefore I ask Mae to keep me company, and to stay near me. We squat just inside the open kitchen door.

Phor asks Luke many questions. I translate for both of them the best way I can. This is very difficult for me because I don't really understand all the details of Luke's business here in Thailand. Also I don't always know the correct Thai words for the job Luke does. Of course I know he owns a computer company selling communication software to banks. Luke is a very clever man. He anticipates the communication needs of banks. I am very proud to explain this for my dad.

'How farang can tell what banks wanting?' Phor's frown lines are becoming very deep, his eyebrows already grey.

I notice my dad is already looking like an old man, though not having many more years of life than Luke. 'He only having small company, Phor.'

Luke's eyes become bright. He is very proud of his success in business. He turns to me. 'Tell your father it's not that hard. I put myself in the bank's position and ask myself what would make their life a lot easier. Then I try to supply it.'

My dad and brother are listening hard to what we are saying, then: 'Meaning Luke miracle worker, and banks very happy with this?' Phor's face shows he doesn't believe me.

Also I see my dad watching Luke struggling to scoop up rice and chicken with his fingers. He tries imitating me but he isn't very skilled. I already taught him to eat in the Thai way with sticky rice. That type of rice is very easy to mould into a spoon shape, but Jasmine rice is much too flaky, the grains do not stick together, therefore Luke must chase them all over his plate. My dad tries hard to hide his amusement for this. He doesn't believe Luke can succeed in what Phor calls 'miracle business' any better than Luke can eat in Thai way.

I am very sure Luke does not understand exactly what my dad is saying, therefore I smile very sweetly, adding much politeness to my translation.

My mum is really hungry. I can tell from the way she clears her throat, then spits and gobbles the food very fast as though she is starving.

Also Luke always finds it strange that Thai people eat bones. Mae embarrasses me by making loud gobbling noises, squawking like a gander as she chews chicken meat and crunches the bones with her teeth. This is happening partly because her teeth are not so good now, they make a tearing sound as she chews. The way she slurps when she swallows rice and papaya salad is already hard for me to take, and then she breaks wind with a very loud noise. I cannot bear to look at Luke, so I shut my eyes in shame.

While she is busy putting more chicken into her rice I suggest, in a very low voice so no one else can hear, and very nervously: 'Maybe you try making small noise when you eating, Mae. My dad and Luke talking.'

'The telecommunications industry has to learn to supply the right services for the financial markets,' Luke continues as he puts tiny pieces of chicken into his mouth. 'So far it has resisted it. That's where small companies like mine come into their own. There's a great opportunity for them to do well because they can adjust quickly to new ideas and leave their larger competitors standing.'

My brother Pi Chong is also very hungry. He puts the last piece of chicken into his mouth, leaving only rice for Luke. My dad is still a little bit unsure about Luke's business and I see Luke noticing this.

'My programmers write the new routines the banks require. They don't need to be brilliant, just practical. That way we get a few months' advantage.'

'And then what you do?' Phor asks me to translate, shutting his eyes, eyebrows meeting. 'Then big companies taking over and your farang businessman losing all that business.' Phor scoops one more handful of rice and crams it all into his mouth. Several grains stick out at the sides, like small fangs.

'Not really.' Luke turns with a surprised expression to look at Phor.

Maybe he thinks my dad is just an ordinary villager, and not very clever. No true. I already explained that my dad is the head man of our village, but maybe Luke has forgotten, or maybe he does not understand that that s very important.

'I'm negotiating with a large company at the moment. They'll

38

take on my products and I'll be able to sell through them. They'll keep a percentage, of course. But I'll have the benefit of their customer base. It works well for both parties.'

At last Phor's eyes open wide and he nods. Little bits of spittle collect in the corners of his mouth. I already pointed out to my dad that I know Luke is an excellent businessman because I see the way his colleagues treat him.

'What are you telling him, tilac?' Luke puts some papaya salad into his mouth. His face turns very red, small tears collect in the corners of his blue eyes. 'Compliment your mother, Taiella. This is the best papaya salad I've ever eaten.'

'I tell my dad I know you are doing good business in Thailand because your colleagues invite you to join them for karaoke. Also they invite you to many parties at the best hotels in Krung Thep.'

'You're exaggerating, Taiella. I've never been near such a place!'

I giggle. 'You forgetting already, Luke. We never calling Bangkok, that Western name. Even Krung Thep only first part of very long name, longest name of any city in whole world.'

Luke grins at me. 'Right you are, I did forget. So what's the whole caboodle then?'

I understand very well that he is testing me, thinking I do not know the name because I am not well educated. He is mistaken. We were always singing that long name to a popular tune, in the military school in Udon Thani, the special school my dad sent me to until he could no longer afford for me to go there. 'We call it *Krung Thep Mahanakhon Amon Rattanakosin Mahinthara Ayuthaya Mahadilok Phop Noppharat Ratchathani Burirom Udomratchaniwet Mahasathan Amon Piman Awatan Sathit Sakkathattiya Witsanukam Prasit*. The first three words we often use in important legal documents.'

Luke's face loses its grin. 'I'm impressed,' he says, and looks at me with grave eyes.

Mae starts yawning, giving the clear signal she wants the evening to finish and to go to bed. I explain to Luke that we go to bed early, at the time of the sound of the drum, what he calls twilight. The reason is very clear; it's because we get up at late strike, what he calls dawn, when the first morning light brightens the sky. All village people work in the paddies before the sun gets hot. We do not do much in the evenings in Dumden Village, there is no light. Though we dance and have parties for weddings and birthdays, and even for funerals when the time is right for that.

'Fetching extra mat and spreading for Luke in kitchen,' Mae says, laying the mat for my parents out in the big room and setting up the mosquito tent.

'In kitchen?' I worry what Luke will think about that. Will he consider my parents inhospitable, then decide not to bother applying for his divorce? 'That not very polite, Mae...'

'Frog near snake mouth, big temptation.' Her eyes are hard, her lips tight, so I say nothing more. 'When person shot by passion they running around like headless chicken. Whole village knowing man not part of family sleeping here.' Big nostrils widen, eyes go like steel.

She is correct. We are very old-fashioned in Northeast Thailand. Village girls stay virgins until they marry. They guard their virtue very fiercely - they never allow a man to be with them when they are by themselves. Even when they have an invitation to go to the cinema which always comes to the village once a week, or when going for a walk, our girls always take a girlfriend along. This is our custom, and many young girls obey this rule even in Krung Thep. If a boy climbs into a girlfriend's house at night, visiting, and her parents discover this, they send for the police and that boy is held in prison for one day, often for longer. It is considered a very serious matter.

I try hard to explain our sleeping arrangements to Luke. He does not look as though he is worrying. But he has problems with the heat staying in the charcoal my mum uses for cooking. This makes the kitchen very hot, and the big room is much cooler. I take care to lay the straw mat for Luke in the most distant corner of the kitchen, and set up the mosquito tent for him there. Phor orders me to lie down on my mat, and he locks the door leading to the kitchen.

I am worn out with translating, and at the same time keeping my parents and Luke happy, so I fall asleep very quickly.

WHEN IN A PLACE WHERE PEOPLE WINK, WINK WITH THEM

I wake from a very deep sleep because of the huge noises – banging and shouting coming from outside the house, close by.

The big room is dark and shadowy but I can see my parents and Pi Chong climbing out from under their mosquito netting. 'What happening? What all this noise? Bandits coming?'

I hurry to get up, pushing away my mosquito tent, and rush to the kitchen door. Whatever is going on I wanting to be with Luke, so that we can face any problems together. Besides, he is already up and banging on the locked door. I open it and see he is dressed.

'Frog eating moon!' Mae cries out, her voice a big shout from a hoarse throat. 'Hurry! Must help frighten away.'

Now I understand what is going on. 'Come and help, Luke! We must make lots lots noise. Big frog in sky very hungry, and taking bite from moon!'

I pull down one of Mae's cooking pans hanging from the ceiling, and take hold of a cooking stick, giving them both to Luke. I take another pan and stick for myself. Phor is already outside, firing his rifle at the sky several times, reloading as quickly as he can. Because my dad is the head man of the village he has permission to own a rifle. The police not allowing any other villagers to own firearms, this is a very strict rule. It is lucky for our village that the police have so much respect for my dad.

'A frog?' Luke shouts at me so I can hear above the racket. 'You're trying to frighten frogs threatening the crops?'

'Big frog in heavens,' I yell, loudly so he can hear above the enormous din all around us. 'Celestial frog very hungry, he eating moon. All must help stopping frog before moon disappear.'

Luke and I are outside now. He looks up at the cloudless sky. The large circle of the copper-coloured moon, nearly full, has a creature slowly eating away at it, turning itself into the swelling, fattening shape of the cosmic frog. It is moving across the moon, not taking any notice of shots and rattles and bangs all around us.

'Almost swallowing whole moon!' I cry out, tears running down my face. What can happen if the frog eats the whole moon? Will our world disappear, leaving no trace? And afterwards, will the celestial frog gobble up the sun as well? Then we will not have light, or warmth, or even plants. We will not be able to live, and all the animals will also die. If all that happened I think it would be the end of our world.

Luke grabs my hand which is holding the cooking stick and banging hard. He stops the noise I am making. 'You don't need to worry, tilac. There isn't a problem.'

I snatch my hand away, very upset, and beat harder than before. I have told Luke many times already, so I am angry that he is touching me. The spirits will not think this proper behaviour for an unmarried girl. 'Make big noise, Luke! Frog swallowing whole moon right this minute!'

'Honestly, Taiella. There's nothing to worry about, it'll all be over shortly whatever you do.'

Luke sounds very calm but I not believing him. Maybe it would be all right in his world, but he does not understand our world, he thinks it is the same as his. That is not so. I cannot stop crying now, and I go on banging as hard as possible. 'Beat!' I beg him. 'Make lots noise!'

Luke tries putting his arms around me, he wants to hold me. My mum has always warned me that the bamboo's own fruit is what kills it, so I try escaping his embrace. He grabs me tight, kissing the top of my head, holding me so I cannot move. I must not allow this. He does not understand that the cosmic frog is

42

more powerful if we break Thai traditions about not touching, and touching the head is very bad indeed. The spirits are watching, bad luck will come if he does not let me go. I finally see from his eyes that he understands what I am trying to say. He lets go and moves away a little.

'Make big noise, Luke! Before too late late!'

He laughs out loud, now nodding, banging his pan as hard as he can. He does not believe what could happen if we stop making big noise, so he laughs for a long time, thinking it a good joke. It is not funny, it is very serious. I know what is going on because this happened before. When I was working in the paddies as a young child the same celestial frog came and tried to eat the moon. Making a huge noise is the only way to make the frog disgorge its moon food. All our neighbours know this is the only way we can rescue our moon. How can a farang know about our world?

We bang for a long time. At last our reward comes, when the moon is very weak – almost two-thirds gone – and starts to grow strong again. A long time passing until at last the frog disappears altogether. We are very lucky because the celestial frog ate a large part of the whole moon, it looked as though it would not stop. Now, because we worked hard and behaved correctly, we frightened the frog, scaring it so it spewed out all it ate.

The village dogs bark and yelp. The banging continues for a long time as the villagers make sure the threatening frog disappears for good.

'There wasn't any need for any of this, tilac. It was just an eclipse of the moon.'

I have never heard the eclipse word before, and I do not believe Luke. But I say nothing now that the celestial frog is no longer here. If I argue with Luke it might come back.

At last we lie down on our sleeping mats again because everyone is worn out. In the consequent disorder my parents do not notice that I leave the kitchen door unlocked. I lie close to this door, as near as possible. Maybe the frog will come again even if Luke and I are not touching. I want to be near Luke if that happens. I wish with my whole heart that we will always be together, in good luck and in bad.

The rest of the night I toss and turn, I cannot sleep. I think about what to do, how to manage our situation. I am angry with Luke for asking me to bring him to meet my parents because it is very clear that Mae does not wish this. Her anger has sweet tops born of poisoned roots. She is becoming anxious because now she knows I have a farang boyfriend. She does not like strangers coming to Dumden Village, she thinks they spy on her. She is a very nervous lady, she does not want people to see what she is doing.

PICK A FLOWER IN THE SKY

Mae not understanding why I want to marry a farang. She thinking he will treat me like a bar girl, if not now, then later. I know she is very wrong, because I have known Luke for long time now, more than six months, and he is always honest. I have watched him at parties and in business, and he never telling lies.

I believe Luke that, though he is not able to make me his first wife right now, because he is still married to his English wife, he is working hard to get a divorce. Of course I understanding there are many problems in arranging a divorce in England. Not like in Thailand, very easy here and can be arranged in few days if both parties agree. I thinking Luke's wife will agree because they not having any children, and she not wanting any.

Maybe Mae not trusting Luke to honour his promise. But I already know he is a very good man and therefore he will not break his engagement to me. I am very sure.

Does Phor understand why I want Luke for a husband? He thinks all farang make Thai girls into whores, that they do not show respect. This is a big mistake, and it is happening because so many farang visiting our capital city behave without honour.

I know it depends on the individual. It is not only farang who break their promises; Thai men often do not keep solemn pledges. I remember one time very well. Four years ago, before I moved to Krung Thep to live with my older sister Pi Sayai, Phor arranged for me to marry Pi Jan. He is the son of the head man in a nearby

45

village. This was a very good deal for Pi Jan, because my parents only having two daughters, and I am the younger one. Therefore when I marry my husband will live with my family, to be a son to my father. We therefore inherit everything my dad owns: the house, the lake and all his land. Because I have no younger sister no other son-in-law will be coming along, and Mae is now too old to have more children.

Pi Jan and I, we planned our future. He agree I should take job in Krung Thep to earn money for our home. While living in the big city I shared a single room and kitchen with my older sister Sayai and her little boy. I was working long hours and saving money for my marriage while Pi Jan was learning about growing rice and vegetable crops from my dad. Phor is exceptional at this, and very keen on having a son-in-law to help – which is the custom in our village, with Pi Jan being submissive to his father-in-law's authority.

Of course my sister Pi Sayai already broke with village traditions. I know Pi Jan was very nervous about this. My dad did not tell Pi Jan that my sister is a minor wife to Lung Palem. But Pi Jan is not stupid, he worked out she is not Lung Palem's first wife because then her husband would be the first son-in-law living with my family, moving out when Pi Sayai's younger sister marries. So when my older sister stayed in Krung Thep and no husband arrived in Dumden, I think Pi Jan guessed Pi Sayai is a minor wife to Lung Palem.

Pi Jan married another girl from his own village, Nong Nam. Mae told me about this, not Pi Jan, which made me very upset. Mae said she was sure the reason Pi Jan decided not marry with me was that Nong Nam has beautiful pale skin – Mae is always laughing at my dark skin – and also because Nong Nam's dad did not ask for such a big wedding gift as Phor asked for me.

I think the real reason Pi Jan abandoned me was that he thought Nong Nam would stay in the village, helping her parents until she married, and not disappear to Krung Thep. I think he preferred to marry a traditional girl, thinking she would make an excellent submissive wife. Pi Jan may be correct in this.

Maybe Phor thinks it is OK for me to be Mia Glang Tasee – a

bought wife – for Luke. Village people believe all European farang are very rich, and therefore will send good money to parents of any kind of wife, because it is our tradition to support our parents in old age. Even bar girls do this, that is why their parents are not afraid to sell them. We believe if you do not support your parents you have an unhappy next life.

That is the reason why Phor is suspicious of Luke. He does not understand why Luke wants to divorce his English wife and make me his first wife instead of buying me. Therefore he thinks that maybe Luke has other reasons for coming to Udon Thani, that perhaps he wants to buy land for doing some kind of business in Northeast Thailand. And farang are not allowed to buy land, but I could buy it if I was his wife.

My mum and dad both think like Thai. They cannot understand that farang have different traditions from us, that they have other ways of thinking.

Even before meeting Luke, after the first shock, I did not really feel upset about Pi Jan. I was happy in Krung Thep, my older sister Pi Sayai was glad of my company. She spends much much time alone with her young son, her husband only calling when he is not with his other wives. He is a rich businessman and can afford one first wife and three minor wives. When he visits I sleep in the kitchen with my nephew, giving Pi Sayai privacy.

So then I make up my mind not to bother to look for a husband. I never enjoyed life in the village, it is a very hard life working in the fields and cooking for the family. Also, after living in Krung Thep for a long time Dumden Village seems petty and like a prison. I prefer to be a career girl. Maybe my skin is a little bit dark, and therefore not beautiful, but I have a pretty face and a slim figure. Another thing – the ZenZam Centre department store consider me exactly the type of assistant they like to employ. I am a big hit with their customers, they always come back for more toys just to have the opportunity to make jokes with me. Their nickname for me is 'Smileegirl'.

Now it is early morning and Mae will soon wake. I creep across the room and lock the kitchen door. At last I see her pushing back the opening to her mosquito tent and getting up.

'Fetch water for rice, Taiella,' she instructs me. 'I go waking Luke.'

I go to fill the bucket from the storage tank downstairs, under our house. When I come back Luke is already up, trying to make my mum understand what he is saying by using the very few Thai words he knows. She cannot understand him. He uses hands to show his meaning, but Mae is impatient. She is very busy cooking the main meal for the whole day. She will take this out to the fields for Phor and my older brother Pi Chong. She is too busy for talking. She thinks he cannot even be bothered paddling, he will just hang his feet in the water and not do any work. She thinks Luke is a big problem, a stupid farang who wants something from Thai and is not willing to pay for it.

I decide it would be a good idea if Luke and I do not stay in Dumden for long. We plan to take the afternoon songthaew back to Udon Thani, then catch the late flight to Krung Thep. Luke has an important business meeting tomorrow. He is leaving for England the day after that. I concentrate on how we should spend the next few hours in my village.

Maybe it would be a good idea to show Luke how Phor works on his land, and show off his excellent vegetable garden and the banana plantation for which he is famous in the whole area. Now is almost the end of dry season. Our rice crop for this year is already harvested, so village people have leisure time. Some villagers grow vegetables, others do clearing-up work.

Maybe Luke and I will also admire Mae's mulberry bushes and her silkworms. She is famous for her silk, and for spinning beautiful silk yarn to weave into cloth.

When it becomes really hot at noontime I plan to take Luke to sit under the banana bower Phor made. Small, sweet bananas hang down for plucking and at the same time the big leaves will protect us from the very hot sun. Phor is very clever man with plants. We say he has warm hands.

'Girls herding water buffalo,' I explain to Luke. 'You want to see how village people live? Nong Wuadon taking my dad's buffalo to deep wells, together with own family buffalo.' I am standing on the platform outside my dad's house and calling to Nong Wuadon. We are good pals together. She is a friendly girl and looks up at me, wai-ing.

'Sawatdee Kha, Pi Taiella,' she calls up, 'I have important question I must asking you.'

'Sawatdee Kha, Nong Wuadon. Better asking now. We leaving on afternoon songthaew,' I warning her.

'Why you standing like lazy girl, gossiping, Nong Wuadon? Your job getting buffalo to deep wells!'

This is Are Mak speaking, and he sounds very angry. He is the younger brother of Lung Ban, husband to my mum's sister Na Att, which is why I call him uncle. I have no idea why Are Mak is making such a silly fuss about my greeting Nong Wuadon. He knowing very well she is my cousin because she is Na Att's daughter. Even though she is an adopted daughter, she is still my cousin. Are Mak knows exactly that we have been good friends since she arrived as a baby. Also, normally Are Mak uses sugar words with his favourite niece. What has changed?

Nong Wuadon waves to me. 'OK. Bringing back buffalo early.' She flicks her palm branch at the buffalo rumps, herding my dad's animals to join her family's. 'I wanting go Krung Thep, Pi Taiella, but not wanting pay for this with…'

'Nong Taiella,' Are Mak shouts at me now, very loud, very discourteous, 'why you interrupting Nong Wuadon's business? She having work she must do. She not lady of leisure, like some persons we knowing.'

'See you when you coming back,' I call to Nong Wuadon. I never liking Are Mak so I ignoring him. Nong Wuadon is only sixteen, but already she is a very attractive woman. She is extra careful to keep her skin pale, protecting it from the scorching sun. She wears a huge bamboo hat, also a cotton cloth wrapped round her face and neck in spite of the intense heat, with only her eyes showing.

I know Mae is the person who dyed this shimmering blue-green cotton dress, because my mum is the only woman in our village who knows how to make such an unusual colour. She is always making dresses for Nong Wuadon. She never made anything for me, I must always wear my sister's old clothes.

The dress covers Nong Wuadon's arms and reaches all the way to her ankles. But she is a very lively girl, dancing behind the buffaloes. Has Luke noticed that she is very pretty, more beautiful than me? I think not, she is so covered up he cannot see even a tiny bit of bare skin. All he can see is the brilliant material she is wearing, covering her body all over and not showing any shape. Until I remember he saw her last night, when she was visiting Mae, then ran past us when we arrived and went to greet my mum. But he only glimpsed her for a very short time.

Luke is watching as a stream of water buffaloes goes past, with many other girls besides Nong Wuadon driving them to the deep wells out in the paddy fields. He looks puzzled.

'Why don't they just let the buffaloes graze on their own? Are you afraid of cattle rustlers?'

'Like cowboy film?'

'Exactly.'

'Is true we do have such brigands. But main reason is because water buffalo not having sweat glands. Must keeping cool in hot weather. Girls taking to deep wells, pulling up water, throwing over animals' bodies.'

'There's no water in the village?'

'Wells near village not having water at end of dry season. Government send tank for drinking water every day, we keeping in large vat you already see. We having permission to take as much as we like, but we do not have containers big enough for holding water for giving to buffalo. So we walking out to fields, to deep wells. Buffalo cannot get water on own!' I do not want Luke to take an interest in the girls and their buffaloes. I try to think of something more exciting. 'Mae is working with cocoons. Want see?'

'You mean silkworms?'

'Moths breaking out of cocoons soon soon. Mae needs help reeling the silk thread. She puts the cocoons in boiling water to kill new moths before they ruin the fibre. Also moths making good snack we eating when she killing them. Today she reeling silk fibre for cleaning later.'

'No problem, tilac. Of course you must help your mother.'

Many villagers are staring because Luke using the Thai word for sweetheart. This is not proper behaviour, but I do not have the heart to keep telling Luke he should not be using it. Also I liking to hear it.

'Not sure I can face seeing cocoons dropped into boiling water, let alone watch you eat the insides. I'll join the buffalo girls for a bit. Take my radio and enjoy the scenery. They don't go far, do they?'

'You not minding the strong smell, tilac?' I go quite close so villagers cannot hear me speaking and using the word tilac. I know buffaloes stink a lot in the heat, but the true reason I am worrying is because Luke will be going on his own. I promised to help Mae so I cannot go with him.

'Fresh country air.' He is laughing at me.

I am not happy with his choice. Nong Wuadon is so very beautiful and also charming. My mum is always pointing out that her skin is light and delicate, with small pores. My cousin never had to plant rice, like my mum forced me to do when I was young child, because Nong Wuadon's mum did not allow it. Did Luke notice her after all? Is he joining the girls because he wants to meet her, play the ears and the eyes with her?

I try not to think of such a possibility. They are girls together, they will keep an eye on each other. And Luke promised me I will be his Number One wife. I know he is an honourable man, keeping his word. He already proved that when he turned down buying me from Phor. He is acting positive, and I am proud he does not think of me as his slave wife. Also I am sure he will keep his promise to follow the Thai wedding customs when the time for the ceremony arrives at long last, and I must learn to wait patiently for this. Therefore I must trust him.

'Not near near,' I explain. 'Dry season nearly finishing, must look for wells still having water. Is long walk in heat. When arriving girls sit in shade beside buffalo. Gossip.' Still I worry that Luke is hoping to sit with Nong Wuadon. She is not just pretty, she is also very young. In my mind I can hear Mae saying: 'Old bull eating soft grass.'

51

I know Nong Wuadon is too immature for Luke, he is not so young any more, but men do not think this way. I stop myself having silly ideas and wave good-bye as I see him walking behind the girls and their buffaloes.

GIVE THE TREE A CHANCE TO FALL BEFORE JUMPING OVER IT

Luke is away the whole time I am helping Mae boil water and dip cocoons. I am so happy to see him walking back, unhurried, smiling. I run out to greet him. He tells me he spent time with the girls, allowed them to listen to his radio. Then he became too hot and decided to walk back, slowly, because of the strong sun.

'Enjoy seeing buffalo, tilac?'

'It's fascinating to see your way of life. We no longer have that kind of pace. Our farms all use machinery – combine harvesters, milking machines, chicken factory farming. Even the small farms use contractors for much of their work.'

I leave Mae to finish reeling her silk fibre. Helping with this work is not as tiring as planting or harvesting rice, but it is still hard physical work which I am no longer used to. Selling toys in an air-conditioned store is easy work.

I find Luke some cool water to drink from the big container Phor made. My dad always stores rain water which we use for drinking in the dry season. It is very sweet tasting. We only use the government water for washing. Now Luke and I wander over to Phor to watch him working with his vegetables. He is planting a very big field of aubergine – the small, round, white kind which is so very popular in our village. He offers Luke some sweet finger bananas, very tasty. I show him Mae's favourite beans, purple cabbages, coriander, lemon grass. Then we walk to the hut overlooking my dad's lake. My older brother Pi Chong is there, keeping an eye out for thieves. Our neighbours can get hungry, but we cannot feed them all. We join him so that Luke can fish. Luke loves fishing. Pi Chong shows him how we do it in this village, and my clever Luke catches enough catfish for our last meal with my family.

As we return to the village we meet several girls coming back with their buffaloes, laughing and chattering, pointing at Luke. They answer the few Thai words he calls to them with two or three English words they picked up from American films they have seen – hello, happy, handsome. I can tell Luke is big hit with them, even if some of the older villagers are not enthusiastic. I feel proud, but I am surprised that Nong Wuadon is not with the other girls. Maybe she is waiting at my parents' house, but when we go back she is not there. I go looking for her at Lung Ban's house but cannot find her. My dad's buffaloes are not back, so she must still be in the fields. I find this very strange. She said she would be back early because she wanting to talk to me, and it is very important

My dad is back from his vegetables and he and Luke sit in the big room while I help Mae. She cooks some fish, very tasty, and we all enjoy it, Mae and I sit inside the kitchen door like last night. My mum fries the medium-size fish whole, which means Luke can eat it with his fingers. He is obviously hungry and eats plenty, licking his lips. Then the door bursts open and my brother Pi Chong walks in, looking grave. He waves the food away.

'Nong Wuadon missing,' he tells us. 'She not coming back from pasturing buffalo.'

'What about other girls?' My dad holds a handful of fish. As he looks at Pi Chong he squashes his fingers together, so that a fish head hangs out with rice on its top, giving the impression of white hair. 'They not staying with her?'

'No. They not seeing for long time. She telling girls she leaving early for talking with Nong Taiella. Na Att already crying, she very worried.' Pi Chong looks at each of us in turn. 'Who seeing her last? You, Mae? I know you feel like second mother to Nong Wuadon.'

My mum looks anxious, but shakes her head.

'What about you, Nong Taiella? You telling her about big city, making her envious, maybe she coming to see you?'

'No.' I remember again how Nong Wuadon said she wanted to talk to me. 'Yesterday she running past Luke and me, no time for talking. This morning saying she very keen talking with me after she coming back with buffalo...' I stop. When Luke was walking in the paddies he must have seen her. I know he spent time with some of the girls, he told me about lending them his radio. Already I am very nervous.

'You seeing Nong Wuadon when in paddy fields, tilac?' I ask Luke. He does not understand what Pi Chong is telling us, so he continues eating. I think that even if he did not talk to her he must have some idea where she went.

'Nong Wuadon?'

'Girl you seeing with my mum last night, same one I pointing out to you in morning. Taking my dad's buffalo as well as own family animals to deep wells.'

He frowns, looks like he is trying to remember. 'I've no idea. There were at least half a dozen girls.'

'In long blue-green dress. Very pretty.'

Luke shakes his head. 'Don't think I noticed any particular girl. Why?'

'She not coming home. Buffalo not coming back also. We all worry.'

'A missing teenager?' Luke looks around, then smiles. 'Maybe she simply took off for Bangkok? Perhaps your turning up, telling everyone all about your job and that, seeing your city clothes, made her restless. Happens all the time in the UK. The youngsters take off for London.'

He is being very foolish, not understanding our village situation. 'How can she leaving? Songthaew not come yet, she must wait until near sunset time.'

'You mean she was seen after the noon truck left? Right, right. Maybe she decided to hitchhike?'

'What you mean? Villagers ride motorbikes, and no one taking her. We not having cars, no strangers come for visit.' Except Luke,

I already can see my parents thinking.

He shrugs; he has no idea how serious this matter is. Village girls are very careful. Brigands roam in the areas around the villages. They sometimes kidnap a young girl, asking for a ransom, sometimes even rape the girl.

'Aren't you jumping the gun a bit? She could have decided to walk to the nearest town, I suppose.'

It is strange how sometimes such a clever man can be quite foolish. 'We have only one town nearby. Udon Thani is long long way in noon heat. Nong Wuadon know we having all kind brigands in this area. She not going on own, she having big fear without other girls.'

'Perhaps she knows one of the brigands; perhaps she has a boyfriend!'

I feel anger growing inside me. He does not understand at all. 'Nong Wuadon good, hard-working village girl. Virgin. Many men show interest already, but she not liking any.'

'How can you be so sure, Taiella? You haven't lived in your village for several years now.'

'I already telling you. My mum aunt to Nong Wuadon, know very well. She sure sure her niece not disappear because of man.'

He shrugs his shoulders, not understanding that the whole village is upset if a girl goes missing. My mum is very worried because she loves Nong Wuadon like her own daughters. Sometimes, when still a child, I thought she loved her more than her own daughter Taiella! Maybe I felt – maybe even feel now – jealous that she wanted her as a daughter instead of me. I think this is because Nong Wuadon is a dainty girl, with delicate features, very like my mum.

Luke looks at his watch. 'Isn't our songthaew due soon, tilac?'

How can he think of such a thing at this point? Then I understand. He does not have any feelings about Nong Wuadon because he does not know her. 'We cannot go today, tilac. We wait for Nong Wuadon coming back. If she lost we waiting for policeman coming tomorrow.' I can hear Luke draw in his breath. Because he wants to leave right now? Because my village is not good enough for him, he does not like it here?

I cannot worry about what he thinks. A missing person is a very serious matter, even more so if a young girl goes missing. 'No one leaving Dumden Village until Nong Wuadon found, Luke. No one.'

'But what about my meeting? Scheduled for tomorrow, and then I'm booked on the plane to London. Can't we get the police now and clear this up?'

'We fetching police if we sure she lost, Luke. For now we all staying in village, everyone helping with finding Nong Wuadon.' Our village never involves the police if we can avoid it. They are not pleasant, they do not treat villagers with proper respect. They often pick on us, accuse us of being drug addicts when that is not true. Sometimes they even shoot and kill people without asking questions. We do not trust the police. But if we know of a missing person we must report it, otherwise when the police find out they come to the village and arrest people, putting lots of the men in jail. Then how will their families eat?

I understand Luke is anxious about his business meeting. But a missing girl means a big search, with everyone helping. Phor is the head man of our village, so his job is to organise where and how we search.

'If it's as serious as that,' Luke says, his face grave and expecting me to translate for Phor, 'I'll do my best to help. Just tell me what to do.'

Phor nods agreement. He forms several small search parties, sending them off in different directions. For his own party he takes Luke, Pi Chong, Nong Wuadon's dad and mum, Mae and also me.

We search for Nong Wuadon until long hours go by, finding no trace of her, no hat, nothing. All the buffaloes she herded are still in the deep wells where she took them this morning.

Phor decides we cannot do any more this afternoon. It is possible that Nong Wuadon fell asleep somewhere and will wander home at the time of the gong. No one speaks. Her mum Na Att, and my mum, are both crying, tears running down their faces. But I am already very sure that one of the marauding gangs of brigands abducted her. They will get in touch for big money.

My mum and Na Att talk together, whispering. They are very

close, because my mum is Na Att's older sister, and always helped her look after Nong Wuadon. They stare at Luke, point, frown.

Why? Because they think Luke is a bad person, that he attacked Nong Wuadon? They know very well that bandits steal young girls, that they often sell them to the service industry. So why do they suspect Luke?

I hope my wonderful fiancé does not notice their attitude. I can do nothing to stop them whispering, or talking with each other.

Luke and I agree with my dad to wait until the morning, giving Nong Wuadon the opportunity to return or the bandits the chance to ask for ransom money. Phor explains to Luke that we only call the police if we hear nothing. My dad is a very strong leader, an excellent head man of Dumden Village.

BUILDING THE OX'S PEN AFTER IT HAS BEEN STOLEN

Sweat starts pouring down between my shoulder blades as I realise Taiella's mother Nanakorn, and her aunt Att, are gunning for me. Their flailing arms are accusing me, their wagging fingers denouncing me. Att's cobra eyes, angry streaks of bronze in dark umber, try to mesmerise me. I twist away, find myself staring into Nanakorn's monochrome brown. Chocolate specks somersault over burnt sienna rings, intense with hostility. I might not be able to speak, or even understand, the Isaan dialect but tension washes over me in great waves of anger-charged looks and spat-out syllables. The sisters splutter at each other, glare at me with snarling mouths and jagged teeth, their feelings unmistakable. Clear as the Isaan dust: I'm the one responsible for the girl's disappearance.

I look at Wirat. He's brushed aside my reasons for visiting Dumden, been suspicious about my going to the paddies. He's even asked Taiella if I'm a government spy. He stands, feet wide apart, prodding thickets of vegetation with a python-sized bamboo pole. I call out to him. He glances at me, nods without much enthusiasm, his face impassive.

Obviously best to put him between me and the two women, but that means passing them. They're kicking the dry earth, sharp needles into my eyes, making it hard to see. That's why I don't notice Att hurling herself at me, she's so quick. I stumble, almost fall, as her body thumps into mine. Around five foot, and delicately built, she manages several convincing punches. I use a shirt-sleeve to clear my eyes as she starts to pummel with wind-milling fists, then grab at anything I can see moving, hold on tight. And yell at Taiella: 'What's going on? What does she want?'

'Aunt very upset, Luke.' Taiella is a blur in blue trying to get to me, blocked by a blob of brown – her mother. 'She thinking you taking daughter, keeping prisoner,' Taiella shouts, struggling to get to me. 'She mad with grief, she not knowing what she doing.'

Att tries to twist herself out of my grasp, spits at me, kicks. I swing her round to face away from me, shake my head to try to clear my eyes, grab her wrists and hold her arms down in front of her body. She squirms, but I hold on. She tries to kick backwards, but I keep her tight against me.

Att twists her head and bites my arm. I pull my hands up, push her wrists against her throat while yanking her head back. 'She's being absurd!' I call out to Taiella. 'Ask your father to stop her.'

Why isn't Wirat doing his job? His camouflage colours are hard to see against the scrub, but he has to be watching. Why doesn't he come over, slap Att out of her hysteria?

He arrives, stomps in front of us, the bamboo held horizontally, a tightrope walker in a paddy field. He keeps the pole balanced as he raises his right hand and waves it backwards and forwards, a gesture I take to mean he intends to speak, and Att is to pay attention.

He speaks slowly, expressionlessly, to Att. She snarls at him, gabbles, begins to cry. I keep a tight grip as Wirat's impassive eyes stare back at her, let her rant. He speaks again, slowly, evenly, balancing the pole. Att's crying calms a little. Eventually Wirat stands the pole upright and she chokes some words, then stops.

He nods to me to let her go. She runs off to her sister's protection, shrieking what I take to be Thai curses.

'What is she on about, Taiella? How could I possibly drag Wuadon off? She was in a crowd of girls!'

'Remembering girls telling Nong Wuadon saying walking back early, on own? Na Att telling everyone you talking sugar to daughter, she going with you, you hiding her.'

I begin to regret my decision to come back on my own. It was obviously a huge mistake. 'Where would I hide her, and what for?'

Taiella is staring at her aunt, not at me. 'In thick bushes. Tie up and leave till later.'

Sounds as though they've been reading the local rag, expounding the dangers of farang foreigners, worse than Southeast Asian ones. 'Leave her for what? What would I want with her?'

Taiella pushes her right shoe along a rut left by last season's rice crop, her eyes avoiding mine. 'Making love when getting dark. Taking with you to Krung Thep maybe.'

'That's absurd. We arranged to leave on the afternoon songthaew, Taiella. Remind Att – and your mother – of that.'

It isn't a question of using reason. Nothing I say will make the slightest difference to what these women feel. The fact is that Att lost her daughter on the day a stranger walked with her to the fields. He came back and she did not. Naturally Att would suspect me.

I watch Taiella push her shoe along the ruts, making them deeper. Does *she* believe I might swap her for Wuadon? What does she imagine I could possibly want with a sixteen-year-old Thai village girl?

They're all so depressingly obsessed with the girl's looks – which, in fact, I've never seen properly. Something I'm beginning to regret! True, I glimpsed an attractive young girl rush past me in the shadowed lighting of the house yesterday, and I saw the same girl this morning, smothered in green-blue cotton, below me on the street. I did notice the dress, probably because it was so different from anything the other girls were wearing. I didn't even see her face this morning, because it was shrouded by the burka-like scarf and that enormous hat. And even if I *had* been interested in her looks why on earth would that turn me into a kidnapper?

I had considered taking the afternoon songthaew without Taiella, earlier on. Another hot night on a hard floor with nothing but a mat under me wasn't entirely appealing. But if I'd tried to leave all of Dumden Village would have been convinced that I had something to do with the girl's disappearance. Quite likely they wouldn't have let me go, would have kept me forcibly. And

I wouldn't want Taiella to get the impression that I don't like her village, or her people. Though I'm certainly beginning to regret my visit.

I thought about it earlier, assumed that one of the many brigands known to roam the rural areas must have grabbed the girl and dragged her off. Perhaps a ransom note would be arriving soon, and beautiful Wuadon would be saved.

Unless, of course, the village can't raise the necessary cash. I breathe relief. That's where I can help out, with whatever I have on me. About six thousand baht, a substantial sum by Dumden standards. I could raise another ten thousand in Udon Thani, using my bank card, surely enough to cover the most outrageous ransom demand by local brigands. Taiella and I would get the chance to leave, Wirat could come on the songthaew with us and bring back the cash back to the village.

What if there's no ransom note? What if they've killed the girl? No point dwelling on that. Nothing I can do about it that I can think of.

'What about several of the men staying out here and seeing if someone comes with a note?' I try out on Taiella. 'If there were enough village men, hidden in the bushes, say, they could take the messenger prisoner. A hostage for a hostage, sort of thing. Why not suggest that to your father?'

Taiella looks down, hiding her eyes. 'Not good idea, tilac. If making trouble for brigands, coming and killing villagers for sure. Brigands very fierce men.'

'Right, right. So we just sit and wait?'

'All go back to village. Mai pen rai – keep calm mind. I am sure if leaving note under Phor house during coming night we finding Nong Wuadon in morning.' She's moved well away from her mother and aunt and is standing by me.

In my view Wirat hasn't exerted himself that much to find the girl, is calling the search off all too soon. Suppose she's fainted, heat stroke or something? Surely they're all taking a rather passive line?

'Why don't we look around a bit more, Taiella? You and your father and I, if he doesn't want to involve the other villagers.'

Taiella walks over to him, talks. He clearly won't hear of it, shouts 'no, no' at me and waves his right arm briskly, with vigorous shaking of his hand across his face. Then he points back to the village. Rapid-fire syllables make it clear that everyone is to go back. Has Wirat understood what I'm offering? Has Taiella? I can't tell, but he's adamant. I wonder why.

'Where continue looking, Luke? Why going on when Phor say cannot find?'

'There could be other reasons for her disappearance, you know. She could have been bitten by a snake, or had heatstroke. She could be unconscious!'

'Nong Wuadon healthy girl, never having heat stroke. Knowing very good how to avoid snakes. Also, other girls near near.'

'Not all the time, apparently. Anyway, why didn't they hear her scream if a bandit was dragging her off?'

Taiella's eyes smoke irritation, but her tone is level. 'Is simple, tilac. Bandit putting hand over mouth, therefore cannot scream.'

'It just seems tame to give up so easily.'

'Better going back to village now, Luke. Lots mosquitoes coming, biting and maybe getting malaria.' She looks at me through her lashes, eyes blinking. 'Also maybe brigands watching. Phor knowing village ways, brigand ways. Finding note tomorrow.'

'What if she's playing games? Teasing her mother?'

Surprisingly, that seems to register. Taiella flicks her hair back. 'Must going back to village now, tilac, quick quick. If brigands coming back, seeing farang, price going sky high.'

The real reason has, as usual, escaped me. How can I be so dense? And why didn't Taiella say all this at the start? I wonder whether we'll ever truly understand one another.

I look around me. These are the paddies where Taiella planted rice when only six, the cracked earth where she looked for little crabs to bring back precious protein for her mother, the rough fields where she took the buffaloes to the water holes in the rainy season and to the deep wells in the dry. These stubbled acres are where she learned to fight bandits and mosquitoes, and managed to survive on a minimal diet.

I grasp that waiting until morning to clear up Wuadon's

disappearance will not seem that much of a problem to Taiella. What's more, it has to be admitted she isn't the one being got at.

'You're saying we should do exactly what your father says.'

Taiella's smile is as lovely as the sun glinting through bamboo. 'Dutiful daughter not breaking branches of tree shading her.'

Such faith in her father, in his ability to control the world around him. The many years of obeying him will never be completely wiped out, certainly not by a few years in Bangkok. She feels comfortable doing what he orders her and the family to do, so leaving all responsibility to him. She's used to making the best of whatever situation she finds herself in – her upbringing, her instincts – all insist she do exactly as her father wishes. For the time being.

I shrug. 'If that's the way you want it, tilac. Just one thing. If Wuadon's parents need cash, tell your father I'll be happy to contribute. I've got six thousand baht on me, and I could get some more in Udon Thani.'

My Smileegirl stands, incongruous in her Bangkok clothes, in the parched stubbled paddies of the dry season, shakes her shoes off, hooks them over her wrist, walks in bare feet.

'Thank you, tilac. Already knowing always very generous.'

When she's translated for her father he walks up to me, stands the pole upright against his arm, and wai-s.

In England the police would be out by now, together with volunteers, to scour the area. After all, the girl is only sixteen. A child, really.

WHEREVER THERE ARE DOGS YOU'LL FIND FLEAS

As we all walking back to my village and nearly there, Na Att becoming more tearful. Mae puts her arm around her younger sister's heaving shoulders and talks low and sweet to her, trying to make her happy. Then Mae stops, flicking at an irritating insect buzzing round Na Att. She tries to swat a very large, yellow fly which is dancing in front of her sister's face.

'That robber fly!' Na Att cries out, voice sounding like her normal self. 'Look at large yellow body, swirling round my head. Robber fly not biting people, but very fierce. It eating other insects, even dragon flies.' She stands still, pulling Mae back. 'See how it staying by me? Flying in circle round my head? It buzzing very loud because it trying to tell me something!'

'You upset, Nong Att...' Mae puts both arms round her younger sister, trying her best to stop Na Att becoming hysterical. My aunt has this reputation – she always making everything seem worse than it really is. Now no one in the village believing what she says.

'That fly inhabited by spirit of my daughter!' Na Att shouting, running away from Mae, very upset. 'I know it talking with me, telling me my daughter already dead.' She stares at the fly with wild eyes. 'That insect is daughter's spirit coming to haunt mother.'

She begins wailing. I try to help Mae calm Na Att down, but she shakes us both off, pointing at the fly which is now acting in a very peculiar manner. This insect has a long yellow body and bulging red eyes, very distinctive. It buzzes round Na Att's head, but no one else's head. And the buzzing seems very loud because, now that it is twilight, there is very little other noise.

What Na Att is saying about this insect is true, this fly is only interested in other insects – grasshoppers, butterflies, all much bigger than any robber fly. That is why we also call it the assassin fly, because it so very aggressive, dive-bombing prey insects while in flight, injecting them with poison so they cannot move.

We all try swatting the fly, taking no notice of Na Att's shrieking to leave the insect unharmed because it is Nong Wuadon trying to tell her mum what happening during the morning of this bad karma day. I understand what Na Att is trying to tell us. It really is peculiar how this insect seems to wait for our swats, then escapes at the last minute. Afterwards it always comes back to fly round Na Att's head, ignoring others.

'You know this is robber fly,' she sobs. 'I sure what that means. Bandits – robbers – carrying off my little Wuadon this morning. Killing her.' She narrows her eyes at the buzzing fly. 'Maybe they also doing other terrible things. My lovely, sweet Wuadon. Beautiful, most beautiful girl of Dumden Village, of whole area! She finding easy to win beauty contest.' She stops talking, takes Mae's hands. 'That explaining everything! Bandits hear about beautiful girl and plan taking her, intending to keep prisoner and putting her in contest themselves...'

I do not say, because that is not of help, that no bandit can enter Nong Wuadon for a beauty contest. Though we know and fear bandit gangs, no single bandit can afford to be identified as an individual. Because, if the police can identify one, they can find and arrest the whole gang, for sure.

We all try to calm Na Att down, try to help her with happy thoughts about her daughter, distracting her. She refuses to stop lamenting, mumbling her daughter's name all the time, now moaning that she knows Nong Wuadon is already dead, that it is only a short time before we find the body of her daughter.

At last we begin to realise that there is something unusual here. We have to accept that something really odd is going and we try to understand what Na Att is telling us: Nong Wuadon's spirit, in the form of the robber fly, is speaking to her mum. We believe in spirits, so it is not so far-fetched to believe that the fly is Nong Wuadon's spirit coming to talk to her mother.

Na Att is a very foolish woman, but we cannot deny that the fly stays with her, buzzing round only her, refusing to leave. Then it changes antics. It lands on Na Att's arm and crawls up it, its buzzing very loud. Mae raises her hand to lunge at the pestering fly but Na Att pushes her away. 'Not hurt this special fly!' she cries out, 'It already talking to me! My little daughter try hard to tell me something.'

We believing that a dead person becomes a spirit. We also believing that we must appease all spirits so that the dead person can rest in peace. But, though almost all Thai people build spirit houses for their dead, or maybe keep a particular tree as a special home for their family's spirits, we do not expect them to communicate with us.

Na Att is getting very excited now. 'You seeing fly behave this way before? First making little dance for me, then walking up my arm, now dancing again. I must follow where she leading!' And she turns right round to go after the yellow fly which now looks as though it is flying back to the paddy fields, or maybe to the dry scrub beyond.

'All right, Nong Att. Wait for me and I going with you.' Her husband is among a small number of villagers watching Na Att and the fly. 'We never getting peace until you recognising your foolishness.'

Luke, walking by me, cannot understand what is happening. He asks me to explain what is going on. He seeing that Na Att is having a great deal of attention from other villagers, but he does not understand why.

'Really? She actually believes her daughter's spirit is in the fly?'

'Not in fly. She *is* fly,' I tell him. 'Na Att very sure. Heart and soul.'

'Right. Let's go and help find her daughter.' He is very happy because he does not like just waiting. Also I knowing he wants to return to Krung Thep as quick as possible. Maybe he even believing in spirits, I do not know, we have never discussed this.

'Even if she's mistaken about the spirits, maybe following the fly will lead us to Wuadon,' he saying as he starting to follow Na Att.

Phor also deciding to come with us. Na Att is now very clear that Nong Wuadon is leading her, showing us what happened to her. Lamenting her daughter loudly she follows the fly which buzzes, very fast, ahead of us.

'Dark coming soon soon,' Na Att gulps. 'Must hurry, go fast we can.'

It is very strange, very remarkable. When Na Att slows down, or stops and weeps, the fly also stops. It buzzes on again when Na Att regains sufficient strength to follow it.

We move at a steady pace to the fields holding the deep wells, the exact same path where Nong Wuadon was herding her buffaloes this morning. How can a fly know which way the girls and Nong Wuadon went unless it really is Nong Wuadon reincarnated?

The fly moves on, away from the wells. All of a sudden the insect disappears into thick bushes on the far side of the low dyke of dried-out paddy covered in rough rice stubble. The light is already beginning to fade and it is only because the fly has such a bright yellow body that we can see it. Loud, angry buzzing guides us to a dark mass of overgrown bushes.

Now the fly disappears, we cannot see it anywhere. Is it in the bushes? Maybe it went in there for special reason? Then I think maybe this is just an ordinary fly and that we are following it because we have primitive ideas. Are we willing to believe in spirits, like always in our past, because we are upset and nervous? Maybe we are just following a foolish woman, the fly is not really Nong Wuadon, it is just the way some ignorant villagers think.

Now there is no more sign of the fly. Even Na Att cannot hear or see it.

'Enough foolishness,' Na Att's husband Lung Ban says, grabbing her arm. 'We can do nothing today, sun almost gone. We go back village.'

'We seeing by moonlight.' Na Att clings like a stubborn buffalo to the conviction that the fly will come back and lead us to her daughter. And she is right, the moon is full, we can see well. It is fortunate that we rescued the moon from the cosmic frog last night. Our reward is now shining very bright above us in a starlit sky, outlining bushes, showing some dense, some thin. But there is no sign of the yellow fly.

'It leaving, Na Att.' I hug her, hope she is feeling better. 'Your daughter not dead. Bandits sending someone with demand for ransom. We all paying small part and so collect enough money, and she coming back soon soon.' Na Att spits on the earth. 'We only imagining fly is Nong Wuadon, Na Att. Yellow insect knowing nothing of human problems.'

As though the fly can hear me and is coming to contradict me I see the yellow body, glowing from light reflected from the moon, buzzing loudly. It is very angry, hovering in front of a thicket ahead, dancing on one spot, wings whirring, its body moving very fast, up and down. We cannot help watching it, all eyes going to that one spot.

'Fly telling us she over there!' Na Att moans. 'Robber fly saying she inside that bush!'

Then I see it, and Mae also looks at the same thing and recognises it as well. A small piece of cloth, a tiny fragment of rag hanging from one of the branches of the bush. We recognise a piece of cotton dyed in the shimmering blue-green colour Mae uses for her silks. It is very possible that it coming from Nong Wuadon's dress, because Mae does not use this colour for anything except for Nong Wuadon's clothes. Where else could it be coming from?

Now I see that the bushes, very rough, are also showing signs of recent disturbance. Some branches are bent and others are broken, and I can see that the inside of the wood is not yet dark, because it is freshly cut. Then I also notice some pushed-back branches used to hide the cut ones.

Lung Ban and Phor understand what Na Att is saying. They use machetes to slice the bush into two sections, pulling tangled branches apart. Phor grabs one side, Lung Ban grabs the other, and Luke helps, pulling back some of the cut and broken branches.

Then all three men stop at the same time. They shout, Lung Ban cries out, bringing us three women running up to them.

69

We see very clearly now that the branches are out of way, with moonlight shining brightly. And what we see makes us all silent, not even Na Att is sobbing any more.

Lying in front of us on blue-green cloth is the pale, naked body of a young girl, her legs splayed wide and bloodied, her head at an odd angle to her right shoulder, a blue-green neck scarf covering her motionless face. We cannot mistake Nong Wuadon – her long, wavy dark-brown hair, her pale skin, my mum's dyed scarf. She not moving. We not needing a doctor to tell us she is dead.

Na Att's voice comes to life. She wails in horror, in fury, in despair. No one can comfort her, she is past helping. Her husband removes Mae's arms from round Na Att, grabs his wife and pushes her in front of him, pointing her back to the village.

Phor takes his shirt off to cover Nong Wuadon's body, then stands and looks hard. Whatever he thinks, we are clear he cannot know what happened earlier today, and now it is too dark to search for clues. He must wait till morning when he can see more. Now we all know this is murder, so Phor must alert the police soon as possible or the whole village will be in very big trouble. Phor knows no one must touch this body or anything nearby. If he does not guard the body then the police will blame Dumden villagers, might even imprison Phor for not doing his civic duty. They will hold him responsible.

'Daughter, take Luke and your mum back to village. I staying, guarding this body against people and animals. Tell Chong and Nong Lang what happening. I need them here, helping me, soon soon.'

This is a most terrible discovery, and Phor cannot act in any other way. We must wait till morning, then notify the police. We will send someone from the village to leave at first strike, taking a motorbike to Udon Thani. Then we will wait for the police to arrive, to look for clues, to start working to catch the murderer. I worry a good deal because I am sure it was not brigands who killed Nong Wuadon – excessive greed loses the windfall, and brigands are not stupid.

I explaining to Luke what my dad is arranging. Luke looking very grave, and says he agrees with my dad. He also understands

70

why he, Mae and I should now walk back to the village. He thinks it a good idea for some village men to come to help Phor, and agrees it would be a bad idea for Phor to ask the help of a stranger who is also farang.

Mae walks to Dumden with Luke and me, she wishes to help Lung Ban look after Na Att. Now she is with us as chaperone, so I cannot hold Luke's hand and I am feeling very nervous. I wish we had left for Udon Thani early in the morning, before all this happened. Especially because I waited so Nong Wuadon could speak with me which she was anxious to do.

My heart is heavy for Nong Wuadon. Such a gay, loving girl I thinking of as my younger sister, I always bringing her gifts from Krung Thep, I always happy to spending time with her. There is a feeling in my chest as though something is crushing me, stopping my heart from beating. I cannot cry, I cannot speak, it is difficult for me to breathe.

Nothing making sense now. Yesterday I came to see my parents with big pride. Is that why Nong Wuadon died? Because I thinking marrying farang is most important thing in my life? Because I forgetting I am just village girl, not necessary to wear beautiful clothing and looking after hands and hair? That is just vanity. I should be proper younger daughter, stay in village, doing my duty to be the person looking after my parents when they getting old.

Then I start thinking about Luke. Already knowing he very much in love with me, wanting the best for me, wanting to behave like proper man and meeting my parents. Therefore not possible that he is responsible for Nong Wuadon's death. He hardly seeing her, it is foolishness for me to think he thinking about her.

And now Luke is in a difficult position. I knowing he has business meeting tomorrow, this very important, is special meeting, it meaning his business may not succeed if Luke not arriving.

Naturally I am also worried that he is upset with me, with my village, with my parents. What does he think of Thai people now, murdering young girls in the village? Maybe he thinks we are not civilised, we are wild and out of control? Perhaps it now meaning he does not wish to make me his number one wife?

A WOMAN'S MOUTH IS LONGER THAN A CROW'S BEAK

'This is very first time, tilac. Never happening in village before.' Taiella's right hand covers her mouth. Troubled eyes roam to her mother.

'Never?' My instincts tell me this isn't true. I remind myself: Thais do not assert what we see as facts, they say what they see as saving face. 'You're sure?'

She blows a long breath through her nostrils. 'Not since family living here. Mae telling never hearing of murder in Dumden Village.'

Surely I'd been told the police weren't slow to gun down a villager or two, no questions asked? And that this had happened in Taiella's village. Or is what the police do not considered murder, but justifiable homicide? I'm only too aware that I'm among people with a very different outlook on life from mine. I feel sweat trickle down my forehead.

And turn to look at Nanakorn. No movement at all on her closed moonlit face. 'But such things have happened before, haven't they? In other villages perhaps?'

Taiella shifts behind the solid body of her mother. 'Family living here sixteen years. Cannot remember what happening in old village family coming from.'

'Right.' She was very young when they moved, a seasoned

worker in the fields. 'So what about your father? He must occasionally get together with the head men of other villages. Has he heard anything?'

'Phor head man four years now, taking on position when old head man die.' She walks on a few yards, her feet crackling the stubble, looking down. 'A tree, cut down but with roots left in soil, sprouting again.'

I finally remember that direct questioning never works. Thais consider it confrontational and retire behind bland generalized pronouncements. Taiella walks over to me, but keeps what is, presumably, a decent distance.

'Like suffering when cause not dealt with. That how village life working.'

She's telling me this has happened before. In Dumden, in another village, perhaps across the border in Laos. Thais aren't what I'd call time literate. This year, next year, sometime, never... Changing tactics can produce surprising results. 'So rape happens quite often.'

She shies away, waves her right hand sideways across her face. 'No chance for rape. All girls knowing leaf wrapped round rotten fish taking on rotten smell, in same way person spending time with bad people becoming rotten. Nong Wuadon very proper girl.'

As we trudge along the dry road to the village, this time without the excitement of following the fly, the gruesome picture of that poor innocent girl keeps coming back to me. The long hard slog does nothing to make me feel any better. I look at Taiella in revealing moonlight. My Smileegirl's face is expressionless. Her eyes are glinting, empty, her nostrils wide. If I'm so affected by Wuadon's death – and, though I didn't know the girl, I really feel the horror of such a tragically young and innocent life being destroyed – Taiella must be in terrible shock, must be finding it hard to cope.

My instincts are to comfort her, to put my arm round her shoulders and hug her to me. She shakes me off as soon as I approach, as always refusing to hold my hand. 'Forgetting again, tilac. Not proper in village,' she whispers. 'Sorrow leaving people overcoming unworthy thoughts, like water dripping from lotus-leaf.'

Why whisper? Nanakorn doesn't speak or understand English. She shuffles several paces behind the two of us. Is she being discreet, the Thai way, or is she plotting something more sinister? Waves of dislike, perhaps even of hate, feel like a cloud of locusts massing on my back. Am I becoming paranoid?

'Cannot touch because not married, tilac,' Taiella says softly, one slow foot in front of another. Heat, dust, mosquitoes – all exhausting. I'm not used to coping in this climate without the comforts of a hotel room and air-conditioning. And I crave some physical contact, anything, however discreet. With only that glum mother around I see no reason for this charade.

'Doesn't your mother understand? Haven't you told her we're getting married as soon as my divorce comes through?'

She stumbles, scuffing clods of earth. 'Telling Mae, not telling Phor. Small dripping drops of water can fill big pot in time, so person can become sinful with small wrongs.' She buttons her blouse to the top in spite of the suffocating heat. 'If Phor knowing then locking away from fiancé, from all.'

'What d'you mean? I wouldn't let him!'

She brushes her skirt straight, pulls it down. 'If Phor forbidding seeing fiancé, then obeying. Parents highest form of worship for children. Phor father, therefore daughter duty to obey until marrying. Then obeying husband.'

The Taiella in Bangkok has only a small resemblance to the one in Dumden. What do I expect? Twenty odd years of village life aren't going to be wiped out by a few years in Bangkok. I bless my minimal Thai. I could so easily have screwed up with Wirat. Fascinating, of course, that Taiella told her mother about us. That explains why glum Nanakorn is so against me – because I've seduced her virgin daughter!

Doesn't make sense. Even if she isn't a smiling Thai but a glum Laotian, surely she should be happy for Taiella, not glowering like a tigress?

That means she has to be blaming me for what happened to Wuadon which, in turn, means Att will now be raging her accusations in the village to anyone willing to listen. I've already told them: I didn't speak to the girl, never even went near her. In fact it seemed to me that her buffaloes stank even more than the rest! I did kid around with a couple of the other girls, but not with the murdered one.

I feel my throat tighten as I grasp I'm in a Thai village with not a single other westerner around. Will they attack me? I scold myself for stupidity. They'll wait for the police. Injuring – killing? – a farang would lead to drastic measures. The Thai government is very aware that tourism is Thailand's biggest industry.

Nanakorn, I've been told time and again, has this special relationship with the dead girl, is devastated by what's happened. Almost as much as Att. I wonder whether Wuadon was actually Nanakorn's love child – born when Wirat was in Saudi, during the few months when she was 'ill' and retired to Laos for six months. One thing is sure: Nanakorn's fury has spilled onto my sweet Taiella. The mother trudges doggedly behind us, avoiding any contact. I stop a couple of times for her to catch up. She stops, too, scowling and kicking dust into the air. It makes me feel sick – and nervous. I'm very aware there's no Wirat to protect me in the village.

Coming into the outskirts I hear a murmuring sound, people gathered together, talking. As we come nearer the talk turns to shouts, then bellowing Thai curses. I see several men jumping around, shaking machetes, one or two boys copying them with sticks.

Nanakorn comes to life, transformed from a glowering buffalo into a crocodile with a catch. She sprints ahead, into the centre of the crowd, rapid-fire syllables spluttering out and ricocheting from the houses on either side of us.

Taiella, no longer worrying about touching me, shouts as well. I hear 'Mae' repeated several times, as well as 'Lung' and 'Na' – uncle and aunt. One of the burlier men grabs hold of me and pulls me into the centre of the crowd. My whole body is engulfed in sweat as two other men push up to me, grabbing an arm each, while a third comes in behind me so I can't twist away. The first man spits into my face.

Nanakorn runs up to me, glares, teeth bared, loathing in every feature, her arms flailing encouragement at the men.

Taiella pushes towards me, as near as she can get, shrills words I can't understand. The man who spat at me pushes her away. I hear the whistle of clods of earth, or stones, as they fall near us. I've heard of stoning in the Middle East. Are these Thais intending to stone me to death? I taste bile in my mouth.

My height, my skin, my hair, my eyes – I feel their alien look in this place, try to cringe out of the moonlight into the shadows. Nowhere to hide. The moon shines full and merciless, the crowd around me churns and yells. I remember the silent stares of yesterday, the unspoken resentment now expressed.

They've been convinced all along, as soon as Wuadon was missing. Yesterday's stranger is the pervert who raped and murdered their beauty. No need for the police – they've already decided on perpetrator and sentence. I'm in no doubt what that would be as terror turns to fury.

Taiella pushes through again, near enough for me to hear her. 'They saying farang, coming village only yesterday and already trouble.'

'But I haven't done anything…'

'Walking with girls in morning. What reason having for this? Maybe wanting opportunity to be with Nong Wuadon!'

The men on either side of me twist my arms behind me, the third has found some bamboo thongs to tie my wrists together. The stuff slices into me, cuts off my circulation. In spite of the heat I feel the chill of terror.

'Say luring Nong Wuadon into bushes, then raping. When proper girl resisting, strangling for keeping silent, then hiding for covering up crime. Mae very angry, say no good man, seducing daughter when virgin.'

The tears in Taiella's voice, the hubbub, the stark truth which she'd normally water down. 'You mean they think *I* killed Wuadon? That's impossible! I never even talked to her!'

'Not believing, Luke. All farang want sex with beautiful young Thai girl.'

The two men on either side jerk at the bamboos binding my wrists. The pain is searing, continuous. 'But they know *you're* the girl I'm with!' I try to bellow, knowing any sign of weakness is an

76

admission of guilt.

'Already old for marrying, ugly because of dark skin. When seeing Nong Wuadon thinking fiancé liking young girl, wanting swap for beautiful cousin. Already many men in village, also other villages, wanting marry Nong Wuadon.'

Somehow Taiella has managed to come right up to me, her arms spread out to protect me. She won't be able to. Short of her father turning up I'll be lynched. I twist my head round, looking for an escape, trying to think of something – anything – to convince the villagers it wasn't me.

I see Ban, Wuadon's father, a few feet away. He catches my eye and starts towards me, machete held high. Taiella pushes herself right into me as a stream of words pour out of him.

Several men grab hold of him. Not to protect me – I'm clear about that – but to stop him killing Taiella before he gets to me. Not for her sake. They consider her a whore because of her relationship with me, so they'll be only too glad to get rid of her as well. It's clear it's her father's position as head man which saves both of us.

I summon all my strength to twist and turn.

'Not struggle, Luke,' Taiella hisses at me. 'Make more angry. Forcing listen.'

She starts screaming herself into a frenzy. Just a matter of time before one of them grabs hold of her and tosses her out of the way.

Ban's face is contorted as he swings his machete wildly round. Then one of the other men snatches Taiella and shoves her aside. She lands with a loud thump, under her parents' house.

'What's *she* done?' I yell out, desperate to get away and go to her. The voices grow louder, more raucous, more bodies crowd on top of me.

Then, quite suddenly, there's the sound of a rifle shot. The effect is immediate, the grey forms around me stiffen, stand still.

I recognise real gunfire. Where has it come from? Have the police already been alerted, somehow, and arrived?

FASHIONING A NEEDLE OUT OF FLINT

I already using one shot from the rifle my dad make ready the night before. Now I do not know what I should do, my whole body is shaking very hard. This happening even though I went to military school and know how I should handle firearms. My instructor showing me how to fire rifle, but she not able to teach me how I shooting people I know, even if their angry shouts hurt my ears and threaten my Luke.

It is very dark in the centre of the village now, the houses hiding the moon. The air is becoming a little bit cooler because the sun is gone and it is time for the sound of the drum. But many neighbours arriving carrying tamarind branches wound with blazing petrol-soaked cloth, making heat and light. The very hot air coming in billows from so many villagers hits me in the face, making a thick cloud over my thinking.

I know I must stay calm, must work out how to save Luke. Maybe I am also in danger. The people of Dumden are not happy with me, they think I am like the many village girls leaving home for Krung Thep to go into the service industry there, and so disgrace their families. They do not believe that I have a proper job in a department store, they badmouth me to Mae and Phor. They are convinced my parents taught their daughter to be a good girl, always showing me how to safeguard my virtue, but they do not believe I obeyed them. They cannot grasp that I am no longer a village girl, that I live in the modern world. They do not understand that their values have no value in Krung Thep.

I have never missed Phor as much as now. I long for guidance from a strong person. I look for someone to listen to me, but I cannot think of anybody. Mae is not willing to help. I can feel her hating eyes on my back the whole time we walking to the village. She makes her flapping lips shout bad words, stirring all our neighbours up to copy her. Maybe she is sure I have become a bad daughter, have betrayed my family, my village and King Bhumipol. I am upset to the full top that the King might think I am a bad subject.

I cannot change anything now, so I must work out how to act forcibly on my own. I have always had the dream to escape from Isaan, to leave my village and to make a career in the big city; to become independent of my parents and my village. Now the time has come to test if I am capable of this.

I walk out of the shadows from below my dad's house, his rifle loaded for a second shot. I look around to see who is willing to help me. A man close by me has his face lit up by the flame of a torch swinging nearby.

At first I am very frightened, then I realise this must be my older brother Pi Chong. He nods, recognizing me at the same time. I slip my left hand back and forth on closed lips to warn him not to betray me. I remember what Phor instructed me to tell Pi Chong. I am sure my brother will help Luke and me if he knows what my dad wants.

The crowd begins to shift again, soon noticing it is me holding the gun. Some men begin to laugh and I can tell they think it will be easy to take the gun from me. They do not believe in my resolve to shoot my parents' neighbours. Maybe they are right, maybe they are wrong. Even I do not know at this time.

'Pi Chong,' I say into my brother's ear, 'Phor giving me important message for you. You sending Pi Lang and one other man of your choice to go and help him guard Nong Wuadon's body.' My dad cannot know I desperately need Pi Chong to help me here, so I must interpret his instructions. 'Phor remaining in nearby bush so no clue lost before police coming.' This last part is exactly what Phor telling me.

Pi Chong turns his head towards Luke. I am very nervous, and can feel the rifle slipping in my hand running with sweat because I do not know what my brother is thinking.

'You understand how to lead the people of Dumden Village, Pi Chong. Phor trusting you to take his place. Also you know that if village harm farang police coming to take all top workers to Udon Thani. Police beating, maybe some die, some going in prison, leaving family without fish and rice. You helping me right now, OK?'

Lung Ban steps out from behind the banana tree, his sharp ear growing big. He recognizes what is happening for sure. His head swivels round on his mango neck, his eyes are tight slits to see in the dark. He comes running, elephant feet pounding on the ground, I can feel the vibration.

'Nong Taiella holding father rifle!' he trumpets. 'Farang whore wants save bastard farang. That man coming our village, raping and killing my daughter! He thinking he having permission to do anything he wanting because we only poor village people.' Lung Ban twists on one foot, like a runner on the starting line. I try aiming Phor's rifle, cannot even point it.

'Lung Ban!' I cry out, my voice wobbling. 'Stop! You are not head man, that is my father's job. Pi Chong taking place when he not here!'

My brother moves like a turtle, sideways, slow and deliberate. He flicks the rifle from me, pushes me aside, his body now close to Lung Ban. 'What Phor telling you I must do?' he hisses at me out of the side of his mouth, but standing upright and strong. Now I remember what Buddha said, that the virtuous have the appearance to be mighty, even from far away, as far as the Himalaya mountains.

This is my only chance, I cannot be as gentle as in the past, I must be strong woman. 'Phor order sending two men to stay with him till morning, guarding Nong Wuadon body.' My voice starting out squeaky like that of a monkey, but becoming loud and strong because I feel strength growing from inside. Sorrow falls away from those who accomplish hard tasks, like drops of water gliding off a lotus leaf.

I see Lung Ban raise his right arm to Pi Chong. My brother's hands tighten on the rifle, he lifts it to his shoulder. 'Listen to Pi Chong,' I shout now like someone cracking coconut shells, my voice very loud so all the people around can hear. 'My older brother taking my father's place. My father head man. Your duty is listening to Pi Chong!'

My older brother now points rifle at Lung Ban. 'Listening! We make citizen arrest. We keep farang prisoner,' Pi Chong shouts. 'When time of strike coming we alerting police. We must fetching soon possible or they thinking we greedy village people, we kill farang for money to putting in own pocket.'

Lung Ban grabs the top of the gun barrel, pushing it up and down, not afraid. 'Forget police! This village business, we settling in village way...'

'You do what my father says,' Pi Chong trumpets like angry bull elephant. He pushes the gun into Lung Ban's neck, cocking the trigger. 'We keeping farang prisoner in my family house until sunrise. I order you go with Nong Lang helping my father guarding body of your daughter. I staying here.'

Lung Ban does not have much choice, the village elders agree with Pi Chong. Two strong villagers now push Luke up Phor's ladder, into our house and the big room. I follow, watch how they truss him like a pig ready for spit-roast. But they do not try to kill him because they know my brother is taking my father's place. They become fearful when they see Pi Chong stabbing the rifle into Lung Ban, holding it ready to shoot, his attitude very fierce.

I wait now for the remaining villagers to go back to own homes, then I also go into my dad's house. I guessing that Luke is very uncomfortable and hungry for water and wonder how I can help him. If I ask permission to give him water maybe this will make the guards even angrier, if I do not then maybe Luke will become very ill. I think hard, then have an excellent idea. I go to the kitchen, prepare some drinks I know they liking, come back into the room and offer them to the three guards – my brother Pi Chong, his good friend Pi Nan and also Pi Win. All three are happy about this, I can tell. I stay for a short time, joking with them, asking about their children. At last I offer to fetch water, and I also bring some for Luke. They do not say anything, maybe they do not notice what I am doing. I take the opportunity to give Luke water.

He already talking to me, very upset, raising his voice. I do not answer, I know that would be very bad idea. But I look at him for long long time, my eyes big, my nostrils wide and finally he getting my meaning. At last he stops talking, I can see he is very upset, but I also see he understands I have a special plan.

I hold the coconut shell full of water to his lips, he cannot do this because his hands are tied. I know he is in a bad situation, not understanding what the men guarding him are saying, only that they are angry.

He says very softly, between sips. 'What on earth are they on about, Taiella? Are they all accusing me of this horrific crime? I thought that brigands...'

It is a hostage state of affairs, and I must reason with Luke like a negotiator in a Hollywood film. But I do not have permission to speak, though I know that the only way to diffuse the situation, to save face all round, is to calm Luke.

I turn to Pi Nan. I have known him for long time, he always had the eyes and the ears for me. 'It saving trouble if I asking prisoner questions before police coming, Pi Nan. Otherwise hard for me translating quick quick.'

He looks at me and I turn my top smile on him. My teeth are very even, very white, perfect like California teeth. I know I am still sugar for him. He smiling back.

'You cooking special for me, Nong Taiella? You bringing for me?'

I give him another big smile. 'Very happy cooking for you, Pi Nan. I remember you liking very hot curry. I make for you first class.'

Luke watches, cannot understand the words, but he can see I have calmed down one of his guards. He scanning my face and eyes for clues about what is going on. I busy myself wiping the water dripping down his chin because I tilted the coconut shell, this giving me a chance to talk.

'You with girls on own, Luke,' I explain to him. 'You can see that looking bad. Then we finding Nong Wuadon dead, seeing she

82

victim of rape, of murder. Her father sure you culprit.'

Luke looking very sad, very tired. 'He can't possibly know for certain that she was raped, and why pick on me as the one to have killed her?'

It is not hard for me to sound angry, because he does not understand the village way of thinking. 'We all know she with no clothes, two legs spread out. Can mean only one thing.' My voice is quite loud.

Luke struggles hard against the bamboo, making the men guarding him grin and pull it extra tight. I can see he is losing strength. 'Why pick on *me*? What makes them think...?'

'You stranger. Farang stranger. Pi Chong and me protect until police coming.'

'It's crazy to assume I raped and killed that girl!' Luke explodes. 'Why would I do that to a young girl I've never even met?'

Pi Nan and Pi Win look at him hard, even Pi Chong watching with suspicious eyes. Luke getting angry is a good idea, they think I say bad words to him. My voice is still fierce, I know they cannot understand English. 'She knows you my friend, she not afraid, she very beautiful. And you *there*, Luke. You with her.' I do not even pretend now, I remember my anger, like a blade of grass handled in the wrong way and cutting my hand.

'Exactly,' he answers, excited by making his point. '*With* all the other girls.'

'You say with many girls. *They* say you alone.'

'Absolutely true, as far as it goes. I left them – by myself. That's the point. I didn't leave with Wuadon.'

I think back now, how Luke returned to the village from walking out in the paddies. He showed no jumpiness, I saw no scratches on his face or arms, his clothing was not torn, there was no blood on his hands. I know Nong Wuadon would have fought for her virtue like a tigress, leaving many marks on the attacker. I am also sure that Luke is speaking the truth, because the flavour of truth surpasses all other flavours.

I must leave now, to cook, to make red curry. But I think hard. If I am not clear about what happening before the police coming they will not believe Luke. I put sticky rice on to heat up, chop vegetables, cut up the chicken Pi Chong killed, pound chilli paste, add lemon grass. Then I see in my mind's eye how Luke walked slowly back from the paddies, smiling when he saw me, very happy to be near me. How could he have turned from angel to demon? That not making sense. Good karma never causes regret for the doer. I have now known this lovely man for more than six months, and have never had reason to complain. Luke is not the one who killed Nong Wuadon. I am absolutely clear about that.

Just one thing is true. Luke having the opportunity to commit this terrible deed. And because the villagers believing he had a motive it is possible the police may also think that.

I pretending to fetch water. This way it is safe to go outside to the special tree where our family spirits live. I pray, asking them to show the police the whole truth. I promise that if the police can prove Luke is not responsible for Nong Wuadon's death I will come back to Dumden with much gold, much more than they have ever seen in all the years they have lived in my family's house of the spirits. I also promise that I will put gold leaf on the back of the Buddha, that is I will not tell anyone about my good deeds.

HATE EELS BUT EAT EEL CURRY

Wrapped in bamboo slivers like a silk moth in its cocoon allows only one freedom – thought. I let mine burrow deep into Taiella's gentleness, her smile. That's what drew me to her that first night we met. That, and her sweet nature. She's clearly put that aside tonight, for my sake, to get us out of this hole. The bamboo cuts deeper as I try to squirm free.

Chong's two heavies heaved me into the main room in Wirat's house. I landed, clumsily, on the floor, my long legs stopping me from sitting, pulling me into a squat. Hardly what I'm comfortable with. I'm used to chairs, and beds, and other decadent artefacts. I roll onto my side. Chong says something, comes over and loosens my ankle fetters sufficiently so that I can sit, knees up in front, hands tied behind my back. Wood flooring is damned hard.

Taiella slips by, into the kitchen. My guess is she's preparing a meal to keep everyone sweet. Blending aromas of red curry being cooked tendril through the thin door and into my nostrils. I'm not hungry, but I'm determined to eat to prepare for the looming police ordeal.

The kitchen door opens. My stomach churns noises, a universal language which provides simple entertainment for the men crowding me. Taiella carries a bamboo tray with shallow aluminium cups and a deeper one slopping liquid. Three cups. Soup for the troops?

Thin, sloshing liquid. No steam from the large bowl. Fiery

approval which doesn't need the niceties of language, Thai or Lao, explodes around me. Smacking noises click from one bamboo wall to the other, silvering cups are dipped into the big bowl and raised to click. Chok di – good luck. Not mine; maybe not theirs at that, but I think they're not thinking along those lines.

Taiella clearly has a plan. Wirat's home-made sato, made by fermenting sticky rice with water and yeast, is reputedly forty percent proof - and spells possibilities. The big bowl is pretty full. Would being drunk make my Thai guards more or less dangerous?

Chong kicks the kitchen door open, scoops up two bamboo receptacles of sticky rice, then humps a huge bowl of curry and sets it on the floor. The sato shows its strength in spilt sauce as the men start eating. Taiella appears with coconut drinking bowls filled with water.

'Me feed,' she announces, squatting beside me, moulding gobbets of sticky rice into bowls for the curry. 'Know you liking red curry, Luke. Mae teaching younger daughter to make very good.'

Pungent chillies hit the back of my throat, increasing the large drops of sweat caused by the infernal heat. I decide to relax, allowing Taiella to take over. For the time being.

I know we have to talk, to get my story straight before the police strut into the village. Bribery isn't unknown in Thailand. Referred to as 'eating', something of a clue to Thai attitudes. There'll be someone to pass the odd thousand baht to. Goose pimples erupt in my armpits, in spite of the heat brought to boiling point by the effects of red curry. I remember the snag about offering a bribe: it's never how much to offer, it's always about finding the right person. And I haven't a clue.

Chong, baleful eyes checking, sees the other two captors' eyelids drooping, sees them slump sideways, stretch out on the floor. He frees my legs. It takes a little while but I manage to get up, luxuriating in a stretch.

'When are they going for the police, Taiella?'

'Everything OK, tilac. Police sort out early morning.'

'What about untying my hands so I can sleep properly. You could lock me in the kitchen, keep guard outside.' I doubt even

86

Houdini could make it to Udon Thani in the dark. Trekking thirty miles over dirt roads almost indistinguishable from scrubland in daylight, let alone at night, would be quite a feat for a Thai, let alone a Brit unused to rural Thai ways. And even if I managed it, a dishevelled farang trying to book a flight to Bangkok would undoubtedly be intercepted.

That fluttering, comforting smile. 'OK, I making loose, you holding hands together in case men waking up. Everything OK tomorrow, Luke. You sleeping now.' Taiella picks up the remains of the meal and disappears.

I lower myself on to the nearest mat and stretch out. My brain refuses to stop conjuring up self-important parochial policemen. Thais hold their Royal Family in deep respect and, through them, their laws. The King might be on the throne, but cash is a formidable rival. Do I have enough on me, at least enough to buy the use of a phone?

Teng Japhardee, my ever-trusty agent in Bangkok, is authorised to get cash out the business account. I think back, now, to what he said: "Maybe not the best idea to go to Thai village, Luke. How you going to run down some lines with rural Thais?"

I tossed his misgivings aside, but clearly he had a point. He'll have to fly to Udon Thani the moment he collects the money so that I can bankroll a police feast. Fortunately I've had some business practice in satisfying Thais with their favourite food in all its winsome variety.

The copious sweating has left me desperate for water. I try rolling over to the container, pretending I'm still pinioned, and lapping some up. Chong stares at me, eyes morose.

'Nam,' I say, sticking my tongue out and panting. Thai enunciation isn't my greatest skill, and the Lao intonation is probably beyond me. No response. I switch to slurping noises. Chong nods, brings a coconut shell, holds it to my lips, spilling liquid all over me.

Discomfort, heat, humidity and my captors' obvious hate keeps me from sleeping. Dozens of possibilities race through my mind. Am I feeding the wrong crocodile? Am I, in fact, the dupe who's landed himself among a village of brigands in the wilds of

Thailand? Unable to mop up the sticky sweat trickling down my face I find myself even doubting Taiella. Has she lured me to her village so her family can rob me? Was Wuadon's death staged, meant to terrify me into submission? I've seen a body – not proof that it was a corpse. Am I their master plan to get hold of a large sum of money?

I catch my breath, irritated with myself. I have to stop panic taking over. Taiella'd never do anything to hurt me. She tried to warn me off going with the girls, it was my idea to come to the village, my idea to meet her parents. She tried to get out of all of it, I was the one who insisted. Once we arrived she clearly worked overtime to convince her parents I'd make her my first wife – no ifs or buts, a done deed. Why would she jeopardise all that?

I've been surprised by her faith in me. The divorce will take time. I see the divorce papers lying on my London desk, pristine, unmarked. Two years, the solicitor I consulted estimated. Two years unless Helga would actively cooperate. That's the problem. Taiella doesn't know Helga. Unlikely my Smileegirl has ever experienced the full fury of emancipated womanhood.

Something is nibbling at me – small tucks, not really bites. I feel regurgitation in my throat when I see an army of cockroaches moving around. They prefer the Thais. Because they used their fingers for sticky rice, and didn't wash.

I'm very aware that Helga will fight every clause of any settlement offered. Let her. I'm going to get that divorce however many legal tricks she throws at me. After all, it's hardly an unusual situation. . .

It isn't because of Taiella that I've became allergic to Helga, to her nagging, to her criticisms. What surprises me now is that it took me so long. I can't work out why I've spent so many years in futile attempts to please her.

It's over. I've already relegated my highly educated, presentable, professional European wife to the past and prefer to spend time with a girl who knows nothing of my world. So what? I revel in Taiella's smile, I bask in the way her eyes light up when I come into a room, the way she sees only me, the way she chooses the choicest pieces of food and heaps them on my plate. She listens to me, doesn't criticize, makes any points that need making gently, pleasantly. And makes sure I don't lose face.

Easterners give a lot of value to not losing face. We do the same in the West, but we pretend we don't.

Of course I also have another thought. Maybe Taiella will even give me children. I never really grasped why Helga always refused. Presumably she didn't think my DNA up to scratch: no doubt in her view my children would have terrible taste, be incapable of earning large amounts of money, wouldn't live up to her standards. Taiella is happy to reproduce my genes. She's prepared to have children now, even before we're married. We've never used birth control.

Maybe my Smileegirl is already carrying our child. That will leave her exposed to village wrath. I have to be there for her. The only plan I can come up with is to convince the Udon Thani police to let me out on 'bail', and to allow both of us to take the next flight back to Bangkok. Forget my business meeting, forget the UK. After all this Taiella and I will need a pre-nuptial honeymoon.

A PIG IN A POT

I see Luke is sleeping when Pi Chong leaving at first light to fetch police. The two guards also still sleeping, because my dad's sato working very well. He always saying he making best sato in village, and now I see he very right.

'Make sure Luke not running away, Nong Taiella.'

My brother ready to leave. His duty to fetch police, but he also acting as headman, so he very responsible and worry that Luke try escaping.

'Not necessary to be anxious, Pi Chong. Luke wanting police coming, he very worried about angry villagers attacking him. Everything OK, he waiting here with me, no problem.'

Pi Chong nods head and prepares for leaving now, since sun is rising and daylight here. I can hear ordinary village noises of neighbours going to work. I very aware Luke and two guards will be waking soon soon.

When Luke awake I telling him that Pi Chong long gone on motorbike to fetch police, and he coming back at hok mong chow – at the time of the sound of the gong. That is switch over between night and day. We always signal daytime with gong, while night time we signal with drum.

'When is that, exactly?' Luke asking me.

I cannot know exact time, I can only say it will be some time during this morning. Also I cannot work out whether police thinking our village important enough for coming immediately. It is possible they thinking it of second rate importance. They could be coming any time before noon, maybe not even till the time of the drum. 'Maybe ten o'clock, Luke.'

'Quite a long time, then. Right.'

He looking at me. He very exhausted and filthy, and I thinking he must be terribly uncomfortable. 'I fetching water for washing, Luke. Also making breakfast.' I bringing him a face cloth and soap. Not only because of discomfort for Luke. Not a good idea for the police to see an untidy man.

Luke looking at me, trying hard to smile. He speaking very low so not to wake the guards. 'It'll take Chong about an hour and a half to get to Udon Thani, at least, even if he can go much faster than the songthaew. Then another couple of hours for the police to get here, I suppose. You're right. Around ten.'

I can tell he very uneasy that villagers might attack him while Pi Chong away. 'Not necessary worrying, Luke. Village knowing police coming, they afraid of policemen, nobody harming you now or they get in big big trouble.' I can tell this making Luke feel a little bit better, but he nervous because he knows Thai police can be very rough.

I worry that they might behave badly with farang. They might not allow me to translate what Luke saying, they might not even try to understand. Good thing Luke has sufficient baht in his business account. Bad thing that maybe he does not have enough money in his pocket. What will he do then?

'You'll come with me and translate, won't you, tilac? Even if the police interrogator has a smattering of English he may not understand what I'm trying to say.'

'Of course I coming with you, explaining to police everything is big misunderstanding. All working out OK, Luke.'

Now having a new worry: that my mum may be coming back soon soon from staying with Na Att and comforting her. Perhaps Mae wanting to come to own house. Then we having trouble because she waking guards, telling them to treat Luke very bad. Maybe she even beating him. I wondering how I stopping this, so hoping Na Att so upset my mum staying long time with her.

I have no idea how many baht Luke bringing for this trip. Offering too little to police is very dangerous. I say I have work in the kitchen, but really it is an excuse not to talk to either Luke or the guards. But I insisting that Pi Win take Luke outside to toilet. I give Pi Win a bowl and cloth so he can wash, promising wonderful food if he treating his prisoner well when he takes him outside after he finish washing.

Pi Win coming back quickly, complaining of headache from too much sato. He is happy to wash and eat, then go back to sleep without bothering Luke. Pi Nan still snoring. I do not think he will wake up soon.

I untie Luke's wrists and ankles, tell him to go to toilet outside. When he coming back I rub coconut cream into skin. He very raw from the bamboo which is as sharp as a knife when wet. I also bring a comb for his hair and smooth Luke's clothing. It is very important for him to look neat when the police coming.

Luke giving me a hard time when I saying I must tie his wrists again. I tying them as loosely as I dare.

My big worry is how the police will treating Luke. They are often brutal people who behave in ways farang cannot know about. I have seen English police on TV and in movies. They are very polite and do not carry guns. When they see his hands are tied with bamboo slivers Thai policemen might even beat Luke. My hope is they will expect him to give them plenty of baht to eat, and treat him with proper respect because of that.

IT'S EASIER TO CATCH FLIES WITH HONEY THAN WITH VINEGAR

Taiella disappears, leaving me between two snoring guards. Time crawls hot and damp. I'm very anxious about coping with what I'm pretty sure will be a distinctly hostile interrogation by the Udon Thani police. Will they provide, or even have, a senior officer who might speak some English?

The sound of an approaching motor jumps hope into my throat. The morning songthaew rattles in, which does give me a bearing on the time – around eight. How much longer are the police going to be?

The stuttering, intermittent blasts of Chong's motorbike arriving include a background of combustion engine noises revving loudly, and of a more refined, though not spectacularly refined, type. Some sort of army vehicle unsure where to park?

Taiella runs in, shakes my sleeping guards awake, tells them to take me down the ladder. I suggest alternatives which aren't even acknowledged.

They manhandle me down, push me to a particular spot. I've no idea whether that's significant. Anyway, I'm not keen on standing waiting, flanked by two guards, a picture of guilt. I can't get Taiella to understand it would be fairer if I was simply waiting there, on my own, not offering resistance.

Three four-wheel drives brimming with dark grey uniforms

skid to a stop inches away from us. Am I considered dangerous enough to warrant a posse? A small army of men jump off – except for one. Also dressed in grey he sits in the front passenger seat of the front jeep and looks down on me. His shoulders, burdened under the weight of his stripes of office, are rounded towards a rotund belly. Two stripes: a captain. The Thai police take rank in US-army fashion. Sudden death isn't that unusual in rural Thailand so I take it the exalted rank is in my honour. I'd have been happy with a sergeant, but with any luck the Captain speaks English – and hence the honour.

I stand tall, head held high. And smile. Can I counter the effect of an unshaven face, crumpled clothes, straggly hair? I wouldn't bet more than a hundred baht for my chances in appearance-conscious Thailand.

The Captain stands up in the jeep, delivering a stream of Thai with a grave face. It isn't clear to whom – at least not clear to me. He looks around for a response. There isn't one. He sets his features into sterner mode, tries to climb down but can't see his feet and misses his footing. He grabs the steering wheel to steady himself, spits. A glistening gobbet lands at my feet and shudders.

Safely down at last he struts over to me and taps me on the shoulder with his baton. A wise move; his arm might not have reached. Taiella's translation, grudgingly allowed, is that I'm to be taken back to Udon Thani under armed guard.

The usual firearm is slung in holsters around each policeman's waist but I also glimpse one man shouldering a rifle aimed at me. He clicks the safety catch off.

'Khun Captain going to see Phor, looking at evidence in field, also in Dumden Village, tilac. He ordering one driver and two guards taking you to Udon Thani.' Taiella is wearing her Bangkok working clothes. The effect is at once official and decorous. She could be mistaken for my secretary.

'Ask them if you can ride back in the jeep with me, Taiella. Tell them you'll be the interpreter.'

'OK, Luke. I try.'

Taiella turns to the Captain, speaks in a low, infuriatingly obsequious manner, and smiles a great deal. The discussion seems to go on for a long time.

'Khun Captain saying costing money for me accompanying you. Extra petrol for extra weight. Also must pay for interpreting.'

I recognise an ace negotiator glinting behind Taiella's quiet smile. 'How about one thousand baht? Will that cover it?'

The discussion is now brief, the nod reluctant and given with a frowning brow. Time to show the quality of my 'food'.

'Take my wallet out of my trouser pocket, til – Taiella. Give him what he wants. And give the driver and guards five hundred each if they'll let me ride without being handcuffed.' Stick to Taiella's name, I prod my unconscious. No hint of Thai endearments while this charade is going on.

She looks anxious, but I see her eyes flicker as she takes in what I'm thinking. 'Maybe five hundred more for Khun Captain, Luke. Five hundred for driver, three hundred each guard. This way not upsetting to head man.'

Unfortunately the six thousand baht I have on me isn't going to go very far at this rate. I'll be left with three thousand four hundred when I get to the police station – an insult best not offered to an official of high standing. How do I raise enough cash to persuade the Udon Thani contingent to let me use a phone when we get to Udon Thani? Another worry: will Teng be in the office so I can contact him?

Hands freed, and able to anchor myself with my feet grabbing the central well, the trip back to Udon turns out to be less uncomfortable than the trip out in the songthaew.

Taiella, in the front passenger seat, twists round. 'Persuading driver to stop at hotel, Luke. You shaving, washing. Meanwhile ironing shirt.' A great smile and then some.

Many Thai men pluck out their relatively few facial hairs – a chore Taiella often does for her father. My Smileegirl isn't just a pretty smile. She's fully aware I'm an identikit of Barabbas if I don't make myself presentable.

'Agreeing giving driver and guard five hundred baht each, sweetheart. Thinking this good insurance.'

The Police Major's office is guarded by two golden lions with jade claws and ruby eyes. Their tongues stick out, displaying dazzling diamond shapes. Made of glass. The Major himself is less impressive. The enormous sash across his manly breast is truly colourful, but it lacks jewels. He makes up for this with a ferocious scowl and a threatening posture, twirling an officer's stick in a nervous right hand.

'Why visiting Dumden Village?' he asks in Thai.

I can make out what he's saying because I'm expecting it. The stick stops twirling. Instead, he flicks it intermittently at his left hand, hard enough to make the gun in his holster move menacingly up and down.

'Tell him I went to see your father to arrange our village wedding,' I instruct Taiella.

Eyes buried in layers of fat open a little, but the Major doesn't seem to be listening. He's inspecting Taiella, starting at her bosom, moving slowly down her body to her legs, then flickering at her face as she finishes talking. He doesn't bother to conceal his contempt – a city-suit clad, mid-twenties, Thai village woman isn't worth further inspection.

'OK. How much you pay?'

'Tell him we're getting married…'

'How much you offering to pay *Khun Major*, Luke.'

'Oh, right. What about twenty-five thousand?'

Taiella's tongue licks round her lips. 'Start fifteen thousand OK.'

The Thai exchange goes on for several minutes. I study the body language – Taiella's widely displayed whiter-than-white teeth, upturned mouth, expanding arms, the Major's hardening lips, snorting nostrils and, eventually, triumphant eyes.

'For twenty thousand Tan Major giving bail. Show passport now.'

I can't help myself, I grin with relief. 'Brilliant. If he'll let us use his phone we can get through to Bangkok, contact Teng Japhardee. He should be in the office all day today. I'll ask him to get the cash out of the bank and fly up here with it right away.'

The translation is received with impassive indifference.

Thank God I can trust Teng. Of course I know better than

to conduct business negotiations in the Asian world myself. Thai culture is as hard to read as any other, perhaps harder, particularly because Thais like to appear to please without actually giving anything away.

A further, relatively short, exchange. 'Tan Major say costing lots money using phone.'

'Fine,' I take my passport out of my jacket pocket, put the last two of my thousand-baht notes inside, pass it over. 'OK to use the phone in this room? Two calls: one to my bank, one to my office.'

'No problem,' Taiella assures me, her smile reaching her eyes. 'Tan Major understanding farang. Phone friend to bring money soon soon. Tan Major very busy man.'

I'm glad to hear there's no rush, though surprised. A Thai meeting arranged for three in the afternoon could mean anything from one to five – they come early if that's convenient, don't consider themselves late two hours after the appointed time. An odd anomaly. If I want to get out of here I'll have to work out why he's not worried.

The Major sits down, gets up again almost immediately, pushes piles of paper from one side of his desk to the other. Volcanic eyebrows accompany barking noises crackling the intercom, impatient swinging sends his enormous chair crashing into the back wall. He stands, hand on gun, snarling at Taiella in harsh, guttural tones. I finally get it: he doesn't want phone calls made from his office. Perhaps they're recorded. Why do I have to work everything out? Why can't he just say? OK, I'll suggest somewhere else.

He riffles through each page of the passport before opening it at the photograph page. Baleful eyes glitter from my present face to the five-years-before photograph. He crushes the document shut, throws it towards me on the desk. It lands on the floor. Nothing falls out. He's taken the money, but will he let me make those calls?

One of the guards turns towards me, face blank. So this is it. The two thousand is an insult. I'm finding it hard to breathe. The guard stoops, picks up the passport, hands it to me.

We have to get out of here, and now. 'Perhaps the Major would be kind enough to allow me to go to an hotel to make the phone calls?' I suggest via Taiella, smiling as genially as I can. 'Of course I would book a room. Naturally I would expect to pay for a policeman to stand guard outside the door. That way I can't escape.' It would mean I could contact Teng and charge up my mobile.

Brown eyes brush dismissively over me to the men on either side of me. The Major flicks his palms backwards. The two guards move forward, grabbing my arms. The order is short and succinct.

His index finger points at Taiella as he speaks rapidly, then flicks his palm. She wai-s, moving backwards out of the room.

'He say you very good-looking,' she mouths at me, a faint smile flickering on and off.

I bow to the dumpy figure in the bulging uniform. The braid band across his chest is stretched to bursting point. He must be uncomfortable in the heat. I flip the passport surreptitiously. The two thousand has definitely disappeared. I'd thought about how much money to bring. Too little, and I could regret it. Too much and it might be stolen. Unfortunately I hadn't allowed enough margin.

'Taiella, please tell the Major how much I appreciate the polite way he is treating this affair. I'm sure his men will solve the crime very quickly, and will apprehend the murderer.'

The brief translation leaves me in no doubt that she's left out the last part of what I said. She wai-s again and says something else. Probably how splendidly the Major's uniform suits him. Why didn't I have the sense to think of that?

'Go to hotel now. Call friend for money. Stay waiting in hotel.'

He sends me off with the two guards but no handcuffs. They march me to a five star hotel, check me in. All four of us go up to my room. Taiella persuades the two men to stand outside the door. There's the promise of two thousand baht – promises are more expensive than cash in hand. I give them my last four hundred.

'You are a murder suspect, Kuhn Luke?' Teng's hyena chuckle doesn't improve over the crackling line. 'You have unsuspected talents.'

'Never mind the jokes, Teng. Just get fifty-thousand baht out in cash and take the first flight to Udon Thani, OK? No time to mess about. The Major could change his mind at any time.'

'You are with Tan Police Major?' The respectful title, and the note of awe, doesn't improve my morale.

'No. I'm in a hotel room with a police guard outside the door.'

A pause as Teng registers his latest assignment. 'Mai pen rai – no sweat, Kuhn Luke.'

Teng's devotion to 1960s US slang, introduced by the US forces stationed in Udon Thani during the Vietnam war, can be heartwarming. At the right time. It can also be incredibly irritating. He spent his childhood up here, in Northeast Thailand, and comes back for holidays in the area to improve his English, relying on improving his American from expatriate US citizens settled here.

'I will make sure everything is right on.' A slight, unnerving pause. 'I am hurrying to shut the office. I will leave pronto.'

I don't much go for the sound of that reaction. Hurry is not part of the Thai vocabulary. 'You might as well book the return tickets for all three of us while you're at the airport.'

'Are you not enjoying our historic city of Udon Thani, Kuhn Luke? You do not want the low-down on the Bronze Age excavations, or the caves nearby?'

'Just get on with it Teng. I'll warn the bank you'll be taking out a large sum of money. They shouldn't give you any hassle.' If they did my main investor, Howard Spelter, would hear about it and take his business elsewhere. 'Call my mobile if there's a problem. I won't be sightseeing in the caves.'

WHEN THE PEAS ARE COOKED THE SESAME IS BURNED

My brother Pi Chong making a citizen's arrest yesterday is, I think, OK. But I expecting the police to issue official warrant for taking Luke prisoner. Khun Captain explaining me he not needing formal warrant because this offence is of such serious nature. I am very nervous that Tan Police Major might have some other reason for not using a warrant – I thinking that perhaps because in this way there will be no record of how he treating Luke.

Of course I am happy we are in good class hotel and Luke is no longer in police custody. He is hotel guest like any other farang, but with a police guard. I am very happy that Khun Teng Japhardee will be arriving at the sound of the drum time, and will accompany Luke to the police station. Khun Teng is very efficient colleague for Luke. He always working everything out to help Luke understand Thai ways. Khun Teng is first rate at knowing how to act in such situations.

I very happy that Luke looking almost like usual self. 'You go sleeping now, tilac, OK? Chance for good rest. In just few hours I am sure you having telephone call from Khun Teng confirming that bank giving him money and he catching plane to Udon Thani.' Luke smiling, relaxing. I can see he expecting to be free man soon soon, so he not upset.

'Good idea. I could do with a decent sleep on a bed.' He

looking at me with sidelong eyes. 'I've heard it does wonders for a bad back, but in my experience sleeping on the floor takes some getting used to.'

He putting arm around my shoulders, hugging me, kissing me on mouth. I move away because I am nervous that Nong Wuadon's spirit watching us.

He stopping, taking arm away. 'All these traumas must have worn you out as well. Did you want to eat something before we take a nap? We've got plenty of time. I'll ring for room service.' He picking up telephone right away.

'I no can stay, tilac. I must go to pay respects to Nong Wuadon's spirit, and to comfort Na Att. I taking songthaew to my village now and return on songthaew leaving before yam kham, that is before sun setting.'

Luke's eyes grow very round and blue, then squeeze into pretence smile. 'You're just going to leave me to it?' He sounding disturbed, almost angry.

It taking much courage, and very heavy heart, to tell Luke that I must go back to Dumden Village now, that I cannot stay with him. Of course I understand why he not wanting me to leave. Very difficult for Luke to communicate with police on his own, but they will not bother him, I am sure, because they knowing Khun Teng coming on the evening plane, bringing plenty baht. Tan Major not making mistakes about that, I am confident. He knowing he will not get his food if he does.

'Mysterious, violent death making person's spirit very angry, tilac. Therefore important for many people to pray and pay large amount respect. Relatives of dead person have special importance. Na Att is my aunt, Nong Wuadon is my cousin. I must go to be with them.' I understanding that farang cannot know or understand village customs. Even Thais from outside Isaan not knowing how village people treat sudden death.

Luke is looking sad, but he says nothing. 'We trying to arrange for Nong Wuadon's spirit to live in peace, tilac. All friends and family light incense sticks, give Matakabhatta food, say prayers. All this must happen on first day. Also monks coming to give blessings. These ceremonies lasting three days and three nights.'

'If that's what you have to do, Taiella, I won't even try to stop you.'

'Khun Teng coming soon soon, tilac. You want us go back to Krung Thep – Bangkok – together early morning time? Then I must going my village now. No other way we can catch morning plane to Bangkok.'

My choice is very hard, but it is most important that I show respect to Nong Wuadon. We always cremate the dead, but Nong Wuadon's death very exceptional. In this case we must bury her, because her spirit leaving her body in a violent fashion. In such cases we putting the dead body in grave within one day because bodies decomposing rapidly in our hot climate. That explaining why I cannot go to Dumden Village at any other time. If I do not go today her spirit will not be free to leave to be reborn in new human form – all near relatives must be there the first day. Nong Wuadon's spirit is already in big trouble because of her brutal death, even though that not her fault. I feel compelled to go, or Nong Wuadon will remain prisoner in Dumden Village for always, and never able to find a new life.

Luke saying nothing more, but his bright blue eyes are dull. He avoids looking at me, staring instead at the floor. His shoulders are very round, his face turning pale. I running to hug him but he not responding. I leaving quickly so that I cannot change my mind.

First I must run to a shop to buy incense sticks before the songthaew leaving. I run to explain situation to driver. He agreeing right away to wait for me before setting off.

Dumden Village is very quiet, no one to be seen, not even any dogs prowling around. Very big sound of wailing coming from temple. I go into parents' house but nobody there. I not expecting seeing them but I wanting make sure. Can hear sounds of someone climbing our ladder. Pi Chong coming in to change into clean clothing because he is also going to the temple to show respect to Nong Wuadon. We leaving together, arriving at temple together.

Many people are already crowded inside this small temple. They are standing near the body lying in a beautiful coffin in centre of big room. People are walking around, dipping green branches into coconut water and sprinkling this on Nong Wuadon's body to purify .

Nong Wuadon's face looking very peaceful, beautiful. Her eyelids are covered with a pure-white strip of silk so she cannot see the wicked murderer. Her lips are held together with an expensive silk cloth underneath her chin – I will never now know what she wanting so much to tell me. Many tears come to my eyes as I thinking back to only the day before today. I remembering Nong Wuadon dancing behind buffaloes, looking like beautiful butterfly in the brilliant-coloured cotton dyed by my mum. I try wiping away my tears, but more running down my cheeks.

A big urn at the bottom of the coffin is full to brim with sand. Incense sticks are stuck into the sand almost filling it. This telling me that Nong Wuadon's family and friends are already here for a long time. All incense sticks are almost burned to their ends, the big room already filled up with smoke. So now I know Nong Wuadon's body already lying here for several hours. That meaning police bringing body back to village early today. I very nervous that they not examining the corpse in detail, which is usual for police procedure. I worry that they believe they already know who the murderer is, who killing Nong Wuadon. I am very afraid they already decide Luke is the murderer even before the trial.

Almost the whole village is together in the temple and surroundings. When I walk in people move away, making space, showing their backs, not wanting to touch me. I can tell they think it is my fault that Nong Wuadon dead, that it is my fault for bringing farang to our village.

I knowing this is not true, so I not allowing neighbours to stop me going up to Nong Wuadon's body. I noticing how Na Att dressing her daughter in her favourite dress. My cousin looking peaceful, serene. The heavy gold necklace Mae giving her as present when Nong Wuadon coming to our village for first time is round my cousin's slim neck on top of the scarf. The heavy gold bracelet on her right wrist is a present from Nong Wuadon's uncle Are Mak, Lung Ban's younger brother. He always giving Nong Wuadon presents, even without any special reason. He always playing with Nong Wuadon when she was a little girl, he always trying talking to her when she young girl.

Mourners making way as I moving through to Nong Wuadon's mother, Na Att, wanting to embrace her. She rigid as a rock, both eyes shut, mouth tight. She not answering when I speaking to her. I try embracing her and she acting as though she a statue instead of a live woman. Other women coming up to us, using their bodies to move me away, nobody speaks, they are all crying and sobbing. The air is hanging heavy with incense smoke, so it is as hard to see as if clouds were coming down low from grey sky. Maybe the phii spirits are already in this room, swallowing each sad sound, greedy to take strength from the grieving family, the grieving village. Phii spirits can be evil, always coming when someone dies in a mysterious fashion, or when the funeral rite is not conducted in proper manner. Village people try hard to appease such spirits. Therefore it is not just because of the heat, this is another reason why we bury accident or murder victims in a single day. Otherwise the spirits can become very angry, which is not good for relatives or the village, or for the dead spirit herself.

I can see that even some male villagers are crying hard. Looking towards the temple door I recognise Are Mak coming into temple wearing working clothes, remaining at the back, not coming forward to pay respect to Nong Wuadon's body. He is shifting from one foot to another, his eyes swivelling round, never staying in any one place.

Now I notice him making swatting motion with his right hand, then both hands. He covers his whole face with the palms of his hands, turning round in a circle, then running outside with the gait of a staggering monkey.

A feeling comes over me that I must follow Are Mak. Na Att does not care whether I stay or not, my own mum does not even look at me. I hurry outside, see Are Mak rub his hands round his face, and running. As I follow him I see him grab a green twig, the kind we use for dipping in coconut water and, instead, twirling this round his head.

Away from the crying noise and incense smoke I can see with a clear eye, hear with a sharp ear. I make out the loud buzzing of a robber fly, I see its yellow body circling round Are Mak, dive-bombing. I knowing right away why: Are Mak is the one killing

Nong Wuadon! Now knowing without a shadow of doubt that he is the murderer – I am very sure!

Remembering now that Nong Wuadon never liking Are Mak. He always following her around, putting tiny pieces of food into mouth when she was small child. She always spitting them out. When she older he always running after her, giving presents. Maybe he angry she not liking him, maybe he killing her for that.

No one apart from me noticing the robber fly. The police still in the village, standing by Lung Ban's house, making sure Nong Wuadon's body not moved away from here. If I telling Udon Thani police my suspicions maybe they laughing at me, calling me an ignorant village girl who believes in spirits. If I do not tell them they maybe assuming that Luke murdering my cousin.

'You killing Nong Wuadon!' I shouting at Are Mak. 'You murderer and rapist!'

He turning round, face like a snake about to strike, then quickly picks up a stick fallen on the path and charging at me.

'You whore, you trying to save farang. No one in village even talking with you.' He sprints towards me, but I see policeman watching and I run to him for protection.

The policeman stopping Are Mak with baton. 'You village people not civilized. The law here now, you stop attacking this woman or I arresting you.'

Are Mak stops. The robber fly is already gone. He stands still, makes hating eyes at me, spitting. I walk away to Lung Ban's house.

Phor coming out of Lung Ban's house, standing beside me now.

'Several pieces of cloth on bushes hiding Nong Wuadon's body,' he tells me. 'We seeing very clear when sun rising.' He looking into my eyes. 'Blue cotton from working trousers, same as many villagers wear.'

Standing next to my dad I notice Are Mak's trousers in shreds round their bottoms, several jags torn away. All pointing to this man being the guilty one.

'You think the same way I do, Phor.' I explain to him about the robber fly coming again. Even if he thinking I am very stupid I decide to tell him. 'Maybe you pointing out to Tan Captain about

Are Mak trousers?'

'Daughter, already telling him.'

'And what he saying?'

'He thanking me for help, but already knowing how to conduct murder enquiry. He reminding me that head man of village not in charge, not having permission to take part in police business.'

'He still considering Luke as chief suspect?'

'How I can tell what he thinking, daughter? But I thinking he already have prisoner, so case is easy to close.'

'But Luke not having any motive!'

'Luke having opportunity, that very important. Police not allowing you to stay with him? They have official translator?'

'They allowing Luke to leave if he paying bail. He sleeping in hotel, waiting for colleague bringing money from Krung Thep.'

My dad's head shaking. 'Life of village girl not important for police. Aunt young enough for having another daughter. Perhaps Nong Wuadon being born to her again.'

Phor not knowing that Na Att is barren because Lung Ban also working in Saudi Arabia when Mae bringing Nong Wuadon for Na Att from my mum Lao village, so cannot know she not pregnant when he away. Lung Ban always wanting daughter, therefore he very happy he having daughter to welcome him when he coming back from Saudi Arabia.

Mae joining us now, finding it big problem looking straight into my eyes. I cannot forget she accusing Luke for no reason except he farang and he wanting to marry me. Her attitude hangs like a monsoon cloud between mother and daughter.

'You staying with us, daughter?' Phor asking me.

'No. I taking next songthaew back to Udon. Luke and I flying to Krung Thep on first plane tomorrow.'

'You still wanting marry this farang?'

'You not liking him?'

Phor rolls his own tobacco in banana-leaf, puts rolled leaf into his mouth, inhales. 'He showing proper respect. I think he OK.' He nods as cigarette end glows red.

'Luke very impressed how you handle difficult situation. You liking me marry him?'

Phor looking sad. 'To your mum and me it meaning losing a daughter, losing a son-in-law living in our house, looking after parents in old age. Farang no good for this.'

I cannot help how my marriage will affecting them. My sister living in Krung Thep, she also not there for them in their old age. When my brother marrying he will live with his wife's family, or maybe he will also leave our village. Our traditional customs are all changing, Thailand is changing. There is nothing I can do about this.

'I always sending money helping you and Mae,' I tell Phor.

'Maybe when far away, in England, you forgetting own family.'

'I never forgetting, Phor. I always thinking of family. Whole family: father, mother, brother, sister and sister's son. If not living with you always sending money.'

It is a very sad idea, to leave for a faraway land. However, my mind is always with Luke, whether he in England, or in Thailand, or when I joining him in Hong Kong or Singapore. Thailand is a very beautiful country, but that is not enough. I need to live where my heart is, and that is with Luke.

KEEP MUDDY WATERS INSIDE WHILE YOU PUT CLEAR WATER OUTSIDE

Trouble is obvious from the knock. Not the maid's tremulous tap, nor the respectful rat-a-tat of room service. A peremptory bang, demanding admission.

Not Teng, then. I'm waiting for his assured rap, carefully honed with the touch of submissiveness his Thai culture requires him to adopt. I check the time. Two thirty. He'd only just be collecting the money from the bank.

Don't like the sound of whoever it is one bit, so I jump out of bed, scramble into my trousers, grab my passport and wallet and put on my shoes. The second knock follows almost immediately. Doesn't just shake the door – the whole room reverberates, followed by the door knob being rattled. That's lousy news in the land of mai pen rai – take it easy.

So what's up? There's really only one thing which excites Thais about foreigners – the number of available baht. To the Thai involved, that is. Could reception be worrying about their money?

Not likely, and they wouldn't behave like this if they were. They'd have sent a suave manager to discuss it. Something horrendous, then; I'll need help. Teng, hopefully on the next plane, won't be here for several more hours. No sign of Taiella, either.

I don't want them breaking down the door, that would just create even greater antagonism. 'Who is it?'

'Dtamruat!'

The police? Thought that had been taken care of? Far too impatient for comfort. The door handle sounds like an inebriated rattlesnake.

'Bpert reyo reyo!'

Demanding I open up immediately. No choice, really. I turn the handle, keeping the length of my arm between me and the door, jumping back as soon as the lock tumbles. The door crashes wide. A curdle of uniformed Thais catapults through. Four raised batons, four pairs of glittering eyes. Not a time for heroics.

'Grom tamruad!' a heavily-beribboned man bellows.

Go to the police station? When none of them speak English and neither Teng nor Taiella are around to interpret? I opt for the soft approach.

'All OK – mai pen rai. Khun Police Major agree staying in hotel till money coming.' I hold my hands out, palms spread up, forcing my lips into a grin. 'Guards outside. Can't escape.'

'No OK! Come!'

They grab a limb each, pulling my arms behind me and handcuff my wrists, shackle my ankles and push me out of the door. My heart gallops, my bowels threaten to loosen. How am I going to communicate? Can't even play for time. Neither Teng nor Taiella will know where to find me when they finally arrive.

My only hope is the receptionist. The four men surround me as I walk out of the lift, but they aren't actually holding me. As I clank into the lobby I make a sideways lunge towards the desk. The man who signed me in that morning shrinks against the wall behind him.

'This big big mistake!' I shout out. 'When Khun Teng Japhardee arriving tell go police station quick quick!'

That turns the four men around me into human leeches. They grab my arms and hold me tight, halter two ropes around my neck. One man leads, pulling the rope. Two more hold on to an arm each. The fourth man, holding the second rope, stays behind me.

The terrified, closed face of the clerk turns away. I catch a brief glimpse of a girl Taiella asked to buy some razor blades for me. 'Tell girlfriend police taking me!' I shout out to her in Bangkok

Thai, hoping she'll understand.

This time they hit me with their sticks. I shuffle off with them, silent and passive.

'Why have you come to Thailand? Perhaps you think it is easy to make money from our people?'

The office I was dragged to is the Police Major's. The man standing righteous behind a splendid desk is dressed in dazzling white. A broad, blue ribbon stretches diagonally from his right shoulder to his left groin. A riot of braids falls across it, and an assortment of medals fills in the left-hand side of his manly chest. Three stars, buffed to a sparkling shine. This has to be the man in charge of the Udon Thani Police Department, but why is he in military uniform? Then I remember. The Thai police are a quasi military force. They do not just take their ranks according to US army protocol – they model themselves on the US army. A Lieutenant General, no less. And a man who speaks excellent English. My liberty – perhaps my life – depend on him.

I try to get my head lower than his – not easy because of my height and the tension of the rope around my neck. A small nick down, then a straight look into his eyes. 'I develop software for banks. It makes it possible for any bank, whatever its size, to compete with the conglomerates in Europe and America. And Japan and China,' I add. Thais are not overly endeared to either of these closer nations. 'It means that Thai banks can compete on an equal footing.'

Tortoise eyelids open wide. 'You deal with Thai banks?'

'Yes.' The golden baht will save me. Which ones have I sold to? 'Bangkok Bank, Krung Thai Bank, Siam Commercial Bank, Thai Farmers'...'

The eyelids drop slightly. 'You do business with the Thai Farmers' Bank?'

The double-furrowed brow is evening out. Have I struck lucky, named his bank? 'A very interesting bank. Forward looking.' The return of the furrows makes me gabble. 'I think they try to help the smaller farmers...'

'Peasants do not have bank accounts. Middlemen use the

banks. Peasant farmers, often illiterate, sell their total annual rice crop for a pittance, barely subsistence level. The middlemen and the banks make all the profit.'

Helping banks, even Thai banks, isn't the way to win this man's approval. Am I dealing with an unusual man, an incorruptible?

'So. You are an important man, dealing with our bigger banks.' He sits down, shuffles papers, drums a pencil on his desk. 'What were you doing in a back-stream Thai village?'

My motives as far as Taiella are concerned are unassailable. Relief makes my legs buckle. 'Could I possibly sit down?'

He motions with manicured fingers. A chair is brought.

'I wanted to meet my fiancée's parents, her whole family.' Confidence oozes out as I smile relief. He's the sort of Thai who will understand what I'm saying.

The pencil moves over a page, filling it. Even at this distance I can tell he's writing in Thai, translating rapidly for himself. 'You are engaged to marry a Thai girl?'

'Yes. I met her in Bangkok. She lives with her married sister, and works in the toy department of the ZenZam Centre department store.'

His unusually round eyes gleam. 'You met because you were buying toys for English children?'

'Unfortunately I haven't got any children. My wife...'

Tortoise turns to crocodile. 'So you already have a wife?' The drumming pencil pauses to make another note. A faint smile curves unaccustomed lips.

How could I be such an idiot as to let that slip? Or is he a brilliant interrogator I can't hope to best? 'I'm getting a divorce.'

'Will your Thai fiancée be your second or your third minor wife?' His head nods as he writes yet another note.

'No, no. I'm divorcing my English wife and, as soon as the decree absolute comes through, I'm going to marry Taiella Motubaki.'

The pencil stops. 'Will you be taking her to England to marry?' Even the crocodile smile has gone. Traditional Thais don't approve of their compatriots developing deep relationships with Westerners. They tend to look down on fraternizing Thais, suspect them of ulterior motives, consider them betrayers of their culture.

'First we'll have a registry office marriage in England, to make it legal there. Then we're coming back to Thailand to be married in the Buddhist way.'

The Police Lieutenant General's face seems to lighten, broaden. 'You have some understanding of Buddhist principles? You try to live by them?'

'I do admire the Buddhist attitudes to life, yes.' I dig feverishly round my memory for one of Teng's many devout utterances. 'I do believe one reaps what one sows, for example.'

'Indeed.' The pencil moves again, his lips tighten. 'That is something Christianity also preaches.'

He's false-footed me again. I'll have to censor everything I say.

He raises his right hand, clicks his fingers. The four men move, silently. The ropes around my neck are slipped off, the handcuffs removed. 'Does this mean you are a Christian who wishes to become Buddhist?'

Thais generally concede Western superiority in economic matters, but they see Christianity as an inferior religion and don't admire the story of the crucifixion. 'I'm only a nominal Christian. Actually, I enjoy reading about Buddhism. I find it illuminating.'

The pencil stops. 'Illuminating in what way?'

'I believe you have a saying: someone blessed with forbearance is called a true follower of the Buddha, and reveres him with the highest kind of worship.' I rub my wrists to bring back the circulation. 'I agree with you that Buddhism and Christianity hold a number of tenets in common.'

He's flicking through my passport. 'It says Church of England in the slot for religion. So you are a practising Christian?' The momentary sparkle has gone. A short, composed, self-assured man, the General has now trapped me again, and clearly finds me pathetic. He looks at his pencil, makes another note.

'A matter of form. I go to church occasionally.'

He nods, unimpressed. 'So, do you enjoy having many girlfriends?'

'Not at all. I like this particular Thai girl. Not because she's Thai, but because she's charming, good-humoured, adaptable,

112

intelligent without being academic...'

'And beautiful.'

'She is good-looking, but not the most beautiful Thai girl I've come across.' I try not to think about Wuadon whom, after all, I'd only glimpsed.

'You have come across quite a number, I dare say? And the murdered village girl was more beautiful than – what did you say her name was?' He consulted his notes. 'Taiella Motubaki.'

'I've no idea, I didn't see Wuadon when she was alive. Apart from her eyes. Her face was hidden behind a scarf wrapped round her. To keep her skin as light as possible, I was told. The rest of her was covered up as well.'

'But you knew she was exceptionally beautiful. Your girlfriend will have told you about her.'

'Yes, indeed. But there are thousands, hundreds of thousands, of beautiful girls in my country, too. So what?'

'Well, perhaps you wanted to have sexual relations with her. And, being a properly brought-up girl in a traditional Thai village, she said no. So you took her by force, then killed her to stop her telling her mother.'

'I did *not* kill that girl! I never even spoke to her.'

He shrugs. 'A good man should model himself on the bee. It takes its food from the flower without hurting its beauty or its fragrance.'

He makes a few more notes, not looking my way. A brusque command and the men around me move in unison. As they try to manoeuvre me out I put up as much resistance as I can. I have to get across to this man that I've been promised bail.

'The Police Major promised me bail!' I shout, turning my head as best I can. 'Nothing has been proved against me...'

The short man with the big ego stands and walks towards me. 'It is better to keep a cool heart, Mr Narland. Giving in to anger brings its own suffering.' He's lowered his voice. The menace is unmistakable. 'I am investigating this whole matter myself. You must understand: you have to remain in police custody until I have had the opportunity to look into this case. That is the normal procedure for an arrested murder suspect. Your indignation is preventing you from understanding cause and effect.'

'But what about bail?'

'An innocent man knows how to control himself, a guilty one is tarnished by his sin. If you have been honest with me you have nothing to fear.'

Defeated, I allow the guards to take me down a corridor and through a gate. They unlock a door which leads into a sort of windowless anteroom, large and partitioned into two by solid, vertical bars. A door is unlocked and I'm pitched into the space. It is empty except for a separate section in a corner: the toilet. That consists of a concrete floor with a hole, together with a cement trough filled with a greenish liquid. Water? The floor is filthy, the smell revolting. I vomit into the hole, then back off as far as I can, away from it.

DON'T USE YOUR KNEE TO BREAK THE HANDLE OF A KNIFE

As I leave my dad, walking to where the songthaew will soon be leaving from, I see an expensive car driving into my village. We never seeing this type car here. The trek to our village is very rutted, not suitable for a Bentley car. The monsoon can start any time now, so it very dangerous for such vehicles because once the rain starting roads turn to mud in just a few minutes, therefore making it impossible for such car to drive back. That is why I am very curious about a stranger coming to my village while using this kind of transport. Maybe Nong Wuadon has rich relatives I not knowing? Not possible.

The big car stopping nearby Na Att's house, close by our village temple. Many people from Dumden, and from several nearby villages, are all crowding round because there is not enough space inside the temple, so mourners are sitting on the sacred ground outside, on mats, without shoes, hands folded for devotion, listening to monks chanting sacred texts. Of course everyone here has come to pay respect to Nong Wuadon's spirit, therefore I am expecting people getting out of the car to join in with our prayers. Because it is such a special car I assume the passengers will join the close relatives inside the temple, even though it is already very crowded, because I think they must be very important and special guests.

Now I see the driver getting out. He is in police uniform. Is Tan Police Major coming to see for himself what happening yesterday? Maybe he is already investigating this crime and has already worked out that Luke is not the murderer his is looking for.

But now I see that the important man coming out of the Bentley is not the Police Major that Luke and I meeting early this morning. This man is wearing a white uniform, the kind of clothing I have only seen once before. I not knowing if this is police uniform, it looking more like army uniform, but I remembering this uniform for sure. It showing a very high army rank. Any kind of star denoting some kind of General. This man is wearing three stars, therefore he must be a Lieutenant General. I am very grateful to my dad for sending me to military school which teaching me so many important things. I only attending there for two years, then my dad running out of money so I cannot continue at this school for becoming an army officer. That is the reason why I am not in the Thai army now, and therefore I knowing I cannot salute. I wondering how to greet this man now standing beside the Bentley. I see his watchful eyes observing, looking straight at me.

I wai, eyes down, moving away to a place from which songthaew will be leaving soon soon. It is already very late, and I worrying in case it is not coming at all. Then I see it lurching into the village. No one stepping off, all villagers already here for the special ceremony. I walk over, lift down the flap, prepare to jump in. No one else is going to Udon now.

'You, young woman! Where are you going?'

The important man in white uniform is calling me, walking up to me. I wai again, now frightened. He not knowing me, so why he addressing me? 'Udon Thani, my Excellency.'

'You a young woman from this village?'

'Yes, my Excellency. But now living in Krung Thep, with older sister.'

He looking at me with direct long gaze. I know right away I must telling whole truth when talking to this man. 'You are here now. Living in such a small village means you knowing the dead girl. No one else is leaving now. Why are you preparing to board the songthaew instead of paying proper respect to the murdered girl?'

116

'I coming from Udon Thani this morning, my Excellency, especially for paying respect. Nong Wuadon is my cousin I love very much.'

He now making motion with arm for me to approach him. 'A person acting on impulse always regretting this. It is not becoming to rush off when first mourning day is not yet over. It is proper for you to stay until the burial.' He is looking at me very close. 'Why are you leaving? You have reason to feel guilty?' Penetrating eyes scrutinizing my face for a long time. 'Perhaps you harm this girl because, it is possible, you believe she was more beautiful than you?'

He is making me feel very nervous. Why did he come here, why is he asking these questions? Luke and I already answering many questions from Tan Police Major in Udon Thani this morning. What is this man doing here?

'That is not true reason, my Excellency. My fiancé waiting for me in Udon Thani. We taking plane back to Krung Thep first flight tomorrow morning. This is the only songthaew I can take back for meeting him, no other coming today. I cannot return to Udon Thani any other way.'

Important man shaking head. 'If he your fiancé he also should be paying respects. Why you thinking to marry such a man? Do you not know that it is most important to safeguard virtue against decay so that, like salt, there is never danger of losing its flavour?'

'He is farang, my Excellency. He not speaking Thai, therefore not understanding our customs. I helping him, translating for him.'

'He is farang?' My Excellency is looking my body up and down, eyes very stern. 'So, your fiancé is the man accused of murdering the dead girl? The same man now in police custody in Udon Thani? That is the true reason he cannot be here?'

Head of Northeastern Thailand Police has the rank of Colonel. Now I realising this man is not from Isaan, but somehow attached to Udon police, somehow working on this case. I do not understand how, or why, and am very nervous because he now knowing I left out an important fact when answering the questions he putting to me. Everything looking bad for Luke and also for me.

'My fiancé arresting by angry villager, my Excellency. Tan

117

Police Major Monkahn interrogating him this morning, agreeing to allow my fiancé leaving if he paying bail. He waiting in hotel under police guard until colleague coming from Krung Thep with money for bail.'

The important man now squints his eyes shut, making nostrils wide. 'Tan Major Monkahn not in charge. I am the senior person investigating this crime.' Now he is staring at me with eyes which finding it easy to read my mind. 'It is my responsibility to interview all suspects. Bail is not appropriate for a prime suspect. He remaining in police custody now, then standing trial.'

'He truly innocent, my Excellency!' I not having any choice, I must tell this man everything. I must have the courage to do what I needing to do, that is the only way I not suffering remorse for breaking styrax tree branch without care. 'Please forgive presumption, but I knowing who is person committing this crime, my Highness.' I keeping my voice very soft, bowing my head low. 'He is not my fiancé with name Luke Narland.'

At this moment a very long line of people, headed by monks and pulling ropes attached to the coffin, all coming towards us. I recognising Lung Ban, Nong Wuadon's father, head shaved and clothed in saffron robes, he becoming monk for this sad occasion. That is our traditional way of honouring a dead relative. He is walking behind other monks leading the procession. Nong Wuadon only having one other male relative, her father's younger brother, Are Mak. Evidently he refusing to become monk. All other people following behind, first Na Att with my mum helping her, still crying and stumbling. Other women helping to hold her up, everyone ready to process round temple three times while asking the spirit of Nong Wuadon to be happy, to be at peace and to go to heaven.

Now I understanding that this important man arriving in Bentley must be Police Lieutenant General from Krung Thep. He also waiting, head bowed, joining in at end of line of mourners. He beckoning to me to walk with him. Songthaew driver also joining us, clearly not leaving until procession is over.

Strong villagers are already digging a grave inside the temple area. Our custom is to bury everyone in temple surroundings.

This making people afraid to walk there after dark when spirits are roaming. Now villagers are even more afraid to walk in this area after dark because Nong Wuadon is a murder victim.

After we circling the temple with the coffin three times we chant more prayers.

'You stay with me, young lady,' my Excellency Police Lieutenant General orders me. 'When monks finishing their prayers you telling me who you think is the murderer, and you telling me your exact reasons.'

What is going to happen if I telling such important man that I believe Nong Wuadon's spirit, in shape of a robber fly, pointing the murderer out to me? He surely thinking me an ignorant, crazy village woman, and he keeping Luke in Thai prison, maybe to execute him for murder.

We walking round for last time, then my Excellency Police Lieutenant General nodding at me to accompany him away from the crowd.

'How many male relatives does the dead girl have?' he asking me.

'Father and uncle.'

'I see only one new monk.'

'Lung Ban, my Excellency. Father of dead girl.'

My Excellency Police Lieutenant General's eyes searching all round. 'It is certainly surprising that the uncle not becoming monk to honour the niece.'

I can tell he is not only an important man, he is also very quick in thinking. 'He is afraid, your Excellency, because becoming a monk means having a clear heart, nothing on his mind, being very white. It means making many promises of virtue; telling truth is one very important vow.'

'Maybe he has other reasons as well.' My Excellency looking very hot in white uniform. We are nearby my dad's house. I dart underneath to find his knife.

Tan General is watching me, not showing fear. 'You thinking to kill me? Maybe not uncle and not fiancé guilty. Maybe you are the murderess?'

'I think to cut coconut leaf for fan for you, my Excellency.'

He smiling for first time. 'Thank you.' He taking fan, making

119

air move like very strong breeze.

'Murderer is Nong Wuadon's uncle, my Excellency. Mak Kamuki, younger brother of Ban Kamuki, father of dead cousin. I am very sure.'

'So this is your thinking. However, being uncle is not a crime, even being younger brother of dead girl's father is not a crime.'

'He is garland man, not working enough to attract wife. Always he pestering Nong Wuadon, like old man with snake's head. When she little girl, he feeding when she not wanting. When she grown, he giving always presents. She not liking him. She avoiding him. He getting angry.'

'Wuadon Kamuki already sixteen. Why he waiting so long to murder her?'

I also wonder about this, why he killing her now? Then I begin to feel faint, late day temperature is very high, why I not having enough sense to fetch coconut leaf for me? I worry that maybe I fainting and his Excellency interpreting this to be a sign of guilt.

Suddenly I feeling a cool breeze, but no wind stirring branches of plants and trees around. Just cool air flowing over arms and shoulders, caressing me. I regaining strength, feel better. Also now understand this wind is Nong Wuadon's spirit. She wanting real murderer to be caught, she has come to help me.

I hear soft voice of Nong Wuadon in head, telling me what to say. 'Nong Wuadon very keen asking me many questions how I like working in Krung Thep. Already I telling her on previous visit: my life much better than when living in village. At that time I promising to try finding my cousin job in department store where I working. I know she very sweet girl and pretty sure they employing her. Also I inviting her living with my sister and me. Big problem is we never having opportunity to talk with each other before she dying.'

Breeze now gone. I feeling very hot, my colour going high. Maybe my Excellency thinking I losing my mind.

'This explanation not helpful, young woman. Why her uncle thinking about this now? Nong Wuadon knowing your story long time already, if she wanting to leave she already arranging to go. How you explaining why he waiting so long?'

I feel no cooling wind to help me, but I must help Luke or he soon dead in Thai prison. 'Is very simple, my Excellency. Motive for murder happening now is because I coming to my village with farang. Reason is very clear. Are Mak – my uncle Mak Kamuki – is very jealous of farang. He thinking farang inviting beautiful young girl to go to Krung Thep, offering making second wife with myself first wife. Then Nong Wuadon not going just for job and coming back to village for visiting, she going for always.'

'In that case better to murder farang!'

He is right. Tears coming now because I cannot think. Then breeze coming back, with soft voice telling me what I should say: 'Are Mak thinking if he cannot have Nong Wuadon no one having her. Very good time to have sex with Nong Wuadon, maybe only chance he ever having. He thinking that if she resisting he killing her because he knowing village blame stranger, accusing farang for sure.'

'You think this is so?' My Excellency stopping, looks at me, fans himself.

'Village people not liking farang, they thinking he wanting beautiful village girl, taking her by force. So excellent time for Are Mak killing Nong Wuadon and telling whole village farang is murderer.'

White uniform now greying with village dust, military stars sparkle in afternoon sun. 'Maybe Mak Kamuki telling truth, maybe farang wanting this girl and she saying no.'

He not believing me! 'Luke is very gentle man, loving me. He not having scratches on face or arms, but Nong Wuadon nails having skin and blood underneath. Clothing Luke wearing not torn. Are Mak's trousers shredded at ankles, and this same material on bushes where we finding the body. My father discovering when sun rising.'

My Excellency Police Lieutenant General nodding his head. 'Maybe difficult to see scratches on Luke Narland's hand. I noticing they rubbed raw by bamboo bands used for tying.'

I wonder how he knowing this, but do not have time to think about it. In any case rubbed wrists are not Luke's fault, but not helping if I say so. 'He showing great forbearance when villagers attacking him.'

My Excellency clears his throat. 'So there is no cause to worry. We calling person with forbearance a true follower of Buddha. He always feeling lucky, honoured and happy.'

'Of course, my Excellency,' I say as I bowing head. 'But perhaps we should consider that, along the path of life, such a follower may come across jealousy which leading to destruction.'

'Correct. You are acquainted with some of the Buddha's teaching.' My Excellency smiling at me, nodding, then turning grave. 'I intending to interview Mak Kamuki. Not wanting to become monk for this funeral is very suspicious. I ordering guard taking him to Udon Thani.'

Now I cannot stop my tears. I see songthaew already gone, meaning I cannot return to Udon tonight. How can I help Luke? I try not to weep, but cannot stop. My Excellency walks up to Police Sergeant standing nearby. I hear my Excellency instructing sergeant to arrest Are Mak.

'Now we returning Udon Thani. You, young lady, sitting in back of car with me, telling me complete background of village, of family.'

My tears flow fast. 'Thank you, my Excellency. You gaining much merit today!'

Then I see robber fly buzzing nearby, buzzing round policeman's head.

'Tell him how you finding body!' a voice saying in my head. 'My Excellency Police Lieutenant General Thomupi is good man, good Buddhist, believing in spirits. Tell him my spirit is in robber fly!'

'All right, Nong Wuadon. I telling him everything that happening.'

'You speaking with dead girl, young lady?'

Then I cannot stop myself. I tell my Excellency the complete story, everything I know.

WHEN MOSQUITO SWARMS CHARGE AT A DRAGON THESE INSECTS CAN'T EXPECT TO LIVE

My watch and mobile are still at the hotel. No window in this black hole, no kind of light. Mid-afternoon, judging by the heat. I settle on the rough concrete and hug my knees. Last night's wooden floor feels as though it had been a feather bed. I know Taiella or Teng will eventually turn up, but how do I cope with this hellhole now?

The place is stifling. Mid-April, the end of the dry season, just before the monsoon. Down here the air is putrid. I'm desperate for something liquid – all that sweating and nothing to drink since Taiella left the hotel.

'Hello!' I shout. 'Hew nam! Hungry water!'

Nothing but my own voice, twangy and flat. The great General has abandoned me. Are the guards just going to leave me to die of thirst? I'm completely on my own, and out of bargaining power – can't even demand to see someone from the British Embassy.

I shout a bit more, my voice getting hoarser, my thirst acute. No sign of anyone, no noises off. Entombed in a Thai jail, not even another prisoner to talk to.

Shifting my weight to avoid too much discomfort, my only occupation is hunting the bugs and lice which know a good meal when they come across it. They're probably keeping me from going crazy. Eventually I realise mosquitoes have joined the feast. I grasp it must be dusk: around half past six. The last songthaew from Dumden would get into Udon around eight, which is also the time Teng's plane is due to land. I make bets with myself as to who will arrive first, plump for Taiella.

Wrong. I can hear Teng's cajoling voice, the one he uses so successfully for business, winding towards me. Ultra polite, but still insisting that he has to see me.

'Kuhn Luke,' he says, walking into the space now lit with what seems a dazzling light, making my eyes smart. 'I thought you had arranged to stay in a top-drawer hotel, with a police guard outside your room. I thought you were rolling off a log, waiting for me to arrive.'

'Did you bring the cash?'

'Seventy-five thousand baht, just in case they put the squeeze on and fifty is not sufficient.'

Brilliantly capable, as always. 'Thank God you're here, Teng. There's been a coup, or something. The chap I made the deal with was, I thought, the top man...'

'Tan Major Monkahn *is* the cat's pyjamas here, Kuhn Luke. I was talking with him a few minutes ago. It is most unfortunate...'

I jump up, hurl myself at the bars. The man is back again, and he's left me to rot in this cesspit? 'They've been lying to you, Teng. The chap I made the deal with wasn't anywhere to be seen when they dragged me back here.'

'No, no Kuhn Luke! I have covered the waterfront...'

'Some other man, dressed in white with a lot of braid and stuff, and three bloody stars, had me dragged over from the hotel like a common criminal. Interrogated me!'

'Stay calm, Kuhn Luke. It is always best...'

'For God's sake, Teng! Calm? You try staying calm locked up in this stinking hole!'

'I can explain...'

'The man in white looked as though he was pukka Army of some sort. Stiff upper lip type. No chance in hell of negotiating with him.'

'Hang in there, Kuhn Luke, or you will shoot yourself in the foot. I have checked it out. Tan Major is having a surprise inspection from Bangkok. My Excellency Police Lieutenant General Thomupi flew up here today – which left you a dead duck. He is hung up on the letter of our law, a very proper individual.'

'You mean they're reforming the Thai police force?'

'Making sure there is no jaywalking.'

'And this General what's-his-name, he's superior to the police head in Udon Thani?'

'He is the muscle of the whole of the Northeastern Thailand Police Force. The TNPD – Thailand National Police Department – is top-brassed by a police general in Bangkok. He has three deputy directors general and five assistant directors general, who all hold the rank of Police Lieutenant General. They are VIPs. One of them arrived here today for a shake-up on the locals. Tough titty for your side of the street.'

'What the hell d'you mean tough titty? I haven't done anything wrong!'

'You are the headliner in an extremely serious crime, Kuhn Luke. A private citizen from Dumden Village fingered you because he sussed you for a violation, that is the reason you were taken to the police station on the double. The Police Major should have cut you an arrest warrant, and held you in the slammer. He did not have the clout to offer bail.'

It takes a few seconds, but I get the gist. 'Am I supposed to be responsible for that?'

'No way. But while you were plunked down it was his duty to look into the pipeline in the village. After that he might have been able to offer bail.' Teng shrugs. 'The Police Major is a sleazebag, which is why he has not come to see you. He is passing the buck to my Excellency Police Lieutenant General Thomupi.'

I feel my legs softening under me, clench the bars to stay upright. Teng is a trusted colleague, but it won't do for him to see me quail. 'Fine, Teng. Very laudable. But why is the great General leaving me to rot in this god-forsaken piss pot?'

'Please try not get the jitters. I can only give you a hand if you get a handle on your feelings.'

'You're saying you can't get me out of here.' I'm beginning to lose hope. My voice sounds reedy.

'I have explained. I have brought seventy-five thousand baht to give it your best shot. Some leeway just in case.' He puts his hands on mine clutching the bars. 'I can assure you that if my Excellency finds another patsy he will bring in the big guns to get you sprung on bail.'

I snatch my hands away. 'And just how is he going to do that?'

'It is simple. He has already taken off for Dumden Village to get the low-down. He takes the biscuit for an investigative hot shot.' Teng takes out a whiter-than-white handkerchief and flicks at his shoes. Possibly a mote of dust might have lodged there. 'I think he is happy he can have a field day finding such easy meat. He can check out how the local fuzz deal with a murder investigation.'

Bloody bad luck to be saddled with an incorruptible Thai. Should I get Teng to contact the British Embassy right away? I've got enough sense left to see the snag. If I don't show I believe in my own innocence, show I don't need any crutches, I'll be even worse off. I'll concentrate on matters Teng can see to. The General's working methods can't, after all, be faulted.

I clear my throat, steady my voice. 'Look, Teng. I've been held here for hours. It's dark, it's filthy, there's nothing to sit or lie on, and only a disgusting toilet. I haven't had any water for hours. You've got to sort the basics – now. The General can't know the conditions I'm being held in.' Teng's mouth opens and shuts like a fish on dry land. 'Tell him it's something else for him to inspect, and bring up to decent standards.'

Wide nostrils pucker into disdain. His eyes flick over to the toilet area, the filthy floor, the lack of furniture. I see him checking me. My Adam's apple is working overtime to keep the saliva flowing.

His chin sticks out, his cheeks suck in. 'You are right on the button, Kuhn Luke. This is a bad goof. I am certain my Excellency Police Lieutenant General Thomupi has no idea what is going on. I have put the heat on the guard to bring fresh water. Now I will raise Cain for decent grub, a mat for the floor, I will even try for a chair.'

'Good.'

'You get the hang of it, I am sure. The Police Major is not top dog now, and my Excellency is kicking up a storm in Dumden Village. I am certain he will be touching base very soon, he will not stay there after dark.'

A uniformed constable appears, produces a jug of water and a glass. Local water will probably give me dysentery, but not drinking it could kill me. I gulp the first glass greedily, drain it, refill it and empty the next one too. I use the rest of the water to splash over myself. Teng holds the empty jug out for more. The constable bows, takes it off to be refilled.

'I will hunker down for my Excellency in the Major's office. I will chew his ear off as soon as he returns.'

'Hold on a minute, Teng! What about Taiella? Why isn't she here?'

He looks away, shifts his eyes. 'Maybe the songthaew has not come back to Udon Thani yet. She is taking a long time shower that wastes money.'

He knows she should have been here by now. I stare at him until his eyes drop.

'I have not forgotten Taiella, Kuhn Luke. I asked about her at the hotel, gave it my best shot. No one there has seen her.'

Has admitted to seeing her, he means. No surprise. The hotel staff would get it wrong, as usual, assume that because she came with a farang she's a common bar girl. They certainly wouldn't try to be helpful.

I'm worried about my sweet girl – really worried. There's a murderer loose in that village – Taiella knows that just as well as I do. What if he decides she came back to find *him*, that paying respects to Wuadon was just a cover? *Was* that what she planned? Did she know how dangerous that could turn out to be? My Smileegirl is always ruled by her heart rather than her head, always tends to act on impulse.

'She should be here by now, Teng. When she found I wasn't in the hotel she wouldn't need telling where I was.' Should I get Teng to hire a car to go to the village and search for her?

'Dumden Village must be very small. My Excellency will have

worked out right away that the head man is Nong Tiaella's father. My guess is he is spelling out what he has in mind to both him and his daughter. I guess that is how she came to miss the last songthaew.'

Could be. The General might even have arrested her, displeased she'd been consorting with a farang, assumed she was of questionable morality. And the great man, annoyed with the local police, might just have wanted to make sure everyone understood who was in charge. For all I know he has decided not only that I'm guilty but that Taiella is my accomplice. But at least she'd be safe from the murderer.

'It's a possibility.'

'Probability, Kuhn Luke. I know how a high ranking Thai general will sugar pill the stump-jumpers. Mai pen rai — do not worry. He will have her brought back tonight, you will see.'

'If you say so.' It's a likely scenario. Just as the murderer is unlikely to attack again. That would wreck his chances of pinning the crime on me. Sending Teng off into the dark, even if he could get someone to rent him a car, isn't sensible. 'D'you think you could stay around for a bit, Teng? They'll leave the lights on if you're here. And even with a chair, and water, there's nothing to do. Gives me too much time to brood.'

'I will stay for a short time, Kuhn Luke. But I do not wish to be out of line with my Excellency when he returns from Dumden Village, so we must separate soon. I am very eager for him to get a grip on your accommodation tonight. This place is creepy. I am positive he will bust a gut to spring you out of here.'

I watch Teng go, gripping the sides of the chair to stop myself screaming at him to go to Dumden and find Taiella. He's right to make sure he catches the General on his return, as much for Taiella's sake as for mine. Anyway, surely her father would look out for her?

The light has been left on, I have a chair, and a clean mat to lie on together with a mosquito net. The jug has been refilled with water. The temperature has dropped a little, and I've even been brought a plate of sticky rice with a little fish. I haven't eaten for hours and it tastes wonderful. I curse myself for not remembering my watch, then decide to try to get some sleep. For all I know the General might summon me for interrogation again. A highly articulate, intelligent, upright man is much more to be feared than the Major.

No chance of sleep, I'm much too nervous. Taiella's image pops up at me – what's been going on in that village? Something has, otherwise she'd have stormed over by now, unabashed by surly policemen. I'd have heard her, even down here, voice shrill, demanding to see 'Tan Major', anyone in charge. Not at all like her village contemporaries, like the downtrodden Pi Lai. When smiles no longer work Taiella reminds me of stories of Japanese samurai.

Then the crime itself circles endlessly in my head. How can I prove my innocence? No alibi, the tag of a male farang. How am I going to convince them that the last thing I'd ever do is force a woman against her will?

Only Taiella saw me come back from the fields, only she knows I looked and acted as usual, not like a man who'd just committed a heinous rape and murder. It takes a psychopath to pretend anything else.

My mind churns over yesterday's details. Snippets of blue cloth on the spiky bushes where the body was hidden. And, Taiella is convinced there'd be skin and blood under the poor girl's nails. Delicate little Wuadon wouldn't just have given in, she'd have clawed whoever attacked her. My limbs are sunburned, but smooth, my shorts dusty but not stained with blood or other fluids. In England the police would test the man's DNA from the spilt semen or whatever tissue was left under Wuadon's fingernails. They'd eliminate me in no time at all.

Just two small points. Do the Udon Thani police know how to collect samples, and if so, do they have the resources to test DNA?

One thing I've worked out, have thought about time and again. I'll insist the General take the appropriate swabs and test all the men in the neighbourhood for their DNA. Long-winded, time-consuming, expensive – but I'll insist.

I jump up out of the chair, terrifying an enquiring rat attracted by the few grains of rice I've left. There has to be a specific Thai or European DNA constituent which would eliminate me right away. Bringing up such racial differences might require delicate handling, but striking and important biological variations do exist among human gene frequencies. A trivial one: ginger hair isn't just genetically transmitted, it's mostly found in the British Isles and some areas of France – certainly not in Asia! Skin colour, too, and the colour of the iris. I'm also quite a bit taller than any Thai I've come across. Simple to exclude me, and the General has Bangkok resources. My limbs relax, my eyelids droop.

For a few seconds. Then I remember that Thais cremate their dead. The girl's body is already ashes. One small hope. Their fires aren't strong enough to burn the bones, they keep those, reverently.

I feel sick again as I see that young girl, so full of life, dancing light-heartedly behind the water buffaloes, calling to Taiella, laughing. How could anyone silence that?

If DNA can't get me out of this mess I want to die. I know the British Embassy can do nothing except find me the best legal representation. The Thais, I've gathered from drug trials making the headlines, are adamant about foreigners standing trial and, if found guilty, serving their sentences in Thailand. Just the idea of long incarceration in a Thai jail drives me mad. I use the chair to pound the bars of the cell.

ONE LOG ISN'T ENOUGH TO MAKE A HOT FIRE

My Excellency dropped me near the hotel. I feeling happy talking with him because I believe he understanding Luke's position very well. I run into reception with a light step, skip over to the lift.

'Where you going, Miss?'

A sharp tone from the receptionist. I turn; this is same young man who seeing me arrive with Luke earlier today. Maybe he not remembering me. 'Room 234, where Khun Luke Narland staying. I coming here with him noon time.'

The receptionist looks at me very glum. 'Not remembering any young lady. Farang coming with police.'

'Police accompanying him only to make sure he safe.' Why is this receptionist sniffing the air as if he has noticed a bad smell? Maybe he does not like farang.

He shifts sideways to the other end of the long reception desk, picks up a small bell, makes it ding, ding very hard. Maybe he is making the same mistake as the Krung Thep receptionist, and taking me for a bar girl. Not very likely because I am wearing my office outfit.

He staying at far end of desk, his eyebrows meeting in one line. 'Why many police coming, putting handcuffs on farang, forcing him go with them?' His voice very loud and angry. 'You leaving now, Miss. Right away.'

It is hard for me to breathe. My Excellency cannot know Luke has already been taken into custody again. Perhaps because Tan

Police Major is back in charge while my Excellency was visiting in Dumden? I realise that cannot be the real reason. Tan Police Major is a sane man who allowing – even encouraging – Luke to stay in hotel, waiting for Khun Teng to arrive with many baht.

'Khun Luke Narland not leaving with Thai colleague coming from Krung Thep?'

Another receptionist coming in, rough-looking man, with many tattoos on arms, staring at me very black. The first receptionist turning his back to me, leaving.

I look around and notice same young woman I talking to at noon today. She hiding from receptionist behind huge plastic vase containing large flowers. I watching as she wagging finger hiding behind slim stalk, pointing outside. I walking near to her.

'Police coming, putting your man in handcuffs, treating very bad.'

'What time this happening?'

Receptionist with tattoos lifting hatch and walking toward me, fists balled. 'We not wanting girl like you in this hotel.'

I run towards door. So now I knowing exactly that Luke needing me very badly. Maybe I very foolish to leave, I should stay to help Luke by remaining by his side, leaving Nong Wuadon's spirit to roam. I walking outside, see young woman following me.

'No colleague, no person from Krung Thep coming?' I ask this kind sister.

'Man from Krung Thep asking questions, receptionist telling him farang go to police station. Farang try fighting, but too many men holding him. They treating very bad. Not good idea fighting with police.'

I stand, staring, not able to move. I feeling very sick, putting hand in front of mouth, too late. Gobbets of bad-smelling liquid splashing onto hotel entrance steps. I not waiting to see what happening but running away fast, to police station. I reason Khun Teng already there, trying to help Luke.

As I enter the police station I see Khun Teng standing by reception, talking with policeman on duty. Khun Teng smiling out of side of mouth, walking over to me.

'I worry about you, Nong Taiella. I thinking songthaew from village already back, but you not on it.'

'Where is Kuhn Luke?' I turn to talk to policeman behind counter. 'I wish visiting Khun Luke Narland.' I say this in low voice, but in tone which expecting obedience. Teachers showing us this method in military school. Speak up, not too loud, look at person straight into their eye. This going against Thai tradition for village women, but I cannot see other way to help Luke. Policeman understanding right away I mean business. He beckons me to follow.

'Kuhn Luke is in holding cell, Nong Taiella. Please not making trouble for him, I have arranged everything to work out...' Khun Teng sounds very worried.

'*You* arranging? You mean you know Khun Luke already arresting again?'

'Receptionist telling me when I asking for Khun Luke at hotel. Then waiting for you, but you not on songthaew.'

'No. My Excellency Police Lieutenant General Thomupi bringing me back in own car, in Bentley.'

All at once I understanding situation very well. My Excellency not knowing about what going on, but Tan Police Major becoming nervous because my Excellency arriving from Krung Thep, maybe finding out Tan Police Major already eating many baht. Maybe Tan Major worrying that Khun Teng not bringing money before my Excellency returning from Dumden Village. This making Tan Police Major angry with Luke, and so he ordering his men to arrest my innocent Luke.

Kuhn Teng looks at me with respect. 'In official car? Really?'

'Yes. We talking long time.'

'You understand situation, then. You cannot visit Khun Luke tonight. He...'

'I wanting see *now*!' Maybe already beating my lovely man, even killing. It of first importance I seeing Luke. I am determined to ask my Excellency for help. 'Honourable Police Lieutenant General Thomupi knows me! He giving permission...'

'Nong Taiella, mai pen rai.' Khun Teng places two fingers on right hand, very gently, trying hard to calm me down. 'Please believe me. I taking care of everything, everything in order. My Excellency taking personal charge of this case – but already knowing this. He coming to visit Khun Luke tonight, having long talk. I am sure he releasing soon soon on same basis as Tan Police Major.'

Several policemen now standing around, starting to make jokes and laughing. Khun Teng holds Luke in high esteem, he not telling me lies.

'We go to hotel, Nong Taiella. I already reserving room for me, asking reception to keep best suite of rooms for you and Khun Luke.'

'In same hotel?'

'Is very hard getting room day before Feast of Songkran, Nong Taiella. I prefer to make sure we having decent room.' He wais at me. 'My Excellency promising to do everything possible to release Khun Luke to hotel tonight. It depending now on how Khun Luke behaving with my Excellency.'

WHEN YOU FOLLOW THE OLD MAN THE DOG WILL NOT BITE

'You are crying like a turtle being grilled, Mr Narland. It is not useful to lose a cool heart.'

Calm, infuriatingly collected, Police Lieutenant General Thomupi's controlled syllables float through the bars of my cage. The splintering of teak against metal overwhelmed the sound of footsteps, of voices, of rattling doors. Such lack of control on my part could add years to a prison sentence.

I put the chair down; teak is a strong wood, and it still has the appearance of a chair. I slick raw fingers back through my hair, adjust my clothes. The little I'm wearing. How do I address this man? Why didn't I check with Teng?

'I'm sorry, General. I thought you'd forgotten about me. No one's been near me for hours. I decided that making a nuisance of myself was the only way to attract attention.' I cough to clear my tight vocal chords. 'My colleague, Teng Japhardee, was here earlier. He promised to find you and persuade you to place me in more appropriate quarters.'

The small, controlled nod signals distaste for my methods but, I decide, shows a soupçon of understanding. 'Very regrettable, Mr Narland. You are quite right. This holding cell is not appropriate. You have my assurance that no future suspect will suffer this indignity.'

Great: so the real murderer will be able to wait for his trial in comfort!

'I have come here in person to suggest we have another talk.'

My blood churns through unaccustomed arteries, making my temples throb. He's known all along that I'm in this stinking hole. "An honest person learns how to control himself" I could hear Teng mouth. This was the General's high-ranking Thai way of hammering me into submission, then putting on the charm. An oriental version of the hard/soft police play. I presume he's working out a way to trick me into some sort of confession.

'You mean tonight?'

One can't exactly call them raised eyebrows, since his eminence's brows are virtually non-existent, but I get the gist.

'Perhaps you have a pressing engagement elsewhere?' Slatted eyes and a tight mouth are international signals of disdain, but suddenly I catch a glimpse of amusement. Does he know I have a make-or-break meeting with the Krung Thai Bank tomorrow? Is he enjoying my anxiety?

Deep breath in, count till ten, think of something peaceful, radiate calm. 'Not at all. Of course I'll be delighted to talk to you again.' The loosening of tension switches off exhausted muscles. I try, but I'm too weak to keep standing and, grabbing the bars, slide to the floor in spite of my efforts to hold myself upright.

'You are not well?'

'A little weak. The lack of water.'

The positive side gets through to my addled brain. He could have sent his heavies, have had me dragged upstairs. Coming down to this pit-hole himself, and suggesting a further talk, has to mean he's uncovered some sort of evidence. Which might not exonerate me, but might well have sown some doubt into his exalted mind. Even such an eminent personage won't risk treating a respectable European businessman discourteously.

'I understand. A most regrettable experience. Perhaps you would prefer to wait until tomorrow?'

Spend a night in this pit-hole? My grimace will have to act as a smile. I breathe in deeply to steady my voice. 'Of course I'm entirely at your disposal. Actually, I was thinking of you.'

136

A mosquito laden with my blood lands on his white uniform. He swats it off, leaving a dark smear of brown-red. 'I don't quite follow.'

'My colleague told me you'd gone to Dumden Village yourself to make enquiries. You must be exhausted.'

That sideways smile Thais use to disarm, but I think I catch a glimmer of acknowledgment. 'I can see you are as a mountain of solid rock, unshaken by any storm. But you need not concern yourself about me. It is my job.' His eyes, small slits, range over me, linger on my ankles swollen with mosquito bites. 'Perhaps you would enjoy an opportunity to wash and change into fresh clothes. We can talk after that.'

The man's English is impeccable. Who, exactly, am I dealing with? 'I'm afraid I haven't got my things...'

'Naturally I have arranged for all that.' He beckons to the uniform hovering in the background. 'Come with me now. I will leave you in Police Major Monkahn's office for half an hour. Then I will arrange for a meal to be served.'

'Very good of you,' I stammer. He's trying to placate me. Has he *solved* the crime? Is it all over?

A set of my own clothes is waiting, neatly folded, in the Major's office. Razor, after shave, toothbrush, toothpaste and soap are in his bathroom.

Teng is there. 'I thought it would be helpful to bring a change of gear as well as front-money, Kuhn Luke. So you have your ducks in a row for my Excellency.'

I must have underestimated him. It's far too easy to misinterpret people from a different culture. 'How on earth did you arrange all this?'

'I cannot claim it was due to me. My Excellency had already got a handle on the situation by the time he returned from the village.'

'Top marks for bringing the extra togs, Teng. How come there are all these privileges all of a sudden – has something happened? Have they found the real murderer?'

'My Excellency did not put me in the know. I think some clues

137

are in the can. I do not know whether that gets you out of hot water. I know my Excellency was not just whistling Dixie with Nong Taiella.'

'You mean he interviewed her father?'

'Nong Taiella hit the nail on the head with him. A person who upholds the cause of justice, especially one who respects the spirits of the dead, finds friends in time of need.'

'He's talked to Taiella?' How did he come across her? Or did she see him in the village, work out who he was, and then approached him?

'Hurry to wash and shave, Kuhn Luke. Get yourself spiffed out.' Teng runs water into the basin. 'The earth is a long way from the sky, England is a long way from Thailand, but the nature of a virtuous man can be seen to be farther still from that of a wicked man. I am sure my Excellency will catch on, but for now go along for the ride and do not keep such an important man waiting.'

'Have you seen Taiella, Teng? Is she OK?'

'She is cool. I pulled strings for her comfort in the hotel you checked into before.'

I realise that's all I'm going to find out for the time being. 'Teng, how do I address the General?'

'We say my Excellency, sometimes my Honour. You might also like to use the term "sir".' He stands back, tips delicate fingers against each other. 'Remember he is the only game in town, Kuhn Luke. Stay on the ball, and do not keep my Excellency waiting.'

WAIT UNTIL THE TREE FALLS BEFORE JUMPING OVER IT

'It is not necessary for me to put you under guard, Mr Narland. You are an intelligent man, you know you cannot run away. We will act in a civilized manner. A Thai meal will be served while we discuss your case.'

'You're very kind, your Excellency.'

A small, upward twist of the lips, a macro-second of enlarged pupils. The General motions me to a chair on the other side of the Major's cleared desk. White damask tablecloth, western-style cutlery for two. Aromatic Thai food arrives, served by bowing waiters. There's bottled water to drink.

'Please – sit down.'

'Your English is incredible. Have you lived in England?'

The grin is mischievous. 'I read Philosophy at Oxford. Brasenose.'

Ridiculous, but that information induces a feeling of relaxation, of comfort. He knows the drill. And he wouldn't be treating me like this if he still thinks I might have committed the murder.

'First of all I should explain why I am taking over this case. The whole of the Thai police force is being reorganized. Instead of having provincial police departments under separate heads all departments are now under the control of the Bangkok Headquarters. I have come to Udon Thani to explain how we do things in the capital.'

'So this is quite an upheaval.'

'It was unfortunate for you that you were caught in the middle of it. On the other hand you might have fared a good deal worse with the Major. They're still pretty backward here. We use modern methods in Bangkok.' I think I see his eyes focus on my ginger hair. 'Forensic tests, that sort of thing.'

'How very interesting. That's quite an advance.' Leading up to the DNA! If the samples are still around.

'First of all I would like to congratulate you on your choice of a future wife. Taiella Motubaki is an intelligent young woman. I understand she spent two years in the military school in Udon Thani, so she is reasonably well educated.'

'Yes. She couldn't finish her time there because her father ran out of money. A bad rice harvest.'

'Quite so. But she learned the basics, she knows how to conduct herself. She holds our Royal Family in high honour, and she is a dutiful daughter.'

'I understand you've met her?'

'A fortunate encounter. I noticed her just outside the temple grounds of Dumden Village and knew right away she had to be involved in the case. She told me all about her relationship with her cousin Wuadon Kamuki, and the reincarnation of the dead girl's spirit.'

Surely this cold, collected, high-ranking policeman, educated at Oxford and, presumably, in the best establishments in Thailand, doesn't actually believe in spirits?

'I see you find it surprising that I believe in spirits.' Direct eyes sweep over me. 'You already mentioned you are a Christian.'

'Yes.' That complacent feeling that comes from going to church on a reasonably regular basis. Well, at least four times a year.

'I see.' That smile again. 'Possibly you have never considered the implications.'

What's he talking about? Do unto others? If you have not charity you are as nothing? Do not kill? I tell myself off for being flippant, look expectant.

'You believe quite extraordinary things, you know. You believe

140

in God, a spirit whose existence cannot be proved by analytical means. You believe he had a son by a woman who was a virgin.'

'Well, yes...'

'Producing a being who was half God, half man.'

'Not exactly. We believe Jesus Christ is the Son of God, and therefore *is* God. We believe He was born of woman, and therefore *is* man. So He is both God and man.'

'Quite so. And you believe further that he died – a quite horrific death, incidentally, worthy of the direst horror story – then rose again from the dead.'

Complacence has turned to discomfort. I nod, not looking at him.

'You also believe that his mother's body was assumed into Heaven. These are articles of faith, not fact.'

'Not all Christians believe that.'

The eyes go steely. 'Nevertheless, a large number do. So why would our belief in the existence of spirits surprise someone who believes these extraordinary things?'

'I beg your pardon. Of course, you are entirely right.'

'However, though belief in spirits is widespread in Thailand, we also believe they can only guide us, and consequently that their actions cannot be used in a court of law.'

'I see.' Simply humouring me, amusing himself.

'But, once alerted, there are other, more international, methods of detection. My attention was drawn to the dead girl's uncle, Mak Kamuki.'

'Oh?' I do remember Taiella mentioning him a couple of times. Not very favourably.

'Yes. He was not paying proper respect to the dead girl: he was not in the temple with the other mourners, and he refused to become a monk which, as you probably know, is expected in Thailand for male relatives of the recently deceased. That certainly roused my suspicions. The head man of the village – your future wife's father...' He pauses, makes a note on his pad. 'Where was I? Ah, yes, Wirat Motubaki mentioned scraps of material on the bushes where the girl's body was found, then pointed to Mak Kamuki's trousers. That was enough for me to take him in for questioning.'

'I suppose he might have a perfectly reasonable explanation for the torn trousers. He does work in the fields there.'

'You are correct. I did not say it was enough to arrest him. I did, however, require him to come to Udon Thani for interrogation. He is here now.'

'Right.' The food isn't particularly spicy, but I have a hard time not choking.

'Your future wife told me the story of the robber fly, and how the search party discovered the body of Wuadon Kamuki because of it.'

'That was extraordinary. I was quite overwhelmed by that myself.'

'While I was there the same kind of fly buzzed round Mak Kamuki's head. That is not the way these insects normally behave.'

'Are you saying you will be able to use these events as proof against this man?'

Exasperation widens nostrils considerably less broad than most Thais'. 'Naturally not. It is not scientific proof. As I said, we use modern methods in Bangkok.'

'Of course.'

'That is why we are also collecting samples of tissue, semen and so forth, for DNA testing.'

'I thought it would be too late for that, that you cremated your dead almost immediately.'

'Not in the case of victims of accidents or crime, that is people who meet a violent end. No, here in the Northeast of Thailand we bury those people, to give their spirits a chance to calm down.'

'Oh, I see.' I feel tension draining out of me. 'So your courts accept DNA testing results?'

'I am here to show the local police that such samples can provide extremely valuable evidence in cases of assault and rape. Even when the victim is not killed she may not be able to recognise the person who attacked her because of the trauma involved. And, as in this case, even if the girl had lived, she might not have wished to name the person – a family member, for example. That is why we are now basing our procedures on the precedent of US laws.

These are not law in Thailand yet, but we can inform the suspect that they soon will be.'

'I see.' I lean forward, dropping a piece of octopus into peanut sauce, splattering the General's sleeve.

He daubs at it with a corner of his napkin carefully soaked in water. 'You have something you wish to say?'

'If your courts accept that DNA testimony might become relevant, you need not actually use it to incriminate anyone in this case. You could simply exonerate *my* involvement by testing *my* DNA.'

'Really?' Acute-angled eyes jump to attention. 'And how do you suggest we do that?'

A particularly fresh-looking, transparent fish, tiny but tasty, dangles between his thumb and forefinger. He dips it into fish sauce, flicks it precisely into the receptive cavern of his mouth, drops his eyelids and smiles. When he lifts them again, like stage curtains revealing actors assured of their applause, the dark irises fire salvoes. A cornucopia of fun. Testing me is dessert.

This might be my last chance for a decent meal for some time. The little fish, plump curls spiced with lemon grass, are irresistible. I scoop up three tails and plunge their tops into the sauce, savour them. Delicious. 'People having the same Alu sequence at the same spot on their genome must be descended from a common ancestor.'

I note that his Excellency flicks neat fingers at the remaining fish, sucks it slowly into his mouth. He nods, waits.

'Virtually everyone in Dumden Village is related in one way or another.'

He adds a gobbet of sticky rice with the fish, chews slowly while I wait for him to admit my little victory.

'I think we understand one another, Mr Narland. If you are innocent you should have nothing to fear.' His eyes open wide, his nod is vigorous.

'Thank you, your Excellency. Are you saying I'm free to leave?'

'Not at all.' The fish has all gone but a basket of deep-fried locusts arrives, crisp and golden. 'The investigations will take some time.' He cants his head to one side as he examines the new dish. 'You are still a suspect. However, I think now, in your case, bail would be appropriate.'

I can't stop a wide smile. 'Wonderful! Teng has brought the money...'

He picks up a locust, waves it from side to side. To cool it, I presume. 'It is not nearly as simple as that.' He crunches the locust in his teeth. 'Have you tried this Thai specialty? It is superb.'

'It's been a wonderful meal. I don't think I can eat any more.'

'What a pity. You are missing a treat.' He crunches two more insects. 'I think we really shall have to ask for rather more bail than you agreed with Police Major Monkahn.' A white elephant smirk – Thais are, after all, famous for finding a way to combine freedom with serfdom – acknowledged with the appropriate smile.

I not only know the story of the white elephant, I appreciate it. So I know exactly what he's telling me. I clatter my cutlery down on my plate, wipe my lips with the napkin. 'I see.'

Two more locusts are impaled on sharp white teeth. His eyes roam my face. 'You must understand our position. That sum is not significant for a man of your standing. In Thailand bail is set according to the detainee's ability to pay.'

'I suppose it would be. But surely it also depends on the detainee's ability to find the money?' How does he expect me to get hold of more money in Udon Thani? Surely Teng must have told him...

'You understand my position, I do not doubt. If I do not make sure that bail is appropriate you could simply go back to England and forget all about this case.' This time he takes a little rice, cleaning his mouth with it. 'We have not yet established your innocence.'

'I wouldn't think of running. And my dealings with Thai banks form quite a large proportion of my business.'

The smile of a lizard basking in the sun. 'No doubt we have rivals: Singapore, Hong Kong, the Philippines...'

'Furthermore, I wish to marry a Thai girl who will want to return to her country to visit her family.'

'I do not doubt you are an honourable man, Mr Narland. However, I am acting in an official capacity, not a private one.'

'Naturally.'

'Unfortunately I also have to make you aware of a further problem. Normally I would be happy for you to pay a cheque into official police accounts after an expedited inquest. That would be quite acceptable.'

'But?'

'It is Songkran the day after tomorrow. These are our New Year celebrations, as I am sure you know. It means everything is closed for several days. Up here these celebrations start early and end late.'

I nod. Precisely why I'd arranged the meeting in Bangkok for tomorrow, precisely why I wanted to fly back to England the following day. Business-wise nothing happens in Thailand during this holiday, and it goes on for a good week in some parts. 'So what do you suggest?'

He raps the table for the waiter to clear the debris. 'Stay in the hotel and enjoy our festivities. Even if I allowed you to leave you would not be able to get a seat on a plane.'

'I took the precaution of booking early.'

'You are a man of vision, Mr Narland.'

'But I will be free to fly to Bangkok as soon as the banks are open again?'

'After the inquest, and when we have received the money. Certainly.'

'Assuming I have enough money in my account to pay the bail.' I grab my glass of water before the waiter takes it away. 'What were you thinking of?'

Relatively delicate nostrils twitch. 'That is for the judge to decide. All I can do to help is to arrange the inquest as soon as the Songkran festivities finish.'

His eyes have shut down, his voice intones dismissal. I realise I'll have to get onto a firm of bondsmen in the UK in case I wouldn't be able to raise the money. 'Assuming I can find the bail, are you also saying I have to stay in Thailand until you're ready to bring a case?'

'Unless you are indicted at the inquest you will be free to leave the Kingdom.'

'That's marvellous! I am so grateful...'

'We say a person who gives rice gives strength,' he nods at me. 'I am simply an official fulfilling my function. There is one further point I have to make you aware of. As I said, you may leave for England after the inquest, but we will require your English address and telephone number. We will contact you in due course. Even if the investigations eliminate you as a suspect you must return for the trial – as a material witness.'

'I see.'

'It is my duty to point out to you that if you choose not to return you will never be able to revisit Thailand. If you did, you would be arrested on charges of contempt of court.'

BUDDHIST HOLY DAYS DO NOT TAKE PLACE ONLY ONCE

'Perhaps we really should be thinking about finding me a lawyer.' Luke is walking up and down in our room, not very happy.

We had good sleep in best rooms hotel can offer. Receptionist was very respectful when Khun Teng and I returning from police station night before. We waiting for Luke. He ringing from my Excellency's office to say he coming tonight. Hotel giving Khun Teng room Luke and I staying in before, moving us to very expensive suite. Only one left is honeymoon suite. Same receptionist as before booking us in. I still upset at way he treating me before, but understanding no other hotel having any rooms free on eve of such important festival, so agreeing to stay.

'You mean finding a lawyer here, tilac, in Udon Thani?'

'Well, this is where I am, whether I like it or not. What if the General changes his mind and decides to take me into custody again? What if I can't get bail?'

'I think my Excellency very fair and honourable. We having long chat together, and he being very reasonable. If you using lawyer – Udon Thani lawyer not very good for farang – I think you having big problems. We free now to enjoy Songkran, so be happy for few days, forgetting all problems.'

Luke looks as sad as a village buffalo not wishing to pull a heavy plough. 'The mai pen rai philosophy writ large: bend with the wind, keep smiling, keep your cool, never mind, no worries, take it easy, everything OK.'

It is true that in Thailand we like this way of thinking. Luke walks round our room throwing pillows on floor, banging doors of wardrobes, not keeping a cool heart. 'It is excellent philosophy, Luke. Everybody knows you are innocent, the only question is how you finding enough money for paying bail day after Songkran finishing. Khun Teng bringing plenty baht for few days of festival. We can enjoy.'

'I suppose it does give me a chance to ring the UK and try to make sure of a source of cash.'

'You not have enough in your bank?'

His laugh sounds like the bark of a snarling dog. 'I haven't been given any indication how much I'll need, but I wouldn't think so. I don't hold much cash. I run a business!' He looks at me sour-sweet, makes more laughing barks. 'Don't suppose there's anyone in your family who knows how to help me out.'

He is right. My family having no money, no connections. Already my mum spending all own money for two weeks on special Jasmine rice for Luke, thinking that sticky rice not good enough for farang.

'We not having money, no. But we looking for documents for my dad's land. That worth much money. I am sure my dad very happy helping future son-in-law.'

I know Luke's look of present happiness is result of merit done in life before present one.

'Really? You think he'd do that?'

In our villages we believe that the giver of happiness always gains happiness. 'We always helping family members.'

'I'll see if I can arrange something with my bank. If not, we'll have to see what your father can do.'

He is looking glum again. It is not useful to be sad. I remind him of the happy times we having together, travelling to Hong Kong and Singapore.

Happy memories bring back a laughing Luke. He suggesting now we relax, then calling Khun Teng for coming to room. Meanwhile I trying hard to convince Luke to enjoy celebrating Songkran in my country. Because he forced to stay here in Northeast Thailand, this giving excellent chance to see our customs first hand. Khun Teng and I explaining everything for him.

'You often asking me introduce you to Thai customs, tilac. Now you can see exotic Thai tradition. Not only Thai; also celebrating in Laos, Burma and Cambodia. Also Chinese living in Hunan Province.'

Luke looking at me with small, sad smile, then sighing. 'OK, then. What happens, exactly?'

'Main thing is, time for everybody to be happy, Luke. Smiling whole time, people enjoy throwing water at each other. You thinking great fun, I promise.'

He holds me in his arms, very affectionately. We making love for very long time, feeling extra good. We having shower together, then dressing.

'Right, then, Taiella. We'd better get together with Teng and go out to play.'

Finding Khun Teng sitting in lobby reading newspaper. We making up mind we all having lunch together to discuss what we doing.

'Well, we're stuck here for three days at least, so why don't you two tell me what Songkran is all about?'

'You want the do-gooder story of how Songkran came about?' Khun Teng looks at Luke with laughing expression.

'Maybe a short version.'

'The story does not stir the action, it is quite similar to many European fairy tales. Rural people become high as a kite during Songkran. It shows why the local farmers started the take on this.'

'Sounds as though an early beer might be appropriate.'

'I join you with non-alcoholic beer.' Khun Teng is leading the way to comfortable seating in the hotel foyer.

'Basically, it is the story of a rich man accused by a neighbour, Kabilabrahma, of going down the tube because he had no kids. The rich man started merit making in a big way, and prayed for help. Finally a son he named Dhamabal was born to him, who turned out to be really on the ball, to the tune of understanding bird language.

149

'First crack out of the box, Kabilabrahma worked on testing the grown Dhamabal's smarts by coming up with three bummers he had to finagle in seven days. If he could not, he would kick the bucket, but if he did good, then Kabilabrahma would go down in flames and chop his own head off.

'As per usual, Dhamabal had his ears to the answers – checked out a bunch of eagles, where he got a handle on the patter. He answered all Kabilabrahma's questions on the ticket, which meant the jealous one had to do the deed.'

I see Luke not really listening. 'End of story? Bit tame, isn't it?'

'It was not the end of the story, Kuhn Luke. Taking the chopper to his own head was not peachy. The head had super-duper potential. Crashing to earth meant scorching the land, exposed to air it would suck up all moisture, and landed in the ocean it would give really deep trouble: the waters would dry up. The only defence was for seven dames to play hardball, trekking the head on a dish around Mount Prasumeru. After that the head was stowed away in Kantabuli cave at Mount Krai Las for 365 days. At the end of each year one of the seven dames would parade the head round Mount Prasumeru once more.'

'And this happened precisely on April 13th?'

'Exactly. Seven dames, so it did not matter which day of the week Songkran fell on, they would max out.'

Luke laughs. 'As you say, usual stuff. So what's all this got to do with the festival?'

'Well, it explains why we make such a big production at this time.'

'It does?'

'During the rainy season our plains are deluged enough to choke a horse. When the waters even out they leave pools. When these dry up baby fish get trapped inside. Farmers catch the small fry and keep them alive until Songkran Day, then give them the heave-ho into the canals. In other words, firing one shot gets you two birds: great merit is gained from giving away the fish.' He smiles at Luke. 'No doubt you have sampled the basic chow in the village, rice and fish. Giving fish away is the clincher for high class fish stock for another year.'

150

'Right. So what actually happens now?'

'Tomorrow you will see humdinger preparations, bubble-gum music in the streets. The day after, April 13th, is the kicker. We let it all hang out.'

'Eat, drink and be merry for tomorrow we die,' Luke says, strong face little bit sad. But he cannot stop Khun Teng talking.

'Another tradition is throwing out old clobber and other schlock. Keeping it would bring bad karma. This is a form of merit making.'

Khun Teng not knowing like I do how we celebrate in Udon Thani. 'We not throw out old clothes here, in Isaan. On April 12th we go to temple and wash Buddha image with fragrant water. On April 13th we have big parade, carrying Buddha round, washing again. We keep smiling all day long.'

'In my village young people hit the road to pour scented water into the hands of their elders as a mark of respect, give it a shot for a blessing,' Khun Teng telling us. 'On April 14th people bring food for monks so that they can live in tall cotton. The first day of the New Year means people stay in the straight, keep a cool tongue. Otherwise they will attract very bad karma for themselves.'

'And you forgetting, Khun Teng. People buying birds in cages and live fish for releasing to make merit.'

'You *buy* caged birds and caught fish, and when you release them you gain merit?' Luke almost laughing.

'Why not, tilac? Is paying money to do good deeds.'

Khun Teng smiling at Luke, offering more beer. 'Nong Taiella knows more about the local doodads than I do. We city slickers buy live fish to release into the canals.'

'Another custom is my dad talking to his trees, spraying with water. He saying 'Wake up, wake up,' to banana tree, mango tree, all his crop. 'This year you will grow more than last year, you having big crop.''

'That a fact? I have never heard that before.' Khun Teng smiles.

I am already exciting at the thought of the festival. 'April 15th excellent day for festivities. Street party, people throwing water at everyone they meeting. Getting very wet if going out that day.'

Khun Teng looks serious. 'Some old superstitions say that

Nagas – a kind of mythical serpent – brings rain by putting on the Ritz, spouting water from the oceans. So the custom could be interpreted as getting on the bandwagon for rain.'

Luke forehead in deep lines. 'What I can't work out is how the farmers can afford the time away from their land.'

'That is why we celebrating Songkran at this time, tilac. Very hot, earth cracking because lacking water, cannot cultivating. Farmers have plenty time in dry season, nothing growing. Waiting for rainy season, everything starting again.'

'If there's this shortage of water, where do they get it from?'

'You already knowing, tilac. In my village we have plenty wells, very deep, but long way away. Taking long time to fetch water, we pray for wet season. Every year I telling rain-water butt: 'Wake up, wake up, fill quick, overflow with water.' If I not do this I having to work very hard fetching water from far-off wells.'

A SINGLE HAIR'S BREADTH CAN HIDE A DISTANT MOUNTAIN

Teng and Taiella, engrossed in the Songkran reminiscences and preparations, don't notice my slipping away. The UK banks are due to open in around an hour, just when Helga will be finishing breakfast. Taiella might be right about the lawyer, but not arranging for a substantial amount of cash isn't a prospect I'm willing to consider.

I know I can ask Howard Spelter, my main investor and a good friend, as a last resort. My other source of cash is the joint savings account with Helga – about twenty thousand pounds. Over a million baht – surely that's enough to see me through? What I do know is that there's no chance with only half that amount.

A startled gecko scampers out of the stone wall of the temple grounds. I'm looking for a quiet spot, but the term is, at best, relative. I gaze at elaborate monuments – small, pyramid tombs of the rich in vivid hues of green and gold – but fail to find inspiration.

The dilemma is this: do I simply move the savings into my business account, or ring Helga and discuss it with her? I know the money will be returned in a relatively short time. I don't think she'll put any obstacles in the way once I've told her my predicament, and how I'll be exonerated as soon as the DNA results come through. Or sooner, if the murderer's left other clues.

Couple of snags. Even if I lie successfully about my reasons for visiting Northeast Thailand – and get away with such a blatant untruth while talking to a skilled cross-examiner – I'm planning to start divorce proceedings as soon as I get back. She's bound to spot my hesitations, bound to cross-examine. And, however hard I squirm, she'll hardly fail to spot the implications and deduce the real reason I'm here.

I feel uncomfortable, but it doesn't seem the right time to bring all that up now. Especially not over the unreliable phone lines from Northeast Thailand.

I slough off my sandals, walk into the cool of the temple, luxuriating in feeling the marbled floor under my feet. The Buddha image looks at me reproachfully. I stick some gold leaf on its back, but its eyes haven't changed when I move to the front again. The Buddha isn't fooled, and I'm unnerved by a suspicious monk. He smiles uncertainly, indicates a place to deposit baht. I rummage for some change. That only merits the smallest candle.

So, should I blurt out I've found a new love and still expect Helga to help me out? Hardly needs Freud to tell me that that would be a serious error. She'd be more likely to block my share of our savings as well as hers.

The saffron robes swish past, return, settle. The monk lifts the corners of his mouth but keeps his eyes veiled. Does he think I'm going to steal some of the gold leaf? He points to a text written in English: 'Watchful among the careless, wakeful among the sleeping, the wise man gallops ahead like a warlike steed, leaving behind the weak.' I nod, fishing out more baht, not even waiting to see what size candle he will light.

What surprises me is that Helga hasn't already guessed about Taiella, sniffed her on my clothes, found her in my sudden passion for Thai food. She's even accepted my absence over the Easter weekend without comment. Does she, perhaps, have someone else? Am I the one who's blind?

So, should I go ahead and transfer the money, knowing I'll pay it back before Helga even notices? And what about Taiella? Will she walk out on me if she finds out I haven't let Helga know about us, or what I'm planning?

There isn't anyone I can talk to. The Spelters are no use to me. Geraldine is Helga's best friend, and Howard won't necessarily view bail, or me in jail, as a good business proposition. I've dropped a few hints to my parents and sister – taking them out to a Thai meal, praising the country, that sort of thing. No idea whether they got the message. My parents looked vaguely puzzled, my father said spicy food wasn't to his taste, but my sister avoided my eye. I guess she got it.

I have to do something – today, now. The probabilities of international phone calls connecting from this part of Thailand aren't favourable. From tomorrow they'll be non-existent. I saunter back to the room at the hotel, ring reception to dial my home number, and raid the mini bar. It's the time Helga will be getting ready to leave for her Chambers.

'Helga! So glad I've caught you. It's me, Luke.'

The welcoming chuckle she hasn't used in years. 'Well, hello there, stranger! I tried your hotel all day yesterday.'

'I told you I wouldn't be back in Bangkok until today.'

'Travelling, poor darling. You must be exhausted in all that heat. So how was the trip to the Northeast? Big success?'

Deep breathing as my legs buckle and I land on the bed.

'Are you OK?'

'Not wonderful. Couple of problems, actually.'

'What d'you mean? You haven't caught one of those tropical diseases, have you?'

Is she talking AIDS, or Hep C? She's been on safe sex alert ever since I've been travelling to Southeast Asia, particularly Thailand. 'I'm fine physically, Helga. Look, we might get cut off any minute.'

'I know, I know...'

'So let me just explain as quickly as I can. I'm not flying home tomorrow; not for some time, in fact.'

I hear the rattle of the receiver. She always unwinds the cord when she's stressed. 'What does that mean? I'm missing you! When *will* you be back?'

'That's the point. I don't know exactly.' My mouth is dry, my throat seizing up. I guzzle more whisky. 'Hold on a second, I'll get a drink.' I pour some water down my throat. 'It sounds ridiculous, but I've had some trouble with the police.'

155

'What! What sort of trouble? Immigration, you mean? Wrong kind of visa? You want me to come out?'

'Not your field, I'm afraid. I'm accused of murder.'

The receiver bangs against something hard, is retrieved. 'Did you say murder?'

'It's all right, just a mistake...'

'A mistake? Dead bodies must be as unmistakable in Thailand as in England!'

'Let me try to fill you in. I'm in Isaan, a very rural part.'

'Chiang Mai, you mean?'

'Udon Thani. That's...'

'It's the notorious place the US sent their troops to relax during the Vietnam War.'

Why didn't I remember that? Teng and his US slang. Helga's so damned well-educated. 'I'll go into all that later, if we get a chance. The point is I need some money to put up as bail.'

'Bail?' I hear the kitchen tap splash water. 'Are you in prison?'

'Not as bad as that. But nothing functions till after the Songkran festival, so I've got to arrange for the money to be available when it's all over, on the sixteenth.'

'I see.' Her voice sounds ominously quiet. 'How much?'

'Don't know yet. My guess is around twenty thousand. The inquest won't take place till after Songkran.'

'You mean that Water Festival they go in for? I thought the whole point was you were leaving Thailand before that. No business for at least a week, you said.'

Helga is so bloody clued up she's better informed about Songkran than I am. Probably knows more than Teng and Taiella put together. And she's certainly not going to take kindly to my swapping her for a relatively uneducated Thai girl from an Isaan village.

'That was the plan. That's why I have to set up the money before tomorrow. D'you mind? Is it OK if I transfer your share of our savings into the business account? Just for a couple of weeks.'

Nothing for at least ten seconds.

'Helga? You still there?'

'You're not having cash flow problems, are you, Luke?'

'Nothing like that. You know Howard would help me out on that one. There's just this idiotic idea that I murdered a young girl.'

'A Thai girl, you mean?'

'Of course Thai. I'm in the Northeast of Thailand.'

'My God, Luke, how could you get yourself into such a mess?'

'Just bad luck...'

'If you need bail they must have good reason to think you're involved. Even in the back-of-beyond Thailand.' Her voice sounds forbidding.

'It's a long story. Yes, they did. Now they only think I'm a material witness.'

'Right.' The barrister is kicking in, fast. 'Tell me what happened.'

'I went for a walk and got caught up in a group of peasant girls herding water buffalo. It's the end of the dry season, and water is scarce. They were driving the animals to the deep water holes to keep them healthy. I was merely taking in the local scene.'

'Doesn't sound like the place for a murder.'

'It isn't, normally. I got hot and bored, and walked back to where I was staying, on my own. Later that day one of the girls was found to be missing. Her body was discovered that evening, lying in some bushes, obviously raped and definitely murdered. I was immediately suspected...'

'What? You can't be serious. Why you?'

'Because the villagers knew I'd walked with the girls, because I'd arrived back on my own, and because I'm a foreigner and therefore suspect. That's what made the locals think I must have done it.'

'I see.' The muffled sound of leather kicking wood. 'And did you?'

'Presumably that's not a serious question.'

'It is a serious question. I have to hear your answer.'

'No, I didn't. I never even talked to the girl, or been anywhere near her on my own.'

'Right. That's good enough for me.'

I found it hard not to choke as tears well out. 'Thank you, Helga.'

'Nothing to thank. I think I'd know if my husband was a

sociopath. And I flatter myself I can detect a lie when I hear it.'

Always spot on. 'So is it OK with you if I ask the bank to transfer the money? Shouldn't be needed for more than a couple of weeks. A month at the outside.'

'I don't care about the money, Luke. I care about...'

I replace the receiver and disconnected us. She wouldn't – couldn't – know how to reach me. There's no way I can go through the whole relationship thing now, over the telephone.

I dial reception, ask them to get through to my bank. When I finish with them I ring Helga back. She's gone; she never likes to be late for Chambers. I leave a soothing message on the answering machine.

LIFE IS SO SHORT WE MUST MOVE VERY SLOWLY

'Were you able to arrange lots of dough, Kuhn Luke?'

Taiella and Teng have been waiting patiently and aren't showing any signs of irritation. Thais seem to be able to do this – an amiable calm, a sort of living proof of mai pen rai. Whatever the reasons, their poise calms me down, makes me feel able to consider taking part in celebrating the traditional Thai New Year.

'Yes, everything's under control.' I decide against sharing any concern I might have about Helga, or mentioning notorious bank inefficiencies of the past. 'Now let's get down to the serious business of enjoying ourselves.'

Taiella giggles appreciatively, and Teng finishes his latest non-alcoholic beer with a particularly wide smile. He stands, his short figure swaying from side to side. He has foresworn alcohol – or so he insists. After all, one of the five precepts in Buddhism warns against taking intoxicants causing heedlessness. Well, it is Songkran – and he's on holiday, if you can call a forced trip to Udon Thani that. And, ever zealous, he's found us a couple of medium-sized water pistols – perhaps through the intercession of the spirits or some other method he doesn't disclose. I suspect an excess of baht which ensures that our water-soaked arms will be able to spurt more water back.

Twangy, crackle-punctuated Thai music blasts through enormous loudspeakers mounted on pickup trucks. The chances of finding a sound-free oasis are slim. The only defence I can think of is locking ourselves into our hotel room vibrating with air-conditioning, drawing the curtains and wearing earplugs. A large supply of food – better still, anaesthetizing alcohol – might get one through the next few days. Not an entirely attractive solution, and I'm positive Taiella wouldn't go for it. She's looking forward to the merriment.

Excited crowds mill round as we move through streets overwhelmed with cut flowers. Taiella giggles as we try to escape the occasional spray from an early water pistol squirt. Our aim is finding bigger and better pistols for S-Day. Much too late; everything's sold out.

An irritating buzz around my face brings me to an abrupt stop, forcing several merrymakers to sidestep me. I flick at the buzzing insect. It seems large, and very un-Thai in its persistent targeting of my face. What is it, anyway? No others to be seen. The buzzing is driving me crazy. I look round for a place to buy a fly swat, turning hotter and redder every second, while waving away offers of inferior water pistols, buckets, even rain capes.

'Is robber fly, tilac! Something very wrong!' Taiella's shrill scream is deafening my right ear. She's pointing at the spiralling insect. Identification of flies isn't a major talent of mine but, now she's drawn my attention to it, I see it's just like the fly which buzzed us to that unfortunate girl's body. No need for a degree in entomology to know it has no business in a town, with no prey in sight – or any smell.

'You think it's Wuadon again?'

'Nong Wuadon try telling something much much important, Luke! Must listening.' Taiella's voice is verging on the hysterical. She's not exactly the calm collected type under stress. Inclined to jump to conclusions.

I look around me. Do all these people really believe in spirits? Here I am, reasonably confident about being a contender in the technological world, and Taiella is expecting me to deduce meaning from the antics of a fly. Right.

I try to put my arm around her but she backs away. I swish at the fly again. 'OK, tilac! Mai pen rai – keep calm! I expect the fly has simply come to say hello to you, that Wuadon is all right in her new world, that...'

'No, tilac! Can see something very wrong.' She wrenches herself away from me, is jumping up and down, screaming that the fly is Nong Wuadon. People around us, fascinated, stop to stare.

The fly *is* weaving around my head in what I have to assume is an unusual fashion. Is Taiella panicking? Or is she asserting a knowledge of fly language – as opposed to bird language in the Songkran story I was told – expecting some ghoul to appear, wielding a Thai sword to decapitate me?

She pushes me away from her again. 'Not believing, Luke! Wrong wrong. Not normal this type fly coming to Udon Thani, buzzing round face.'

I try to pat her head, remember too late that that's another no-no. 'So what's it telling you?' Bangkok is difficult enough for a foreigner to understand, but Northeastern Thailand has an extra dimension of eccentricity to unnerve the unsuspecting farang.

She draws herself up, eyes blizzarding. 'Fly cannot speak, Luke. Presence here giving warning, telling danger near near.'

'OK, then.' I swat again, ineffectually. 'Where, exactly, is the danger?' The insect is going berserk, buzzing at frenzy pitch, moving up and down right in front of my nose. Sweat is pouring down my face as I try hard not to react.

'Mai pen rai, Nong Wuadon, listening!' Taiella grabs the hand holding the swat and strokes it. 'Danger all round. Much much danger, tilac. Must try understanding what fly telling, or big tragedy.' Her eyes swivel round. 'Fly knowing what we cannot know ourselves.'

Teng makes a valiant attempt to stand upright, with only moderate success. How does one get drunk on non-alcoholic beer? Presumably Thai-style non-alcoholic beer. 'What is your problem, Nong Taiella? We wishing to enjoy Songkran, why are you making a song and dance about a fly?' He lunges at it with an arm so wide off the mark it hits me on the shoulder. He looks stricken. 'I am so sorry, Kuhn Luke. I did not mean to...'

'It's OK, Teng. I understand. Why don't we all go back to the hotel and have a rest.'

Taiella's mouth opens wide, soundless. When the scream

comes it freezes the people round us. I follow her gaze. A distinctly wild-looking Thai is emerging from behind a thick palm tree trunk. Long wavy hair is kept under control by a band around his forehead and, unusually, he has a full beard. He looks like someone who sleeps rough, clothes covering him haphazardly, layers of rags hanging round formidably muscled legs.

'That ghost catcher! He coming to catch Nong Wuadon ghost in fly body!' Taiella grips my arm, proprieties swept aside. 'Must rescue fly, Luke. Otherwise Nong Wuadon spirit becoming prisoner.'

I'm trying to understand why the danger has, miraculously, switched from me to the dead girl. Taiella's inconsistencies are part of her charm for me, but not, perhaps, right this minute. Putting myself in the way of this ruffian wielding, I now see, a hefty-looking bamboo pole, is not my idea of Songkran festivities. On the bright side, his chances of killing the fly with such an implement are remote. He isn't, as far as I can tell, carrying a fly swat, though the rags allow plenty of leeway for concealment. Nor is he coming towards us, but I have to admit he's watching us intently.

'So what d'you suggest we do, Taiella?' Wuadon's spirit is prancing a dervish. 'Even if we caught the fly what are we going to do with it?'

'Fly leaving Dumden Village for warning us! Must taking back.'

Is she saying the insect is warning *us* of Wuadon's – I'm getting as bad as Taiella – its own danger? 'Don't you think it would be dangerous to go to the village? At least there's a police department here.'

'Police cannot help with spirits, Luke! Ghost catcher very strong man, catching robber fly, killing if someone not saving. Thinking all in bad danger, but now see Nong Wuadon is target. Spirit of Nong Wuadon asking *us* for helping!'

'We need magical abilities, someone strong enough to protect us from evil demons,' Teng is stuttering, eyes bulging on bamboo stalks, suddenly sober. 'I think we must go to the nearest temple, make lots of merit and ask the monks to get us out of the woods.'

'You're both insisting that this rough-looking man has come to Udon to catch this fly?'

'Why else fly dancing in front face, tilac? Already explaining, Nong Wuadon having scarf over eyes so departing spirit cannot see face of killer and coming back to haunting. Now she searching for murderer.'

'So this ghost catcher is supposed to stop that?'

'Yes. Ghost gate only open for one two days, soon soon after deed of execution. So now if ghost catcher succeeding then Nong Wuadon spirit haunting Dumden Village for always, and dead cousin not able achieving being reborn for new life.' Tears are streaming down Taiella's face. 'Big tragedy for Na Att, Nong Wuadon mum, big sorrow for whole village. Cannot allow this happening. Must helping.'

'Terrible thing to do. We all on the line, will reap what we have sown. We must face the consequences of our actions and take the bull by the horns.' Teng, in Buddhist mode, is taking this ghost catcher business as seriously as Taiella. He looks sombre, the careless jollity of a few moments ago a wraith.

The ghost catcher stands watching us and, presumably, the pestilential fly. Suddenly he turns and walks away. 'He seems to have lost interest,' I say, grabbing Taiella to me, stroking her hair while she tries to twist away. It's hard to remember that's an unforgivable no-no, hard to remember cultural differences at times of stress.

She struggles free. 'Is trick. Ghost catcher waiting for good chance.'

All the same, her breathing relaxes, she appears calmer. The fly, meanwhile, continues its antics in front of my eyes, buzzing as though its life depended on it. Which, according to both Teng and Taiella, it does.

'We must follow through, Kuhn Luke, take the bull by the horns,' Teng croaks. 'Just as the ocean is filled by great rivers flowing into it, so charity must be dispensed by the living to be received by the dead,' he pronounces in renewed religious mode.

There's a small explosion, like a fire cracker. Not scheduled till the day after tomorrow, but that, I know, wouldn't stop the merrymakers from setting them off today. Another explosion - and I realise it's a second shot.

The crowds scuttle into doorways, shops, restaurants – any of the flimsy shelters around. A man dressed in the distinctive blue working trousers and tunic I'd seen so much of in Dumden has emerged from behind the palm tree. Baring his teeth he levels a shotgun and points it at me, eye to the sight.

'Is Phor gun!' Taiella screams out. 'Is Lung Ban with Phor gun!'

A double-barrelled shotgun, and he's already emptied the two chambers.

'Let's just get out of here, Taiella, Teng. He'll reload in a minute.' I grab them both and start away, towards the hotel.

'I think we must get off the dime.' Teng shakes me off, twists round and starts towards Ban. He's fumbling with the gun, clearly has no idea how to handle it. And he's swaying. Teng sprints up to him, grabs the gun and chucks it out of reach. I kick it further out of the way.

Ban turns on Teng, work-hardened fists ready to strike. Teng, nimble as a lizard, jumps aside, twists round and lays Ban out cold with a couple of Thai boxing blows. The villager's body lies on the street, inert.

'We had better get the goods on this man to the authorities,' Teng says, a triumphant Thai boxing smile lighting up his eyes. 'This hayseed attempted to wipe you out, Khun Luke. We cannot enjoy high-jinks with this low-life loose in the town.'

The understatement of the whole crazy farce.

'Leaving quick quick now, Luke. Finding policeman arresting Lung Ban.' Taiella tugs at my T-shirt, pulling me away. The fly has disappeared.

I hail a tuk-tuk, surprised into action by the unexpected space around us. Teng has already persuaded a policeman to come over, shown him the weapon.

'Damned if I'm going to hang about for the police to question me again! Let's get out of here.' I clamber into the tuk-tuk and Taiella follows, leaving Teng to sort things out. It feels good to be speeding away from Ban – well, relatively speaking. We can't be doing more than five miles an hour. Better than trying to push through the crowds on foot.

'Now understanding what happening,' Taiella shouts above the din. 'Lung Ban angry police taking younger brother Mak to police station. Lung Ban still believing you killing Nong Wuadon. Therefore Lung Ban paying ghost catcher to kill Nong Wuadon spirit so cannot protect anyone.'

Taiella's convincing, if unreliable, theories have changed again.

'But if Ban gets the fly killed, he'll be killing the spirit of his own daughter!' I point out. Though logic is hardly a strong contender here.

Taiella's delicate shoulders heave. She's sure of Ban's motives. 'Nong Wuadon not Lung Ban flesh and blood, already telling. Nong Wuadon coming as baby from Laos – not Lung Ban true daughter - somehow he finding out now. But Are Mak true younger brother, therefore Lung Ban very concerned.'

'If you say so, tilac. But Ban brought Wuadon up, he must have *some* feeling for her.' Thais are particularly keen on their own progeny, suspicious of any child not their genetic offspring. I've been told they're very reluctant to adopt. They think adopted children might murder them for their inheritance once they're grown. 'So you think Ban borrowed the gun from your father?'

Taiella's voice rises again. 'Phor never giving gun. Only head man of village having permission for gun. If Phor lending, not allowing have gun again. Lung Ban must stealing.'

'OK, Ban stole the gun from your father and set off for Udon Thani. So who arranged for the ghost catcher?'

Only a slight hesitation. 'Also Lung Ban, because Nong Wuadon spirit protecting farang.'

'You're telling me he'd want to kill me rather than wait for the real murderer to be caught? That's a bit unlikely, isn't it? Even if it does turn out to be his younger brother.'

'Lung Ban not caring for truth, tilac. Only wanting protect younger brother.' She looks at me carefully. 'Also thinking your fault Are Mak killing Nong Wuadon.'

'That's a rich one. How does he work that out?'

'Because farang coming to village, Luke. Mae telling all villagers stranger marrying with her daughter. Lung Ban thinking farang showing new life for Nong Wuadon, much better than in village. Nong Wuadon already telling her mum wanting go Krung Thep. Making her mum very sad.'

'You're saying everybody assumed Wuadon was going to Bangkok because of me?'

'All people thinking you taking as second wife.'

Not sure how these Thais manage all these wives. I have trouble handling one! 'I already told your father...'

'Thinking way Thai men thinking, tilac.'

'I think I have pulled the plug on this nonsense, Kuhn Luke.' Teng has joined us at the hotel in a surprisingly short time. 'The police cannot refuse to put the squeeze on Ban for snitching a gun; even possession is illegal. No chance of a cop-out.'

'Well done, Teng. So Ban will be in that fragrant cell while we enjoy Songkran.'

'One more thing we having to do, tilac. Must finding ghost catcher. Pay catcher for not killing Nong Wuadon spirit.'

Another load of baht.

MUD FORMS A CLUMP ON
A PIG'S TAIL

Police Lieutenant General Thomupi, impassive in the front row of the courtroom, corrects the interpreter – frequently, disdainfully. The poor man's voice registers in a lower key each time he speaks.

'Court granting bail, Kuhn Luke Narland khrab. Setting one million baht. Paying instant.' Barely a whisper while his eyes sweep to the General's shoes.

The General, allowing this last announcement without interruption, half-turns towards me. 'You are quite free to leave for the UK now, Mr Narland. I wish you a good journey.' His outstretched hand is manicured, his grip on mine stainless steel.

'Thank you, your Excellency.' I smile, glowing in the remembered friendliness before Songkran, putting the seeming coldness down to pedantry. 'I have to admit that this is one visit to Thailand I will never forget.' The smile fades to embarrassment as the General's sparse eyebrows signal an inferior to lead me out. He nods patrician bounty at me, squares pristine white shoulders. 'If your presence is required at the trial we will contact you. My assistant will escort you to pay your bail.'

I force my features into a rigid mask, determined not to show supercharged relief. I am able to cover the bail – the twenty thousand pounds was transferred, miraculously within three days, into my business account, and bail was set at exactly that amount. I congratulate myself on working that one out.

There's just enough time to make a dash for the evening flight to Bangkok. 'Tell the clerk to wait a minute,' I instruct Teng, and arrange to meet him and Taiella at the airport.

Even after walking down labyrinthine corridors to reach the right office my signature is a barely recognizable scrawl as my hand shakes ink. My feet hustle out of the court buildings, slow to a dignified crawl to hail a taxi. Reality takes over. It sobers me to know I might be back at some stage. As a witness. The time scale might be unclear, but timeless Isaan has already proved more expensive than the fanciest parts of Bangkok. The seventy-five thousand baht Teng originally brought barely five days ago just about covered hotel rooms, expenses and, of course, the ghost catcher. At least Wuadon's freedom from molestation in her spirit world is assured, her father banned to Dumden Village, her uncle suffocated into jail.

The battle of Greater London, though not about to be fought with such deadly weapons as the battle of Isaan, is looming uncomfortably close. Helga has, most unusually, come to meet my flight. I'm not expecting her. It's a shock to see her rush at me, constrict two strong boas around my neck. Almost impossible to breathe.

'Luke, darling! I was so worried about you. How on earth could you have got caught up on a murder charge?'

'Helga!' I twist my face away, knowing my breath is bad, but mainly because I can't pretend to be glad to see her. 'Not too near. I think I've caught a cold.'

She loosens her grip, I pat her back, slip the luggage trolley between us. I expected to have a little more time to psyche myself up on the underground to Hammersmith. Still haven't worked out how to get across what I have to tell Helga, at least not in the right way. I want to take the blame on myself, tell her it's all my fault – but I can't. She was the one who started it, belittling me, reducing my self-confidence to zero. And I can't cope with a major attack right this minute.

I bare my teeth into a pseudo smile which, I believe, can't fool a blind woman, let alone an astute barrister. 'How sweet of you to go to all this trouble, Helga.' She'll expect an added darling, or at least a dear. I can't force the words out; even my voice sounds false. Surely she'll notice, demand to know what's going on?

'I've missed you. God, how I've missed you.' She pushes the trolley aside, wraps her arms around me again. A determined mouth finds mine.

I grab the trolley handle, knock off a piece of luggage, extricate myself to pick it up. 'What about your court schedule?'

'When my darling husband's finally home, just out of the clutches of Thai criminal law?' Her face takes on that steely look. 'Not that they've got a decent system, not by a long chalk, but in a way that can be even more dangerous.' She stands back, eyes lynxed. Nothing can possibly escape her. She's determined to leech blood. 'Of course I had to meet you. Only gave up a minor case, anyway. Swapped with Kate,' she waves that away.

How come I'd admired this Brunhilde, adored her, when all I can think of now is petite, delicate Taiella? What did I enjoy in that cool, composed, blue shimmer when all I now want is to melt into gentle, yielding, cinnamon depths?

Her arm snakes mine. 'I thought we should celebrate. Not every day my husband escapes a murder charge! I'm taking you out to a slap-up dinner.'

'They served a full meal on the plane...'

'On Thai Airways?'

Have the lines between her eyes deepened since I last saw her? Turned into daggers of accusations to bloodlet my brain?

'You didn't eat that rubbish, did you? What you need is good, solid, English food after all that Thai spice.' She stands away from me, pulls at my shirt now hanging loose. 'You've lost at least ten pounds.'

'It's really sweet of you.' Eat? Even the thought makes me feel sick. 'Sorry, Helga, but I don't think I can handle that tonight.'

'Why on earth not? It's only five!'

'It's been a long trip. Udon Thani to Bangkok, then straight on to the London flight...'

'Nonsense. I've already invited the Spelters. We're all longing to hear what really happened. How *did* you get involved in such a mess?'

169

I'm surprised. More my friends than hers, if you count the starting gate. But Helga's taken over Geraldine since then. Howard's still the biggest investor in my business. Well, Geraldine's money, Howard's management.

'I'll tell you all about it. But not right this minute.'

She pushes her upper lip over her lower one, blinks. 'Fair enough. Anyway, best cure for jet lag is to carry on in the time zone you land in.'

I nod, too depressed to argue. Right theory, wrong practice – as so often. Helga never allows for the unforeseen. Or am I underestimating her? She's renowned for brilliant court tactics.

'So are you still a wanted man?'

I knew it! That incisive brain has macheted through the jungle of overwhelming growth, has cleared the ground from under me. She knows; of course she knows.

She pulls me to her again, a strong hand claps my back. 'When I told Howard about the murder charge he nearly choked on his blue sirloin.'

Upright Howard and uptight Geraldine I've dubbed them. Howard is into the Atkins diet while Geraldine virtually doesn't eat. 'I told you, it's all under control now. The real murderer is in jail.'

A bottle of mineral water pops out of her bag, is opened, then proffered as though to a baby. "All men are babies, really," she's patronised so often in the past. "One's enough for me, no need to go to the trouble of having more."

Taiella and I have given ourselves to each other wholly, without hindrance or artificial barriers. Not planned at first, then agreed without a word. Sweet darling assures me she'll be happy – thrilled – to have my baby, married or not. She's the true love of my dreams transformed into reality. I forget the past when I'm with her, allow us to sink into bliss. I long for my seed to grow inside her, wait for the magic words to confirm our love. Ironic that nothing's happened so far.

I take the bottle – reluctantly. I have a perfectly good mother, no need for Helga to fill that role. I've always been embarrassed by her insistence on choosing my clothes, telling me which films to see, which plays to go to. Because, she always maintains, her taste is impeccable, mine tawdry.

Helga walks briskly towards the car park, dragging at the cart I propel so slowly. 'Geraldine is thinner than a beanstalk now. I've suggested Diana.'

'Do I know her?'

'You must have heard me talk about her. Our medical expert in the anorexia case. You remember; I took on the case of teenager who died. National Health completely screwed up.'

Price of a daughter in pounds sterling – thirty thousand. "Such a good outcome," she'd bragged for days. I stand back and drink the water – good little boy – anything to shut out the harangue I know is coming. How am I going to start?

She stops in mid stride, annihilating a young woman carrying a baby. A dummy with a red knob flies past me in a wide arc. I catch it, hand it back to the bewildered mother.

'These women use their babies as battering rams! I ought to sue her.' Helga has, mercifully, reached her turn for the parking ticket machine. It refuses to take her money. She kicks it, gives it several slaps. It dutifully swallows previously rejected coins.

'You know, you really are looking decidedly peaky. A Thai jail can't have been a pleasant experience.' Steely blue punctures my face, would have read the message in my colour-defused irises if I hadn't turned away. 'I rented that film – the *Bangkok Hilton* – to get some sort of idea. Checked on the internet as well. Is that what it was like?'

'I haven't seen the film.'

She turns, mouth clenched, towards me, exit ticket fluttering. I push the luggage trolley away, deliberately hard. She catches up in two strides, embracing part of the trolley as well as me. 'You don't even know where I'm parked! We need the lift.' She takes over. 'How long were you locked up?'

'Just one day – only eight hours, actually. Nothing to get excited about.'

'How d'you mean, eight hours? You were in Udon Thani for five days!'

'I told you when I rang you. Songkran. Everything shuts down

171

for the festivities. The man in charge of the case released me on the promise I'd stay in Udon Thani until the inquest.'

Her nostrils spread into disdain. 'Their New Year – yes, you did say. So what happened, exactly?'

'I'm worn out, Helga. Let's do Thailand later.'

'Poor Lukikins, all on his lonesome. No Helgi to look after him.'

I feel her stare, start to sweat. I'm pretty sure she'd have antagonised the general, prolonged my stay in jail.

'Well, I suppose Teng was there. Did he help?'

Now! Tell her now! 'He arranged to bring up enough baht to ward off the first policeman. Meanwhile the big wig from Bangkok turned up. Very correct, not into bribes. Went to Brasenose, would you believe.'

'Oxford? Really?'

'Perfect English. He was the one who caused all the problems.'

'Well, if he went to Oxford, surely he was reasonably civilised.'

'Exactly. Insisted on my applying for bail at an official inquest. Not to be held, of course, until after Songkran. But he did set it on the day after.'

'Phones didn't work either, I take it.' The well-remembered pounce.

'No.' If lies are kept as short as possible even sharp cross-examiners can be gulled. I edge out of touch. No sweaty palms to give me away, the car park lighting blissfully dim.

'Look, sweetie. D'you really have to go on doing business in that country? Don't you find Thais rather – well, distasteful?'

Projecting problems onto Thailand now. Cross-examination is sure to find me out. 'No.' That answer is making me feel guilty, as though I'm betraying Taiella. 'Matter of fact I think it's a great country.'

She ramrods to full height. 'You never did have any taste.' She grabs my arm and twists me round. 'Bangkok – well named! – is an unsavoury haven of bought sex and tawdry trinkets. I suppose all those bright colours and false gold fire your imagination.'

'Bangkok's temples and palaces are a unique architectural and artistic experience, equal to any in Europe, or the rest of the world. Even you can't deny that.' We visited Bangkok and Phucket together the first time I did business there, made a holiday of it. Not Helga's scene. She pronounced both town and country unhygienic, sexually exploitative, hot and smelly, with questionable food and backward inhabitants. And a horrific climate.

'I'm not saying anything against the past. I accept that was spectacular. The rot set in when the Americans came over from Vietnam. Think of the way all those Thai bar girls practically threw themselves at you even though I was there...'

'All right, Helga!'

'So what happened?'

'Everyone joins in for the Songkran celebrations. All very jolly and friendly. The main event was shooting water at each other – from water pistols. Great fun, actually.'

'If you happen to like that sort of childish behaviour.'

We've reached the car. She zaps it open.

'So a few unfounded allegations of murder and rape are the first steps to a deep affinity, that your line of thinking?' The long sinewy neck I used to admire, fondle, kiss, swelled angry red against the memory of Taiella's smooth, slender brown.

Helga's long arms, honed to concrete by her daily work out, tentacle out again. I try not to recoil. She hasn't shown affection for years, and now I can't handle what feels like an attack. I haul an inoffensive piece of luggage off the trolley, lever it on again.

'What the hell's going on, Luke? I know you're jetlagged, but presumably you're intending to put that luggage in the boot?'

I shove my gear into the boot. 'It was about to fall off.'

She pushes the trolley separating us, grabs my arm, pulls me to her and kisses me on the lips – again.

I clamp my mouth shut, step back out of reach. This charade has gone on long enough. 'Time I told you the real reason I was up there.'

Her neck jerks abruptly back, her blank face masks her feelings. A deep breath taken in, exhaled. Another breath. 'The Northeast, you mean? You don't have to tell me anything you don't want to, sweetheart. I know you've had a really rough time...'

'I don't *want* to tell you, no. I have to.'

Her shoulders hunch forward. She's grown her blonde hair longer. She prefers a gamine cut, so she must have grown it to please me. The new style accentuates her high forehead. Twice the size of Taiella's, I'm pretty sure, housing a formidable intellect. An Eiffel tower to Taiella's village hut. Will I be able to counter Helga, protect Taiella?

'Not tonight, Luke. Let's just celebrate your being home again.'

Of course Helga suspects more than business problems, must know something personal's involved. She's a barrister, expert at separating fact from fantasy. She can't know for sure how serious it's become – with no connection to Thailand she can only guess.

Helga puts on a determined smile. 'You're worn out, poor darling. You do far too much travelling. Why not give yourself a chance to relax, sweetie? Jetlag isn't conducive to making decisions.'

'The decisions aren't in the future, Helga. They've already been made.' My voice sounds far off, dreamlike. I expected fireworks, psyched myself up for a fight – and got protestations of love, of sympathy. Guilt brings bile to my throat. "You are stained by your own evil deeds," I remember Taiella translating for me in a temple. How true; how irritatingly true.

'Not sickening for one of those tiresome tropical diseases, are you, Luke?' Assessing eyes sweep over my face, my body. 'I suppose you took the Lariam?'

'Do stop fussing, Helga. Let's just get back.'

'I did tell you to take some other anti-malarial drug, sweetie.'

Clenched hands on the steering wheel, slur in her voice I've only just noticed. Did she start on the gins before she drove to Heathrow? Will she crash the car?

'That one's renowned for side effects,' she insists.

I stay silent as I wait for some bloody medical term to account for my reluctance. Is she going to suggest a claim for damages against the drug company? File that the Lariam I took led to psychosis, anxiety disorder, depression – maybe even schizophrenia! Which, in turn, has led to a sexual entanglement I'm incapable of ditching...

Why can't she scream abuse the way she's done so often in the past? I have to get on with it, tell her the truth, convince her it's really happening.

174

It isn't in Taiella's, or my, interests to antagonize Helga. I want a settlement, not a court case. Am I up to handling Helga personally? Should I do everything through a lawyer?

I'm going to see this through myself, leave dependence, become the one to be depended on. "Good karma leaving no cause for regret," I hear Taiella translate.

I've read somewhere that there are many different types of intelligence. Helga's is undoubtedly intellectual, Taiella's definitely emotional. Which one will triumph? And where do I fit in?

DON'T FEED A SLEEPING SILKWORM

'Luke, old man. I hear you've been accused of murder! And there I was thinking you were holed up in a tin-pot little country, sweating your guts out selling our software.' Howard's hand is held up in a High Five. I don't respond. 'This is so much more exciting.'

'Not really. The actual murderer's in prison, Howard. I've been demoted to witness status.'

'But Helga, I thought you were so worried...'

'I should have known it would turn out to be a false alarm. Racial prejudice isn't confined to Caucasians, you know. Anyway, the phones weren't working over that holiday they make so much fuss about.' Helga sweeps her hand dismissively across the table, her mouth a thin red line. 'I should have guessed it would all have been sorted out quite quickly.'

So harsh, so cold, so competent.

'Good show.' Howard's long tufts of grey, plastered across his advancing bald patch, shake disappointment. 'But they did accuse you, Luke. You're going to sue, I take it.' He eagles Helga, eyes reflecting the table candles.

'Absolutely not.' I think back to sweet, gentle Taiella, look at the three people who've been my closest companions for the last ten years, shrug. 'The Buddha teaches that the wise man allows anger to diffuse and shoulders no regrets.'

'Well said.' Geraldine, a stick insect pecking at food, nods at me, her eyes enormous in her bony face. 'And the Kingdom of

Thailand is not tin-pot, Howard. It's a highly civilized country, with a majestic past.' She glares at her husband. She was curious about our holiday in Thailand, that time I went with Helga. Even Helga's dismissive reports didn't take the potential magic away from Geraldine. She pestered Howard to take her there on their next break, then promptly fell in love with the place. In the past I've dismissed her as tricky, bad-tempered and spoilt, but her present passion for all things Thai endears her to me.

'Luke's such a sucker for anyone interested in his programmes. Thailand's a bloody white elephant, if you ask me.' Helga fills her wineglass almost to the brim, twiddles the stem. Trickles spatter red dots onto the white tablecloth.

Geraldine turns, eyes now alight with righteous wrath. 'We weren't, actually.' She uses the menu to fan herself. She'll order salad – no need to look. 'Anyway, you're nearer the mark than you think.'

'Waiter! What about some celery sticks while we're waiting?' Howard's belly, wobbling above his belt, oozes onto the table and moves his plate away from him. 'Don't take it out on Luke, Helga m'dear. All businesses have their ups and downs. And Thailand sounds a good enough market to me.'

'You don't even know where the expression "white elephant" comes from, do you, Helga? If you did, you'd have more respect for the Thais.'

Helga's eyes squint into full alert. 'Really? And why might that be?'

'It shows how subtle they are. How ingenious.'

'You're being ridiculous, Gerry. It's a developing country, at best.' She twiddles her reading glasses hanging on a chain around her neck. 'And it *is* well known for exploiting the GIs during the Vietnam shindig.' The sniff turns into a snort, loud enough to startle the waiter uncorking another bottle. 'And, in so doing, the Thais turned Bangkok into the sex capital of the world. There's greatness for you.'

Geraldine's fingers threaten to break her wine-glass stem. 'You're blaming the Thais for selling sex rather than the GIs for buying it?'

'They could only buy what they were offered.'

'That's like saying a starving man is a thief when he filches bread from a dust bin.'

'And so he is!' Helga bellows. 'Exactly my point.'

I cringe. How can I expect to win against her?

Geraldine's face glows unaccustomed passion. 'Seems to me it was the GIs who exploited the Thais. The mighty greenback, and all that. How can you expect an impoverished population to resist fistfuls of dollars?'

The blue eyes shine, fervent with assurance, a case Helga is about to win. 'Your charming Thais sold out to the Japanese as well. The most charitable thing you can say about that nation is that they bend with the wind.'

'And stopped their country from being devastated. Look what happened to the Koreans.'

Helga grins triumph. 'I'm not even going to try to change your mind.'

'Maybe I can change yours.' Geraldine speaks softly, caressing her wine glass. 'Let me tell you how "white elephant" became part of the language. Not just theirs: ours, too.'

'Must you?' Helga's frown lines really are so much deeper than I remember.

'I think you'll find it informative, Helga. Seeing the world through a barrister's glasses isn't the only way, you know.'

'Good enough for me.'

'Wait till you've heard the story.' Geraldine shakes her serviette out, spreads it on her lap. 'At the time when two states dominated Southeast Asia – Burma and Siam – the elephant was the key to military success. And the rulers of both countries chose the biggest and most magnificent animals for pageantry.

'Now the *white* elephant was something else again. The Buddha's mother dreamt of one on the eve of giving birth to him. Since then these animals have had sacred powers and fertility attributed to them. Laws were passed that they could only belong to the king, that anyone finding such an animal had to catch it and take it to the king immediately. It was – *is* – treason for a commoner to own one. These animals were one of the wonders of Siam.'

'Gerry, my precious. We're having dinner to celebrate Luke's homecoming. We don't want a history lesson!' Howard grabs a handful of celery stalks, bites into them, crunches them to a green pulp swirling round his half open mouth.

'I'm getting to the point, Howler. One of Siam's great kings became furious when his most outstanding minister became too rich and influential. Why, he was in danger of eclipsing the king!'

'What to do? He couldn't sack a faithful minister, or execute him without a cause. That's when he had his brilliant idea. He made a great song and dance about how wonderful his minister was, and how he was going to give him a fantastic present. So what d'you think that was?'

'Any chance we can stop you telling us?'

'He gave him one of his white elephants!' Geraldine's eyes sparkle. 'Now *that's* what I call class!'

'No idea what you're talking about.' The remaining celery sticks are crushed under green teeth. 'So elephants are highly prized in ancient Thailand. So it was a great honour. So?'

'Not any old elephant, Howler darling – a *white* elephant.'

'Jolly good, then, a white one. If the king had several what was the big deal?' Howard shakes his head. A sheaf of hair is now hanging down by his right ear.

'Before we go on I need to know whether white elephants actually exist.' Helga's wide arms threaten innocent side plates.

'Absolutely. They're albinos – actually means they *lack* pigment. Their eyes appear pink because you can see the blood vessels normally covered by the whites and the corneas, their mouths are pink for the same reason, so are their toenails. They've got transparent hair which appears white when seen against their bodies. And their hide, being thick, looks a very light grey.'

'Go to the top of the class!' Helga pours herself another glass.

'Well, now, old girl, I have to defend my lady wife. White elephants *do* exist, and they *are* rare.' Howard eyes a forbidden roll, grabs it, breaks it in half and spreads Geraldine's butter pat as well as his on it.

She passes her second butter pat over to her husband. 'Deuce of it is, white elephants have to be housed, fed, decorated. Diamonds

179

on their foreheads to ward off evil spirits, precious stones set into their tusks. Gold plaques round their necks, no less, inscribed with their titles, golden pendants in their ears, golden umbrellas to shield them from the sun, gold feeding troughs.

'The good minister couldn't refuse the gift, but the animal could only be housed by the king. So the loyal subject had to pay a king's ransom to decorate his elephant and to stable the sacred beast in the royal palace grounds.'

'Is there a point to this story?' Howard's eyelids flutter as he devours the other half of the roll.

'The king's gift was a subtle move...'

Howard grins, displaying teeth with bits of roll intertwined with green.

'Well, you have to admire the strategy. The king was ruining the man he called his favourite by showing him the highest form of friendship.'

'We *can* work it out, Gerry, old girl.'

Helga's eyes turn opaque. 'That *is* quite a story. I'm impressed.' She looks at me over her glass, drinks deep and long. The battle has begun, and she's been alerted to Thai tactics. Which I'm not altogether sure I know how to deploy. And my Thai girl isn't here to show me how it's done.

'Exactly. Don't go confusing Thailand with a tin-pot country.' Geraldine actually eats a crouton from her salad.

'Makes what I heard all the more worrying, my dear chap. You really were in a spot of trouble, weren't you?' Howard's eyes open wide, then shut, as though he already knows precisely what happened. 'Slammed in the clink, I gather.' The sort of grin I've seen on many of the male tourists in Thailand splits his face. 'Do they put everyone in together? Men and women, you know? Female guards?'

'Don't be ridiculous. If you must know I was on my own. Just for a few hours. All because of some mix-up in the village.'

A Freudian slip, or have I done it on purpose?

'Village? What village?' Helga's normal hold on her temper when with our friends turns into half-screech, half wail. 'I thought you were selling software to banks!' Little specks of spittle escape

180

her lips, dart down her chin. She swipes them off with her serviette, overturning her wine glass.

A waiter comes running.

'Can't you see we need another bottle?'

'Yes, madam.' He holds his hand out for the serviette, blots up the liquid, disappears.

As though on a prearranged signal Howard and Geraldine both begin to talk, their gestures wild, their words erratic and unnecessarily loud.

The waiter brings another bottle. Helga holds her glass up imperiously. He starts to fill it but, watching her, spills a little.

'For Chrissake! can't you even do a simple job like pouring wine? Get me the head waiter.'

'I'm sorry, Madam.' He withdraws the bottle, produces yet another serviette.

'Let's not go overboard, Helga,' Howard sugars in. 'Just pour some wine, man!'

I watch, mute, helpless. At least she knows now. At least I won't have to explain. I hold my glass out for Dutch courage.

'Celebrating the Thai New Year in a village, were you? Gone to see the real thing, I expect.' Howard giggles. 'I've heard they make quite a sarong and dance about it all, and yet they keep the same calendar we do.'

'It's a festival, Howard. And they're called charongs in Thailand. That's for the men. The women wear phatongs. You really should get your facts straight.' Geraldine's eyes flutter to Helga's face. 'Songkran is just like Christmas. A little livelier, that's all.' She looks around the table. 'What's the difference, when you get down to it?'

'Christianity is the difference.' Helga puts her glasses on, fixes her eyes on Geraldine. 'The Thais are just a bunch of superstitious pagans.'

'Don't be ridiculous, Helga. Hardly anyone in this country ever goes near a church. And most Thais are Buddhists. Practising Buddhists. Did you know virtually every Thai male becomes a monk at one time or another in his life?'

Helga's mouth rounds, a volcano on the brink of eruption.

'What on earth were you doing, Luke, cavorting with Thai villagers? Researching water buffaloes to see how much money they'd generate for your latest Thai bank? Perhaps you've written a programme specially for them!' Her laugh crackles across the table, leaps into my wine, turns me to jelly. 'I think the heat must have mashed your brain.'

Has she decided to simply refuse to believe anything I tell her on the grounds of mental disturbance? Is that how she intends to deal with me?

Clearly I have to make her see. And just as clearly not right here, right now.

SWEET MOUTH, SOUR BOTTOM

'I think we should get a divorce, Helga.'

She's setting out her breakfast ingredients in meticulously ordered clusters. A knob of butter, measured by the cubic centimetre, sitting beside two rashers of bacon waiting in soldierly order on a plate by the frying pan, itself centred on the front right-hand gas ring. One medium egg, one slice of bread in the toaster. A daily ritual.

The cube of butter slips from knife-tip to cooker surface, missing the frying pan.

'Haven't heard what you said. Can't you see I'm busy?' The flame is turned down and what remains solid of the errant butter rescued with a spatula, then deposited in the pan. She shakes it, making enough noise to cover any attempts at conversation. She keeps her face turned away, scoops up the melted butter with a kitchen towel, rinses the dish cloth, wipes the cooker clean, places the bacon precisely in the pan.

I've chosen my time carefully. I know she has to get to Chambers by nine, has to be in court by ten, that she'd want to cook and eat, get her briefcase sorted, put on her coat. My timing means I can say what has to be said and make sure she has time to think about it away from me.

I watch belligerent muscles twist her body round. The bacon sizzles. Her mouth opens, her lips part. No sound at all.

'I've been trying to tell you for ages.'

She sweeps the working surface with her arm, watches the coffee splatter across the floor, empties the creamer onto the mess. Her favourite cork tiles, the ones we'd chosen so lovingly together, the ones she paid for because I'd recently started my business and wasn't earning, while she, highly qualified, was already making good money. I feel my eyes water for a past love I can't save.

'You must have sensed something.' My voice gravels low.

She stands, stretches to full height. Only a couple of inches shorter than me. Her mouth is closed, her eyelids tight...

'There's someone else...'

She swallows hard, presses her napkin to her face, flings it on the mess, presses her palms against her ears

'I'm sorry, Helga.' I have to say what I have to say. If she isn't going to listen that's her choice. 'I assumed you already knew what I've felt for some time now. After all, you were the one to bring it up, remember?'

She grabs the kitchen table cloth, pulls, scatters cups, saucers, spare cutlery, glasses, condiments on top of the mess on the floor. She runs for the door, grabs her coat and briefcase set ready in the vestibule, and is gone. The door stays open.

I turn off the gas, start to pick up the debris, stop. I can't face clearing anything up, not even the crockery. What does she mean by all this? Is she saying she'll abandon the house, leave me to get on with divorce proceedings? Or will she fight?

I long for Taiella, her heart-warming smile, her cherishing words, her fragile body in my arms. She'd be back from work, at her sister's. No phone, of course. And Teng would have left the office, gone to eat.

I need someone to talk to, but Helga and my friends are mutual friends, my relatives have no idea what's going on. At least, not officially. My sister's guessed, I'm pretty sure of that. Not that she's particularly keen on Helga, but I want a firm ally, not a lukewarm one. And Helga, whatever my family's private thoughts about her, is my wife. They might feel obliged to support her.

I go to the office. Allow time to calm Helga.

'There you are, honey bun. I decided to come back early. Left

Patricia to hold the fort. Still jet-lagged, or feeling better?' Her sweetest smile. 'I did suggest you don't go to the office today.' She comes right up to me, her eyes soft and moist. 'I told you Lariam is dangerous.'

'It's not the Lariam, Helga. Or jet lag. I've thought about it long and hard and come to a decision. Our marriage isn't working any more.'

The upturned lips, the softened eyes, turn to concrete. 'You never mentioned it before.'

'You did. Several times.'

'You never said a word.'

'I wasn't sure at first.'

'But now you are.'

'Yes.'

'Just like that?'

'I've thought about it for at least six months, if that's what you mean.'

'But never bothered to tell me what you were thinking.'

What can I say to that? True, but not the truth. Expressing opinions to Helga always ends in a major cross-examination which invariably defeats me and resolves nothing. 'Pretty obvious. We haven't made love for six months.'

'Not because of me...' She starts towards me. I can't help myself, I cringe. 'I see. Maybe we should just take some time away from each other. I'll go and stay with Patricia – she's got that huge house out in Hampstead...'

'I already know. I told you...'

'Not in a hurry, are you? After all, we've been married for ten years. It isn't right to simply turn our backs on that, is it? Till death us do part, we said. You were the one who wanted a church wedding.'

'It hasn't been working for some time – years, actually. You were the one who pointed that out.'

'Heat of the moment.'

'And you're the one who refused to have children.'

Her jaw gaps down. 'You never said you wanted any!'

'After I'd been told my genes are crap?'

'I never said that!'

'Not directly, no. But I have no taste, no education, I'm hardly civilized...'

'Anyway, that's supposed to be the reason? You never even mentioned an interest before. And you know I'd make a rotten mother.'

'I don't know anything of the sort. And I'm happy to take my chances on what sort of father I'll make.' I should tell her about Taiella, now. What's stopping me? Why can't I simply say forget the separation, there's someone else, I love her and I've become allergic to you? I clear my throat, croak – nothing. The words simply will not form, let alone express.

'Let's relax for a bit. Go to a film.'

'You're making this very hard. The last thing I want to do is hurt you.'

Her chin always dimples when she's determined. I used to put my finger in the small indentation, laugh, kiss. Not any more. The dimple disappears, her chin trembles 'Right. I'll get a few things together.'

I don't want to do this to her. I don't want to hurt Helga, I simply want to be with Taiella. Why couldn't she have found someone, left *me* to flounder for a bit?

'I'll help you.'

She turns, her eyes blazing the way I've got so used to. 'Can't wait to see the back of me, that it?'

Maybe that is what my unconscious is saying. I didn't mean it that way, I'm genuinely trying to help. The least I can do.

'Right. I'll just clear up this morning's...'

'That's right. Get the house nice and clean. Never lifted a finger before, and now it's got to be all spick and span. Doesn't take Stephen Hawkins to figure out why.'

So she does know. I don't argue, just go into the kitchen and start cleaning up the mess.

186

LITTLE BIRDS BUILD NESTS ACCORDING TO THEIR SIZE

'Tilac! So good hearing voice.'

I bribed Teng to taxi to Sayai's house and take Taiella back with him to the office phone. Can't wait to tell her the news.

'Worrying much much when Khun Teng fetching at end working day, Luke. Thinking maybe something very bad happening when Kuhn Teng saying must telephoning England.'

'Not bad, tilac. Good news, actually. Helga's moved out.'

'Meaning first wife leaving house? Already?'

'Yes. She's gone to live with a friend of hers.'

'She having boyfriend, tilac? That very good news.'

'No, not that I know of. A girl friend; a colleague who has a large house she and Helga are going to share.'

'So first wife having company. That very good news.'

'Why not apply for a visa to come to England, Taiella? You can come and live here, in my house.'

'Meaning finish with job in ZenZam Centre?'

'Well, you won't want to work in Thailand once we're married, will you? And we can just live together until the divorce comes through. No big deal these days. As soon as it does we'll get married in a registry office over here, make it legal and all that, then have a Buddhist wedding in Thailand. In the village, with your parents.'

'Not worrying about that, Luke. Worrying first wife coming

to old house, seeing new woman, very angry. Maybe coming attacking new girlfriend.'

'Don't think attacking you physically is her style, tilac.' I laugh at the idea of a fight between Taiella and Helga, then brush off an uneasy feeling that it just might happen. Wouldn't like to bet on the winner. 'It's OK, tilac. She's having all her things packed up by a moving firm. She won't be back.'

'How getting visa? Not very easy.'

'I've been thinking about it. Get a tourist visa to start with. Maybe you can work for my firm, translating between Thai and English. We should be able to get you a work permit.'

'Not needing. Khun Teng doing translating for company.'

'Not in Thailand, in England. You speak Lao, too, don't you? And didn't you say you also have a smattering of Cambodian, and Burmese? I could use that. You could be a great asset to my business.'

'Not doing business in such places.' She hesitates, says something in Thai I can't follow. 'Not very sure, tilac. Still worrying about first wife...'

'And I'll take you to see my parents. They live right in the country, in Devon. They have a big garden and grow all their own vegetables. Not that different from your family – few more mod cons, that's all. You'll love their place, and they'll be delighted to meet you.'

'How can you be sure English parents liking Thai girl from Isaan village?'

'They'll like you, Taiella. They'll love your smile and the way you are.'

'Must thinking hard hard, Luke. If giving up job cannot get back. Very good job, Japanese liking, offering position of supervisor.'

'Job? I'm offering you a job – in England. I'll pay you far more than you can earn in Bangkok.'

'Not for money, tilac. If plan not working out, if number one wife not divorcing, then what happening?'

'There isn't that much she can do about it, Taiella. I'm starting divorce proceedings. If she doesn't like it she'll just have to put up with it. She can't force me to stay married to her.'

'In Thailand easy getting divorce if parties agreeing. Can happen in few days. In England can taking long time if one party not willing to divorce.'

How does she know that ? Did they teach her that at the Military School in Udon Thani? Bit unlikely.

'Knowing this from Pi Panjim. I already telling you about Bangkok friend, Pi Panjim, taking me to party where meeting? Pi Panjim having boyfriend who knows an English businessman wanting to divorce his first wife to marry a Thai girl. First wife not wanting divorce, but no problem. He can get a divorce he living separate from his wife for five years.'

'I've done my homework too, tilac. There are ways to speed it up. In our case I can say that Helga refused to have children. That means the maximum time we need to wait is two years.'

'Still very long time, Luke.'

'I'll try to persuade her to make it sooner. After all, the sooner she's free, the sooner she can find someone else.'

'Thinking Helga still loving husband, tilac. Cannot blame!'

'Two years at the outside, sweetheart. Meanwhile we can just live together. What difference does it actually make?'

I know Taiella wants to be my first wife, my only wife, and I'm just as keen that she should be, just as keen to get everything done properly. Otherwise why would we be bothering at all? What I also want to suggest is: let's get serious about starting a family.

Helga may lie about refusing to have children. Actually, I'm not sure it was ever brought out into the open. She might find some legal loophole to prolong the divorce procedures – her expertise. Better to leave that for a while. But I'm nervous, almost superstitious. I can't understand why Taiella hasn't conceived yet. Is it a sort of punishment because I slept with Taiella while married to Helga? Do the spirits disapprove and are they taking their revenge? I try to wave such ideas aside as ridiculous. A worse thought: did Helga actually not bother with the pill, and just didn't conceive? Because I'm the one that's infertile?

Well, if there are going to be problems in that area, whatever their cause, I'm hoping Taiella and I can get the medical profession involved sooner rather than later.

OUTGOING TIDES SHOW
UP THE STUMPS

Luke having beautiful house, modern bathroom and kitchen, but I am finding many problems living in England. Is not only language, customs very different from Dumden Village, even from Krung Thep. Also Luke going to office for whole day, and very busy whole time.

I spend many hours cleaning and cooking. Then what I do? Also I am not happy staying on own all day long. In village seeing lots neighbours whole time. Remembering when working hard in paddies planting rice, or tending buffaloes, or watering vegetables, all girls working together, laughing together, enjoying company.

Outside Luke house garden very beautiful and cool. After finishing cleaning go outside for cutting grass using electric machine Luke showing me how to start. But it go on running away from me quickly when I begin to mow lawn, knocking hard into apple tree. Coming big gash, not good for tree but I not knowing how to stop machine. It going into flowers, cutting, making wide path. I becoming very nervous now, so stopping motor.

I put mowing machine away in little wooden house at side of garden, taking big scissors Luke giving me to cut down too big plants. Copying what I watching my dad doing for many years. He outstanding gardener, my dad, warm hands making all plants he touching grow. Remembering very well how he doing this, and imitating.

After cutting down flowering plants I going to vegetable

garden. Luke having many bushes with branches carrying little black berries, but many other branches which only having leaves, no fruit. First tasting berries, very sour, not yet ripe. Then cutting down empty branches so plants keep plenty strength. Leaves from this plant giving off very strong smell I not recognizing.

Now starting to rain. Not such good day for gardening, but right day to collect water. Even if Luke having running water upstairs, where he keeping storage jar for drinking water? I no can drink water from what Luke calling tap – tasting horrible. In village collecting rain water during rainy season, very sweet soon after rain starting. Luke water tasting full from chemicals. Still cannot find storage jar, so putting washing-up basin outside for catching rain.

Now thinking good idea to go inside again and wash clothes, polish furniture, make whole house beautiful for Luke. He has many machines, very clever, but I not understanding all English words so not knowing which powder going which place. Deciding by closing eyes and pointing to two packages – whichever coming first putting in washing machine, second powder in dishwasher.

Now phone ringing. Luke telling me I must always answering in case he ringing, or coming an important call from Home Office because Luke helping me to apply for a work visa. Authorities are not allowing me to go to Luke's office until approving my work visa application.

'Hallo?'

There is strange exploding sound, maybe phone dropping. Then 'Who on earth's that?' coming into my ear in very loud voice of woman, strong and harsh. Knowing right off this Helga mum. Luke telling me she very fierce lady, ringing often.

'Who calling, please?' Making voice soft soft.

'Who the hell are *you*? What are you doing in my son-in-law's house?'

Already feeling nervous and frightened. Will she coming to this house, beating me? 'Please excusing, not understanding. My English not so good.'

There is sound of barking dog, then strong voice coming again. 'Never mind your English. What are you doing there?'

'Using machine for cleaning – vacuum cleaner, madam.'

'Don't be impertinent! What are you doing in that house?'

Very loud barking dog unhappy for mistress, I can tell. 'Mr Narland not here, madam. Going to office...'

Dog yelping very loud now, like something frightening him. I worry maybe this woman coming to Luke house, bringing fierce guard dog, telling to bite me. Thinking best idea to put phone down.

Ringing again right away.

'Don't you dare hang up on me! Of course I know Luke's at work. What I want to know is what you're doing in his house?'

'I maid, madam. Cleaning Mr Narland.'

A little pause, then I hear laugh. 'Well, I daresay he can do with a bit of that! No, Roger, you can't eat the phone...' More noises, receiver falling, sound of person picking up. 'So, where d'you come from?'

'Please excusing, madam. Working for Mr Narland. You wanting take message?'

'What's that? You can write, can you?'

'Not very good, but try writing down what you saying, madam.'

'Then tell him this. I know what he's up to, and it won't do him any good. My daughter is a brilliant lawyer.'

Not necessary for me to speak again. I hear crashing noise and the phone is dead.

This woman not sounding pleasant. Now understanding Luke having two big problems. Going to front door very quickly, pulling bolts and putting chain in hook. Lucky no one can enter house except by front door. Many houses in this street built in a long row, joined together, you can only get to back and to garden through house.

Soon hearing big banging at front door. Going to bedroom window, looking down in case Helga's mum – or Helga. Not opening door even if making terrible noise. Looking out and seeing Luke.

'Coming tilac!' Running downstairs fast as possible.

'Why on earth is the door bolted?'

Telling him all details about phone call, dog noises. Luke

putting arms around me, kissing me.

'Don't worry, tilac. I'll take you to the office tomorrow. You can just sit in reception, reading a magazine or something. I can't let you do any work, not even making tea. If the Home Office found out they'd deport you.'

'OK, coming office tomorrow.'

'So what d'you think of my house?'

Knowing Luke very fond of house, very proud. Having all kind of machines, good furniture, lovely garden, and also house very near bus stop for going shopping. But not like village. No neighbours calling out greeting and talking, just looking and when seeing me smile looking away quick quick.

'I cutting grass with machine, tilac. Little bit problem, running away and not knowing how to stop.' He very busy looking at letters arriving today. 'You want I making dinner now?'

'Lovely. Did you pick some of the courgettes? No? I'll get a few for you. And there should be plenty of blackcurrants for dessert.'

Opening dishwasher as he going out. All dishes looking dirtier than when put in, many funny bits all over. Better to wash by hand. I starting washing dishes just as Luke coming back in. He looking little bit glum.

'Been out there with the secateurs, have you, tilac?'

I not really understanding what he saying. 'Very pretty garden, tilac. Roses looking pretty good on wooden ladder bending over...'

'You mean the pergola!'

'Seeing weeds growing between bushes so cutting down and digging up.' I smile at Luke, thinking he very pleased with my work.

'So that's what happened. That was my new Jackmanii – a climbing plant we call clematis. About to flower for the first time! It climbs up through the roses.'

'Not weed?' Now feeling very sick.

'No, tilac. And you've cut down all the new growth on my blackcurrant bushes!'

Blackcurrant – thinking maybe meaning little black fruits, very sour. 'Strong smelling plants down bottom of garden? Is OK, tilac. I cutting out all branches not having fruit. Not good for shrub, it making more room for branches with fruit if thinning out. Needing sun and air, my dad always explaining. He very good gardener.'

Luke sighs. 'It's not the way those plants grow, Taiella. For those bushes you cut down the old wood after fruiting and leave the new growth for next year's crop. Well, never mind, there's an awful lot for you to take in.' Coming over now, he looking into dishwasher. 'What's all this mess?'

'Putting in lots powder, tilac. This machine not cleaning well. Washing by hand...'

He looking hard, shaking head. 'You put in salt instead of cleaning powder, that's why.' He leans down, cleaning out bits while I washing dishes and making supper.

At last we both finish. Luke starting washing-up machine with proper powder. I setting supper on table, spoon and fork. Luke putting knife and spoon on right hand side, fork on left. We never using knife and fork, we always using spoons or chopsticks in village. Knives only using for cutting vegetables and meat for cooking.

We laughing while eating, laughing very hard when I telling Luke story about Helga's mum and very angry dog.

'It's going to take a little while, I can tell.' Big chuckle. 'I think my house is strong enough to cope with your ministrations...' Then seeing my face, noticing I nearly crying. 'I'm not annoyed, tilac! It's just so funny. And I think you've made a brilliant start!' He pulling me on lap, kissing again. 'Tell you what. It's time you met some of my friends. I'll fix dinner with the Spelters. Howard's been on at me to come over for dinner for days.'

GOLD WRAPPED IN RAGS

'Luke, old man.'

Hearing trumpet noise, like small elephant.

'Very good to see you, old chap. Where've you been hiding for the last couple of weeks?'

'Hi, Howard. Been a bit pre-occupied.' Luke turns round, pushing me forward from hiding behind him. 'I've brought the reason with me. This is Taiella Motubaki.'

I see large-bellied man with wobbling, red-veined cheeks pointing his big nose down at me. It is very swollen, a shade of purple I never seeing before. His glowing white shirt reflecting the light, very stiff, with a black bow tie, and a velvet jacket of a dark green colour. Not easy to see the fat man's eyes, wrinkles all round, but I feel him staring hard at my body, up and down.

Already know this old man is Luke's colleague, and very important for him. He is a big investor in the software business Luke is running. He waves his cigar in a circle. I can see he is not expecting to see me.

'Well, now.' The old man is smiling with a lop-sided face. I can see he is thinking this girl is like flowers near the path, ready for easy plucking. His wet mouth already showing saliva on lips, sucking. I take a step backward, bumping into Luke. He pushing me forward again, holding both shoulders so cannot go back.

'Taiella, this is my very good friend Howard.' Luke nudges me through grand door of an expensive apartment. Two lacquer vases, elegant like old Chinese vases, are guarding the entrance. Polished parquet flooring is covered with a Chinese rug, has gleaming subdued greens matching the vases. A large chandelier like a crystal cave gives good light.

'Taiella's just over from Thailand, Howard. She's only been in England a couple of weeks, so there's a lot for her to take in.' Luke laughs in a funny way, not comfortable.

Why did Luke not tell his friend he is bringing me? That makes it very hard for me to know how I should be behaving.

'Savatdee kha.' I smile, wai-ing because I cannot help it, that is how my mum and dad always teaching me to greet strangers when I growing up in my village. In Thailand it is super important how you greet people.

The old man watches me, eyes a little bit soft. 'Delighted to meet you, m'dear. Charming, charming.' He puts out his hands, touching mine, clears his throat many times. Finally he putting out his cigar in a jade ashtray, pointing that we now go through to the open plan living room area, past the front entrance. It is not like Luke house, there is no corridor. Here is a very big room with many windows and walls all painted white. Many curtains, also white. The whole floor in this room is covered in fluffy white fitted carpeting, also furnished with white leather chairs and sofas. I am uncomfortable, stand on one foot, wondering if necessary for me to off shoes, or not correct to do so?

Luke pushes my shoulders, I take very small steps and go in, very slow. Many big paintings hanging on the walls, I can tell similar to pictures hanging in a gallery, but very strange, not showing people or animals, only patterns. Big chandelier hanging very low from ceiling above a long ebony table with a large flower arrangement, very tasteful. Lights showing hundreds of little glass pieces twinkling, turning in the smallest draught. Now I can also distinguish rugs hanging on the walls, like paintings, but these are silk carpets from Iran, the same type I seeing in department store in Krung Thep. Europeans always buy very expensive carpets in Thailand, even when Thai assistants telling customers they will not survive well in the rainy season.

How do I address this man? He takes up a beautiful glass bottle already filled with amber liquid, pours more liquid into his glass and drinks all in one gulp.

'Geraldine's still in the bedroom – sorry, boudoir. Making herself beautiful.' He is looking at me very hard, nose now bright red. 'Bit of competition there, I'm afraid. You're enchanting, m'dear.' Grinning now at Luke, one eye winking. 'So that's what you were up to in Udon Thani.'

Standing close to Luke, very close, wishing I was not here. How long do we have to stay?

'Sit down, do, no need to stand on ceremony.'

Old man points at one sofa. I pull Luke's hand to make sure he will be sitting beside me.

'What'll it be for the little lady? Cocktail, perhaps? A Pink Lady?' Suddenly laughs very loud, so I am startled. 'I think some Buck's Fizz is called for!'

He not waiting for an answer but goes behind a bar in the corner of the room. 'Always keep the champers cooled, don't y'know. Just in case.' Taking out a bottle with a big cork, I recognise it is the same champagne Pi Panjim's friend is always drinking. 'You open it, old man. I'll get the glasses and the orange juice.'

Howard comes back, takes the bottle from Luke and begins pouring into four glasses, then putting olives and crisps on the table. I am not happy drinking alcohol, I prefer fruit juice.

'If OK, maybe I just having orange juice?'

Howard looking at me for long time, until heat crawling all over body. 'Orange juice. Right you are.'

I'm sitting in a chair which is very big for me, so I almost disappear.

'What about ice? Can you manage that?'

'Thank you. You very kind.'

I hear a door open, then shut, high heels clicking on the parquet floor. Because it is an open plan apartment I can see a stick-thin woman coming right away. She looking much older than husband. I can see immediately that she is wearing designer dress, very expensive, very beautiful, her shoes also high class. Round her neck she having huge diamond necklace, on wrist matching bracelet, and also enormous engagement ring above her wedding ring. I thinking maybe she very rich, richer than husband.

'Luke, my dear! Where *have* you been in the last little while?

You never answer your phone, and your secretary always maintains you're in a meeting!'

She not seeing me first thing because I sitting in deep chair, with Luke standing in front, blocking me. I notice she looking down at glasses on table, little frown on face, then I thinking she noticing my gold sandals.

Beautiful golden head freezing in air as she turning to Luke. 'I see we have another guest. Perhaps you'd make the introductions, Luke.'

I not knowing what to do, stand up or stay sitting? I cannot go against training my parents teaching me, so I jump up, knocking table so that big vase wobbles, spilling water. 'So sorry, fetching cloth...'

Her thin hand is rising up like a traffic cop's, meaning stop. She fixing my body in strong glare, her hand makes pushing down gestures, showing she not wanting any movement. 'Howard will see to all that. And you are?'

'This is Taiella, Geraldine. She's staying with me while we wait for a work permit for her. She's going to be my translator into Thai, Lao, Burmese and Cambodian.' Luke is grinning like a monkey, showing all teeth. 'Quite a splendid addition to my staff.'

Thin lady turning away from me, talking to Luke. 'Taiella, did you say? What kind of a name is that?' Saying very soft soft, not looking for answer, just showing feelings. Face lined but made up by high-class professional, that is very clear. Grey hair coloured a very good blonde, not harsh, and styled like a young girl's. 'So you're a polyglot? Congratulations.' She turning to me, eyes cold like a crocodile. 'You're from Laos I take it?'

Maybe my English not very good, but cannot misunderstand scornful tone, can see mouth tight as closed zipper.

'Taiella is from Thailand, Geraldine. From Isaan.'

Geraldine picks up a glass, takes a sip of Bucks Fizz. 'I see we're celebrating. Anything special?'

Howard and Luke both start talking. Geraldine lifts her glass, making mocking eyes. 'I never would have guessed Thailand. Your features are quite Laotian, aren't they?' Eyes nearly closed, like a turtle basking in the sun.

'My mum from Laos.'

'Indeed. So you celebrated the most recent Songkran with Luke, did you? In your village, was it?'

'Not in village, no. In Udon Thani. Big town near my village. Thirty miles.'

'I know where Udon is. Howard and I were in Chiang Mai last year. Also for Songkran, so we know quite a bit about it.' No more smiling now, lips so tight round glass I thinking she will take a bite.

'People celebrating much more in Chiang Mai than Udon Thani.'

'So I understand.' Draining glass she now holding out to Howard, at same time looking at Luke with angry eyes. 'So, how did you two meet? Or are you telling me you went up to the Northeast on the off chance of finding an interpreter, Luke? Those border languages are so important for your business, I know.' Eyes hooded now, like snake about to strike.

Luke takes a big gulp of cocktail Howard already pouring into his glass. 'Matter of fact we met in Bangkok. At a friend's party.'

'What an extraordinary coincidence. Your friend, or Taiella's?'

Luke looking like water buffalo bull with wounded back. 'Both, as it happens. You know Teng Japhardee, of course. He dragged me along. And Taiella was invited by a Thai friend of the Norwegian businessman who was giving the party. His fiftieth birthday, I believe.'

Beautiful, plucked eyebrows are meeting in an ugly furrow. 'Teng knew you were looking for a translator to bring back to England, and that she'd be at the party, is that what you mean?'

Luke now looking stern. 'No, Geraldine. It was a party. Lots of people there.'

'You don't say. So how come you were in Isaan together?'

I feeling very nervous, this woman not liking me, she knowing Helga and on side of number one wife. If Luke explaining he coming to meet parents Geraldine knowing right away he already planning we marry before telling Helga he wanting divorce. Very bad karma. Helga is clever lawyer and can make big big trouble.

'Looking into business, Geraldine. As always.' Luke making

excellent sculpture out of water. 'As I said, Taiella is a first class linguist. She speaks several Southeast Asian languages.'

I sip orange juice, look down at my lap.

Geraldine is preparing to raise tigers and crocodiles. 'I thought Teng was your interpreter. You're always saying how brilliant he is.' Staring at Luke, challenging. 'Quite hefty on the company payroll, at any rate.'

'Teng translates from Thai into English. He doesn't speak Lao or Burmese. Those countries border Thailand, you know. That's where Taiella's skill comes in. I was hoping to...'

Geraldine turns, looks again in my direction, Buck's Fizz shaking in her glass. 'I see. So where did you learn your English, Taiella? Went to a good school, did you?' Crocodile eyes devour clothes, stockings, sandals, finally face and hair.

'Yes. I going Military School in Udon Thani.'

'Really?' For first time eyes not glaring. 'Of course. Thais use female guards to protect the King, don't they?'

'Very great honour to guard honourable King. He not choosing girl from village.'

'I daresay not.'

'Learning English as young child. Children in my village learning each week. Important for Thai government. They sending young man teaching people in villages English, important policy for whole country. All village children always trying hard learning because knowing excellent method for getting good job.'

'Or an English husband.'

I feeling like handing out betel nuts. Instead looking straight into Geraldine eyes. This woman not having any business judging me. 'Not thinking of husband. Thinking of better life than parents. My dad making big sacrifice, sending to military school for good education.'

'So this English teacher came to your village every week?' Howard brings more orange juice, spilling some on my dress. I wiping off with handkerchief.

'Yes. All children watching American movies, wanting same standard of living. When young people having money to buy pair jeans they going city quick quick. Hard hard life in paddies.

Planting rice, tending buffalo...'

Howard nods. 'And who can blame them?'

'All this bleeding heart stuff,' Geraldine snarling now. 'You can hardly expect me to fall for that. What kind of business were you after, Luke? As far as I know the only business there is opium – the Golden Triangle. Is that what you're into now?'

Howard makes gurgling noises, turning to wife. 'Darling, you don't say things like that even in fun. Remember, we're shareholders in Luke's business. And that's strictly selling software to banks.'

'So many of them in that particular area. Renowned for it.' Geraldine sits on second sofa on other side of the table, beautiful shoes kicking at rug, hard enough to make hole.

This lady having great looks but bad breath. How long we staying, I wonder? All this juice making me needing to go to bathroom. How I asking where to find?

Doorbell ringing. I very happy hoping maybe more friends arriving, taking attention from me, making Geraldine busy.

Howard jumping up like stung by scorpion, moves to front door, but Geraldine abandoning shoe in hurry to stop him. 'I'll deal with this.'

She limping to door, opens little bit, but already I can see tall, blonde woman coming in. 'Geraldine, sweetie.' She embraces Geraldine, giving big kiss, looking quickly to Luke. 'Hi there, Luke.'

She not seeing me first thing, because the two men standing in front block me. Then I hear her taking in a big breath. Maybe she catching sight of bright colour silk dress showing between dark materials of suits the men wearing.

'I see you already have another guest.' She looks at Geraldine, I thinking maybe she even considering hitting her. Instead, she throwing big bouquet of flowers so Geraldine must catch. 'You might have told me.'

'Helga, my dear. Let's just go to the kitchen to put the flowers in water.'

'We had no idea, Helga.' Howard walks over, putting arm round blonde woman twisting away.

'Whatever. I'll see you both another time.' And she is already out of the door as she saying this, banging it shut, making lots lots noise.

AS DIFFERENT AS AN ELEPHANT AND A MOSQUITO

Geraldine has arrived in my office, uninvited, unannounced. High heels tangle in my jumble of wiring.

'I really think you should have a meeting with Helga, talk to her, Luke. There isn't any reason not to, is there? She's still your wife. And you're both civilized people.'

I can think of any number of reasons to keep well away from Helga, but the main one is that I don't feel like being trampled by a herd of heavy harangues delivered in punctilious legal language. Maybe not even all that metaphorically, either. What is there to say, anyway? Our marriage is over, a finalized divorce just a matter of form. Whatever delaying tactics she employs, however brilliant her legal arguments, there's nothing Helga can do to stop it, nothing more I have to contribute. All we'd do if we meet is regurgitate old resentments.

'I do appreciate you want to help, Geraldine. But my marriage to Helga is over, finished, kaput. Be a good friend and tell her that, convince her. Anything else will just make things worse.'

'Worse?'

Do I have to spell it out? 'Make her feel worse, prolong the discomfort.'

'But she's the woman you chose to marry! You've always been such a devoted couple, so adult in your relationship.' Geraldine is tripping round the room, blundering into printers, threatening computers. 'You can't just forget all that.'

'Of course not. Yes, I thought I was in love with Helga, I thought the world of her, admired her brilliance and her personality. I'm sorry all that has changed.'

'Helga hasn't changed. You're the one who started all this!'

Not exactly true, but is there any point trying to defend myself? 'It wasn't all my fault.'

Geraldine's cheeks spike red, her lips purse disdain. 'Two sides to every question, six of one and half a dozen of the other. So original.' She tosses the coiffured hair. 'She lived with you for ten years! There's got to be more to you than a dreary set of aphorisms!'

The intercom cuts off the rest. 'Call from Thailand for you, Mr Narland. Teng Japhardee. He says it's urgent.'

'I'll get back to him in ten minutes.' I switch off the intercom, the phone, my mobile. 'All right, let me put my point of view, Geraldine. Helga's been getting at me, belittling me for years. However hard I tried, I was never good enough.' I leaf through the morning's mail, tear a reminder to shreds. 'And she didn't hesitate to do it in front of you, did she? And others. No amount of yackety-yak, however high-flown, is going to make a darn bit of difference.' I toss my paper cup into the bin, splashing forgotten coffee.

'You're a damn bloody coward, Luke.'

'Sorry, Geraldine. The Bank of Siam...'

She gets up, clutching a small handbag to her lack of bosom. 'You're besotted with that smiling face, with a much younger woman. You're making a huge mistake.'

I stand, towering over her. 'Is that so?'

'You're infatuated, Luke. You're being ruled by your hormones. Which means you're not thinking straight.'

I walk over to the office door. 'Rubbish. I'm in love with an enchanting, sweet young girl who's given up her world for me. You think she's got nothing to lose...'

'You told us. She's been promoted to supervisor in a toy shop. Hardly the same as a top barrister.' She takes in my grim features. 'Of course I'm sure Taiella is a fine young woman. But you're quite a bit older than she is, you come from two very different cultures, different backgrounds. Have you really thought it all through?'

I stab the letter opener at the mail. 'Naturally not. I know nothing about Thailand, haven't been up to the village, haven't met the parents.' Am I talking to the admirer of all things Thai, who pestered Howard to buy a place there? Only thwarted because foreigners aren't allowed to own land in the kingdom. 'You must think me a complete idiot.' I stand, my hand twisting the door knob.

'Just let me finish, Luke. You are impulsive, much more so than Helga. She's known you for many years and, apart from loving you and hoping to put all this behind you, wants to stop you from making a ghastly mistake. For your sake, even if you don't get back together with her.' She puts a tiny, scarlet-tipped hand on my arm. 'Otherwise she'd hardly lay herself open to being rejected again.'

I twist away. Would my meeting her serve any sort of purpose, make Helga feel better or something? 'I don't think...'

'You're so wrong. You've never even discussed things face to face.'

'She was the one who took off!'

'You owe her a personal explanation, not cowardly tactics hiding behind lawyers.'

Rich one coming from one of those lawyers! 'What good could it do?'

The bird-like feet patter around me. 'You've never given Helga a chance to tell you how *she* feels about all this. You owe her that at least after ten years.'

I twist the door knob back and forth. 'It wasn't working, Geraldine. Every time she saw me Helga had some sort of criticism – I wasn't earning enough, I wasn't smart enough, I had no taste in clothes or furnishings, I never knew what I wanted...' Except, of course, this time. I certainly know what I want. I'm crystal clear on that.

'She could be right!'

Doesn't that say it all? If she's right, or feels she is, why would I stay with her? Why continue to make each other miserable? 'If it was only me, all my fault, how come I'm having a wonderful relationship with another woman now?'

'Hormones, Luke. And, however sweet she is, a Thai village girl is hardly in a position to rate you. You just can't see that at the moment.' She takes my hand off the door knob, opens the door. 'Give Helga a chance, Luke. That isn't asking too much, is it?' She twitters in front of me and teeters out through reception.

CONFUSED LIKE A CHICK
WITH SHATTERED EYES

I now having very great longing to go back to Thailand. Every day I thinking of my country, how happy there, how many friends surrounding me. This is very troubling and I not knowing what is right for me to do —staying here, or visiting sister in Krung Thep, or maybe returning to my village for thinking through what I should be doing.

I understand very well that Luke is very happy when I living in his English house. I knowing this because he always coming home singing, every day. Only sad time is when phone ringing. Then Luke worries because he thinking Helga or Helga mum calling him. If he answering they shouting abuse. So he finds very simple solution: he not answering telephone. He buys me a mobile phone so we can talk with each other without problems. But he asking me not to call at the office, he very busy right now because extra important he making more money now Helga no longer paying share of household bills.

I do exactly what Luke asking, but I finding very uncomfortable to listen, often for long time, to phone ringing maybe twenty times. Then knowing right away this is Helga or Helga mum calling. If we setting on answering machine they leaving long, rude messages. Of course I understand they cannot reach me, but still this ringing making me feel nervous in case maybe they ring door bell instead of using telephone.

Luke already applying for work permit for me so that I can

be in his office, but is very long time coming. Also Luke tries hard to find something I can do during long working day. He arranging English classes starting late in September this autumn time. So looking forward to studying, meeting students from many countries. But most of all I hoping to meet Thai people.

In meantime he suggests I act like tourist in London, there are so many interesting excursions I can take part in. However, I am not happy sightseeing on own self, therefore I have no choice and must stay in Luke's house, alone. To occupy my time I cleaning for many hours, and gardening. But Luke's garden not very big, so not taking that much time. I even started crocheting big big blanket, for something to pass boring time.

Now is afternoon, and at last I can think about what I making for dinner. I decide to go shopping, this having also advantage of leaving house. Good house, but beginning to feel like prison cell.

It is short walk to nearby Tesco. I walking slow slow, taking as long as possible for trip so filling some of long hours when by own self. Living this way not easy after village life. There, many girls and women always together in groups, talking, laughing. Even in Krung Thep many other girls work in same department store, we having much fun chattering and giggling. Thinking such thoughts, walking along busy Shepherds Bush Road without looking at other people, suddenly hear voice, quite loud:

'Sawatdee Khrab!'

Now I am smiling full face to hear words in own language. Not only words. Is Thai voice having strong Isaan dialect, so right away I knowing this person coming from Northeast Thailand.

'Sawatdee Kha!' I saying right off, almost dancing in street I am so happy to hear Thai. Already sadness forgotten, only wishing woman and not man giving greeting.

Man looking at me straight, eyes checking hair, face, figure. 'What you doing here, younger sister? Living this street?'

This man speaking Thai language from village, I knowing right away he not having much education. Intonation is of Lao person, like my mum. Also noticing clothes very new but also very cheap. Thinking he coming to this country short time ago. After a little I knowing he looking a little bit rough type man, but so happy hearing Thai words I forgive him for not combing his hair, for dirty shoes. 'Not living Shepherds Bush Road, no. Living in side street, Cromwell Grove, house number seventy,' I explain, already excited. 'You living nearby, older brother?'

'Renting from relative living in apartment in house end same street.' Smiling all over face, nodding. 'House having number eighty-two.'

End of Cromwell Road is all council houses. Luke telling me people living there not allowed to have tenants. Maybe this man OK because he is a relative.

Seeing doubt in my face. 'Is OK because living with daughter of younger sister of mother. My cousin having two small children. You also having children?'

'Not yet.' Every time thinking about this I am a little bit sad, I cannot stop smile running away in sadness. Why am I not having a baby? I want that very much, and Luke also wanting so much because Helga refusing having children and he not wanting to be age of grandfather when he at last becoming father. But nothing happening. Luke already suggesting maybe we visit doctor in Hammersmith Hospital. This place world famous for treating problems when not having children.

'Maybe you lonely, younger sister? Husband working daytime, and you all by self?' Looking at me with eyes a little bit slit. I not understanding why, but instincts warning me that I not liking this man. Still, he from my country so I am happy to talk with him. 'Then maybe you having time visiting my cousin and little boy and girl?' he asking now.

I smile again, but decide to say nothing. Maybe his cousin is a pleasant woman I would like, and also I would be very happy to see the children.

'You coming with me now, younger sister? Good time for visiting.'

I am not clear why I am very anxious, feeling nervous. Wanting to meet Thai woman very much, want even more to play with kids. Starting to open mouth for saying yes, we can go, when cloud of small insects buzzing round head and into mouth so I cannot speak.

Luke telling these little insects called midges always flying in clouds when weather wet and warm. I seeing them in evening time in Luke's garden, but they never flying into my mouth before. Right away I am nervous, thinking perhaps insects are Nong Wuadon's spirit, warning me against Thai stranger? Maybe I liking cousin of this man, but I knowing very well I not wanting to be with this stranger on own.

'Husband coming home soon soon, older brother. Better I wait for visiting with him.'

Face changing to angry, I seeing even though Thai stranger putting hand over mouth and eyes, then through hair, so hiding emotions very quickly. 'Is small apartment, younger sister. Not easy fitting in lots people.'

His voice sharp, but he calming down. Something in eyes reminding me of someone I know. Maybe in Dumden Village, maybe in Krung Thep. Or maybe because I am lonely, remembering Thai friends and family, therefore anyone from my country bringing memories of what I am missing. Very hard to know what I do now. I not wanting to leave this man but also I not wanting to go with this man.

'Of course I understand such difficulties. Maybe good solution for you and cousin and children coming to my house? Having big space, husband owning whole house.'

Thai man looking sideways, little bit strange, as if finding surprising what I am saying. 'You already married, younger sister?'

'What you meaning to say?' How he knowing I am not married?

Standing so close I cannot move without touching him, this making me very nervous. 'You looking too young to having husband, younger sister.'

This not good answer, it makes me worry more. Nobody mistaking me for very young girl less than sixteen years. Thai brother now has lips very wide, teeth showing big and white, eyes hard. This is smile of liar.

Why this stranger caring if I married or not married? Already knowing I only talking with this man because so happy to hear voice reminding of home when so far from Dumden Village.

Now man closing lids over eyes, hiding thoughts. 'Cousin and

I happy visiting you and husband. Give phone number and cousin ringing you.'

Eyes wide open now, he looking not so bad. Maybe I making mistake because midges buzzing round me and therefore I finding it hard to think straight. I understanding very well this man having same kinds of problems as me. He is also foreigner in unknown land, and now I feel sorry for my bad thoughts. But what is the right solution? I cannot give this stranger Luke telephone number, we not answering. Not understanding why, but having very strong feeling not to give mobile number. 'OK,' I decide. 'You give me your cousin number. Grocery shopping taking long time. I calling when returning home.'

When coming back from Tesco with many bags, turning corner of Shepherds Bush Road and Cromwell Grove, seeing red BMW parking outside Luke house. Recognising Helga's car right off.

Stop on pavement, go back to Shepherds Bush Road, thinking very deep. Turning round I seeing Helga at front door of No 70, trying key in lock. Luke already changing lock, but now I do not have the opportunity to go inside because this is a terrace house, no back entrance. Therefore I walking away to other side, my head down, towards higher numbers. What was Thai brother saying? House number eighty something. I not remembering which house, I not knowing his name, but having telephone number. Dial very quick on mobile. Little bit strange, but not knowing what else I can do.

'Yes? Who calling?'

Voice of woman, but not with Thai accent. More like Indian, maybe Bengali or Pakistani. Why a villager from Isaan having an Indian cousin? Not having any choice, now must do something so Helga not seeing me.

'I meeting your cousin short time ago, sister. Coming from Thailand. He saying good idea we meeting, becoming friends.'

First is only silence, then child making noise, mother shushing in language I not understanding.

'Sorry if not convenient, sister. Ringing later.'

'Not cousin, sister. Having lodger. He coming from Bangladesh, not Thailand. Maybe here for two weeks. You girlfriend? Wanting I take message for him?'

'No problem, sister. Having wrong number.' My suspicions are very correct. Something wrong with this Thai man, giving a number he inventing.

Shopping bags now feeling very heavy, but cannot go home. Remembering I can sit in Brook Green playground, watching children. Lots mothers with prams, toddlers climbing on frame, having fun on swings. I enjoy seeing children play, maybe also have opportunity to meet a Thai mother. So longing for having family, holding baby in my loving arms. Meanwhile enjoying watching mothers play with their children.

I wondering if I telling Luke about meeting Thai man? Still I worry about midges. Not same as robber fly, but I becoming very frightened. If I telling Luke he thinking me foolish, superstitious woman from Thai village. Then maybe he changing his mind and not marrying me.

AN ANT WATCHING OVER A BUNCH OF MANGOES

I walk into the Café Rouge, search for the right table: away from other diners, but not too discreet. I've deliberately come early so Helga wouldn't spot a set-up.

She's already sitting in the corner behind the door, half a carafe of red in front of her. She must have seen me look around, but didn't call out. Now she's inspecting my shoes, my trousers, my jacket, finally my face. 'Hello Luke. This is a surprise!'

I ball my fists inside my trouser pockets, squeeze my face into a kind of smile. 'Helga. How are you?' The carafe is almost empty, her eyes have that uncertain look.

'Thirsty. Let's order a full carafe. The house wine's very good.'

'Not for me...'

'Waiter!'

I dig my nails into my palms, splutter in the smoky air and look across to the non-smoking section. 'D'you think we could move over to...'

'Christ, Luke. Sit down! Always such a fuss. Allergies are in the mind, I've told you that dozens of times.' She twirls a chair. 'At least this side keeps the kiddies at bay.' She pours the rest of the wine, gulps it down.

I sit, as near the door and fresh air as I can get.

'Waiter! Another carafe – make it a litre.'

'It's lunch time, Helga. I've got to get back to the office later.'

'So what are you doing here, then?' Somewhat blood-shot blue eyes narrow into me, California nails click her glass, she crumples a menu. 'Meeting someone for lunch? A lady friend, perhaps?'

'I'm on my own. What about you?'

She twirls a beer mat on its side, spinning it like a top – rather impressively. 'Just whiling away time until the next case. Not till three this afternoon.'

Her Chambers are in the City, she's living in Hampstead. Hammersmith is at least six miles from either. I grab another menu and try to read. The only dish that I reckon I can stomach is scallops choo chee with pad Thai.

'Don't know how you can stand that stuff. Those spices completely ruin perfectly good scallops. I'll have the Coquilles St. Jacques au poivre de Széchuan et au saké.' She pushes the menu at the waiter, drinks from her refilled glass.

My scalp itches irritation. A waitress brings cutlery, serviettes. 'Carlsberg, please. Half a pint.'

Helga opens her handbag, takes out a compact, pats her cheeks. Still that heavy flush. 'So, what d'you think?' Her eyebrows turn into question marks. 'Don't say you haven't noticed.'

I blink. Has she sent through something about the divorce?

'My hair, slow coach! What d'you think I'm doing here? Spying on you? Of course you don't remember – as usual. Nina's the only one who can get the colour right.'

I've forgotten she dyes her hair and has a local hairdresser. Now there are red-gold streaks mingled with shades of blonde. A darker shade would have toned down the crimson glow.

'Same old Luke. You could use a good hairdresser yourself.' Clawed fingers feel the material of my coat. 'Can't afford to let yourself go, you know.'

I check my watch, twist the menu, put it on the table behind me.

'Am I keeping you? I assumed you'd come in for lunch.'

Saintliness was never one of my virtues, but spelling out Geraldine's plan would be nudging suicide as well as upsetting Helga for no reason.

'Helga, please. We've got the chance to have a friendly chat, talk things over. Or just catch up. We don't have to be enemies.'

'No, we don't, do we?' Highlighted tresses sprawl over the hands covering her face, red nails peeking through. 'I love you, Luke.' She pushes back her hair, her hands sneak over to my right hand innocently straightening the cutlery on my side. She envelops it, holds it. 'You know there's never been anyone else, that I'd do anything for you.'

Blood speeds through veins I didn't know existed, blooming sweat even to the tips of my ears. I rescue my hand, fish out a handkerchief, wipe. Why did I allow Geraldine to bully me into this charade?

'You do know how much you're hurting me, don't you?'

She's already tipsy, aggression mere seconds away. She tilts the carafe over her glass and spills wine into it, drinks it in one gulp, then fills it again. 'Waiter! A packet of Players Medium.' Blood-shot, watery eyes fasten on me. 'You haven't become teetotal, have you? Foresworn pork?'

'Taiella is Buddhist, not Muslim. And I'm a Christian, if you remember.'

'Of course I do.' Her teeth are showing that yellow tinge tobacco ads don't mention. 'Till death us do part.'

'And for the procreation of children.'

'Taiella. That's her name, is it? Bit trite.'

'It's a Thai name, one her parents gave her. Just like our parents chose our names.'

'Whatever.' She drinks the rest of the contents of the glass, looks around for the waiter. 'They're so slow here.'

'Helga...'

'You know you're the only man I've ever loved, the only one I can be happy with. You know that, don't you, Luke?'

With millions of better-looking, brighter, richer men in the world she can only love me? Am I a pea-brain to fall for that? What does she think she's talking about? 'You've always said I have no taste, Helga. I'm sure you're right.'

The waiter brings a packet of cigarettes, opens it, offers one to Helga and produces a lighter. She inhales, sighs.

'I must tell you I was very disappointed.'

'In what way?' What is that supposed to mean?

'When I saw your choice. You're trading me in for a nobody, a girl from an obscure Thai village in the north, a country bumpkin with no inkling about the western world. How long d'you think that's going to last?'

Shades of Taiella's father! 'I don't trade wives, Helga. Our marriage hasn't worked for years, and now I've found someone I think I can be happy with. I'm not saying it's because of you...'

She puffs, blows smoke into my face. 'Thought it was because we didn't have children. She's pregnant already, I expect.'

That honed instinct always on target. 'I would like children, yes. But that isn't really what it's about. We don't get on, Helga. You've told me dozens of times how useless I am, how uncultured, a low earner.'

The cigarette end glows red. 'Well, you are. But I was willing to overlook all that.'

'So kind.'

She splutters, drinks more wine. 'Just what d'you think you have in common with some bar girl from Bangkok? You'll be bored the second the sexual excitement blows over. And it will, I absolutely guarantee it. A few months at most.'

'Taiella is not a bar girl, she's been made supervisor in the toy department of the ZenZam Centre in Bangkok.'

'Wow. The toy department. Got the teddy bear already, have you?'

'She does come from a village, yes. And she hasn't had much formal education. But she's bright, quick to catch on, and charming.'

'Fantastic.'

'None of that matters. She loves me for what I am, not for what she would like me to be. That's what it's all about. She's not after some mythical superman, someone I have to live up to. She's settled for what she's got.'

'That's what you think, is it?'

'It's what I know.'

'Stubborn as always. Wrong as always.' She pours another glass, gulps it down, stands. 'I've no intention of wasting any more of my time. My clients pay three hundred quid an hour, you know.'

She takes another drag at her cigarette, stubs it out, pushes back her chair and walks as briskly as the amount of red she's drunk will let her.

The waiter's eyes follow her. He shrugs, puts the pad Thai in the empty place, the Coquilles in front of me.

I toy with ringing Taiella, decide against it. 'The bill,' I say, pushing the French-style scallops away. 'The lady isn't coming back.'

ESCAPE FROM THE TIGER AND END UP WITH THE CROCODILE

'Looking all over!'

The Thai man I meeting two days gone is running across the street, waving. I not wanting to talk, but also not wanting to make scene.

'Sawatdee Kha!'

'You not phoning cousin, younger sister. And calling at house number you giving me but no one answering.'

True, I never answering when someone coming to door, always staying upstairs or in rooms at back of house. I frightened that Helga or Helga's mum coming.

'You making mistake, older brother. I phoning cousin. Sister answering not from Thailand. Maybe from Pakistan, India, Bangladesh – but not Thai.'

He grinning, wide teeth, one missing on right upper side. Making Thai brother look like criminal. 'Maybe you not writing down correct number? Easy putting down wrong numeral.'

'Perhaps. Not having number now. Cannot remember long number.'

'You making mistake, younger sister. No problem coming now and visiting cousin.'

Of course possible I making mistake when dialling number, very nervous at that time because of seeing Helga car. Also I

217

worrying that Helga seeing me standing on street. Not likely she remembering how I look, she only catching glimpse in apartment of Luke friends. But when she seeing a Thai girl in street outside Luke house she guessing I am Luke girlfriend.

I starting to walk towards bigger number houses on Cromwell Grove, but Thai man running forward, turns, stands in way so I cannot pass. 'Cousin not living this road. Living Poplar Grove next road along. We walking along Melrose Terrace and finding.'

It is a beautiful day, green leaves with blotches of yellow on the trees lining the road. Many of the little red cherries are falling down, dropped by the birds. The road is very wet and I nearly slipping when Thai brother coming too close to me, making me nervous. 'Last time you saying address Cromwell Grove number eighty-something. Not remembering which number.'

Wide teeth smile much more like shark when he shaking head. 'Not thinking too well, younger sister. Saying number eighty-two Poplar Grove. Similar Cromwell Grove, maybe why you remembering wrong.'

Small sun in and out of leaves on trees making it hard for me to see Thai face. I not liking sound of his voice, now harsh and not friendly. I feeling cold with fear, looking round at people in street walking by. Will anyone helping me if this man attacking me?

'Why you slow down like this? You not want see my cousin? She very happy seeing you, also her children happy...'

This man's face appearing darker now, sweating very hard in cool English weather. Why is he sweating so much? It is not hot, like in Thailand. A cloud of midges suddenly appearing from nowhere, buzzing around the man's head. He swatting hard with both hands. Now I knowing for sure that this cloud is Nong Wuadon warning me about this man.

'You not telling truth about street. You saying Cromwell Grove.' I walking away from him very fast. He running after me, grabbing me. No proper Thai man would do this. I noticing a white van drive past, so I shout 'Stop!', pulling away from the no-good Thai.

The white van pulls up, and another Thai man jumps out, sliding open the passenger door. 'Get in quick! This man no good.'

I recognise man owning Thai grocery. Already knowing this man very well, very polite person from southernmost tip of Thailand. More Malaysian than Thai. I jump into van, very upset. No-good Thai running away, bumping into tree. I seeing cloud midges all over head, so Thai man cannot see where he is going.

Grocery man slides the van door shut, runs to the other side. I recognising him because he selling me Thai magazines, and also I often talking with his wife. Kind people but not reminding me of my home village, they not from Isaan. 'You very kind stopping and helping, older brother. This man could have accomplices. You very brave.'

Smiling lovely Thai smile he nodding head. 'We going my shop now, younger sister. You sitting in shop, having tea, talking my wife. She keeping you safe until husband coming home.'

ONE ROTTEN FISH MAKES THE WHOLE CATCH SMELL

'You really think he was actually trying to abduct you?'

Surely Helga hasn't hired a kidnapper? Glib promises of a safe, genteel part of London melt like ice cream in Bangkok heat.

Taiella is tearful, desperate to be hugged. I'm just as desperate to do the hugging. 'You telling no problems in this part London if not crossing Shepherds Bush Green after dark, tilac. Therefore walking on Shepherds Bush Road, streets nearby, only during day.'

Runnels of fury charge up and down my arms, hairs stand to attention, sweat collects in pools, saturates clothing, falls into stinging eyes. I lock and bolt the front door, stomp out into the garden, inspect the neighbours' partition fences for signs of abuse. Nothing.

Could Helga really have resorted to this? Is she willing to risk her career for revenge on a younger rival? Ridiculous. Would Geraldine – preposterous. Could there be a Thai connection? Even more far-fetched. None of it seems real.

I've been nervous about leaving Taiella on her own for so many hours every day. Not because I thought she'd be abducted; that never crossed my mind. Other dangers. She's managed to kill the tropical fish by replacing their warm water with cold – clean, as she put it – water from the tap. Water in Thailand is never that cold! I worried she'd do herself damage with unfamiliar machines, or that she'd be lonely. But I know she doesn't need much language to understand the people around her. She proved herself astute in Bangkok when she arrived, straight from backward Isaan. She overcame that distinctive and despised Isaan accent and dark skin to land an excellent job.

The dangers I imagined were coming face to face with Helga or, worse, Helga's ghastly mother. Even that eventuality, I'm sure, would have turned into a purely verbal battle. Abuse, shrieked words – but no sticks and stones.

I can't afford to spend time away from the office. I have to grow the business. Howard is demanding more sales in the Far East. I know I have to go back to Thailand at some stage, so I'm concentrating on finding more business there.

We're in bed, the doors locked, the bolts drawn, the curtains dark against the dusk. 'Wasn't very wise to talk to a complete stranger just because he speaks Thai, tilac. This is London, you know. Can be a dangerous place. He could be a white trader!'

Taiella's shoulder punches my chin. 'Bangkok dangerous city, tilac. More desperate people than in London. Know very well how looking after self.'

'You had to be rescued!' A chance attack by a lonely Thai carried away by Taiella's sweet smile, enticing figure? Not very likely. Instead, it reminds me of the murdered Wuadon. Perhaps there was more to that killing than the jealous rage of a smitten uncle. Possibly some sort of kidnapping gang was involved. But what could they want with Taiella? Hold her as a hostage to get hold of me? And what do they think I know?

Taiella snuggles into a spoon shape. 'Girl trade not worrying. Too old. Thinking maybe knowing this man, but not remembering where meeting this stranger.'

'Someone from Isaan in Hammersmith?' I tilt her head back, kiss from above. I realise that if she's come across him at some stage it means he knows her. Which means she'd recognise him sooner or later. 'You sure about that?'

'No. Not sure. Maybe homesick, wanting see Thai person from village, so perhaps hoping, imagining.'

'Not actually sure what he could have been after, whether he was really trying to abduct you...'

Her feet push into my legs as she twists round and levers herself away. 'What you mean trying? If older brother from Thai shop not there that man grabbing and dragging off street. Not big man, but very firm, big muscles. Not able fighting off such strong man.'

I pull her back, cuddle her. 'Be sensible, tilac. He couldn't have got far without a car...'

She struggles hard, and she's no weakling with muscles honed hard by working in the paddies, then spending hours in the toy department climbing ladders, lugging heavy crates. I have to use full strength. She isn't able to stop me holding her. 'Maybe dragging to house of cousin and locking inside!'

'He might just have been as keen as you to get to know another Thai, reluctant to see you go.'

She kicks my shins hard. 'Stranger try grabbing! Proper Thai man not acting this way.'

'He could have made a genuine mistake with the phone number, you know. Does happen.'

'Giving wrong number, tilac! Knowing for sure.'

'Got the right area code. Why don't we go and have a proper chat with the man who runs the Thai grocery? He's very likely to know about any Thais who've come to the area recently.'

She slithers away, throws the duvet at me to slow me down. 'Thinking spending time there for two hours and not asking? Thinking not talking to wife?'

'Well...'

'Already knowing other local Thais thinking this man no good. Not knowing where coming from, what doing here. Not having friends in area, therefore everybody very suspicious this stranger.'

'You'll be telling me next that he's connected with Ban or Mak, trying to take you hostage so that the Udon Thani police release Mak!'

'That foolish remark, tilac. Know police not doing any such thing.'

'It was a joke, tilac.' Maybe not that far off the mark at that. This man could, somehow, be connected with Mak Kamuki.

I untangle myself from the duvet, slip on some clothes. 'Perhaps he wanted a hostage because I'm going to be a witness...' My giggle tails off. That idea makes more sense than is altogether comfortable.

Taiella's hair spins round as she rushes at me, a dark halo framing a startled face. 'Thinking that right, tilac! Now remembering! Are Mak knowing Lao men Lung Ban calling cousins, inviting for visiting. Remembering now. Nong Wuadon always telling: rough men coming to village, talking to girls. Village girls not liking, too much hiding in bamboo, ambushing girls and kissing.'

There are several other Thais in this part of Hammersmith – waiters in the many Thai restaurants which have become so popular. The grocery draws them like a magnet. Thais only eat their own type of rice – in Thailand they have shops which sell nothing else, offering around twenty varieties. Basmati isn't nearly good enough. The grocery also tantalizes with fresh fruit and vegetables flown in from Southeast Asia. Was it luck that the owner was driving by when Taiella needed him, or does he know more than he's letting on? I'm beginning to imagine Thai thugs lurking under every bird cherry tree on Poplar Grove, fallen fruit running dark red under their thundering feet.

'You're thinking Mak might have had accomplices? That they might have been planning to kidnap Wuadon as part of some service industry they were involved in?'

'Thinking police finding out lots men involving, maybe whole gang. Maybe not just after Nong Wuadon, maybe abducting many girls.'

'So you do suspect girl trafficking.'

'Is possible.' She opens the curtains, eyes focusing beyond the garden, searching the spirit world, seeing beyond intellectual reasoning. 'Maybe gang planning crime police finding more worrying. Maybe trafficking drugs. Honourable Prime Minister very keen stopping drug trade in Thailand.' She comes to sit on my lap, puts firm arms around my neck, rubs noses. 'Thinking maybe I knowing something, tilac. Thinking they would already kidnapping me in Krung Thep if I am target, while waiting for visa. This just a warning, gang wanting to frighten both of us to keep silent.'

'But I don't know anything!'

'Maybe not understanding what knowing, tilac. Village ways different from English ways. Maybe cannot telling how gang members thinking.'

Idyllic fantasies of simple village folk morph into gargoyles of thugs. Mak could be backed by a gang of unsavoury Laotians. Bangkok sex establishments pay well for country girls, particularly virgins. Isn't that what the villagers' angst is all about? Perhaps Wuadon just happened to be the latest victim, murdered because Mak was so crazy about her he muffed the kidnapping. Or maybe Taiella is right: Wuadon was a sideline, the real business is drugs.

'I'm getting panic buttons put in,' I announce. 'Don't go out on your own again, tilac. What with Helga on the rampage and this Laotian character, I want you staying in.'

'Cannot stay in house all day, tilac. That driving me crazy. Maybe good idea returning to Thailand. Maybe you following soon for trial, tilac. Then getting together again that time.'

Why had I gone to that damned village? One thing after another since then to keep us apart. Or is it worse than that? Is Taiella actually unhappy here? Am I about to lose my lovely girl?

'Where in Thailand, tilac? What would you do?'

'Stay with parents, help in village.'

'You can't, sweetheart! You'd be worse off than here! What happened to Wuadon could happen to you!'

I've started to read meaning into those dimpling cheeks. She's determined to go back. I can't blame her. 'Why not go and stay with your sister?'

'Dumden villagers know I always staying with Pi Sayai.' She looks sideways, strokes my cheek. 'Better staying with Pi Panjim.'

'A girlfriend? Don't think you mentioned her before.'

'Pi Panjim taking me to boyfriend party, tilac. Same party you arriving with Khun Teng, on day we meeting.'

'You mean the hairdresser, the one who also works in the ZenZam Centre?'

'No need to worry. Ladyboy, not finding girls interesting except as friend.'

I remember that all right. And I also remember the Norwegian boyfriend as a bisexual with unrestrained appetites. 'What about the boyfriend?'

'Is Norway time. Very safe, no one thinking of me staying in

Pi Panjim place.'

'I suppose so. You will lie low, won't you? No rushing round to the toy department, telling them all you're back.'

'No problem. Understanding Bangkok very good, tilac.'

'I'll be over as soon as I can – ten days at the outside. Let's hope the General's got the trial date set. Maybe I should be getting in touch with him and telling him our suspicions.'

LOOKING FOR LICE TO PUT ON ONE'S HEAD

I finding very uncomfortable living in Krung Thep. Pi Panjim on holiday with family in Isaan, another friend already staying in room so I cannot stay there. I decide to stay with older sister Pi Sayai. No running water, such sticky hot air, many kinds of bad smell and so much noise pressing on ears from all directions I never noticing before. When walking in street traffic fumes so bad almost not possible to breathe.

Luke asking one thing only I must do: to telephone every day from office run by Khun Teng Japhardee. Luke always very kind when I telling that thoughts about Celestial City are different now, after returning from London. Right away he offering money for renting bigger place, with air con. I discuss with Pi Sayai and invite her to move with me, but she not wanting this. She worries about what happening to her and her young son after Luke and I will marry and return to England. She only minor wife and husband cannot afford big apartment excepting for first wife.

I have much time so today I go to hospital to find out why baby not coming. Doctor says nothing wrong, gives medicine to take every day. 'This medicine making you relax, young woman. Next time boyfriend visits you making baby for sure.'

I promising Luke not to visit my friends in department store, or meeting friends in evening. All this meaning I am very bored. Same situation as in London, except now I not having Luke house to clean, or to work in garden, and I cannot look forward to seeing

Luke in evening time. Pi Sayai having own job. She cooks early every morning, then goes out and sells meals on Krung Thep streets while my nephew attending school. This meaning I feel more lonely even than in London.

Six days after arriving I think hard all day and finally I make decision: I asking for an interview with my Excellency Lieutenant General Thomupi in the Metropolitan Police Headquarters of Krung Thep. Is very important he knowing that maybe not only one man is involved in murder of Nong Wuadon, could be whole gang. Maybe also he can now tell me at what time he will need Luke as witness in coming trial.

Of course not easy to set up meeting with such an important man. Big security arrangements always in force in case gunmen try killing dignitary in such high position as Lieutenant General Thomupi. Therefore not surprising that officer at front counter of police station very worried by my request and calling police sergeant for help in such difficult situation. Police sergeant on duty refusing to believe I knowing eminent Police General. He getting angry when I insisting I wish to speak with my Excellency in person.

'How can young woman from Isaan know such important man?' He looking down squat nose so eyes almost crossing. I upset, because wearing clothes I buying with money Luke giving me to look correct. Though now speaking proper Thai maybe police sergeant can still hear a little bit Lao accent in my nervous voice. Perhaps that explaining why he not thinking me proper person for meeting with my Excellence Police Lieutenant General Thomupi.

'My venerable Excellency not wasting time talking to unknown woman asking for meeting.' Sergeant talking, looking with hard eyes, then picking up telephone and waving me away.

I smiling as hard as possible, offer food older sister preparing this morning. She is excellent cook, and aroma of chicken marinated in fragrant lemon grass and coriander entices suspicious policeman to sample little piece of food I offering. Big look of pleasure changes features. He taking more and nodding head.

Now he turning to inferior. 'You leaving for lunch break right now, Nong Constable. Important for me questioning this young woman by own self. I calling when needing you.'

Already I understand older sister's cooking has found favour. I put on special winning smile. 'You almost correct, Khun Sergeant. I not meeting outstanding Excellency in Krung Thep.' I make deep bow, from waist, and do everything to look like well-behaved young lady who very clear Khun Police Sergeant is superior being. 'He visiting Police Headquarters in Udon Thani to check on police procedures there, just before Songkran time this year.'

'You have more chicken?' Khun Sergeant licking lips and looking at Pi Sayai basket. 'Maybe enough for me taking some back to wife?'

I remove cloth from basket, showing not only chicken but also fresh pink shrimps and two bottles fragrant sauces older sister making. He can see these very special, and I take off container lids and offer him to smell. 'I very happy if you take whole basket, Khun Sergeant. Then you and beautiful wife enjoying this special food in comfort, at home.'

Face changing from grim, hard lines to soft curved moons. He comes out from behind counter, putting index finger into one sauce, scooping up and putting on tongue. 'Tastes very delicious!'

'Perhaps you showing exceptional kindness and telephoning secretary to my gracious Excellency.' I smile with lips spread wide, eyes soft and at the same time offer hungry sergeant the whole basket. 'Then you understanding what I telling is truth. Also I have important information for my venerable Excellency about special case he investigating.'

Now Khun Sergeant looking at me with eyes stony like pebbles. 'You knowing something about any case under investigation, your duty to report.'

Scalp beginning to sweat as I realise I making big mistake. Change voice now to very soft, very gentle. 'That is why I here, Khun Sergeant. Perhaps you will be so kind and informing my Excellency's secretary.'

'Unavailable Excellency not in habit of speaking with witnesses direct.' He takes basket, removes cloth and looks inside again. Eyes enlarge, glitter. He picks up telephone and speaks to gruff-

228

sounding man at other end.

'Young woman here saying she having urgent information about negligent Udon Thani Police Major. Important to bring this matter to attention of Tan Police Captain Worluti.'

'If you excusing interruption, Khun Sergeant, but I cannot help hearing what you saying. I do not have information about excellent Tan Police Major in Udon Thani. My information is about – '

'Do not exciting, young woman. Tan Captain Worluti assisting my Excellency with Udon Thani police procedures. He agree seeing you later today. You wait here until he having time for you.' Khun Sergeant picks up food basket and puts under front counter so hidden from people coming into police station. Counter phone starts ringing and he very busy answering. I can see no possibility he talking more with me.

At last he flicks eyes over in my direction, picks up phone and subordinate coming in and taking over. Khun Sergeant leaves, not wai-ing goodbye to me.

I remain patient, hoping I will convincing Tan Captain Worluti that I really do know my outstanding Excellency Police Lieutenant General Thomupi, and also that it is very important that I speak with him in person.

Many hours pass as I waiting for Tan Captain Worluti coming. At last, almost at time of sound of drum, when sun almost setting, young man in brand new uniform opens flap from behind front counter of police station, walking quickly to where I sit and staring at me. I now very tired, also faint from not having any food all day. I asking policeman in charge of desk for water at lunchtime. At first he refusing, but when I telling maybe I fainting he giving me some, all time with deep line down forehead, frowning very hard.

Young man stands right by me, looking up and down body. I rise and wai to him, quite low but not as low as to Khun Police Sergeant. I can see he new recruit, meaning he not very important.

'Sawatdee Kha,' I say in polite but distant manner.

He not wai-ing back. 'You awaiting Tan Captain Worluti?' Eyes half-closed, upper lip in sneer.

'Yes, Khun Constable.' Better using Khun address to give

plenty respect.

He picks up mobile and walks away while talking. I decide to remain standing, leaning backs of legs against chair because feeling quite weak.

'You Taiella Motubaki?'

Still standing, I bow again. Man approaching is middle-aged, wearing full Captain uniform. He is a lizard who likes to show he has a golden necklace. Irritable eyes examine my hair, face, body. 'Yes, Tan Captain.' I decide to flatter with ingratiating address.

'You have information regarding Udon Thani Police Major?'

This sounding a little bit worrying. I know officials in our Heavenly City always hoping to catch Isaan officials out for making mistakes. They assuming we all stupid country yokels. 'I having information about special case my brilliant Excellency Police Lieutenant General Thomupi investigating himself, Tan Captain. He taking over from Tan Police Major Monkahn in Udon Thani.'

Slight shoulders of Captain draw back, eyebrows knot. 'You making serious mistake, young woman. Honourable Excellency only going to Udon Thani for assessing police operations in Northeast Thailand. He not involving with particular cases.'

'Please excuse me not agreeing with you, Tan Captain. My Excellency coming to Dumden Village, investigating murder of young girl, Wuadon Kamuki. Rape and murder taking place outside village, few days before Songkran festival early this year.'

Tan Captain drawing himself up to full height, only little bit taller than me. 'I repeat, young lady. You making very bad mistake. Why my exalted Excellency bother with problems in rural areas? He having important work he doing here, in our City of Angels. He not having time for remote Isaan areas.' Tan Captain whirls body on right heel, away from me. 'I giving strong warning: go home right now, and do not disturb busy police department. If seeing here again arresting you.'

What can I do to convince this man that I have genuine reasons to see my Excellency? I run in front so that he nearly collides with me. 'Please listen, Tan Captain. Big reason his gracious Excellency involving himself is because Udon Thani Police Major accusing farang with name Luke Narland of murder.'

'Farang committing murder in village?'

'No, Tan Captain. He in police custody when My Excellency arriving to investigate Udon Thani police procedures. My Excellency interrogating Khun Narland. Outstanding Excellency deciding very useful case for testing methods of Udon Thani police, so he deciding he investigating murder in Dumden Village himself. This is how meticulous Excellency knowing whether Police Department following correct procedures for investigating village death.'

I mention that a farang involved in this case because I knowing Tan Captain Worluti now listening to me little bit more carefully. Tan Captain standing still, eyes looking into mine. 'Young lady, you telling me farang so important that my Excellency taking on case?' Shakes papers in hand very hard. 'Is that what you maintaining?'

Naturally knowing Luke not important for my Excellency, but my fiancé very important for me. I must think quickly for correct answer. 'Tan Captain, you understanding that diplomatic Excellency knowing not good for Thailand if innocent farang staying in prison. That making very bad impression, and British Consulate becoming involved.'

'This farang, he diplomat?'

'Important businessman, Tan Captain. Having business relationships with presidents of all big banks in Thailand.'

Corners of Tan Captain Worluti's mouth drooping. 'OK, young lady. You follow me to office. Settling this matter without bothering my Excellency.'

'Why my Excellency agreeing this farang not guilty?' Tan Police Captain Worluti asks while waving that I sit on small chair opposite enormous desk filling room.

I wondering about what I should say for many days now, but still I am not sure of good answer. 'Khun Luke Narland my fiancé, man I marrying soon soon.'

Policeman bangs right fist down, making big noise, rubbing hand. 'So, now understanding. You coming here because you having personal interest in case.' Outraged lips pucker out of round, hard mouth. 'This farang now in prison in Udon Thani?'

'No, Tan Captain, that is not reason I asking to speak with astute Excellency. Khun Luke Narland free on bail, now in own country, in England. He preparing coming back to Thailand because having special new programme for presenting to Thai banks. His Excellency, President of Bank of Bangkok, is very eager for having meeting with Khun Luke. My fiancé first in whole world for installing such programme for banks, and he choosing Thai bank for this.'

True this exaggerating little bit, but how can ordinary police captain know anything about bank business? I am sure he not ringing high-ranking president of Bank of Bangkok. Still, Tan Captain refusing to paddle, instead putting feet in river and getting nowhere. 'Wasting time, and police time, is a very serious matter. In what way all this concerning my Excellency? What kind information farang having if living in England? Also, if murderer in jail then already guilty.'

True in this case, not correct in law.

'My fiancé and myself believing Mak Kamuki, man in jail, member of criminal gang committing big big crime, much more than killing one village girl.'

Captain sitting down at desk, picks up pencil and begins tapping. 'Farang remaining in England, now sending you telling Bangkok Police Department uncorroborated suspicions he having? What kind of information is that? Why not here in person?'

'Already preparing to come, Tan Captain. Returning first because Thai man I never knowing try kidnapping on London street. This man looking very similar to man accused of murder and now in Udon Thani jail.'

Tan Captain Worluti opens file on desk. I can see losing interest, I must say something to startle. 'Similar? Meaning related?'

Realising now it very true he reminding me of Are Mak. Maybe he some kind of cousin to Are Mak, and therefore also to Lung Ban. 'Maybe relative of prisoner. Stranger coming also from Isaan, very close to Laos border. I knowing gangs from Laos coming to Thailand for kidnapping young girls from villages, taking Krung Thep for service industry. Virgins fetching good price.'

Tan Captain shrugging shoulders. 'That commonplace

occurrence. Not thinking my serene Excellency involving with something unsavoury Udon Thani police can handle on own. You wasting police time.' Standing now, coming over to chair I sitting on, rocking it.

He is correct in what he is saying. Then the flock of midges fly into my mind, forming the shape of a tall man – then recognising Luke! Thoughts run around in my head, one idea and then more and more. Already suspecting that gang of Laotians only try kidnapping me as decoy, they really wanting Luke, otherwise they already taking me.

Now I can see new possibility. Gang abandoning idea of kidnapping Nong Wuadon that day, maybe observing Luke walking on own, therefore seeing excellent opportunity to take hostage. Possible to get big ransom for farang businessman, only small price for village girl, even if young and very beautiful and virgin. Now I guess that maybe on that day gang member, perhaps Are Mak, asking Nong Wuadon to act as decoy, hoping Luke would follow when she walking to lonely area and then they overpower Luke.

Right away I believe evil plans not working out because Nong Wuadon very good girl, knowing Luke going to marry with me, so guessing she refusing to cooperate with evil men. Therefore Are Mak becoming very angry, so angry he not thinking straight and attacking own niece Nong Wuadon he loving much much. I can see in mind how this murder happening.

I stand, look at angry police captain without fear, swinging foot into thorns. 'Tan Captain Worluti, I thinking very important you informing my involved Excellency that I in police station. Otherwise possible my Excellency becoming most upset if you not telling him. Khun Narland important businessman, but investors in Khun Narland business more important still. I meeting in London and they super rich, making all kinds trouble if finding out Thai police ignoring new evidence I taking trouble to bring to police attention.'

Tan Police Captain starts pacing round room, pushing back hair with hands, face becoming red, perspiration stains under arms spreading to big patches. At last stopping near me, tipping chair so I must stand. Now pointing towards door.

'My Excellency already going home. Leaving note on desk for time of sound of gong. Now you going home.' Suddenly grabbing right arm. 'Leaving number for calling.'

Mobile Luke giving does not work in Thailand, therefore giving Tan Captain Worluti number of Luke office in Krung Thep, because knowing business associate Khun Teng always there in working hours.

Leaving Police Headquarters I decide to visit Khun Teng to make daily telephone call to Luke.

WHEN THE CAT'S AWAY THE MICE TURN LIVELY

Walking along without worrying, looking in shop windows, now seeing two men behind me, watching me. When I move, they follow. When I stop, they stop.

Am I very stupid to think no one was watching me going into Metropolitan Police Station, and seeing I remaining inside all day? Already it is easy to guess what is happening. Tan Police Sergeant I talking with telling anyone offering sufficient baht about my situation: impossible for meeting with my Excellency Police Lieutenant General Thomupi today. Is very likely all other police officers in Central Police Station have opportunity to order very large baht meals, much more than I am able paying. Therefore these people not of interest to me. What is very clear is that someone wishes to prevent me meeting with my Excellency. That explaining why two men following me. I am sure.

Luke office is long way from here, Soi Paidi Madi. This is a lane behind big Suhkumvit Road. Deciding best if I take tuk-tuk. Hail one passing, climb aboard, tell driver to take me quick quick. He moves off right away and I starting to relax, now very exhausted from waiting all day in police station while sitting on hard, uncomfortable, wooden bench.

At first not noticing driver not taking me where I asking to go because thinking about Luke, how I telling him I have meeting with my Excellency within short time, as soon as I receive message when I visiting Khun Teng in the office. Suddenly realising tuk-

tuk going along Thoetdamnri Road, that wrong direction. Possible there is big traffic congestion on usual roads, something often happening in Krung Thep. But I have nervous feeling, stomach churning, so when driver taking turning into Sukhothai Road I becoming very anxious. Why is tuk-tuk driver going to place I not asking to go?

'Where you going, driver? This way not leading to Suhkumvit Road.'

He not turning head round, he hunching shoulders over steering wheel. Asking again, but he saying nothing, just continues in wrong direction. Now seeing second tuk-tuk coming up close behind, then third one settles nearby in front. All three tuk-tuk travelling very close together, all moving forward as one, like convoy. Heart thumping, becoming heavy as I now understanding something very wrong. Three-wheelers not travelling fast, that impossible in our Celestial City where too many angel chariots keeping traffic moving like turtles.

Making quick decision to jump out of moving tuk-tuk. Not difficult because no doors stopping me and I planning to run away quick quick. Tuk-tuk driver watching me in mirror, I can see, so guessing my plan. Putting hand on horn, making lots noise. I foolish hesitating too long. Two men leap out of backs of other tuk-tuks. One jumps on pavement, another on road, so blocking openings of my vehicle. They showing guns as they getting into my tuk-tuk, so not good idea to scream. Now sitting between two large men in tuk-tuk I hiring. I try talking with men, smiling big smiles, but both sitting with blank faces showing no movement.

Convoy continuing until at last arriving in small soi off Pracherat 1 Road, one street I never hearing name before. Very few people walking here, also no other traffic. Three tuk-tuks all stop. Two men taking arms, one each side, and four men walking towards me slow slow, all looking fierce and frightening. I am a rabbit trapped by a cobra.

Two men holding my arms move me to a door other men are opening. Expecting to see very dirty place, like building criminal gang living in. But this house very clean, very modern, with top-of-the range, expensive furnishings. Some sort of overpowering scrubbed smell, reminding me of high-class disinfectant. All walls painted white, all furniture stainless steel. Getting impression of sterile environment, feeling like operating theatre in hospital. Legs buckling, no longer supporting me. Two men on either side catching me as slumping down. Dragging along corridor to double doors at end.

Automatic doors opening wide and I see large desk with a man in a white coat sitting behind, having stethoscope hanging round neck. Therefore I understanding right away he is doctor. Heartbeat calming down little bit. Maybe not criminals. Maybe when I passenger on plane from London I catching disease and now doctors wanting to put me in quarantine? Men on both my sides now leaving me to stand on own.

Man sitting at desk watching me, widening nostrils. 'Taiella Motubaki?' He having piece paper in front, pen moving very quick, filling out form on paper.

My training from childhood is to be polite to all superiors and older people. Man at desk is both, so wai-ing, eyes cast down and bowing very low.

Man wearing glasses, eyes looking over top of rims. 'You healthy young woman? No venereal diseases, or TB?'

Too nervous for speaking, so nod head.

'We need spoken answer.'

'Yes, Khun Mor. Please explaining me who you are, and why you forcing me to come to this place?'

'Forcing?' His frown is very hard, his voice irritable. 'We have a legal document here, which older sister signing, saying you staying with her until right time for you coming here and staying here.'

'That is correct, Khun Mor. I always staying with older sister when in Krung Thep.'

'Maybe in past. Now you agree terms we sending, and life changing to rules here. We provide first-class accommodation and all food and clothing while waiting, together with reasonable salary paid into safe bank account in name Taiella Motubaki. Until time of the operation.' Now reading from document, later investigating eyes sweep over my face, my body. I having a hard time staying upright. 'After recovery you free to do as you wish. All

237

Isaan people very happy coming here. We offer excellent rewards.'

He is searching my face, looking for a reaction, but I do not understand his meaning and therefore my face staying the same.

'Scar you getting will be very small, almost cannot see with the modern techniques we using. Recovery time is about three weeks, and you will not notice any problems with future health.' He looking at me again, eyes puzzled. 'But you already knowing all this.'

'No, Khun Mor. I have no idea what you telling me. What operation?'

'Explaining all this in very clear detail at initial interview!'

'I not understanding. You saying, I very healthy, not needing medical treatment.' It is true I speaking to older sister Sayai about going to hospital for help with conceiving a baby. It is also true that when going to the fertility hospital I signing a document saying I accepting hormones to swallow on my own responsibility. But nothing I signing or saying mentioning an operation in any way.

Now eyes of doctor roll, showing he thinking I am a little bit crazy. 'You coming from Isaan? From village near Udon Thani?'

'Yes, Khun Mor. But not living...'

'Naturally not, this understood. You coming to our Celestial City of Angels, we rescuing you from planting rice, now you can enjoying modern life. Excellent decision, very wise. While you waiting we taking good care of you, arranging outstanding educational programme, you visiting wonderful Grand Palace and beautiful Temple of Emerald Buddha.' He stopping, eyes flicking from notes to me and back again. 'And all other attractions of beautiful city. Maybe you learn speaking English. This education worth more than money we paying. You can find top job in modern Thailand, make interesting friends, meet excellent husband.'

Another door behind the big desk now opening and an imposing farang, dressed also in white overall over ordinary clothes, is walking into the room and taking a chair next to Doctor Number One. The new man looking around with pale blue eyes and I understanding very well before mouth even opening: face of deer, heart of tiger.

'Right! What have we here?' He picking up papers Doctor

238

Number One writing on and reads through. Then looking at me very hard. 'Not our usual type, Napoka. Quite a bit older. Can't be running out of teenagers, surely?' Now shuffles papers and slamming down on desk. 'You Thais are like children, you simply don't consider consequences. This young woman's behaviour since she arrived in Bangkok means considerably more tests, you know. And more expense. I specified virgins for a reason.'

Khun Mor he calling Napoka shrugging, answering in English. 'I leave all that to the agents in the Northeastern Territory, Tan Mor. This young woman seems healthy, I do not foresee any problems. Our village women stay virgins until they marry. She is not married.'

'Excuse me to interrupt, Khun Mor.' Strong man who holding my right arm before, forcing me here, is now in this room, smiling with wide teeth. 'We already having match for young lady. Farang from England, name Luke Narland.'

Match? This some kind joke Luke playing and these people trying to arrange a marriage? For one small moment thinking perhaps Luke... Not possible. Feeling fear turning to terror, whole body now shaking.

Doctor Number One, Khun Mor Napoka, translating what this man is saying.

'Really? I don't remember that name on our list.' Doctor Number Two looking again to me, eyes hard as lizard eyes. Then turning to Khun Mor Napoka. 'Everything been checked out? All the forms filled in and signed and witnessed? We don't want any slip-ups.'

Strong instincts telling me I am fighting for my life. 'I am sorry, Tan Doctor,' I say out loud while moving forward to the desk, courageous because not having any choice. 'I do not understanding what you say. What operation?'

'You speak English?' Doctor Number Two is staring at me, I understanding he not very happy.

'I having as fiancé Englishman name of Luke Narland, Tan Doctor. He coming to Thailand in few days and we marrying soon soon.'

Doctor Number One taking off glasses, rubbing eyes. 'Please

not to bother Tan Mor, young woman,' he says in Thai. 'You consenting to operation one week gone! Agreement already signed.'

'No!' Shouting in English so Doctor Number Two understanding. 'I never agreeing any procedure involving operation. It is illegal forcing me.'

'Changed your mind, have you?' Doctor Number Two mutters, very casual and without any worry. 'Even though, I gather, it's your fiancé who'll benefit. Price of the marriage, presumably. Well, terribly sorry and all that, but we can't accept a change of heart. We explain everything very carefully when we send the recruiting agents to the villages. Once in the system there's no going back.' Now lifting up piece of paper, walking to front of desk, holding paper with writing out for me to look at.

It is not my signature, and also not that of my sister Pi Sayai. Recognising the signature on the paper as belonging to Ban Kamuki. He signing it as uncle, nearest male relation. Naturally this is a very big lie, my father is still living.

'No, Tan Doctor. I did not sign this agreement, I did not meet any agent, I am not agreeing now. The signature on the piece of paper is from my uncle, husband to younger sister of my mother, but my father is still living. All this is a very big mistake, some kind of mix-up. Please to allow me to return to older sister living here, in Krung Thep, right away.'

Doctor Number Two standing up, not even looking at me. His eyes signal to Doctor Number One that he wishing both to leave. Two guards from before sprint over to stand on left and right side of my body, forcing me to walk through another door behind the big desk.

They herding me like a water buffalo along a long corridor. Two men unlocking a door to a room on the right-hand side, then pushing me inside. I hear the lock click shut, now know I am a prisoner.

240

DON'T SHOW A SQUIRREL
THE HOLE IN THE TREE

'Have you seen Taiella, Teng?' My daily call to the Bangkok office is several hours earlier than usual: three in the morning my time. Not that it matters; I can't sleep anyway. My Thai representative is often late, so I'm relieved to reach him before ten. 'I didn't hear from her yesterday,' I carry on, trying to stop my voice from sounding quavery.

Am I imagining it, or does he hesitate before answering? 'I have not seen her for the last two days, Kuhn Luke. I had the hunch she was set on returning to Isaan.'

My throat narrows. I splutter as I try to swallow. So why the hell hasn't he been in touch? I *have* stressed, time and again, how worried I am about her safety! 'What on earth d'you mean, Teng? I specifically asked you to look out for her, to make certain she's OK. Why didn't you call me when she didn't turn up?'

'I have been working all the hours preparing presentations, Kuhn Luke. The Bank of Bangkok…'

'I don't give a damn about the banks!'

I hear the click of the computer keyboard. Playing scrabble? 'I cannot keep tabs on Taiella all the time, Kuhn Luke. Maybe she checked in on her parents. Last time I saw her she was cheesed off. Her sister is out all day, her nephew is at school, even her kathoey friend…'

'Panjim, you mean?'

'Is that his moniker? He is away in his village.'

'All that's irrelevant. We agreed she'd wait for me to join her, and that she'd be in touch every day. Something's wrong.' Panic turns my voice into a disjointed croak. 'I also asked you to find a couple of chores she could do around the office. Did you do that?'

His laugh, thin with nervousness, is overlaid with the fluttering of papers being shuffled and reshuffled. 'I tried. I asked her to man the landline for two hours, while I was taking clients out to lunch. But she cannot be much help, she does not understand this line of work.'

'That's up to me. Nobody was going to hold *you* responsible.' Fury has taken over from panic, but I know better than to explode. Teng doesn't like Taiella. He has the usual Bangkok hang-up about her roots. He's from a 'good' family, and Taiella's from a remote Isaan village of no importance. I begin to suspect he's allowed something to happen to her, maybe is actually involved. 'You were simply asked to make sure she was OK – as a priority. Let's get this straight. When, exactly, did you last see her?' My underarms are pouring sweat, my face blazing. I can smell disaster.

'Perhaps yesterday. I cannot be one hundred percent.'

The laconic tone, the irritating US phraseology, infuriates me even more. Hasn't he just said two days ago? 'She was in the office yesterday but didn't ring me? That what you're saying?'

'I am so sorry, Kuhn Luke. My mis-mistake. It must have been d-day before, then. N-not longer than that, sh-sure thing.'

There's a curious stutter in his voice, nothing to do with his Americanisms though that, too, is deteriorating. He's fudging the facts. So does he know, or is he evading the issue because he's been negligent? 'What made you think it was yesterday?'

'Now remembering. There was telephone call from Metropolitan Police Station. Captain Worluti ringing, asking telling Nong Taiella Police Lieutenant General Thomupi wishing see at three that afternoon. But Nong Taiella not arriving.'

The sudden change to elementary Thai English means he's got something to be guilty about. I feel like throttling him, would enjoy squeezing the breath out of him. I put the image aside. If I don't control my fury and rising panic I might never see my Smileegirl again.

How the hell does Thomupi know Taiella is back in Bangkok? I breathe deeply, pour myself a steadying drink. Only if he's arranged surveillance on her sister's house, or on my office. Too far-fetched. But why expect her to be there on that particular day, let alone presume she'd get such a message? 'So you rang Worluti back, right? Told his secretary you were expecting her but she hadn't come in?'

'No, Kuhn Luke. Why doing such thing?'

It takes me several apoplectic seconds to digest this and try to make sense of it. Thais, whatever failings they may have in our eyes, are fantastically polite, incredibly status-conscious. Teng would only slight the General if the alternative is a substantial threat to himself. 'You're very aware what an important man the General is, Teng. You know how essential his continuing interest in the Kamuki case is for me. After all, you were in Udon Thani when it was all happening!'

'Illustrious General not asking for you.' Evasive, defensive.

'I'm not an idiot, and nor are you. If he asked Taiella for a meeting it must be to do with the case, and it has to be crucial. How could you just allow him to think she didn't bother when you knew she hadn't got the message?'

'I was going to make contact today. Tell the police she has not been in...'

His reactions are completely out of character; he's clearly hiding something. And then it clicks. The only way the General could know where to contact Taiella is if he knows she turns up at my office every day. Who told him? Not Teng, otherwise the General would have had him brought in.

'And it didn't occur to you to go to her sister's place, or Panjim's, to look for her, as soon as you got the message? You must have known how important it was.'

'I am very busy person, Kuhn Luke. You know I am getting ready to introducing new programmes. You already directing me to telling all customers about new routines, and how they impacting on their businesses. I do not have time for going out of central Bangkok and find some apartment set in small soi. The streets are not even named in some of those districts!'

243

His English has recovered sufficiently to tell me he knows where Sayai lives. That's where I took Taiella that first time we met, after the party. Sayai lives in one of those little lanes spidering across the city. I also remember now: Teng knows the district, he's been there before.

'Also, I would not even know when she is at home, Kuhn Luke.'

Stalling, evading. Has he been bribed to forget about Taiella? If so by whom, and why? 'I want you to go to the police station right now. Just shut up the office...'

'Excuse me, Khun Luke, what I should be doing about the Bank of Bangkok deal? My meeting with the sub-manager this afternoon...'

If it is, it's the first I've heard about it. 'I don't care a damn about that. Call them, tell them we'll get back to them when we can. Make some sort of decent excuse; a glitch in the new programme, anything. Taiella is my first priority.'

'It has taken weeks to set up such an important meeting! Excuses will make them think the programme is no good.'

Lucky Teng isn't here in person – I feel my hands choking the receiver, force myself to calm down. 'I'm not going to think about business while she's missing, Teng. I want you at that police station as soon as you can get there. Insist on contacting the General, don't take no for an answer. And when you do get hold of him ask him to ring me, here, in London. Something's very wrong, I can sense it.'

'You must understanding, Kuhn Luke. It may not be possible setting up meeting with such illustrious man. He may not even remembering my name...'

'If he asked Taiella to meet him he will have gone through his Dumden murder notes. Just remind him who you are, tell him she rings me from the office every day but didn't yesterday. Spell out to him that it means there's a problem.'

'It still may not be a cinch for me to arrange a get-together with the General. Someone like that does not see people just because they request it.'

That part sounds assured, more like his old self. 'No more excuses, Teng. You're to see the General, whatever it takes to get to him. Use money to oil the wheels with the underlings. That's your expertise; it's one of the reasons I employ you.' Not enough leverage. I have to threaten him, or he won't even try. What with? 'I'll see to it you never work for a farang again if you don't contact him. Am I making myself clear?'

Not much of a threat, and of course I have no way of controlling other foreigners – and Teng has already been head-hunted. I have to assume he doesn't realise how little I could do to harm him. Suddenly I remember Howard Spelter. He's quite another matter. He's super rich, a substantial investor in Thailand.

'No doubt you remember Tan Howard, a good friend of your Prime Minister. He's very concerned about Taiella.'

A sort of gulp, almost instantly controlled. 'I will trying most hard, Khun Luke. As all time I working for you.'

Fortunately I've always treated my local associates really well, paid them over the odds, invited them to England for their holidays. Teng's been introduced to Howard and Geraldine, knows their high standing. Question is, are these threats greater than the ones he's had already?

I book myself on the next flight to Bangkok, pack, and ring the Bangkok Metropolitan Police Station while waiting for my cab. I manage to get them to put me through to Worluti – eventually. His English is no better than my Thai, but it appears the General's not in his office.

I check into the Tai-Pan Hotel, the one Taiella knows I always stay at. Just in case she turns up, having heard from Teng that I've left London. I make two-thousand baht sure the manager knows it's very important to ask Taiella – should she turn up – to wait for me in my room. Then I order a motorbike for the trip to Sayai's place – I've kept the piece of paper on which Taiella has written the address, in Thai. I haven't been inside, but she told me her sister lives in a studio flat in a nice house. It's in a pleasant enough area, reached by crossing the Chao Phraya River, but set on one of the many narrow side streets – sois – which aren't wide enough for cars.

The driver has trouble finding it. Clearly not a street which gets much call from anyone not living in that neighbourhood. I have the intelligence to ask him to wait for me, and to make sure he checks that I'm standing by the right door.

I knock. Nothing. I bang hard. Same result. I bang again – and again. Thais don't, normally, knock. They walk straight in. But I can't bring myself to do that. Eventually a middle-aged, well-fed Thai flings the door open, wide nostrils dilated and shoulders drawn back into aggressive pose. I'm not expecting a man to answer, let alone such a muscular, earthy type. Still, he has to be Sayai's 'husband', on one of his visits. He doesn't look the part but he is, I've been told, a businessman of standing, otherwise he wouldn't be able to afford four wives. So, with any luck, he's used to dealing with foreigners and speaks some English.

'I am so sorry to intrude,' I start. 'I am Luke Narland, Taiella's fiancé.'

This time the stolid disdainful stare of the successful Thai takes over from the suspicious look of a man who has obviously considered betrayal. No smile, however. Not even a wai. 'OK. Nong Taiella not here. Wife sleeping.'

'I really am terribly sorry to disturb you, but it is very urgent. I think there is something horribly wrong, that Nong Taiella is in danger. Could I speak to Pi Sayai? Find out when she last saw her younger sister?'

'Thinking you leaving now,' he says, a strong solid hand pressing against the door. 'Wife knowing nothing.'

I put my foot in the doorway and see his eyes slit to a thin line, hear his breathing take on an ominous rumble. I might be a foot taller, but he looks as though Thai boxing is one of his hobbies. 'Please. Can I just find out when Pi Sayai last saw Nong Taiella? Yesterday, the day before?'

An imperious muscle-bound arm shows me I have to remove my foot. I take another look at his thick neck and decide not to try anything physical. Sayai lives in a strictly Thai part of the outskirts of Bangkok. I let him shut the door and stand, staring at it, wondering whether to knock again. Maybe surprise him, just walk in and try to talk to Sayai. As I psyche myself up for action he opens the door just a crack. Small enough so that I can't get my foot into it.

'Younger sister here morning three days gone. You leaving right now.'

The door clicks shut decisively. I put my name on one of the hotel's cards and slip it under the door. So that Sayai – or Taiella – will know how to get in touch.

BEAT THE OX BY PUNCHING THE HARROW

'Back to the Tai-Pan,' I snap at the driver. 'Quick quick.'

There's nothing I can do – nothing at all – until tomorrow morning. Except fret. Obviously I'll have to get hold of Thomupi. It's in his gift to start a proper search, but will he? I know better than to trust him completely. I remember very well how he had me put into that cesspit of a holding cell, that he talked to Taiella in his car all the way from the Dumden to Udon Thani and never mentioned that he'd had me taken from the hotel and shoved into that disgusting jail, and that he was barely civil after the inquest. I'd only be able to rely on his help if it coincided with his own plans. I realise all that's secondary. The first essential is getting hold of him. Harder, I realise, than speaking intelligible Thai.

I'll have to bribe my way to him, almost certainly my only option. But even if I have enough cash on me right now to buy my way into getting hold of his private address, the posse of security people guarding him will simply refuse to let me through. Worse than that, they'll arrest me, almost certainly without telling him. Public figures in Thailand are prisoners of their own success. Would-be assassins lurk on every street, in every dark corner. Their services are cheap.

The manager greets me with a wink. 'I am so sorry, Khun Narland. No young lady, no message.' Gleeful teeth display piranha qualities. 'I can find beautiful young lady for you here, in this hotel. No need waiting. We guarantee satisfaction.'

I curl my left little finger, press with my right hand until it hurts, checking the intense longing to knock his teeth out of his head. Instead, I demand my key in colonial-style English, then batter at the unyielding door to the lift. A nervous-looking Western couple stand aside, their shocked faces pretending a greeting. They move out of my way with distant smiles. The lift door stutters open. I jab the sixth floor button in the empty cabin and, when the doors don't shut instantly, stride out again. I decide to take the stairs, two at a time. I want to feel my feet pounding them, to run the length of my corridor and to slam into my room. When I get there I crash into the bathroom while chucking off my clothes.

The shower taps fairground-mirror a bulging torso. Furious, I turn both on full blast and stand under the shower-head, the water spurting tiny arrowheads at me.

My brain hides inside my skull, refuses to provide ways I could search for Taiella. She's been abducted – that much is obvious, even to my jet-lagged brain. The reason escapes me, however much I bash my head against the sweating shower cabinet. My lame – my sole – conclusion is that the London contingent of what I have to presume is the Kamuki gang only got through to their Bangkok counterparts yesterday, maybe the day before.

Crap. Taiella's been in Bangkok a week, staying with her sister because Panjim's on holiday. If the gang knew she was back they'd know where she was staying and would have nabbed her several days ago. They didn't. There could be only one explanation: she'd let them know that she was back in Thailand, and had provoked them at the same time. How?

I lean back, see her as I remember her that time she came looking for me at the Tai-Pan. In her working clothes. The trim, dark blue suit, the lace of her white shirt feathering her swan throat, elegant legs confident on stiletto heels, pointy toes. I see her sway ahead of me, seductive, pert, her dark hair swirling to check I was still following. High-spirited, impulsive – exactly what I so love about her.

The water beats down on my face, pummels it. I hear Taiella's small steps clacking confidently along Bangkok streets, see her trip out of the Tai-Pan, down Soi Suhkumvit 21, into Sukhumvit Road.

Once there the figure seems to float, then fly and we are on the Si Ayutthaya Road, in front of enormous glass doors. I see them open as she goes into – Metropolitan Police Headquarters!

She kind of skirted round the idea several days ago, testing me out. I shouted – yelled at her – to wait until we could go together. She didn't press it, and I thought no more about it. But that has to be what she's done. It wasn't super-detective Thomupi who discovered Taiella was back in Thailand. She was the one who alerted *him*, sent a message by going to look for him, asking to see him. That has to be it. Which means a mole in the police department. A sleek, black mole with a sniffer-dog nose rooting out Taiella, hunting her down, using its claws to grip her so she can't escape.

I turn off the hot tap. Cold water sprays my head. I leave it on until I feel so waterlogged my mind refuses to function at all. And still the questions tumble round. Why did she risk herself, alone? Why didn't she wait until I could go with her?

I turn the shower off. Water splutters down the drain, slowly, blocked by soap scum and hair. I kick at it, impatient, twirling a towel round my body, longing for something, anything physical, I could box.

Taiella must have gone to the Police Station on her own because she couldn't wait any longer, wanted action, movement. And I guess she also wanted to prove that she – a simple village girl – could arrange a meeting with that exalted Police Lieutenant General Thomupi entirely on her own account.

Her vanity could cost her – and me – her life. Who are the kidnappers? They have to be from Isaan, with Bangkok – evidently even international – connections. What do they want? Taiella as hostage couldn't get the jailed Kamuki off the hook – they'd know that. Mak Kamuki isn't the motive. So what is? Revenge? I shrug that off. No baht in that. There has to be some sort of pecuniary payoff – a decent one.

Are they holding Taiella to get a substantial sum out of me? Not usually the way Thais would think. To them Taiella is just another village girl, not even beautiful in their eyes, already past marrying age. They'd soon discover that her father's already put a maximum two thousand dollars on her marriage settlement – not worth the risk to mess with a farang.

Would they realise she's worth much more to me? That I'm madly in love with her and will do anything in my power to get her back? Not a chance. Thai thugs from Laos, or even Isaan, wouldn't think like that. Much too much of a Western concept.

That's what I tell myself, calm myself down with. I unscrew the top of the bottle of sleeping pills I always bring on long-distance trips. I need sleep, oblivion. Tomorrow's going to be a heavy day.

WATERING A STUMP

I reach for the phone with my right hand, splash a bottle of mineral water all over myself. By the time my left hand finds the receiver I'm woozy, but awake.

'Luke Narland speaking.'

'Want see girlfriend alive, come Phetburi Market, hok mong chow.'

'What?' Something familiar about that voice. Ban Kamuki? 'Who are you? Where exactly?'

'Phetburi Market. And wearing green tie girlfriend giving. Hok mong chao or never seeing again.'

'Hold on a minute...'

The dialling tone. Time in Thailand is charmingly vague, especially after seven in the morning and two in the afternoon. Will I get it right? Hok Mong Chao literally means six am. My watch, still on English time, is just as confusing. Reception are clear on seven am. The caller must have said Hah Mong Chao, eleven am.

Cramp in my left leg forces me out of bed, stomping my foot, twisting it into the normal, preferred position. The gang knows about the green tie Taiella's given me. What ghastly things are they doing to her? Last night's Thai Airways food spews everywhere.

I limp to the bathroom, stand under a cold shower in my shorts. Have I lost her? Tears and water run down my face, frustration changes to anger. I twist on both taps with all my strength, endangering the plumbing. I'm determined to get her back.

A farang wearing a green tie will be easy to spot, even among the teeming alleyways and laden stalls of Phetburi Market. No way for me to know who Taiella's captors are. I need help – genuine help. Badly.

Not even eight. Should I ring the police? Thomupi wouldn't turn up before noon. My phone call to Worluti made it clear: pointless to talk to anyone else.

Only three Thais know I'm in Bangkok – Teng, Sayai and her 'husband'. He doesn't know me, and at first I dismiss Sayai as a possible conspirator. Doubts creep through the steady stream of water. Could she be part of it? For a relatively high price?

Well – maybe. Jealousy is a green-eyed dragon breathing fire. A gleaming remembrance of a monster with yellow eyes and blue claws reminds me of the Thai who answered Sayai's door last night. I see the stocky arm again – tattooed! Common in Thailand, where tattoos are said to ward off bad luck, but surely not for the stolid businessman Taiella described as her sister's husband? Why did I assume the man who came to the door was Sayai's man? And then it hits me: *that's* where I heard that voice on the phone before – last night!

I presume there's a gang operating in Dumden Village, quite likely a Laotian one. They're known to be operating in the area. Tattoo Thug could be one of them, maybe its leader. He let me go because it suited him, because he's used to working with Westerners and sensed a way to make substantial sums of money. He knows he hasn't a hope of getting it unless I'm free to get hold of it for him, which in turn means proof that Taiella is alive. I grab a towel, rub myself dry. We still have a chance.

The British Embassy, opening at eight, has to be stop number one. Alerted, they'd know I'm at risk, and will take action if I don't return.

The chaotic Bangkok rush-hour traffic is best tackled on two wheels, though the risk to one's life isn't insubstantial. Almost funny. I throw on a clean shirt and a pair of light trousers, put the green tie in my pocket and make for the breakfast bar. I gulp down some fruit juice, grab the largest water bottle I can see. The booked bike and driver await me on the street.

Dehydration rights itself after I finish the bottle. I feel my brain slip into gear. We putter up Phloen Chit Road. As soon as we turn into Withayu Road I have my little speech ready for the Embassy staff. Nothing fancy: just a few words to convince them that if I don't turn up again by the time they close that afternoon, half-past three, they'll know something is very wrong.

I'm not looking for a royal welcome. Just a tiny amount of attention and sympathy. Crimped smiles, bland assurances. A young chap with slicked-back hair, staring at the photo of a blonde, waves me to a plastic bucket seat by his desk.

'If you were to be missing for any length of time official enquiries would, naturally, be set in motion.' Fingers poise to tap in his girlfriend's phone number.

'You're not listening. If I'm not back...'

'We're not here to prevent possible attempts on your person, Mr Narland. If you suspect such eventualities you should take the necessary precautions.' Baby-bottom complexion, baby-wolf smile. A delicate eyebrow triangles upwards. 'And we certainly cannot involve ourselves with the welfare of Thai subjects.'

Now if Taiella had blonde hair... 'I'm not asking you to! I'm only alerting you to possible problems.'

'Perhaps you should consider employing a private investigation agency. I'm sure we could recommend a local firm.' A single tap, the number registers, the connection is made. Both eyebrows triangle. 'All right?'

'Thank you for your concern.' I stand, shirt sodden, trousers damp. Teng? Storm the police station, insist on seeing the General?

Still two hours before my Phetburi Market appointment, waiting in this steaming city. My stomach pinches, empty, annoyed. Stupid not to tank up; I'll think better if I'm fed. I settle for one of the many restaurants which sprout along every side-street in Bangkok.

A waitress smiles up, gabbling green curry, fresh prawns, beef salad. I love Thai food, order the base of rice and a mild curry, have trouble swallowing. I push another spoonful of rice into my unwilling mouth and stare. A robber fly is hovering around the live prawns watched over by an ancient native. What is this fly doing here, in the centre of Bangkok?

The prawn vendor prepares for war. He blood-curdles Thai swear words at the insect, hurls ice cubes. The fly buzzes to my table, hang-glides in front of me, then flitters towards the road. The waitress, alerted by battle cries, arrives with an enormous swat. I grab it fast, shove a hundred baht note into her hand, follow the fly's demented path.

I keep the fly in sight but remember Taiella, eyes wide and gathering moisture, smiling through and whispering that the robber fly is the latest incarnation of Wuadon. Her image stays with me, her presence strong, her direction delicate but firm, asking me to listen, not to disregard what so many Thais believe.

The fly has taken on the features of an archangel. Like Thomas, I've seen so I believe. Taiella told me, breathless, that the fly buzzed around Mak's head, that's what clinched his guilt for her. He's Wuadon's murderer, a trial unnecessary as far as she's concerned. From a worldly point of view it's also why the General had doubts, why he allowed me to be freed on bail.

The hypnotist fly is forging out into the traffic-choked Phetchaburi Road, leading towards Phetburi Market. I follow. What's a little insanity among believers?

The fly gyrates on, defying fly-slaughter by staying on my side of the road, unperturbed by my inability to keep up. The sun is rising, flaming white. I've forgotten to take more water, am not wearing a hat. Heat stroke is imminent as we pass the farang-oriented Pratunam Market.

Coconut water, accessed through a hole in the shell with a straw, is sold for a few baht everywhere. I throw ten baht, grab one, follow the yellow speck towards the Baiyoke Tower.

Dodging the traffic, buoyed on the coconut, the fly's objective finally crystallises. The Baiyoke Tower houses the Japanese department store where Taiella used to work – in the toy section of the ZenZam Centre. And, next to that, is the hairdressing salon where Taiella's best friend in Bangkok, Panjim Narcoso, runs the hairdressing franchise his boyfriend bought for him.

The fly has disappeared. Did I really follow it, did it actually nudge me to remember that Panjim was someone who'd be truly concerned for Taiella? He was on holiday when she arrived a week ago. Due back yesterday. Obvious, now. Panjim is my best hope: Taiella's Galahad.

Though Panjim is kathoey – a ladyboy – he's braver than many Thai boxers. When I first met him, dressed for that fateful party, I was completely fooled. Slightly taller than most Thai girls, but very beautiful, outshining Taiella from a model point of view, though not ousting my idea of the perfect woman. He/she appeared flawless, with light skin, glossy long hair (which turned out to be a wig), perky breasts and one of the most beautiful gowns I've ever seen. And, another coincidence, strikingly similar to Wuadon in the princess-like way he moved.

Panjim's jewellery proved his boyfriend filthy rich. And, though he girlie-simpered whenever the boyfriend was around, his gleeful taunting humour when on his own betrayed a keen mind behind the bland façade.

I'm energised with new hope. Panjim is clever, he's street-wise, he speaks reasonable English. And he's devoted to Taiella because she's always stood by him through the taunts and insults thrown by many of their acquaintances.

There was just one condition of friendship when I first met Panjim. I was to refer to him as 'she' whenever we were not at his place of work. A small price for the looked-down-on kathoey's understanding of his city, his country and his devotion to Taiella.

LOOK AT THE DIRECTION OF THE WINDS

Now having the time to look around carefully. The room I am in looks exactly like a room in a private hospital. An adjustable bed with a metal-frame is standing in the centre of the room, under a bright light, and there's a tall glass with water on the bedside table. Also a reading light and a TV, and a modern bathroom through another door leading from the right side of bed. Everything is very clean, neat, ordered. I have no idea why the people in this place wanting me here, or what they are doing.

I am very hot and hungry for water. I pour liquid into the glass, drink little bit and immediately feel a terrible tiredness coming over me. Cannot think about anything now; I lie down on the bed, exhausted, and go to sleep.

Some noise from nearby waking me up. At first I have no idea where I am, what I am doing here. Then I remember. Same noise which waking me up is happening again – I think maybe a door slamming in room next to me. Can hearing voices but cannot distinguish what they saying. Trying to open door. Still locked. Now putting my ear to the wall but can only decipher a few words, some quite loud. In English, not Thai.

This room very clean and comfortable, but still I am held prisoner, cannot act as I wish. I am desperate to escape soon as possible. What can I do to get out?

I check around, looking at everything. This must be private

room in modern clinic. Many people come to Thailand for operations because much cheaper here than in United States or in Europe. This building very new, walls thin, I think only ply board. I understanding this is very shoddy building with glossy furnishings, but windows of this room have strong iron struts – no possibility for finding way to escape.

I notice again glass of water standing on table next to bed. Now understanding why I so tired and having to sleep. Very common scam, putting knockout drugs in drinks at rave parties and many bars. Perhaps this water is spiked with strong drug. Now very hungry for water, but do not trust this liquid. I take glass to bathroom and pour down toilet. Now thinking that if I holding glass against wall where noise coming from, perhaps I overhear some conversation going on in next room.

Booming tone must be Doctor Number Two, speaking English. I think he talking on telephone because he almost shouting, using strong language.

'I don't...what... problem... I've *told* you time... got... twenty... You must... samples... now... except... Get on...tests...'

Hearing nothing more, then Doctor Number Two speaking again. 'Don't fuss! Forget... HLA tissue tests. ...anti-rejection... excellent. No... don't want... clutter.'

Then all very quiet, only scraping of something hard, perhaps Doctor Number Two listening to what other person saying.

'... not listening! ...to use... techniques... spell it out... L A P A R O S C O P I C. Much less invasive... tiny scar ... quick recovery...'

Doctors, tests, techniques. Now all coming back to me, what Nong Wuadon saying that morning when I seeing her and she talking to me little bit, before Are Mak interrupting. "I wanting go Krung Thep, Pi Taiella, but not wanting pay for this with..."

Now I think maybe last word she wanting so say was 'operation'. I not understanding at that time what she trying to tell me. Now it becoming very clear what she trying hard to explain. In poor areas, in villages like Dumden, agents coming to villages, offering poor parents – maybe Nong Wuadon mum not knowing, but dad knowing for sure – big money for children becoming living donors of organs. Maybe kidney, maybe part of liver, maybe lobe of lung.

I think possible Doctor Number Two phoning about kidney donation, and Nong Wuadon father agreeing to such action because agents offering more baht than he can earning in five years. Nong Wuadon very afraid, not wanting this, that is reason she try talking with me, that is reason Are Mak so upset at idea she talking with me on own. He thinking she arranging to go Krung Thep with Luke and me. Maybe now I also understand why Lung Ban so very angry when someone murder Nong Wuadon – he feeling guilty about encouraging beautiful daughter to give body parts, wishing to blame farang for own bad deed.

Maybe Lung Ban understanding later that Nong Wuadon killed because gang suspecting her of telling somebody outside local area exactly what they doing. It also very possible he even more angry knowing that he not receiving any money now.

How could he sell own daughter? I thinking he able to do this because he finding out he not real father. Maybe Are Mak telling older brother that my mum bringing baby for Na Att from Lao village while Lung Ban working in Saudi Arabia.

After short silence I hearing Doctor Number Two speaking once more:

'Why *should* they donate... kidney... for fuck all?'

He talking lots more, then big noise of crashing receiver. In silence I very upset thinking about Nong Wuadon not able talking to me when she hoping getting help. If she asking me I telling her not to agree to such radical operation – for sure. Also I begging Luke we taking her to Krung Thep with us when we leaving.

Now understanding very well why Are Mak murdering Nong Wuadon. I thinking he finding beautiful girl on her own, knowing right away that this his last chance to be with her. That is why he raped her, then killed her perhaps on orders of the gang.

Suddenly knowing must stop thinking about Nong Wuadon. Now doctors have me as prisoner, and wanting to do tests because wanting to take body parts from *me*.

I very frightened now. How can I get out of here, escape such terrible fate?

Door opening, and three nurses coming in. It is very clear one in charge, two others there to stop me running away, prepared fighting me. Khun Head Nurse carrying syringes, swabs and other medical equipment in kidney bowl. I seeing right away she preparing to take blood samples, maybe also other tests.

Khun Head Nurse arriving in room, smiling at me, very kind. 'Not becoming alarmed, younger sister. Taking blood samples from you for testing. Not invasive test, not harming. Just take very easy, relax, then not hurting at all.'

'I am not sick! Why you try forcing me for having tests?'

Khun Head Nurse smile fading. 'Please not causing problems. You signing correct papers, therefore must undergo preliminary tests like all others. I promise these tests not painful or damaging, younger sister.'

'What kind tests you planning?'

'You doctor? No? Then you not understanding what must happening.'

Now I struggle against two strong young nurses. 'If you not telling me what you wanting, you must forcing. You wish forcing me?'

Khun Head Nurse setting her neck sideways, staring at me for long time. I staring back, not blinking, showing no kind of fear. 'OK, I explain why doing tests. Need blood for establishing blood group and tissue type for cross-matching.'

I never hearing this word before. 'What is cross-matching?'

'This most important. Mixing some your white blood cells with blood from recipient. If white cells attaching and die we know you not correct donor. This not meaning something wrong with you, or affecting you! Only we must test for donor to be safe.'

'Recipient? What is recipient? You want me giving blood? That is reason you kidnapping me?' I not believing this is all these people want from me.

Khun Head Nurse looking at me very strange, forehead spreading deep wrinkles which run down both cheeks and into chin. 'What you telling me? Not correct you coming here of own free will, because you wishing donate kidney for boyfriend?'

Right away I feel danger signal in my brain. Knowing I must not alarm Khun Head Nurse, knowing I must pretend that I agree to give kidney for Luke. My thinking is if she part of gang it making no difference, if she not part of gang she thinking this a very romantic

260

situation. 'This is place where donating kidney for boyfriend?'

'People bringing you here, they not telling? Such stupid men!'

'Driver of tuk-tuk bringing me, he saying nothing. Thank you for explaining, Khun Head Nurse. '

Khun Head Nurse's wrinkles deepen around eyes as she smiling very soft. 'You showing so much love for boyfriend. Very romantic you agreeing acting as living kidney donor, giving life. Many young people from villages donate body parts, but only for money. Much younger than you, still children. Now understanding why you older. No problem if healthy...'

I believe this woman is just a nurse, she not part of a gang. 'Maybe you explaining for me what I must do?'

She undoes buttons on my shirt, pulling off. 'You thinking through before making decision? You consulting counsellor?'

'I thinking through.'

'Then already understanding our system. Once arriving at clinic you committing to operation, having no choice. We making as pleasant as possible. We must research medical history, take chest x-ray, electrocardiogram, urine test and many other procedures. All non-invasive.'

'And?' I know right off something bad coming.

'Very modern in this clinic. Using CT scan, very simple. Injecting dye into vein, you lying flat on table and machine beaming x-rays through body. That providing us with three-dimensional picture of organs.' Eyes half shut, she not looking at me now.

'And?' Something bad going on in her mind. Not only eyes turning away, whole body turning sideways.

'Two methods we using for taking kidney. One, cutting open body, making big scar. Second more modern, costing lots money. With laparoscopic surgery, incision only two inches long. Such procedure much more expensive.' Now her face turning from serious to sunny, bad teeth showing. 'Your boyfriend rich? Easy for me to arrange laparoscopic surgery. English doctor preferring this procedure, he not liking to use old-fashioned method.' She stops, looks at me with big eyes. 'Machinery very expensive. I can making sure you on farang doctor's list to do laparoscopic surgery. Costing one hundred thousand baht.'

CAN'T SWALLOW IT, CAN'T SPIT IT OUT

'Sawatdee Khrab, Khun Luke! Big surprise seeing you in Thailand.' Bewildered eyes look beyond me. 'Expecting Nong Taiella.'

Panjim Narcoso, the Thai-smiling welcome on his face flattening out as he takes in my expression, rushes over to the sliding glass doors and puts a friendly hand on my left arm. I guessed he'd be in early today, rearranging the salon. His assistant is good, but Panjim is so much better.

Taiella told me that today would be his first day back from holiday, that she'd move in with him right away to keep her whereabouts as secret as possible. Naturally she'd go to the salon right away, so he could do her hair. I'd imagined her sitting on one of the chairs, Panjim holding up her tresses, evaluating what to do.

'What happening, Khun Luke? You looking sick.'

'Taiella's disappeared. I jumped on the first plane as soon as I was sure.'

'Kuhn Teng not seeing her?'

'No, not for two days.' I think back to Teng's closed-up face, have trouble controlling my anger. 'I think she's been abducted by a gang, and that they'll kill her.'

'What you meaning?'

'I think she's been kidnapped.'

'You thinking for ransom?' He leads me to one of his barber chairs and pushes me into it, locks the doors again and draws the curtain across the plate glass fronting the hairdressing franchise.

'Kidnappers snatching on street?'

'All I know is that she's gone.'

'You try talking to older sister, Pi Sayai?'

'Last night, as soon as I landed. A man answered her door and wouldn't let me see her.'

Panjim puts a funnel into a small bottle, busies himself filling it from a larger one, turning his back to me. 'This not sounding good.'

There's only so much an individual – even one pinpointed by the robber fly – can do. I'll need to involve the General as well – but not till after the meeting I've been summoned to in the market.

'Taiella must have told you about the General? The man who got me out of jail?'

I wonder whether a Thai would have more chance of involving him than I have, decide it would be best for us to approach him together.

'Of course. Nong Taiella talking with me about my exalted Excellency, Khun Luke.' He puts a stopper on the smaller bottle, turns towards me. 'My village not far from Dumden, therefore I decide visiting Nong Taiella parents. They telling me surprising news: Mak Kamuki killed in jail. No one knowing what really happening, but villagers saying guard pretending prisoner escaping and shooting.'

I begin to shiver. Was the air-conditioning working over time? 'You've heard Mak Kamuki is dead?'

'Is definite. Guards gunning down in jail.'

The murder suspect's been killed and the General hasn't been in touch to say there won't be a trial? That could only mean he hasn't been informed. Ominous.

'I desperately need your help. I have to find her, and neither my Thai nor my knowledge of Bangkok are up to it.'

Panjim's expression turns into the proverbial inscrutable one. 'You have colleague Khun Teng. He knowing Bangkok very well and having very good English and also connections.'

Panjim's never taken to Teng. Partly because Teng earns quite a bit more than he does, but mostly, I suspect, because of Teng's macho attitude to kathoeys, which really upsets the hairdresser.

'He's in touch with me every day, but he didn't let me know Taiella hadn't come into the office. That's very odd. I'm not sure I can trust him. Taiella's life is in danger and the only man I have any faith in in the police force can't easily be reached.' I've thought carefully about putting it into words, but I feel I owe it to the friend Taiella claims has always stood by her. 'You're a rare friend, Panjim. You have high principles, and you're one of the few people who'd put himself at risk for someone he loves.'

'Herself. You forgetting, Kuhn Luke. Please always thinking me as lady.'

'Of course. Herself.' She, her, herself I drum into my unconscious. There wasn't a word for conscience in the Thai language until quite recently, so it is not a general concept. Their belief in karma conveniently covers many problems. Clearly Panjim's karma has made him – her – more stalwart than many of her compatriots.

She continues setting up her lotions, turning her back to me. 'I have job, Khun Luke.'

'I understand, but I – Taiella and I – are desperate for your help'. I get off the chair and start pacing round. I know that will make her nervous, but I simply can't sit still. 'Forget about money, I'll make it up to you financially – and more. This place managed without you for your holiday, so it can carry on for another day or two, can't it?'

She's still keeping her face turned away. What can I do to convince her?

'It's a matter of life and death, you know.'

'How you knowing this?'

'At first I thought the man who answered Sayai's door was her husband. I didn't take in the tattoos until later, didn't realise he looked more like a Thai boxer than a businessman.'

'What kind tattoos?'

'Some sort of twining forms; something like a mixture of a snake and a scorpion.'

The bottle breaks on the tiled floor, scattering a green liquid. 'You seeing scorpion?'

'Nasty-looking animal. Emblem of some sort, like a member

of a gang. And I was stupid enough to give him the hotel's card! That's how they knew where I was.'

'What kind gang you talking about?' Panjim's got a mop and is slopping the sticky mess into a pail. 'Maybe you see too many movies?'

'They tried to get Taiella in London, Panjim. That's why she rushed back. We thought about it and thought possibly Wuadon's murder wasn't a personal crime. More likely a gang killing.' A slosh of water threatens my feet and I lift them out of trouble. 'It has to be part of something with much wider implications.'

'Buying village children for service industry?' Panjim's on her knees, soaking a cloth, wringing out water, head turned resolutely away. I guess her own experience has been along those lines.

'Commonplace, and local. I think this is on a bigger scale, and much worse.'

'Drug trafficking?'

'No idea. I've been ordered to be in Phetburi Market at eleven this morning if I ever want to see my sweet girl alive again.'

She empties the pail, takes off the smart coat she (as a he) wears to impress customers.

'Phetburi Market not very specific place, farang not going there. So perhaps recognising man coming from his tattoo?'

'It's not a problem. They'll find me. If Westerners don't normally go there I'll be only too easy to spot. I'll be wearing a green tie, one Taiella gave me. That's what he said I had to do.'

She nods. 'This very serious business. I instructing my assistant taking over for today. Then changing clothes. Only taking short time.'

'OK to use your phone? I'll pay, of course.'

She's already disappeared into a curtained-off section of the salon. 'No problem.'

Surges of sweat turn cold in the conditioned air. What kind of idiot relies on miracles? I have to alert the General, make sure he knows I'm back. And somehow pressure him that, if I were to go missing, he'd order a search. So, next stop, call Worluti, put the fear of karma into him.

'Captain Worluti? This is Luke Narland. We spoke yesterday.'

'Sawatdee Khrab, Khun Luke.' Cold, distant, sure he's in charge.

'I need you to contact Lieutenant General Thomupi right away. I've been contacted by a member of the gang who's taken my girlfriend hostage. I'm meeting him shortly...'

A choking noise, covered by a cough. 'You are...you having c... criminal ap...proaching, K...kun Luke?'

Quite a reaction. 'I presume so.'

'Is n...not good idea, K...khun Luke.' An explosive clearing of his throat. 'You s...stranger in this c...country, maybe you letting police – you must letting police handle this matter, for sure!'

'I've already informed the British Embassy, and they will act if I don't get in touch with them by four this afternoon – sahm moang yen – you understand?'

'Bai sahm moang, yes. But I think you must –'

'I've also found out that Mak Kamuki is dead. Shot. Why wasn't I told?'

'M...my Excellency in charge this c...case...'

'Exactly. The General can't know the murder suspect is dead, or he'd have been in touch.'

'You mis...stak...ken. His Excellency asking about c...case many times. He informed very good.'

'I think not, Captain Worluti. The British Embassy know to contact him if I don't return later today. I'm sure you know you should alert him to that.'

A splutter of coughing. 'Of course must check...king facts before telling my Excellency.'

'Check what you like, Captain Worluti. I'll ring this afternoon, and I expect to see the General then.'

'Very busy man...'

'If you don't cooperate I'll go to the Embassy and get them to make an appointment for me.'

I ring off while he's still talking in case he's having the call traced. Then I ring Howard. Somewhere along the line I'll need cash, almost certainly large amounts of cash. I have to rely on his generosity, and his trust.

'The little girl you brought over that day? Abducted? Sounds like a dicey wicket. Anything you need, Luke, old man. Anything at all.'

Of course I know Panjim is kathoey – a ladyboy. I'd mistaken him – her! – for a beautiful woman at that fateful party, when Taiella and I first met, but I'm not prepared for such a radical transformation. She reappears dressed as one of the Thai office girls to be found all over Bangkok. A smart, understated suit just like Taiella's old working clothes – I suspect they *are* her old clothes! There's no trace of glitz and just enough make-up to look the part. And I defy anyone who doesn't know her to spot she isn't a woman.

'This good disguise, yes? In case gang members already knowing Panjim Taiella's friend. Now thinking translator.' The puckish smile dimples her cheeks. 'Maybe now thinking you have new girlfriend. That putting down price.'

I'm impressed. Panjim knows Taiella is in danger, knows we are as well. Wuadon's murder clearly wasn't motivated by an infatuated uncle bent on incest. She must have posed some sort of threat to the gang. And the police have to have been involved – at least some of them, at least after Wuadon was killed.

Once the General finds out what might really be going on he's bound to be personally involved. He is, after all, keen to stop crime, including drug trafficking and the sex trade. Which means the gang will do anything – almost certainly including arranging for several more murders – to prevent him finding out.

That may not be possible, however well organised they are. We have one thing on our side – I'm a farang. If anything happens to me I'll be missed, the police will be forced into a proper investigation, and that would alert the General. So whatever reason they have for getting rid of Taiella and me would no longer solve their problem. I sense there's a chance I can buy Taiella's life.

An assured rat-a-tat on the glass doors. Has the gang followed me, have I put Panjim's life in danger?

She goes over to draw back the curtain and let her assistant in. It doesn't take long to explain that she'll be spending the day with me and Mon will be in charge again. A delighted wai to both of us.

Panjim lifts my collar to loop the green tie under it, does up the top shirt button and puts the tie on like an expert. Then she motions me through the glass doors. 'Mai pen rai, Khun Luke – we take easy. We sharpen slow slow to get sharp knife.' She grins at me, waving a fan in time with her fluttering eyes. 'Fine enough to cut throat of kidnappers.'

USING SHRIMP TO BAIT A PERCH

Making friends with Khun Head Nurse bringing good luck for me. I am very sure. She ready for eating big, and I already know if she asking Luke for money he will be able to arrange finding some from business account. One hundred thousand baht is a very large amount in Thailand, not so much in England. The important matter is my telling the nurse how to get in touch with Luke. I trusting that he has worked out that I am a prisoner, and that the person contacting him knows where I am. Luke is a clever man; I very confident Luke rescuing me.

Instincts telling me money is not main reason Khun Head Nurse acting very kind to me, because I thinking she not asking enough. Maybe she very romantic, I remembering very clear how her eyes were near tears when we talking about loving relationship between Luke and myself. Therefore I thinking she wanting something else, more important than money. More personal.

So now I stop fighting the young nurses and allow one to take blood from my arm.

'I think my fiancé very happy paying for laparoscopic surgery, Khun Head Nurse,' I say as they take lots blood from right arm. That only hurting little bit, but making anxious. Hard for me to stop shaking. All time I thinking maybe the nurses putting poison into my veins so can do as they wish, so wondering why this nurse offering alternative operation? Can be only one reason: she is making money from this choice, because no one else knowing what is going on. So I begin wondering, if Luke offering enough money, maybe he persuading her to help me escape?

Khun Head Nurse having very crooked teeth which show right away in big smile, eyes becoming gentle. 'Excellent result, younger sister. I arranging to put on correct list.'

Heart pounding because now realising something very wrong. Why she not asking me how she contacting Luke? Breathe in deep deep, try hard not to panic. 'Maybe you so kind and giving water in bottle? I not sure if water in taps is for drinking.'

'I very foolish, should bringing before.' Signalling right away to second nurse standing there, one not taking blood. 'Fetch two bottles water. You prefer still or sparkling, younger sister?'

'Very happy with sparkling, Khun Head Nurse.' Hoping is not so easy for adding drugs, maybe they not dissolving quickly.

Kuhn Head Nurse nodding at younger nurse. Now only two women in room with me. Wondering is it possible I running out between them, escape out of unlocked door? Khun Head Nurse looking like old woman, Under Nurse very small. But feeling faint because they taking blood from arm, and I am not very good at coping with medical procedures.

'Everything in good order.' Khun Head Nurse is smiling with a wide mouth. 'Your fiancé is meeting a friend I sending to Phetburi Market hah moang chow – very soon.'

Thinking right away: how can she know this? Trying hard hard to hide my big worries that something is very wrong. If she and her colleague already talking with Luke he must already arriving in Krung Thep. How they knowing where to find Luke? Whole affair looking very serious, cannot be about one hundred thousand baht, must mean Head Nurse will be demanding big money. Sounding more like ransom than operation.

'You want I coming with you, pointing out fiancé?' I try out. I am very sure Luke not giving Head Nurse money unless he knowing I alive and well. Calming down little bit now, knowing I having some time before Nurse and accomplices act.

Eyes showing strong flickers, maybe she angry, maybe she thinking it amusing that I trying such a simple ruse. 'No, younger sister. Staying here. Not hard picking out farang in Phetburi

Market, also wearing special green tie you giving him.'

Now very clear what she telling me: she already contacting Luke, and she working with a partner. Of course I suspect they plan to murder me and harvest all my organs. Who can help? They know my father is only a villager, living a long way from Krung Thep; I know they know he cannot protect me.

'Maybe allow me phoning fiancé? He always carry mobile phone.'

At first I think she will agree, then she sees my trap. 'Of course cannot allow such nonsense. You staying here, enjoy resting, sleeping. I coming back soon soon.'

TOO MUCH GREED MEANS THE WINDFALL IS LOST

It's just on eleven o'clock when Panjim and I arrive on the outskirts of the market. I know Thailand well enough to realise we might have to wait a couple of hours before anyone tries to contact us – the Thai concept of time is very different from the western one. We'll just have to stay around, however tiresome that is. What is much more worrying is that I might not be approached at all if I were seen to be with a companion, even a female one. Perhaps particularly a female one. Panjim agrees. She trails behind me at a discreet distance.

I'm looking out for the man I met at Sayai's and, to be candid, worry he'll have at least two others with him and try to kidnap me, as well as holding Taiella. However, having Panjim in the background does at least mean she can alert the General right away. Surprisingly, we don't have long to wait, though I'm astonished by the person who turns up.

'Khun Luke?' A thickset, middle-aged woman shoves her way past Panjim and over to me at a counter overflowing with a brilliant display of jack fruit, mangoes and coconuts. I pick up a large nut to use as a weapon, just in case. But she doesn't look physically dangerous, merely unattractive. The stallholder is asking for his money. I put the coconut back.

'Yes – khrab.' It always pays to show I can speak a little Thai, and can understand a reasonable amount. Has Panjim spotted I've been approached, or has she been fooled?

'Wanting girlfriend being comfortable?' the woman says in tolerable English. Then leers at me, playing with the friendship ring I gave Taiella, pushing it on and off the little finger on her left hand. 'Must pay!'

'Of course.' Comfortable? I just want her back! Thank God I've got Howard lined up for money. 'You're...' I want to shake her, force her to tell me where Taiella's being held, but know I have to use the soft approach 'You're looking after her, are you? You have some sort of proof?'

Suspicious eyes turn reproachful. 'Not remembering ring giving girlfriend?'

I stare at the glinting metal. Did she hurt my Smileegirl, taking it off? Not likely; it was always loose on her. All the same, visions of hacked-off fingers come into my mind... 'Anyone could have stolen that.'

She huffs away from me, stuffing the ring into a purse. 'Not paying, meaning not seeing for long time.' She twists round, steps sideways, eyes swivelling. She's ridiculously nervous, clearly in two minds about what she's doing, probably about to disappear into the crowd.

Except that Panjim stands in her way, blocking the narrow gangway between stall holdings with a large, leafy plant held in front of her. The woman tries to elbow past and Panjim dances, first left then right, as though she can't decide which way the woman wants to go. The woman swears as she turns back to me, eyes seething a mixture of annoyance and determination.

'How much you want?' I ask, startling the people around by shouting, myself now blocking her way.

Wide nostrils widen even more, her eyes scan round. 'Me Head Nurse in charge of procedures. Two hundred thousand baht for excellent method. No bargaining.'

Procedures? 'You'll bring Taiella when I give you the money, OK?'

'Bring girlfriend?' The scorn spits out in a glob of spittle. 'No. Head Nurse, therefore making sure having laparoscopic surgery instead opening whole body. Leaving only small scar. Also more comfortable, short time for recovery.'

I feel the sweat of terror dripping down my whole body. 'Is she sick?'

The woman's eyebrows meet. 'Not necessary for worry. Girlfriend looking in excellent health. Doing lots tests, making sure all in good order.' Her eyes brush past me, skim the stalls around us. 'Wishing left or right?' A sudden shaft of sunlight through the awnings illuminates a deeply grooved face drawn tight. 'Right side better for carrying baby, left easier for surgeon.' Her mouth twitches as she looks all round again.

She's not making sense to me. I see Panjim is near enough to overhear, to translate for me later. What the hell is going on? Has Taiella gone to some sort of fertility clinic and they think they can get large sums out of me?

Panjim is holding her thumb up behind the woman, tapping her watch, mouthing at me to arrange a meeting place.

'So who sent you?'

She spits. I can see her thinking about pushing Panjim out of the way. 'Arriving for helping girlfriend,' she chokes, shaking a fist at me. 'Why making problems? Very lucky man having generous girlfriend.' She huffs her shoulders, suddenly grins. 'No one sending. Overhearing orderly on mobile, saying meeting farang Phetburi Market, wearing green tie.' Her eyes glitter as she jabs at me. 'Orderly not able change medical procedures, so arriving early before orderly spotting you. Maybe asking for more money, but that man can do nothing!'

I stare at Panjim, unwilling to indicate even with a flick of the eye what was immediately apparent. She looks past me. Panjim puts back the plant, picks up another one.

'So you'll give me your name, and where to contact you?'

Her hand shoots out, grabs my arm, dismissing the idea of any clues as to her identity. 'You coming Pratunam Market today, neung tum, OK? Bigger market, more safe for meeting.'

Seven o'clock tonight. I nod, trying to control my breathing, my heartbeat.

'Coming to stall nearest Phetchaburi Road place crossing with Ratchaprarop Road, OK?' Her eyes disappear between puffy flesh. 'You bringing cash.'

She turns round, pushes past Panjim, who signals to me to let her go. I work out why. We want her out of the way so we can meet the man who'd rung me, the one we know will come to ask for Taiella's ransom – and that will certainly be more than two hundred thousand baht.

Panjim beckons to me to walk further into the market. 'You sick, Khun Luke?' she says, staring at me. 'You needing kidney transplant?'

Not at all what I'm expecting. At first I think it's some kind of Thai joke I don't understand but when I look at Panjim's face I see no trace of humour. 'Is that what she said?' I could feel my breathing stop as I try to think. 'Absolutely not. You sure that's what she said?'

'Not said, but understanding meaning. This woman not criminal, Khun Luke,' Panjim says, standing close to me and almost whispering. 'Because, strange coincidence, I knowing this jar of pickled garlic with legs. I can never forget.'

'You *know* her? That's why you...'

Her face, glistening with sweat, splits into a melon grin. 'She not recognizing me even if she seeing full face. I coming to clinic for operation to remove Adam's apple. She Head Nurse at clinic, walking past open door of room, not interesting in me because not farang.' Panjim laughs – a full throaty laugh of pleasure. 'Now we knowing where they keeping Nong Taiella.'

I freeze, literally freeze. I can't move, not even my vocal chords.

'You understanding me, Khun Luke?' She stares at my catatonic pose, at the face I know to be bloodless. 'Why you upset? Now knowing where criminals holding Nong Taiella. We telling my Excellency Police General, and we fetching.' She frowns at me. 'What wrong, Khun Luke? You not trusting me?'

I gulp, swallow, clear my throat. A sort of wheeze comes out. I try again. 'They've got her in a clinic? That means they're about to perform some ghastly operation on her.' I can hear the screeching tone, know I have to control myself. Thais don't appreciate confrontation, the ethic is to remain calm – mai pen rai – above all, in every situation. If I'm not careful I'll lose Panjim – my only hope of getting Taiella back, literally, in one piece.

Because now I understand exactly what's going on, and can feel myself go rigid. They're holding Taiella to extract a kidney – for me, allegedly. Panjim didn't get it wrong. That's what the woman meant by left or right. I grab at a pole holding up the canopy to stop myself falling.

'So that's their racket, Panjim.' She nods, probably ahead of me. 'They arrange for teenagers from the villages to be living organ donors. That's what was going to happen to Wuadon.' I try, but I can't stop tears coursing down my cheeks. 'They'll murder my sweet Taiella! They'll kill my lovely, enchanting girl to harvest her organs.'

For the first time I feel emotion take over from logic. This time I can't ask my programmers to write a logical sequence to solve my problem. In all the years I've been married to Helga I've never really been touched by her, felt my heart twisted by longings I couldn't suppress, or change. I'd mistaken admiration for love, the exchange of dutiful presents and calibrated smiles as proof of deep feelings. Now I know better, and my body – my whole being – reverberates with feelings I've never even guessed at. Embarrassing perhaps, but I can't stop my shoulders shaking, my tears continuing.

Panjim frowns at me. 'I think you right about scam, Kuhn Luke, but not necessary to worry. We having plenty time for rescue. Thinking nurse not having any idea Nong Taiella not agreeing to operation. In any case clinic must arranging tests, even if you right they plan murdering Nong Taiella. And you forgetting; chief nurse not here *instead* of man calling you, she here on own account.'

My panic subsides bit by bit. Panjim gets us both a drink of coconut water and it calms me. I grasp that, indeed, we do have time. All we have to do is make sure we meet Tattoo Thug and agree his price. He'll know he won't get his money unless he can give us proof of a live Taiella.

And then another thought strikes me. Panjim is right. The nurse is probably exploiting the situation on her own – but so is Tattoo Thug! He might be a member of the gang, but he's seen a way to make a fortune all for himself. As long as we manage to convince him he'll get the money he'll be my best bet to keep Taiella safe. And give us time to get the General on the case.

The robber fly has scored again. But we still have to make sure Tattoo Thug finds me. Otherwise I'll never see my Smileegirl again.

Panjim and I walk round that market at least thirty times, our feet tiring, our throats parched. Coconuts are, as always, plentiful and cheap. Our clothes turn grey with dust and saturated sweat. By now we must be reeking. Wearing the green tie is a small torture I have to bear. Not because I'm not easy to spot – I don't see a single other farang – but because I know I have to keep to the conditions Tattoo Thug dictated.

By half-past one we're beginning to wonder whether he saw me talking to the nurse and decided not to contact me.

Suddenly, there he is. The same burly body, pockmarked face. He saw us together. He isn't pleased but I know immediately that Panjim was right. The fact that she looks like a woman has the effect of calming the man.

'You want see girlfriend?' He stares at Panjim. 'Or having new woman?'

'Friend of Nong Taiella,' Panjim puts in, in Thai. 'Here to translate for Khun Luke. Of course wanting see girlfriend, being with fiancée.'

The man nods, apparently not suspecting anything. The conversation between them is something I can't follow, but I know Panjim will report what's relevant later. What I do gather is that the ransom is set at five million baht, around eighty-five thousand pounds. And that he wants it, in cash, within two days. He'll get in touch as to where he'll deliver Taiella and collect the money.

I feel cold tentacles of despair. I'm not sure that even Howard can produce such a large sum in such a short time. He's an investor, not someone who keeps cash in his bank account.

'In big danger coming here,' the man tells me, addressing me directly, eyes swivelling round in case we're being spied on. 'Doctors planning put girl on operating table soon soon, cannot stop. You doing as asking. If not girlfriend die for sure.'

TALKING WILL ONLY GET YOU A SMALL REWARD

Khun Head Nurse walking into my room, whistling a tune, her step very light, hands smoothing clean hospital gown she puts on the bed. She looks ten years younger than the last time she came. My feet want to dance because I am sure she meeting Luke, but I decide not to question her but to wait.

Her eyes provoke me to ask why she looking so happy, but I prefer not to show how much I care. When nothing happening she smiling with very wide lips. 'Going Phetburi Market before noon. You guessing who I seeing?'

This means she saw Luke for sure. My heart thumps hard. Can she hear it? I sit still, try hard not moving a single muscle.

The smile peels off her face. 'You not have interest knowing?'

I look at her with big eyes. 'Maybe you meeting handsome boyfriend, giving you flowers?'

She laughs, puts her hand on my shoulder. It feels very warm. 'Not boyfriend for me. *Your* boyfriend.' Her eyes search my face, my body. 'He big man, good looking.' Her head leans sideways on her neck. 'Handsome, but not young.' She looks at me sideways. 'Maybe he finding nice new tree when axe already broken.'

'He not so old, only thirty-eight.' Now wish I had not spoken. Khun Head Nurse is only trying to fill the bucket with water when the river is high.

'Mai pen rai, meaning he having sufficient money.' Bright eyes ask for a reaction, but I stay silent. 'Agreeing to pay for laparoscopic

278

surgery. I trusting him to bring money, so we doing scan now.' Her face turns grave in a sudden look like a stone as she points at my hospital gown. 'Khun Mor Napoka ordering scan today. Must doing as he orders.'

My instincts tell me not to have a scan if possible. I not really knowing why, but thinking that without a scan the doctors cannot tell if I am healthy enough for donating kidney.

Already I work out that they will put me on operating table to harvest kidney, then lie and say I died on the table – giving reasons such as a faulty heart, allergic to anaesthetics or to drugs of some kind maybe. Not easy to prove this incorrect, therefore I know I am only safe as long as their tests are not complete.

'All operations having some degree risk,' I say, starting to cry.

She frowns, not understanding what I want. 'But you such brave girl, such good girl, offering kidney for boyfriend for making healthy. You lovely couple, looking like gold branch with jade leaf, younger sister! Why fearful now?'

I must build on her sympathy, on the romantic feelings of Khun Head Nurse. 'Excusing emotion, Khun Head Nurse. Doctor promising boyfriend holding hand before I going to operating theatre. Maybe you bring to clinic for me, only for few minutes?'

She blinks at me, her look soft and dreamy. She enjoying this romantic story, and it is not so wrong. If Luke needing a kidney I would give it to him, no problem.

'OK, little sister, I see if can bring boyfriend here.' She opens the hospital gown for me to put on. 'This only for CT scan, not hurting or harming, only telling us if kidney OK for boyfriend. If not suitable we finding kidney from other donor. No need for worrying.'

'You having lots donors here?'

She is gay, dancing round room. 'Not here, little sister. We bringing from Isaan villages, they coming Krung Thep for new life.' She helps me put on the gown, very gently. 'Parents get sum money, young people get accommodation, education, money while they waiting for becoming donor. Then we offering job in health industry. Is good deal for all, helping families from poor villages, helping sick people.'

'You knowing time for operation, Khun Head Nurse?'

'Three, four days. We cannot schedule until tests complete.' She walks round, plumping pillows, smoothing bedclothes. 'Now, younger sister, if I fetching boyfriend, maybe you doing something for me.'

Somehow I already know she is not talking about money. She has something far more important on her mind. 'I very happy helping you, Khun Head Nurse.'

'How you meeting such handsome farang, not so old?'

I understand at last. She is looking for a husband, but from the way she acting I think not for herself; maybe a husband for a daughter. 'My special friend taking me to party. There I meeting future boyfriend. He with own friends, coming to party for business reasons.'

'And who this friend? He can arrange taking beautiful Thai girls to more parties?' Her face is glowing, the years skipping away.

'He working in hairdressing salon in ZenZam Centre. He excellent hairdresser, so lots clients and friends of clients. Boyfriend...'

Her eyes go cold instantly, and I know big mistake to mention boyfriend because now she knows I am talking about kathoey. Instead of being gentle her hands turning very rough.

'You meaning friend is kathoey, and knowing boyfriend?'

'He not boyfriend to my boyfriend, Khun Head Nurse! He...'

'He coming with farang in market!'

Pi Panjim is helping Luke to find me? Khun Head Nurse is not stupid woman, she right away understands what is going on.

'He helping fiancé find way round Krung Thep, translating Thai,' I say quickly to cover up.

'Boyfriend already speaking Thai. Plenty kathoey coming here for operations. Maybe kathoey friend know where I working, finding me.' She looks round the room. I can see she is very scared.

'Fiancé knowing you helping me, Khun Head Nurse, and very grateful. You having daughter?' I must be careful not to turn into an overexcited rabbit, and forget what I am trying to do.

She looks at me with a little bit of a smile. I see I can undo my mistake. 'Daughter sixteen years.' Head Nurse looking less unhappy now.

Now wrapping my hands round her right hand, smiling. 'We help each other. You bring boyfriend for short time for making me feel good. When finishing all medical procedures Khun Luke taking your daughter England, finding good husband.'

Her face is old again, but she ties the back of my gown very gently.

BUYING A WATER BUFFALO IN THE MARSH

'I've got to contact my friend Howard, Panjim. I need the money in place just in case things go wrong with the police. And then I want to go to the bank and pick up that two hundred thousand baht for Nurse Woman.'

'You panic, Khun Luke. You not need money, my Excellency go straight for clinic and fetching Nong Taiella. Going police station right now, and talking with Police Captain Worluti. Then he will taking us to my Excellency for sure.'

It's a Thai characteristic to take things at face value. I'm a little more cynical than that. Police Lieutenant General Thomupi is no ordinary Thai. He'll take what he can get and then play it the way it works for him. As the Thais so cleverly put it: He's a nun who sets a dried fish free.

'Possibly he will, but I'm not going to take any chances.'

She shrugged, clearly thinking me a fool. 'OK, your cash.'

'After I've arranged for the money I want to contact someone with clout at the British Embassy. Just in case Worluti doesn't cooperate, let alone the General.' I glance at Panjim, at the eagerness in her face. 'And in case the General decides not to act.'

'Not possible. Well-known as campaigning for Thailand to be less corrupt, acting quick quick for sure.'

I decide on the diplomatic approach. 'Or he may be gunned down before we get to him. A lot of people must hate his guts.'

'Slow slow, Khun Luke!' She puts her hand on my arm. 'Why

you not want go police before British Embassy?'

'They close at three-thirty, and I might miss the chance.' I move my arm out of reach, impatient to get on. 'Now, shall I go back to my hotel to make the calls, or can I do that from your office?'

'We go my office. Must changing back to ordinary clothing.'

The magic words 'living donor organs' energised both the British Embassy and Captain Worluti. We are promised a meeting with the General at five. He is not, apparently, available before then.

Miraculously I've got through to Howard without a hitch.

'Don't worry, Luke, old chap. I can get my bank manager to transfer that sum to your business account pronto. Everything'll be tickety-boo.' His chortle sounds threatening. 'I can always take my business elsewhere, don't y'know. Cash should be there tomorrow.'

'You really are a marvel, Howler. D'you think they'll make any problems about letting me have it in cash?'

Howard's familiar chuckle calms me. 'Not that unusual in Bangkok, old bean. I'll stipulate that's the deal.'

I feel my throat constrict. 'You're a true friend, Howard, old man. I'll never forget this.'

'Get the little girl back, that's the thing.' The emotion in his voice sounds wistful. 'You're a lucky so-and-so. She's a gem, a pearl.'

I decide to collect the cash for Nurse Woman while Panjim changes back into her male persona. Then we'll be set to tackle the General.

'Mr Narland, an unexpected pleasure.' The General, full regalia starched to perfection, rises and holds out his hand.

I wish I'd thought to wipe the sweat off. I expected the usual Thai wai, but knew better than to wai first. The General's choosing of the Western form has to be significant. He's been told about Mak Kamuki – my guess is belatedly.

'This is Khun Panjim Narcoso, your Excellency. Sh-he comes from a village only about twenty miles from Dumden. He was on holiday there until yesterday...' He, him, himself!

Peremptory eyes flicker for an instant towards Panjim, then

back to me. 'I have already made enquiries. He actually comes from across the border.' The tortoise smile. 'A village in Laos, I understand.' He waves his hand, glass-eyes Panjim and turns away.

Laos? Panjim is originally from Laos and Taiella's never mentioned that? Wasn't there also some sort of connection between Wuadon and Laos? Of course – she came from there originally!

The General motions me to sit opposite an opulent desk inlaid with mother of pearl. My chair, though comfortable, is noticeably lower than his. Panjim is left to stand.

'Quite so. I have been informed about some disturbing events which have taken place in Udon Thani since I last saw you. I had no idea Mak Kamuki is dead.'

'Indeed. Gunned down, your Excellency.'

His eyebrows disappear into his hairline. 'Exactly. While trying to escape. Most unfortunate.' He clicks at the computer keyboard on his desk, resettles into his chair, waits. 'I sent for a full report as soon as Captain Worluti alerted me.' He flicks eyes at Panjim, widens his nostrils, returns to the computer screen. 'Yes, that appears to be correct.'

'Some time ago, apparently,' I can't help saying.

'So it would appear. We have all that in hand.' He clicks the computer off, sits back in his chair and crosses his arms. 'Now, I understand, you have lost your fiancée. A trifle careless, perhaps.'

Neither the little sideways smile, nor the jocular tone, registers with me immediately. When they do I have to control my temper. 'The first attempt was in London. That's why Taiella came back to Bangkok. Then, the day before I could get here, she disappeared.'

'Of course you are very worried.' His nonchalant look takes in my irritation. 'However, you will be glad to hear I have not been idle since Police Captain Worluti told me about Mak Kamuki's death. Naturally we have Taiella Motubaki's details on record. I sent someone to her sister's place...'

So our scheduled meeting hasn't prevented him from making enquiries earlier. I fume again. 'Did she know anything?'

'Forbearance eradicates all evil, Mr Narland.' His lips all but disappear. 'Do you know the sister well?'

'I've met her a couple of times.'

'And did you form any sort of impression?'

Should I say what I suspect? I see no point in that. 'Not really. A pleasant woman with a young child, the second wife of a reasonably well-to-do business man.'

'Precisely.' He folds his hands wai-style, brings them up to his chin. 'It will be helpful if you bear in mind that anger is like rust eating away at metal.' He scans my face. 'When we went to the apartment no one was there.' He stops, his eyes steady on me. 'A calm mind understands the nature of evil, and can overcome it.'

'Indeed.'

'We found the sister's body, Mr Narland. She had been bludgeoned to death.'

'They killed Sayai?' A surge of panic brings treble to my voice, blood to my face. 'What about the boy?'

'We found no sign of him. Perhaps he hid when he heard the perpetrator, or perpetrators, come in. Possibly he ran off to his father when he realised what had happened.'

I nod, words not being quite under my control. The terrible sadness of a young boy who'd know what to do in such a situation. Taiella will be devastated. I feel her pain. Will she blame me, decide against me?

'Now, Mr Narland, of course you are emotionally involved, and I regret these circumstances.' He spreads steepled fingers. 'There are no secret places for those who sin. We will stop these criminals. I understand you have important new information.'

I tell him the story of how I tried to contact Sayai and all that happened as a consequence. Except, on instinct, I leave out Nurse Woman. Instead, I tell the General that Panjim recognised Tattoo Thug as an orderly from the clinic where he'd had his Adam's apple removed.

'So you know where this clinic is, do you, Panjim?' his Excellency says in Thai, clicking the computer on again. I note that he just uses the first name. No salutation. Insulting.

Panjim shows no reaction, and doesn't allude to the meeting with Khun Head Nurse. 'Yes, my Excellency,' he answers, eyes downcast. 'Taking your men there and rescuing Nong Taiella no problem.'

'You will give us the address, give us details of the exact location.' The General turns back to me. 'We are dealing with a well-thought-out criminal scheme. It will need serious planning to decide how best to approach this clinic. We will arrange to act as soon as possible.'

'But you will raid them right away? Taiella's in terrible danger!'

His head is bent towards the computer screen. 'As soon as possible. We already have some leads about the man who probably murdered the older sister. Your description fits our sources.'

'But you *are* making rescuing Taiella a priority?' I don't want to annoy him, but I have the feeling that Taiella's safety is not paramount as far as he's concerned.

'The human body dies, but fame and honour live on forever. We will act as quickly as possible.' Unemotional eyes indicate his distaste. 'Meanwhile it would be wise for you to go about your normal business.'

Is he expecting me to talk to bank managers, work out new programmes?

'You must understand my position, Mr Narland. I have to get evidence of what is going on, to stop this infamous abuse of impecunious villagers and their innocent children.'

And Thailand's reputation. 'But Taiella's about to be murdered!'

'A poisonous liquid cannot seep into an unwounded body. Evil will not befall anyone who has done no wrong.'

'She's the prisoner of unscrupulous criminals!'

'I think you can be sure that the man who has demanded five million baht will protect her, otherwise he will not get his money.' The measured tones, the affable expression, bring sweat running into my eyes. 'Your girlfriend will be safe until the arranged meeting...'

'My fiancée!'

'I beg your pardon.'

'This man might want to keep her safe, General, but he might not be able to. He certainly isn't the head of this gang!'

'Mai pen rai, Mr Narland. Nothing else will do much good.' He stands, goes to the door, opens it. 'We will meet again in happier circumstances.'

Panjim and I walk out of the police station, silent until we're out of earshot.

'Now you know why I took out the cash for Nurse Woman,' I say, bitterness in my voice.

'Frogs choose boss,' he agrees. 'You right about my Excellency. Because I am kathoey, he digging with mouth and chips with eyes.'

'Exactly. Remember, he had me held in that disgusting holding cell. Quite unnecessary. Now, it's almost time to meet Nurse Woman, isn't it?'

Panjim nods. He does, I'm sure, deeply resent the loss of face inflicted by the General. Not merely autocratic and supercilious – downright rude. Will it affect him as far as rescuing Taiella is concerned? Will he lose heart, or is he used to it, so he'll just brush it off and carry on as before? I can't tell.

'We go pick up money from salon now. Also must change again, disguise so no one recognizing me. Then we go meeting Head Nurse in market.'

While Panjim is changing and instructing his assistant I still have half an hour to get through. I shuffle over to the toy department where Taiella used to work. Perhaps I'll gain some strength from visiting the place where she smiled her wares, charmed her customers. My heart aches in a way I've never known before. Am I about to lose the most precious gift I've ever had? Will we ever be together again? If we have children we'll take them to a place like this, watch their eyes light up, give them the toys they long for. I finger a slinky, one of those mind-numbing gadgets which glide from hand to hand. I try to engage the unsmiling girl who serves me.

It doesn't work. I turn back to the salon, sit and wait for Panjim, unable even to read the English language magazines he keeps for his clients. At first I watch the long, thin hand of the clock tick round, second by second, dragging a minute for each one. I rock the slinky from hand to hand until Panjim looks at me, hard and long.

'We leaving for market soon soon, Khun Luke.' He'll transform himself into a woman again. A secretary type, as before.

FETCH WATER AT HIGH TIDE

You sure boyfriend agree taking my daughter England?'

'I sure,' I say, tears coming into my eyes while thinking about my wonderful Luke. 'You must fetching him, bringing to see me. Just for few minutes, Khun Head Nurse,' I add, because I can see her forehead creasing into deep ruts. 'Remember the Buddha says: If you do good you receive good, if you do evil you receive evil.'

At first I worry little bit in case Luke will not want to come, then I remember he always ringing me, wanted to hear my voice when I not with him. He will come, I am very sure.

Khun Head Nurse has eyes very big now, watching me. 'Younger sister, staying this room. Someone coming in, you say you having bad headache, cannot move. They thinking I giving medicine and go away.'

It worrying me that Khun Head Nurse thinks someone may be coming to fetch me when she is not here. I am sure she is not part of the gang, she is just a nurse paid by the clinic, she not understanding what really happening. But maybe she also is beginning to have suspicions because of my situation.

'I staying here, Khun Head Nurse, no problem. I wanting rest.'

'I locking door for protecting you.'

She leaves, and there is nothing I can do except bite my nails. They are already very short.

'Nurse from clinic arriving, Khun Luke,' Panjim warns me. 'Look

288

on right.'

'Sawatdee khrab,' I say, relieved Nurse Woman has turned up on time.

'Sawatdee kha.' She wai-s, then stares at Panjim.

'This is one of Taiella's friends. She's my translator.'

Her eyes shoot at Panjim, then land on me with the fury of a woman who recognizes she's been duped. 'You think stupid, you think I setting chicken free? This is person accompanying before, recognising kathoey. Such people coming all time to clinic for operations. Recognising this one coming for Adam apple surgery,' she snarls, index finger pointing at Panjim.

'Mai pen rai,' I say, moving my body to cut off her retreat, my elbows wide, ready to stop her physically if I have to. 'Very clever of you to spot that so quickly,' I add, my wide mouth straining my face. 'That tells you we already knew where you work when we met before. We could have come to the clinic and told the doctors you were asking for money to put my girlfriend on the laparoscopic list. But we did not.'

Panjim translates for her. She nods, grave at first, then actually smiles at me, though turning her back on the despised kathoey. At least I take it that the grimace she produces is a smile, a variant of the many Thai smiles, and one I have not come across before.

'You very good man. Girlfriend saying you taking my daughter for England if arranging taking to clinic to see girlfriend. Short time only.'

Am I hearing this right? I ask Panjim to translate and he confirms it. So that's how Taiella got this woman on our side. Helga may think Taiella's a stupid village girl. Not at all. I reckon she's done as well as Helga would in that situation – quite possibly better.

I nod fit to dislocate my neck. 'We'll be delighted to take your daughter to England with us. How old is she?'

'Sixteen. Very beautiful.'

I continue my mandarin act. 'I'm sure.'

Suddenly the grim look returns. 'Giving money now.'

'I'll give you the money at the clinic.' I show her the bag I'm carrying it in, open it, let her see the cash. 'You understand that

I'm longing to see my girlfriend once more before she gives me the biggest present anyone can give.'

The soft look is back. 'In whole life never seeing such love! So romantic Nong doing this for you!'

'Exactly.' I gulp back my distaste, put on a travesty of a smile. 'You can see why I want to hug her, hold her in my arms, before she makes this wonderful sacrifice for me?' It's a tear-jerker playing just for the nurse, a young woman giving up her kidney for her beloved.

'Taking to clinic now.'

She starts off towards the Phetchaburi Road. We follow, hailing a cab. We all climb aboard and she gives the driver an address. I raise my eyebrows at Panjim and she spreads her nostrils in assent.

The roads are clear. It doesn't take more than twenty minutes before the cab pulls up in a side street which looks pretty deserted.

'Make sure he waits for us,' I say to Panjim as Nurse Woman strides ahead. 'Offer an extra tip.' I don't fancy escaping on foot. For all I know Taiella's been given sedatives or worse, and won't be in a state to walk, let alone run.

Panjim cottons on right away, pretends to pay the driver, talks softly to him. I see the man nod.

We follow Nurse Woman to the staff entrance. She brisks ahead of us, walking rapidly through a maze of similar-looking corridors stacked with the usual trolleys and other hospital paraphernalia. I think of Hansel and Gretel, of how Hansel strewed pebbles to lead them back out of the forest. I bend as I walk, placing the odd baht – and even the almost negligible satang – here and there, but soon run out of ammunition, even though Panjim supplies a further six coins.

At last Nurse Woman slows, turns round to see whether we're still there, then clicks a knob to unlock a door.

'Staying only five minutes,' she says, eyes bright with emotion. 'Cannot allow longer. Tan Doctor angry if finding out.' She pushes me through the door.

The room is unlit, the form lying on the bed motionless. I make out a dark head of hair and a short, slim body under a sheet. My heart races erratically, my pulse rockets.

'Taiella?'

The form bolts upright, throws off the sheet and stretches out her arms, a broad smile on her face. 'Tilac! You come res...'

I put my fingers over her lips, remembering Buddhist maxims. 'Don't talk!' I whisper. We have to get Taiella out of here, everything else can wait. My mouth nuzzles her ear: 'I'm going to ask to be left alone with you for ten minutes, with Panjim outside. As soon as she signals the nurse has gone, we'll make a break for it.'

I feel my little girl shudder, but she doesn't say another word.

I look up at Nurse Woman devouring our meeting, hold out the bag with the cash. 'Maybe we could have a few minutes to ourselves? Panjim, can you translate?'

Nurse Woman nods her understanding, moist eyes sweeping over us. 'Not worrying. Arranging correct surgery list.' She turns to Panjim. 'Stay in bathroom. Bad idea other staff seeing.'

Does that mean she's going to lock the door on us? She walks out. The click of the closing door reverberates throughout my body.

I walk up to the window, staring at the impressive array of bars. 'No need worrying.' Panjim prances to the door, opening it. 'Pushing in small knob stopping door locking.'

Though definitely against my normal inclinations, at that moment I could have kissed her. Taiella is wearing nothing but a hospital gown. I grab a towel and wind it round her. We start down the corridor, desperately trying to remember which way to go to find the few coins I managed to plant. There are, I know, several doors between us and the staff exit.

The roar behind us has a familiar tone. 'What fuck doing?' the voice bellows in Thai. Tattoo Thug, seeing his five million baht escaping.

The furnace breath behind me makes me turn to trip him up, though sure I'm not likely to be a match in a fight. 'Run!' I shout at Taiella. 'Get out with Panjim!'

As I twist round I hear the door ahead of us fly open with a gust of wind which nearly topples us. 'Go!' I yell, but Taiella grabs my hand, urging me on with them. We head through the opening just as the blast of air disappears. I turn, mouth wide as I witness an airborne attack on

Tattoo Thug. A yellow-bodied insect – a robber fly! The hoarse bellow chokes into a rattling gasp as, true to its reputation, the assassin fly injects him with a cocktail of nerve toxins. Enough, I hope, to stun him for the few seconds we need.

Another rush of wind seems to propel us through the corridors, the coins glinting at the sides as we're manoeuvred to the exit.

We bundle into the waiting cab. 'Thai-Pan Hotel,' I yell. 'Sukhumvit Road! A thousand baht if you lose us in traffic!'

Panjim shouts a translation. We rock into the back seat as the driver swerves headlong into the Bangkok rush hour. Shocked into silence, Taiella and I cling to each other, desperate to prove that we're really together again. We're incapable of letting go.

'All clear,' Panjim announces. 'No one following.'

Taiella extricates herself from me, turns to her. 'You very special friend, Pi Panjim. We never forgetting how you helping.'

'I try hard.' She puts her arm round the two of us. 'But not arranging assassin fly or wind. How it possible for such strong wind blowing inside air-conditioned clinic?'

Taiella grabs us both by a hand, lifts them up. 'No problem for Nong Wuadon spirit,' she says. 'She coming, helping us. She turning into strong gale, then robber fly, then strong gale. She strong-minded girl!'

FLYING TERMITES FLY
INTO THE FIRE

I look in driver's mirror because I am very afraid people from the clinic are following, but I see no signs. Still, I knowing that gang will not allow us to get away without following. Even before Luke telling me about ransom and deal with Khun Head Nurse I knowing we must leave Thailand right now, otherwise they killing us.

'Maybe Thai-Pan Hotel not such good idea, tilac. Gang knows you staying there, they sending assassins to kill for sure.'

Luke and Pi Panjim look at each other, nodding heads.

'What? Right, good thinking. I'm carrying my passport. They can take payment for the bill from my credit card.'

'Maybe we go my sister house. My clothing there.'

Luke puts his arm round me, holding me close. 'There's some really terrible news I have to tell you, sweetheart. I'm so sorry, you're going to be...'

I feel hot from running, and very excited, but a cold shiver makes my skin taut, my muscles ache. 'Pi Sayai, she OK, Luke?' Tears are coming already, I can feel my elder sister's spirit is not happy.

Luke holds me close, strokes my hair, so already I know without his saying a single word.

'They kidnapping her? She also in clinic? What happening my nephew?'

'Gang from Laos very cruel, Nong Taiella.' I can hear tears in

Pi Panjim's voice. 'They hurting elder sister.' Voice very low.

'They hurting bad?' I can see from Luke's face it is more than bad.

'They killing.' Pi Panjim sits without moving, tears trickling down her face. 'My Excellency telling us. Only one body. Nobody knows what happening to nephew. We think he running away and finding father.'

The muscles in my throat are not functioning so I cannot speak. The muscles in the rest of my body are also locked – I cannot move. I sit silent, tears running down my cheeks, my nose, not making a single sound.

Luke hugs me more, then speaks to Pi Panjim over my head. 'She's absolutely right, Panjim. No one, not even the General, will be able to protect us. We have to get to the airport and get the next plane to London. The only safe place in Thailand will be in the departure lounge, after the security checks.'

'We have no choice. We still must go Pi Sayai's house.'

I know Pi Panjim right, but the tears are coming so fast I almost cannot breathe. I must try to say good-bye to the spirit of my beloved sister, dead because she is my sister, for no other reason.

'You mean because of Taiella's clothes?' Luke asks. 'Don't think we can go there, the police will be all over the place. What about lending her some of yours?'

'Not clothes, Khun Luke – passport with visa!'

'I hardly think the police will just let her pick it up!'

'They cannot refusing Nong Taiella fetching private property,' Pi Panjim insists. 'Maybe pretending I am Nong Taiella, asking for clothing, personal belongings. Police guarding place not knowing what she looking like, also they not knowing she kidnapped. They giving me.'

I clear throat, finding voice. 'I leaving passport in office, Luke. Thinking not safe in m-my s-sister house.' I finding it hard to speak, start crying again, cannot stop.

Luke directs the taxi to his office. Already knowing no problem if Khun Teng not there, Luke has key, and also he knowing combination for safe. But how will I get clothes?

'Stopping in side street, I buy clothing for me,' Pi Panjim says. 'Nong Taiella taking old office clothes, I changing back to man.'

'Teng always keeps a change of clothes in the office, Panjim. To freshen up in case he meets clients. You can borrow those.'

Door to Luke office wide open, furniture upside down, papers all over floor. We finding Teng on the floor behind his desk, very still. Luke runs up to colleague he knowing for four years, always in the past a good friend.

Luke kneels beside Kuhn Teng, sees tie tight around his neck, tries undoing knot. He pulls his Swiss army knife out of his pocket, slits the tie, gives Kuhn Teng kiss of life.

Kuhn Teng not moving, his eyes already wide circles popping out. He is dead for sure. Luke holds a mirror to test for breath, tries for pulse. Nothing. Luke looking very sad, very unhappy.

'So now we know why Teng behaved in such an odd way,' he saying, putting material over Teng's face. 'I was so overcome with worry about Taiella it never occurred to me to worry about Teng.'

'Sorry to tell you, Kuhn Luke. This gang very organised. Not possible for you to do anything to save outstanding Thai associate.'

The gang not finding the safe behind the mirror in the bathroom. We taking out my passport, some baht, some important business papers. Pi Panjim and I change clothes. We leaving office, shutting door and walk out: one office girl, one Thai man in businessman suit, one farang.

'I think we must asking my Excellency to protect us, tilac. If gang finding us, they killing us for sure.'

Luke looks uncomfortable. 'Don't think we can do that. He asked me not to take any action, to allow his people to do it all.'

'But you refuse waiting?'

'Without telling him. I thought they might well operate on you – or worse – if we didn't act as quickly as we could. I didn't tell him about meeting Nurse Woman – Khun Head Nurse.'

Now understanding why Luke is not using mobile phone, telling police he saving me. 'That is why you not ringing my Excellency, telling I OK?'

'Exactly. He could – almost certainly would – stop us leaving the country. There's a really good chance the gang won't find us before we can get away.' He turns to Pi Panjim. 'Safest if we split up now, Panjim. I can't thank you enough…'

'Nothing to thank, Khun Luke. Nong Taiella is best friend I having in Bangkok.'

'You'll come and visit?'

'I always wanting to learn techniques in Taylor Taylor, top London hairdressing salon.'

'No problem. I'll organize it as soon as we get back.' Luke turns to me. 'He can stay with us, tilac.'

'Is wonderful idea.'

'We'll grab a cab to the airport now, try to get on the next flight.'

Pi Panjim wai-ing and Luke wai-ing back.

'If you wouldn't mind doing one more thing for us, Panjim. I'll ring you when we're boarding. Check that the flight's taken off, then get in touch with the police. Anonymously of course.'

We very lucky, there is a flight in three hours, some empty seats on plane. Luke pays with credit card using mobile phone.

That is the exact moment when we hear two police cars behind us, sirens screeching.

'Two thousand baht if you can get us to the airport before the police catch us,' Luke says to the driver, holding out money.

Driver grabs money, puts foot hard on accelerator, swerves nearly off road.

Now driving fast as he can, but police having better cars. Taxi driver moving quick quick to side of road, police driving past, do not stop. They not looking for us!

At last we on the plane, flying back to London. I not knnowing if my nephew still alive, I not able say goodbye to my sweet elder sister Sayai, will not be able to attend her funeral. Will Pi Sayai's spirit find peace? What can I do to help her?

I should be happy being with Luke, and I am happy, but also sad. Why have we had all this trouble? All we ever wanting was to be free to love each other, to marry, to hope to have a family.

Then I remember my teachers telling me: a wise person remains unmoved by praise or blame, by good or evil, just like a mountain of solid rock remains unshaken by the fiercest storm. Like the tree which bears fruit after the roots have been watered, Luke and I intend to give rice to many, and place much gold leaf on the back of the Buddha. Soon our sorrows will fall away from us.

IN HOT WATER THE FISH LIVES, IN COLD WATER THE FISH DIES

I feel really bad about not getting in touch with the General as soon as we'd rescued Taiella. But, as the Thais put it, windows have ears, doors have holes. I reckoned we might never make it out of the country if I'd alerted him.

Will it mean we can never go back to Taiella's home? Why should it. We haven't committed any crime. And I'm pretty sure the police will have plenty of time to raid the clinic and shut it down – if they want to. Harvesting organs is, after all, a good export trade, and Thailand is a poor country.

I ring Panjim, then Howard, as soon as we're safely through the security checks.

'That you, Howard?'

'Luke! Are you all right, old man?' He sounds odd, as though he has something important to say but is keeping it in reserve.

'All of a piece.'

'Is the little girl safe?' There's a pause as he clears his throat. He sounds choked. I wonder whether Geraldine is all right. 'The funds haven't been moved, d'you see. Bit worried.'

'Taiella's absolutely fine. Marvellous, isn't it? We didn't need the cash. You'll hear all about it when I see you. But I'll never forget your coming to our rescue, Howler, old chap. I can't tell you how much that means to me – to both of us.'

'You've got her back, hunky-dory?' The Howard chuckle, purring delight. 'So how d'you fix it? Outwitted the scoundrels, eh? Bit of old Blighty, I'll be bound!'

'Can't take all the glory, I'm afraid. In great part due to one of Taiella's friends. A ladyboy called Panjim.'

'Well, there you are. The fame of the virtuous spreads even against the wind.'

I laugh. The Spelters, apparently, are clearly even more immersed in Thai culture than before. And that in spite of my misfortunes.

'I know, you think we've gone batty about Thailand. Well, maybe we have. We know there are problems, but they seem more on the surface than the murky waters we go in for in the West.'

'And that's a good thing?'

'Easier to counter, old bean.'

Maybe he has a point at that. 'You sound very cheerful. Does that mean you're off to Thailand sometime soon?'

'There's something you should know, old man.'

Is this the brush off? He's going to pull out of my business? Without Howard I'll find it difficult to cope at all; even with him things aren't exactly in the best of health. My Thai problems haven't helped.

'Been a bit of a change of heart.'

I knew it. Fuck.

'It's all these complications you've had.'

'You don't want to be involved any more, that it?' I catch my breath, then go on. 'I can't blame you, Howler. You've been wonderful through it all...'

'Not my meaning at all, old boy! Not a bit of it. Fact is, we've had a word or two with your lady... with Helga.'

Helga? They're taking her side? 'I know she and Geraldine are good friends...'

'Introduced her to someone else, don't y'know.'

'You mean to say...?' I can hardly believe it. 'She didn't stop you?'

'Didn't ask, old boy. Decent chappie we've known for yonks, lost his wife to cancer. Invited them both to dinner. Then had a little chat with her, don't y'know, suggested giving another fellow a whirl. No point hanging about.'

'Well, yes...'

'So here's the long and the short of it: she's not going to contest the divorce. You can be free chop chop, soon as the formalities are done. She'll get it all seen to Bob's your uncle.'

The General does his stuff, thorough and above board. He closes down the clinic, imprisons known members of the gang, alerts rural authorities to the problem, issues dire warnings against reprisals. We understand it will be reasonably safe for us to return to Thailand – in due course.

We spend the months waiting for the decree absolute in planning our Thai wedding. We'll invite the Spelters, and my whole family, for a trip to the Land of Smiles. My people's first experience of the country, of the Far East, in fact. They can sample the marvels of Bangkok, the temples, the Thais themselves. And, finally, they can travel with us to Dumden Village, for the Buddhist wedding ceremony which is going to take place there.

The minibus, the most comfortable transport I can arrange from Udon Thani to Dumden, carries the Spelters, my family and me to the village, where Taiella is waiting with her parents. Wirat Motubaki is standing in front of his house to greet us. This time he receives us, smiling his Songkran best, happy enough with the handsome wedding present I've already given him and his wife. More than the price he asked, the day before the cosmic frog tried to eat our lunar friend so many moons ago.

The whole village crowds round, watchful, silent. We climb up into the Motubaki house and make ourselves as comfortable as possible on the floor, with only the Axe cushions to lean on. And wait for the monks to arrive.

Saffron robes soon fill the room as the monks seat themselves, cross-legged, at the far end. My bride – dressed in a traditional village wedding dress – and I kneel in front of them. We shuffle forward on our knees, presenting food to the monks, waiting for their blessing.

The ceremony proceeds, and we are duly married. Then we all troop outside, laying our tribute around the Motubaki family's spirit tree. Taiella and I walk around it three times, pour water, pray. And as I watch my bride, her slight, sweet figure wrapped in those exquisite Thai wedding clothes, I'm amazed to see a dragonfly buzzing round her. A beautiful, green-blue dragon fly, translucent, exquisite. And not a single villager tries to swat the fly away.

That is when I witness the final miracle, the climax of our hopes: I see the beautiful dragon fly position its body on the choicest gift and lay its eggs there. The fact that it is out of season doesn't, apparently, worry it. And Westerner though I am I know – I just know – that Wuadon has been reborn as a dragon fly, a beautiful, shimmering insect in the colours she loved so much. And I also know that its actions now symbolize that Taiella and I would, eventually, be blessed with children.

That night, after we'd gone back to Udon Thani and were staying at our plush hotel, Taiella wakes early, around six o'clock. She moves quietly around the room but I, pumped up with adrenalin, have only slept lightly, and wake up.

'Very hungry, tilac,' she says, slipping on a dress and some sandals. 'Going out on street buying breakfast.'

'At this hour?'

'Street vendors starting now. Can smell fish cooking. Not going away for long. You want me buy for you?'

'No, thanks.' A dawn breakfast isn't what I'm looking for. 'Shall I come with you?' I start out of bed reluctantly.

'No, tilac. Going by self.' And she's gone before I've even got out of bed.

And back within half an hour. She had this craving and it couldn't be satisfied by anything the hotel has to offer. So she slipped out of the room, out of the hotel, and into the streets of Udon Thani to look for the only thing which would satisfy her.

She found her favourite type of catfish, cooked in the Isaan way, with Isaan spices. She ate it right on the street. To save me from the smell, she said. Then she came back, crept into bed beside me. But not for long. Within an hour she rushed to the bathroom to be sick.

I take the pregnancy test kit out of her toiletry bag, persuade her to pee, and dip the stick in. And there it is – my enchanting, sweet, delightful, wonderful Thai bride is pregnant with our first child.

I hold the test strip up to Taiella, show her the colour chart.

Her eyes grow round, and solemn, and finally half close. And my Smileegirl smiles as I have never seen her smile before.

THE END

THOU SHALT NOT KILL

Tessa Lorant Warburg

PROLOGUE

Guernsey, May 1941

The scream wakes him – he knows it's coming from outside, from the seashore below his bedroom window. He couldn't have heard it through the waves crashing against the rocks, but he knows it's real. He's frightened. Should he call Maman?

The house is perched on top of sheer cliffs surrounding the bay. He grabs his father's spyglass, climbs on to his windowsill and stares down at the beach. A full-moon night, cloud cover hiding the shoreline, then lifting to reflect light from wet sand.

He jabs the glass to his right eye, adjusts the focus, concentrates on the sand lapped by the ebbing tide. Dark shapes are moving by the water's edge. People, not animals. Who are they? Not Guernseymen – it's long past the new curfew decreed only yesterday.

Maybe this is the commando raid they've all been praying for? He goes on staring until he makes out four men in uniform. Sweat trickles into his eyes. Four German officers, their highly polished boots and brass insignia reflecting moonbeams.

Clouds scurry across the moon and hide the figures. He waits, pulse pounding in his ears, until there's enough light to see again. Now the black figures are bunched round a kayak beached on the shore. He sees them drag two people out of it, cries out as he realises who they are: Maman and Papa. Two of the Germans are holding his father. He hears a shot. The other two... A merciful cloud covers the beach.

He flings the spyglass on the bed, opens his window, throws out the rope he keeps fastened to his window frame, grabs his catapult and the ice-pick Maria smuggled out of the kitchen for him. He abseils down the wall merging into cliff face.

The screaming is unmistakable now, daggering into his mind, crowding out thought. He jumps the last ten feet, fingers the ice-pick and begins to run. He's going to charge in attack.

A single rifle shot ricochets between the rocks surrounding the little bay and roots him to the spot. Rays of moonlight reflect from something which glitters at him – a knife? A man – Henri – hurtles out of the shadows and wields something long and gleaming. A bayonet. The one his grandfather brought back from the Great War.

He dives forward, but the four Germans have already scattered, running towards the cliff path. He falls to his knees by the water, weeps. The Germans have gone, but not their legacy.

CHAPTER ONE

I saw him again in that dreary little room used for the monthly coffee mornings. Politely stooped, but still head and shoulders above the sprinkling of ageing family men and spotty altar boys. I watched an uneasy smile flittering on and off his face as he balanced a cup on its unmatched saucer - I could see the water sloshing. The good soul disbursing the kettle's contents had overtopped the instant coffee granules in her eagerness to be the one to serve him.

I went on staring, mouth open, mesmerised. His presence among that motley assembly of uninspired parishioners was totally unexpected, almost ridiculous. What was he doing here? My heart missed a beat as my eyes flicked over his features, my pulse began to race as I took in his every move. He turned towards Father Oncey.

'I'll do my best,' I heard that glorious bass purr across the room. 'I can always play the...'

The end of the sentence was drowned by an infant deciding to bawl for milk. In spite of that reminder of the consequences of carnal bliss I felt my body tingle in a way it hasn't done for years, producing physical reactions I was confident were dead, not merely dormant.

My ears strained to catch the phrases tossed between the two men across the room. Matthew looked dynamic beside the passive figure of the priest bowing his favours. Why was this man singing at St Olaf's when the Brompton Oratory, or any of the other well-known Catholic churches, would consider it a privilege if he were to join their choir? I'd wondered all through mass about

305

that bass. I'd even twisted my head back, looked up at the singers blurred in the loft, to see whether I could find the source of that magnificent sound. But he was hidden in the shadows, his sublime tones overpowering the quavery sounds of desperately squeaking sopranos who swayed, music in hand, in front of nebulous male singers. In spite of that it was clear that the bass had held himself in check.

My staring must have got through to him. The dark head moved up, alert eyes looked in my direction, swept across the cramped space, paused. My knees felt weak. I saw his face light up. He was going to come over. A shiver through my whole body made it hard for me to keep my nonchalant look. I felt blood surge to my face, felt the rush of heat, longed for an Arctic blast to cool me down. I leaned back against the wall, the blood draining from my brain.

It's been years since a man has affected me. The last one to do so, after all, was Jonathan. There'd been no one else from the day I met him. I'd never felt any temptation to be unfaithful throughout our thirty-five years of marriage. And when he lay dying, slowly and tortuously throughout a whole long year, I'd felt completely empty, almost dead myself. All I'd been able to manage afterwards was to try to energise the little spark of life left to me. I thought all passion had died with Jon.

Now here I was, reacting like a young girl, feeling like one. I was past all that, I hissed at myself. My once good looks faded, my once trim figure a twelve where it had been an eight, my once sharp eyes no longer quick and, at last, in need of reading glasses even for the hymns. My mind, imprisoned in this unspectacular shell, did not see me as I could see myself reflected in others' eyes. A woman on her own, poor thing. Must remember to invite her to lunch. Not dinner – no man to partner her.

Tall, dark and handsome, we girls used to whisper to each other in the refectory, giggling and drinking our Nescafé between lectures. I slipped back into that past, felt my body young again, tossed my hair in a remembered gesture of invitation. My eyes softened, my lips parted. I imagined myself the way I'd felt in my youth, fingered my amber necklace, pushed back my shoulders to lift my breasts – and smiled. My physical allure was, after all, drawing this man to me.

I saw him put down the plate of biscuits he was handing round and side-step over to me, skilfully winding between clusters of children well below his vision and skirting a group of huddled matrons, their broad beams rounded petals guarding a central bloom of gossip.

'Hello there.' He was standing in front of me, eyes bright, even mischievous. The purring voice was even headier once he was next to me. 'Ruth Samuels, isn't it?'

I'd been kidding myself, of course. Matthew Frelé had come over to greet me because he and I had already met. Otherwise there wouldn't have been the faintest chance of his noticing me. The magic of sexual attraction, that magnet which used to charm so effortlessly every time I met a man I fancied, no longer worked. My face, though not particularly wrinkled, is lined. No one mistakes it for that of a young woman. Jon, as it happened, wasn't prejudiced against ageing. The harsh real world, after his death, was quite a shock to me.

Occasionally, I'd comforted myself, people thought I was in my thirties. Like the immigration officer, the last time I'd flown to Boston. In fact he'd terrified me, grinning up at me: 'There's a mistake here, surely.'

'Mistake?' I'd been puzzled and then immediately unnerved. How could there be? I'd used that passport for the past six years, I was British now, quite safe...

'The date of birth,' the passport officer had laughed. 'Twenty years out, I'd say.' A wide-toothed grin had loosened into a smile. Meant as a compliment, I realised later. But at the time he'd hurled me back to when I was a child of six confronted by jackboots.

Perhaps he hadn't noticed. Place of birth: Vienna. My passport didn't state my race. How could he have known? His Anglo-Saxon heritage was clear, and he couldn't have been born till after the war. That a legacy of Jewish genes could be lethal would sound like something out of ancient history to him, the Holocaust an episode in a film, a history book, perhaps a TV programme.

I dragged myself back to the coffee morning. Meandering in the past again. Not something that I did when young. I used to be incisive, analytical. My first ambition was to be a detective. Now I was much more inclined to browse tangentially along my tumbling thoughts and feelings rather than to analyse. The time had come to stop kidding myself. The banal truth was that Matthew Frelé and I first met a couple of weeks ago, when I'd agreed to have dinner with his brother Mark. That's why Matthew walked over, that's why he was being friendly.

Liked the beginning of the story? Look for the e-book version of

THOU SHALT NOT KILL

on Amazon from mid-December 2012

Paperback publication will be in early 2013

THORN PRESS BOOKS IN PRINT

The Dohlen Inheritance trilogy - Tessa Lorant Warburg

The Dohlen Inheritance
Paperback: ISBN 978-0-906374-06-1
Hardback: ISBN 978-0-906374-03-0
Hobgoblin Gold
Paperback: ISBN978-0-906374-08-4
Ladybird Fly
Paperback: ISBN 978-0-906374-09-2

A Woman's World, 138-9 Chri Plus, Hilary Jerome
Paperback: ISBN 978-0-906374-00-9

Snack Yourself Slim, Richard Warburg & Tessa Lorant
Paperback: ISBN 978-0-906374-05-4

Inktastic, Andrew P Jones
Paperback: ISBN 978-0-906374-04-7

Wordfall, The 2010 Anthology from Southampton Writing Buddies
Editor Penny Legg
Paperback: ISBN 978-0-906374-26-9

Knitted Quilts & Flounces, Tessa Lorant
Paperback: ISBN 978- 0-906374-29-0

Spellbinder, Tessa Lorant Warburg
e-book, May 2012

All books are available from Amazon worldwide, and from good book shops

www.thethornpress.com

16657200R00184

Made in the USA
Charleston, SC
04 January 2013